LAST

DANCE

OF THE

VIPER

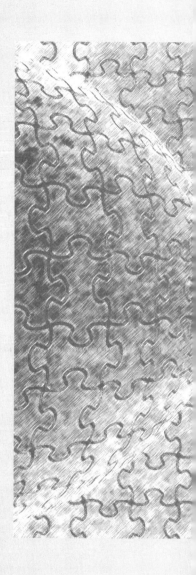

LAST

DANCE

OF THE

VIPER

BRIAN LYSAGHT

A Tom Doherty Associates Book   FORGE   New York

LAST DANCE OF THE VIPER

This book is printed on acid-free paper.

Book design by Jane Adele Regina

A Forge Book
Published by Tom Doherty Associates, LLC
175 Fifth Avenue
New York, NY 10010

www.tor.com

Forge® is a registered trademark of Tom Doherty Associates, LLC.

Library of Congress Cataloging-in-Publication-Data

Lysaght, Brian.
    Last dance of the viper / Brian Lysaght.
       p. cm.
    "A Tom Doherty Associates book."
    ISBN 0-765-30062-1
    1. Police—New Jersey—Paterson—Fiction. 2. Fathers—Death—
Fiction. 3. Boxers (Sports)—Fiction. 4. Paterson (N.J.)—Fiction.
5. Nerve gases—Fiction. 6. Brothers—Fiction. 7. Adoptees—
Fiction. 8. Mafia—Fiction. I. Title.

PS3562.Y4498 L37 2001
813'.54—dc21

                                         2001042315

First Edition: December 2001

Printed in the United States of America

0 9 8 7 6 5 4 3 2 1

For Dennis—
Born There, Lived There,
Died There

It is as true as it is trite,
that there is nothing men differ so readily about as money.

Plunder and devastation ever march in the train of irregulars.

Alexander Hamilton,
Founder of the City of Paterson, 1792

I

Alicia Kent left her quiet flat in Belgravia and walked slowly in the gathering dusk toward Sloan Square: The late afternoon London gloom was deepened by a biting February chill. She huddled inside her expensive coat and bent her head against the raw wind. A couple turned a corner, drunk with youth and love, and immediately stopped laughing when they saw her, as if the world in which she lived was suddenly visible. Alicia glanced at them and the boy flinched. She continued on.

Alicia Kent's mood was even blacker than her appearance. The day before, while relaxing comfortably in the cocoon of her New York law office, she had received the terse, computer-coded order to report to London for an official dinner of the Kensington Dining Council. The message appeared harmless, as it was meant to. Alicia froze at the sight of it, as she was meant to.

When she got to Sloan Square the dead light of the gray-bearded London day gave out altogether and she sought warmth in a quiet pub. The pub was smoke-filled and the men stared at her when she entered. She took off her coat and shook her head to clear the wet softly settling there from the night fog. The bartender slid a napkin down.

"Waitin' for someone, Miss?"

The question was really an accusation, and not very well disguised. Women rarely came into a place like this, and if they did, they came with a man, or caused trouble. The bartender had a heavy Liverpool accent and didn't want any trouble.

"Yes," she lied. "I'll have a whiskey and soda till he comes."

"Yes, ma'am."

She took out a pad and pretended to write, a prop to shield her from the quick, furtive glances of the men, curious yet afraid, like all men. Her thoughts immediately went to Magnus Purcell, her one-time sponsor on the Council, a 350-pound bundle of venom who was in all respects as deeply evil as Alicia Kent herself. But Purcell was also perceptive and once upon a time, to his eternal regret, had identified her for what she was. She was twenty-five back then and a baby lawyer at the prestigious New York law firm. Purcell called her into his office that fateful March day on a pretext. She found him despondent, staring at the city from his perch high above it.

"You look terrible! What's wrong?"

He sighed. "It's the Walker verdict."

She squinted. The Walker case was a great victory for the firm, a $56 million jury verdict in a complicated business case. The firm stood to make almost $20 million in fees.

"What about it? I was at the celebration party. I thought it was . . ."

"It was," Magnus said, shifting his huge bulk. "However, now there's a problem. The judge . . . well, he's convinced our client corrupted several jurors. Our intelligence says he's about to enter a judgment in the defendant's favor."

"That's absurd! We won't get paid! I won't get my bonus! Can he do something like that?"

"For the next seven days. After that he loses jurisdiction. But he's already made up his mind." Magnus had smiled weakly. "Our client is in contact with the law clerk."

Alicia's eyes remained fixed on Purcell as she thought it through. "How did the judge discover the bribery?"

"He suspected all along. Our client really had no case. After the trial a juror . . . one who voted in the minority, one who refused the offer . . . called the judge."

"Have the police been notified? Does anybody know?"

"Not yet."

She became silent then, digesting it. There was only one answer and even at twenty-five she knew what Magnus wanted. And Magnus knew she knew.

"The judge is rather old, I understand."

"Yes, seventy-eight. He refuses to retire."

"Accidents happen to elderly gentlemen all the time."

"Yes," Magnus had said. "Except *this* accident must happen *before* he issues his order."

"Of course." She was about to do something that would change her life forever. She would not do so cheaply. Not then. Not ever.

"Our client will be grateful?"

Purcell studied her before responding. He enjoyed being right about people. "I think the figure of five million has been mentioned. To be *shared* of course."

"Shared? Of course. To a degree." She rose, her plan concluded. "Well," she said, "I hope things work out."

Three days later the judge's nude body was found in the trunk of a rental car at the bottom of the Hudson. The police literally had no clue. No motive, no eyewitnesses, no nothing. The last time the man was seen alive was at a tavern named O'Brien's in the company of an attractive, tall, blond woman. The judge had had four martinis and become voluble. Before they left laughing together the judge had bitten the woman's neck in an excess of passion.

Alicia reported to Magnus a day later and neither of them spoke of the matter, nor of the large flesh-toned bandage on Alicia's neck. A week later he summoned her to his office again. He handed her a slip of paper with numbers on it.

"What's this?"

"An account in the Channel Islands. It's just off the coast of Britain. Take the Concorde over to London, my treat. Introduce yourself to Mr. Bernard, the general manager. Not quite half the five million we discussed, but you won't be disappointed."

"Thank you, sir."

"Oh, and Alicia?"

"Yes?"

"When you travel to England to visit your money, there are some very important people I want you to begin to get to know."

And now those days were lost in mists of all kinds. She stared vacantly at the blank paper, her face set, purposeful. Back then Magnus had been her patron, her protector, her life in many ways. There had been millions in that Channel Islands account and many millions more were made over the years. Sometimes in order to make that kind of money, people had to die. Sometimes they didn't. It never mattered to her. She had never failed him, not once. Well, at least not back then.

Seven years after her Concorde trip she had met all the members of the Council and had carried out their instructions to the letter. When Magnus formally proposed her for membership, the vote was positive, and unanimous. Magnus thought he had an ally for life. He was wrong. Within months, at the age of thirty-two she felt her own power, and formed her own alliances, particularly with the beefy American of Russian descent who chaired the Council, Gregor Portov. The credit for the successful projects that had once been his were now hers, and his productivity fell dramatically. The year before, when the money was divided, Magnus' share plunged, a loss he blamed, accurately, on the viper he had taken to his breast. He now despised her, and desperately wanted to destroy her. The threat was supposed to frighten her but never did. She sipped her whiskey and soda and glanced at the mirror. He was standing behind her, grinning maliciously, all 350 pounds of him. Her expression never changed.

"Hello, Magnus. Can I buy you a drink?"

He shook his head. "Not right now, my dear. I think it's time for our meeting."

She accepted his offer of a ride and sat primly in the limousine across from him. He smoked a large cigar, uncaring about the stench he was creating. She never asked how he had found her, and didn't care.

"This is a very important meeting. Have you prepared?"

She knew what he meant. Money had been invested. Expectations had been raised. And now there was a failure for which a scapegoat was necessary.

"I'm always prepared."

Magnus laughed heartily, his heavy bulk rolling.

"Alicia, you've prepared excuses. But these men are not interested in your lame excuses."

She shrugged. "We'll see."

The man inspected the glowing end of the cigar. She knew he was fantasizing about using that glowing tip on her. Once he had, in a room full of men in cloaks and hoods, with candles flickering against a black tapestry. She had held out her white, soft hand that night, palm up, and screamed when the knife cut the symbol of a snake in her vulnerable skin. The men had murmured in satisfaction and glasses had been raised. She had then held out the other palm and raised her head to scream again in fury at the uncaring candles high above her, her wrist tight in Magnus' hand as he burned a scar deep into her hand. Today, if he had the chance, it wouldn't be her palm only that burned. Fine, she thought, let him dream. As long as she had Portov on her side she was safe.

They rode in silence to the manor house. Her deep, dark eyes revealed nothing to him. Magnus was visibly frustrated when she exited the car and walked regally to the elegant front door.

2

There were thirteen criminals in the ornate dining room when she arrived: a Swiss, a Swede, two Britons, three Japanese, two French, an Italian, two Arabs and a Russian. All were themselves scarred, in their own chosen way, as Alicia had been when she was admitted to their dark midst. All were leaders in their own countries, with organizations to support. But as far as Alicia was concerned only one man mattered. Gregor Portov smiled warmly when he saw her.

"Welcome, little viper!" Portov drank vodka in the Russian style, warm out of a wine glass. He left his glass and came to her, opening her hand, tenderly kissing the faint white lines in her palm. The other men ignored her, staring at cash reports and computer runs which were spread out on the table. It had been a disappointing quarter and the faces were rigid. These men had made promises to others, promises that now would be impossible to keep.

A small army of attendants swirled around the members. There were cooks, kitchen staff, waiters, Turk guards, even a tuxedo-clad general manager named Charles. The attendants had all been carefully hand-picked by Portov, and paid well by Portov, and all were intensely loyal to him.

The elaborate meal took two hours to serve and clear away. When the food had been replaced by cigars and cognac, Portov rose.

"Let's begin," he barked when the room had calmed. "We have much to cover and time is short. Mr. Yomoto, your report!"

A Japanese man of fifty rose. His hand trembled slightly as he sipped from a water glass. "I have harsh news. As you know, for the past three years we have been working closely with the Asahara group in Japan. In years past, they bought anything we could sell, wasteland in Australia, odd chemicals they thought would produce bioweapons, whatever. It was a magnificent organization, a wonderful partnership."

Alicia snorted. She knew the truth and knew Yomoto was a liar. Asahara was a crude cult leader, a half-blind overweight, drugged-out pederast who had been a washed-up yoga teacher in Tokyo in the mid-eighties. Then, like all cult leaders, he discovered the bottomless stupidity of man. His hastily-formed religion started pulling in $50 million a year from thousands of naive Japanese, robots who believed hell was in their future unless they signed on with "Aum," or "Supreme Truth" as Asahara called it. Yet it was only when the slaves of this godless religion gave over their life savings, and entered the spartan Aum compound at the base of Mount Fuji, that they truly learned about hell.

"Was?" Portov asked gently. "That term concerns me. What is the status of the group now?"

Yomoto coughed and drank more water. "A brief interruption is all. The guru is in prison."

The rumble of murmurs filled the room. In an odd way Alicia actually felt sorry for the man. Yomoto had been on a slippery slope for a long time, his revenues declining every year. The Asahara cult had once made the Council money, and saved Yomoto from certain death three years before. Alicia suddenly realized she had never seen a "replacement" on the Council, as it was euphemistically called. The initiation rites were elaborate. What would the killing be like? Her sympathy evaporated, and her breath quickened.

Yomoto pounded the table. He was drunk, and frightened, but not yet ready to give up, even as the Turk guards shifted quietly.

"I cannot be held accountable for this!"

"Not accountable?" Portov's eyes widened. "But we haven't been paid. The arrangements failed."

"That was *her* fault!" Yomoto spun and pointed.

Alicia's surprised laughter relieved the tension in the room. "My fault?"

"Exactly. *I* acquired the Sarin. *I* had a buyer in place with ready cash. It was *your* fault the transaction was not completed."

Portov turned to her quizzically. "Lovely Alicia? What can you tell us about this matter? Mr. Yomoto's criticisms are so harsh."

Alicia walked to the head of the table and stood next to her newest patron. Her bearing was serene, a subterfuge for the tension she felt. She had allies in the room but also enemies—the Japanese, because she was about to betray Mr. Yomoto, and Magnus, because she had already betrayed him.

"Sarin is a nerve gas developed by the Germans in the 1930s," she began. "In pure form it is odorless, tasteless, colorless and extremely lethal. The Germans refrained from using it only out of fear of massive retaliation."

The room quieted. She had their attention.

"We were offered enormous fees by a German middleman in Paris to smuggle canisters of Sarin into the United States. We of course did not ask the reason or even the identity of the client. I turned to Mr. Yomoto for help."

"So where is the Sarin now?" Magnus asked. "In the air-conditioning ducts of Manhattan office buildings?"

"No," Alicia admitted. "It is stored in an abandoned factory twelve miles outside New York. It's a makeshift warehouse for us. We would have our money by now if problems had not developed."

"What problems?"

"Several." She gestured to Yomoto. "The Sarin he delivered to me was contaminated, manufactured by the cult, not the military. It was not odorless, quite the opposite. That's why only seven people died when it was released in the Tokyo subways instead of seven thousand."

"The stench?" Portov suggested.

"Exactly. The stench sent the commuters running *out* of the subways and police in gas masks running *into* the subways." She paused for effect. "And the same thing happened at our U.S. warehouse."

The room erupted. Portov held up his hands. "What happened? Tell us!"

"The canisters I received were as defective as the gas inside. Within a month one leaked and the smell drew the attention of the neighbors. There was a security breach."

Now the noise was deafening. Charles deftly shut the door and two Turk guards stood with their backs against it.

"Do not be fooled," Yomoto shouted above the din. "The security breach was *her* fault. *She* was responsible for safe storage of the canisters. Now we are all at risk."

Alicia let the room vent their rage. She only spoke when Portov had finally quieted them. "Of course I chose the factory," she said, her hands open. "And an excellent choice it was. The place had been empty for years. But Mr. Yomoto's leaking gas actually killed vegetation outside. An old man next door became suspicious and broke in.

An Englishman reacted first. "What old man? Who is he? Why haven't we heard of this?"

Alicia brushed her hand in the air. "He is nothing. Seventy years old. He runs a gym next door to the factory for training fighters."

The Italian was nearly-hysterical. "How will this affect payment? I must know! Do you know how many people are depending on me?"

"We all must know," Magnus said quietly.

Alicia Kent pointed to Yomoto. "We have not been paid because of his incompetence. If I had received pure, military grade Sarin, there would have been no problem. No stench, no old man. Just delivery as ordered and a wire transfer of millions to our account." She paused for effect. "We would *all* have our money by now."

Portov again. "I want to know more about this. Has the old man called the police?"

"Not yet. He thinks the canisters have something to do with drugs and the Bracca organization out of North Jersey. So for the moment he's said nothing. He's right about one thing, the Braccas found the abandoned factory for us."

The men understood. The Council had made a lot of money with Angelo Bracca in the last few years. The man was a small-time hoodlum by Council standards to be sure. But he had been a very profitable one thus far.

Portov sipped his vodka, his brow lined with thought. "If we eliminate the old man, and replace the Sarin, can we still get paid?"

"Of course. But I don't want *him* supplying it." Her hand swept derisively toward Yomoto.

"No, we can't make that mistake again." Portov stared at the ceiling. "Sarin in pure form is held by all advanced militaries?"

She smiled. She knew exactly where he was going. "Of course. The former Soviet Union, for example."

"Yes," said Portov. "So let's say I replace the gas. My supplier will want something of like value in return. Can we deliver what he will want?"

"No problem." Alicia thought of the declining defense industry in the United States, with its thousands of underemployed workers. She'd find someone to deliver whatever Portov needed to trade.

Portov slammed his palm on the table. "Then it's settled. Kill the old man. I will replace the Sarin and you will get me what I need in trade. Some sort of restricted metal, I'm sure. Beryllium, zirconium, there's always something Alexeyev wants."

Alicia didn't answer. There was still a problem, and she prayed Magnus wouldn't bring it up. Her prayers were not answered.

"Alicia," Magnus asked quietly. "Why don't you tell the Council the *whole* truth."

Alicia turned slowly to him. There was only hate in Purcell's eyes. "What do you mean?"

The man's voice thundered. "She *lied* to you! She can't kill the old man, not if she wants to keep working with the Braccas. He's under the protection of Angelo Bracca himself! And she *knows* that."

The noise in the room grew. Alicia Kent stood quietly, waiting.

"Is this true?" Portov's voice was soft. "Is this a complication?"

"We have to approach the killing delicately," she admitted. "The Braccas are local hoodlums, nothing more. But they have controlled that area for generations. Once, yes, they were prosperous. Now . . ." she shrugged, "they live in the past. They protect the last of the old Irish and Italians in broken cities. And run crude games. And yet . . . they are so very useful to this affair."

Magnus laughed heartily. "Is that all you're worried about, Alicia? The bruised ego of a common mobster?"

This was no time to lie, not when Magnus knew everything. "Not completely. It's just . . . well, very tricky. The old man's daughter is living with Angelo's son, John Bracca." She stopped to collect herself. "And one of the old man's sons is the famous Miguel Meza himself."

The room got quiet in a hurry. Meza! That was a name they knew. A killer's killer, a shadowy lone wolf with loose ties to gangs of all kinds. Even Portov reacted to that.

"Meza is the old man's son? This is messy. Is he as good as they say?"

Alicia again thought about lying but rejected the notion. Meza was too famous to lie about. "Yes. He is without question the most efficient killer we ever dealt with."

Again, no one spoke. That description said a lot. More importantly, they all agreed with it.

"I told you," Yomoto screamed. "If she kills the old man Angelo Bracca will find a way to retaliate. And what about Meza? It is his father she wants to kill! I'm telling you the whole operation could become public! Can you imagine the hysteria?"

All eyes turned to Portov. Under the rules it was his call.

He sipped on the warm vodka before speaking. "It is a difficult decision," he said. Then he looked sadly at Alicia. "I'm sorry."

She stiffened. She had not expected this. "Gregor!"

A Turk guard pushed her into her seat. She felt a cold gun barrel against the back of her head.

"Gregor!"

"I'm sorry," he said again and gestured.

It was true what they say, she thought in that brief split second. As death is inevitable, life stands still. She closed her eyes and was transported as a young girl to a wood deck high above the swirling Snake River. She felt no fear. And then she heard the loud, single report and smiled. She was the one person in the room who didn't flinch at the sound.

You never hear the one that gets you, the soldiers say about mortar rounds, and the same is true of bullets. Alicia knew if she heard the sound she was safe. She left the Snake River to the dark recesses of her mind and opened her eyes. Yomoto was slumped face down on the table. The soft, dark blood was spreading rapidly. Dumdum shell, Alicia thought professionally. In small, out big, the nose of the cartridge weakened by an intersecting "X" cut in the metal. The back of Yomoto's head showed little damage. She knew, however, that the man's face was all but gone.

"My God," Magnus said quietly. The Frenchman, reaching to a long-abandoned Catholic past, blessed himself and kissed his thumb.

The single bullet did its work and the Turks, lacking all compassion, had the mess cleaned in ten minutes. The remaining Council members were quiet.

"What now?" Portov said.

"Now that Mr. Yomoto is gone," Alicia said, "I think it's time to move on to the old man." She sipped her cognac with a rock-steady hand.

Portov smiled. "Very quickly," the chairman ordered.

3

The meeting broke up at midnight, just after the profits for the previous quarter had been divided. Alicia waited until the last of the men filed out. Then Portov pulled her to him.

"Are you happy with your share, little viper?"

He knew the answer. Alicia's share had doubled.

"I'm immensely pleased. Were there others who did not fare as well?"

He shrugged. "There are always disappointments, some reductions. One in particular. Not quite to zero yet, but close."

Magnus! He had opened his envelope, turned ash white and stormed out. Zero distribution was a death sentence. A nominal distribution was a warning. Good.

"Incidentally," she said. "If a member is going to be . . . replaced, I know of an opportunity which is . . . well outside of Council business."

Portov laughed loudly. "Alicia, you have buried the man before his time!"

"Perhaps."

He lifted her face with his finger. When his vodka-scented mouth touched hers she shivered, like she was supposed to. He misinterpreted it for passion, like he was supposed to.

"You are so beautiful."

"Thank you." She held her breath slightly to make her cheeks pink. She yearned for the day when she'd never have to fake this.

"But we don't have time tonight."

"What! Gregor!" Her voice had the practiced disappointment of a stage actress.

"No, business first. The Council is nervous about this Sarin complication. You must return to New York and dispose of the old man."

"I understand, Gregor."

"Who cares if Angelo Brucca's organization objects. I'm sick of his whining anyway. We have local people in Brooklyn who can deal with the Bruccas." He smiled. "My countrymen, actually."

"Yes, sir."

He let her go, now pacing. "After the old man dies, meet me back here. We will fly to Paris and meet with our banker."

He meant the German middleman who would pay millions for the Sarin coming in and the restricted metals going out.

"Yes."

"Then I will meet Alexeyev in Moscow and replace the Sarin. You will arrange the trade from the U.S."

"Yes, sir." She hesitated. "Plus that other *very lucrative* opportunity, assuming . . ."

He cupped her face in his beefy hands. "You will not stop until the fat man is dead, will you?"

Why lie. "No." She hesitated. "And one more thing?"

"Yes?"

"Yomoto's replacement. It will be his son?" Yomoto's son was a twenty-three-year-old Japanese gang leader with great potential. He was smart and ruthless, head of the Hiroshima branch of the Yakudo, the Japanese Mafia. He and his father had been enemies for years. The son would not mourn the father's passing.

"Yes, I think so. The boy will bring much-needed youth to this group. Why, do you disagree?"

"Not at all. I've worked with him. He's . . . well, vain as well as capable."

"And?"

"And I want to be the one to mark him." Her voice was cold. "On his face!"

Portov roared with laughter as he pulled Alicia close to him.

Magnus Purcell left the manor house with no romantic ambitions, just pure anger. The Turks escorted him to his limousine and his driver jumped out, protective. The Turks laughed and went back to the house.

He sat in the back, lit a cigar and poured a gigantic Scotch over ice. His driver looked back quizzically.

"Soho," Magnus barked.

The car left Belgravia and headed toward Piccadilly, unnoticed in the traffic flow. Once through the roundabout it turned to the theater district, the driver carefully watching the mirrors. When he was sure he wasn't followed he cruised back toward Soho, now locked inside a crush of Korean pedestrians on holiday. At the first discrete alley he turned right. A barker was shouting to the mob of tourists, hawking a sex show inside a shop with a cloth curtain.

Magnus walked past the doorman to the perversion inside. Beyond the dark shroud a young Englishman, barely nineteen, danced naked on stage to a deep recorded beat. Magnus ignored the boy and opened a wooden door.

Behind the door an American waited, dressed in a dark suit, white shirt and pale red tie.

"Red, white and blue," Magnus said as he sat down. "How pathetic." There was a bottle of Scotch and an ice bucket on a primitive table. Magnus went for it.

"Not pathetic," the man said easily. "Patriotic."

Magnus drank deeply. He was now very drunk and his judgment was clouded. But his decision had already been made. After the envelope he received, and the disappointment it created, he only had one choice left to him. He would *not*, whatever the cost, end up like Yomoto.

"I want the boy."

"On stage?"

"Yes."

"He's yours, my friend."

Magnus lit another cigar. He was about to cross a Rubicon. "Let's say we make a deal. What do you want?"

The man laughed. Even his laugh was American, but soft, as befits a long-gone refugee from Texas, now onto other things. An American in Britain, not Paris.

"Every single thing you know, big guy."

4

Approximately twelve hours after Magnus Purcell bared his soul to a man he knew only as Crane—in reality Captain Robert P. Simpson of U.S. Navy Intelligence—Lt. Commander Stephanie Shane walked down a long receiving line to the spot where her father stood waiting. She was dressed in crisp whites, which she hated, and had to be on her best behavior for her father, which she hated even worse than the whites. She sighed deeply, put on a frozen smile, and stepped forward.

Admiral Duncan Shane saw her coming and stiffened like he always did when his daughter was near. She was twenty-nine now, a 1991 graduate of Annapolis, where she finished tenth in her class at the same time as she was trying to qualify for the 1992 Olympic marathon team. She didn't, finishing a half-hour behind the leader, struggling the last six miles with burning lungs and a sprained ankle. She gracefully congratulated the three qualifiers and then slammed her bad ankle into a tree till they stopped her.

That was vintage Stephanie, the driven obsessions that always caused Rear Admiral Duncan Shane sleepless nights. Stubbornness was fine. Determination was fine. But recklessness was dangerous, and that's why Admiral Shane had recently decided to put an end to it once and for all.

She finally got to the end of the line and smiled, this time for real, the light streaming from her pale eyes. Then, to her father's horror, she snapped her heels together and raised her right hand to her cap.

"Stephanie, what the hell are you doing? You don't have to salute your father!"

"Yes, sir." Her hand dropped. "Congratulations on the promotion, sir. I'm very proud."

"Then show it." He held out his arms. She looked at him in shock.

"What do you think you're doing?"

He dropped his arms. "Okay, I'm sorry. Just try to have a good time tonight." He gestured. "There's lots of young officers here, fliers, too."

"That's great. Maybe they'll invite me to the next Tailhook."

Duncan coughed. A harsh blow but fair. "They're not all like that. You're a flier. You've been to Pensacola."

"Exactly. And they *are* all like that. Hormone-driven boys with toys. By the way, on that subject we've got a big problem."

Yes, no friends, no man, no nothing. And none on any horizon he could see.

"What problem? No, first, just tell me, how have you been?"

"You want the truth or you want me to lie?"

He desperately wanted her to lie. "The truth, of course."

"Admiral, I'm pissed!"

"How about 'Dad, I'm pissed.' "

"Okay . . . Dad. It's not fair what you did. I got my wings at Pensacola, just like you did. I flew off the Nimitz for eighteen months. I should *still* be on the Nimitz. Instead, you put me in the stupid Pentagon. Like a file clerk! Naval Intelligence. Admiral . . . Dad . . . this is *boring*. I'm a flier, just like you. I *need* to be flying."

He knew that much was true but he also knew his daughter. And her faults.

"I know, baby. It's just that two women were killed last year in F-14s off carriers. And then you missed the wire twice on your CQ."

He realized that one was a mistake before the words got out of his mouth. Her eyes flashed. "There were *six* men killed off carriers the same year. And I *did* carrier qualify, that same night, on my third and last try, while thirty other *men* got sent home. Did they get grounded?"

"You haven't been grounded," he stuttered. "Just . . . just . . . reassigned."

Her eyes narrowed dangerously. "Duncan, this is such . . . such bull!"

His face was the picture of innocence, even though his mind was racing heavenward, where her mother was probably watching with amusement. Where was his late wife when he needed her? "It's really very routine."

"Really? So when do the men fliers get 'reassigned'?"

"Listen," he said quickly, glancing at the fidgeting people in line. "How about we make a deal?"

"What deal?"

"All I want you to do is take a time-out from carriers. Stay with Military Intelligence for two years. I promise you can maintain your hours with ground launches so you stay current. If after two years you still want to go back to carriers I'll make sure it happens."

"Two years! Duncan, I'll go nuts in that room."

"I know." He had thought long and hard about this and knew he had to make it interesting for her. Otherwise, she'd figure out a way to go around him, admiral or no admiral. "No more security checks, I promise. There's something special that just came in. If you want it, it's yours."

Her eyes flickered, suspicious but interested. "What?"

"Terrorism," he said simply.

She grabbed him by the lapel. "What terrorism? Give!"

He was deeply worried about the whole affair but really had no choice. He had to rely on a guy named Braxton from the White House who assured him she'd be in no danger. If only her mother was alive to make these decisions.

"Tomorrow you report to the administrative office building at oh-seven-thirty. Room eight-seventy-six. You know where it is?"

She tried to hide her rising excitement. The AOB was attached to the White House.

"This is not a navy deal?"

"This is everybody's deal. Wear civilian clothes." He looked her up and down. "Do you have any?"

"Duncan," she said sweetly.

"Yes, baby."

"Next time you say something like that . . ."

"Stephanie, I . . ."

"I swear to God you'll pay."

She had never been there, not even for the public tour, and found herself focused and excited, the combination she loved. She rose at 4 A.M., ran a harsh five miles in the lightless cold and dressed in

what she thought was a conservative business suit. When she walked
in the door and the marine guard looked up, she realized it might
not be conservative enough.

"Can I help you, ma'am?"

"Yes, I'm due for a meeting in room eight seventy-six at oh seven
thirty. My name is Shane, Stephanie Shane."

The marine grinned. "Too bad your meeting's so soon. We could
have a cup of coffee."

"Read your list, Sergeant."

The man's eyes went down the list of approved visitors. Then he
stiffened and sprang to his feet.

"Sorry, Lieutenant Commander."

Stephanie returned the salute. "You're on report. Point me the
right way."

In his face she saw the familiar clenched jaw, the look of resentment she had come to know so well. She also knew he was silently
cursing her. The words "bitch" and more were probably coursing
through the man's mind. Yet there was nothing he could do.

"I'll take you right there, ma'am."

The marine guard led her to a room at the far end of the AOB.
As she entered she saw eleven men sitting around a battered wood
conference table. No women, she noticed. Big surprise. None of the
men looked very happy.

"Mr. Braxton," the guard said. "This is Lieutenant Commander
Stephanie Shane, U.S. Naval Intelligence."

Cameron Braxton rose to his feet. His face had a strange smile,
part welcoming, part curious. "Pleased to meet you, Ms. Shane."

She shook his hand. "Lieutenant Commander, not Ms."

The other ten men smirked at that, then looked up with pretty
obvious glances. Damn, she thought, that wasn't smart.

After everybody said hello Braxton gestured to an enlisted man
standing at attention near a computer terminal. The lights dimmed,
a laser videodisc player whirred and a screen lit up. Stephanie
watched an enormous fat man stroll across the screen in front of
recognizable New York landmarks.

"This man's name is Magnus Purcell," Braxton said. "Do not be
fooled by his slovenly appearance. He is a talented criminal and a
member of an organization with the strange name of the Kensington
Dining Council. The 'Council' we call it."

"Oh, please," a voice said.

Braxton rolled his eyes at the remark. "This is Leonard Simon from CIA. We will now pause while he scoffs."

"I'll do more than scoff. I been hearing about this fairly-tale Council—which I'd call a lot worse if the lady wasn't here—for twenty years. It supposedly controls everything including papal elections. We probably got somebody right in here works for them if you believe the stories. To me, it ranks right up there with Santa Claus."

Braxton's jaw stiffened. His composure seemed forced. "We recognize there's a legitimate debate. But gentlemen—and Ms. Shane—the White House believes there's enough evidence developing to be gravely concerned."

The CIA man just shook his head. "This damn Council has been a rumor forever. There's *never* been any *real* evidence of it, just a lot of rumors. If this Purcell guy is supposed to be a member, fine, let's sweat him till he tells us the truth."

Braxton gestured and the images on the screen changed. This time Purcell wore different clothes and Stephanie could make out the spires of Westminster behind him.

"Three days ago we think there may have been some sort of a Council meeting in London. This is a surveillance video of Purcell on his way to the meeting. Unfortunately, he detected our tail and lost us near Sloan Square."

"How convenient," Leonard Simon said.

Braxton ignored the crack. "We believe the meeting took place at a manor house someplace in Kensington. After the meeting Purcell met his handler from Naval Intelligence. He told us a lot. But he left out a lot too. And I agree we still don't know how much of what Purcell said is real and how much he made up."

The marine typed into the computer keyboard controlling the videodisc and this time the screen showed the graceful, snowcapped majesty of Mt. Fuji. At the base of the mountain was a large encampment of buildings.

"What you see here is the headquarters of what was once known as the Asahara cult in Japan, also known as 'Aum,' or 'Supreme Truth.' "

Leonard Simon seemed ready to burst. "This is very, very old news."

"I know, just bear with me. The Asahara cult are bumblers for the most part. But four years ago they were able to synthesize a crude form of a deadly nerve gas named Sarin. They tried to use it in the Tokyo subways. Seven people died."

The marine typed again and the screen showed chaotic Tokyo subways. Stephanie could clearly see screaming commuters emerging choking from underground tunnels.

"After this gas attack the Japanese authorities finally woke up and the cult was destroyed. Unfortunately only half the Sarin was recovered."

The room buzzed now. Simon's face was taut and he didn't respond. The marine typed again and the screen showed Asahara himself standing next to a well-dressed businessman. The "guru" wore white flowing robes.

"The man with the suit is a Japanese national named Yomoto. It's possible he purchased some or all of the missing Sarin. Until three days ago, we believe he was a senior Council member."

"And now he's not?"

"Now he may be dead, Leonard. According to Purcell he was murdered at the last Council meeting."

Stephanie raised her hand, a silly schoolgirl gesture, but she was new at this. "Why was Yomoto killed? They should have been happy he got the gas. And what are they planning to do with it?"

"All good questions, Lieutenant Commander. We don't know why Yomoto was killed. We do know there are over one hundred canisters of Sarin missing, each weighing seventy-seven point six kilograms. We obviously don't know where it is or who it may have been sold to. We do know the Council itself would have little use for it. They are money people, not terrorists."

Another hand went up. "This is Craig Scott of NSC. Yes, Craig?"

"I'm trying to keep my composure but it's hard. This stuff got sold! I want to know where it is, what group has it, where they've got it hid. And I want to know it *now*! You do remember Oklahoma City, don't you?"

Braxton took a deep breath. Stephanie thought Scott's questions were damn good. "Craig, that's the whole reason this group was formed. That's why we're here! Because yes, we *do* remember Oklahoma City."

"What else did Purcell tell us?"

Braxton pointed. "In front of each of you is a briefing book containing the transcript of the Purcell statement. You also have all the photographs we have. Purcell sobered up before revealing the name of the Council member responsible for the Sarin. We do know the code name of that operative is 'Viper.' Beyond that he clammed up."

"And *where*?" Scott pressed. "*Where* is the gas now?"

"Purcell says it's in an abandoned factory on the eastern seaboard. They're using it as a warehouse. We don't know where. But what may give us a shot here, not much of one but a shot, is he said there's been a security breach."

The room came alive at that. "What breach?"

"Purcell said a neighbor—an old man—stumbled onto the canisters. The Viper, whoever that is, has been assigned to murder the witness and replace the Sarin."

"Replace the Sarin? Why?"

"Because it's contaminated. Purcell says the buyer wants only a pure military version. The Viper is in charge of that too."

Stephanie was so energized she almost forgot her love of flying. No more security checks now.

"What can we do to track this down?"

The screen now showed a blow-up of the eastern seaboard. "We divided the East Coast into fourteen segments extending from Boston to Atlanta. Every man—and woman—in this room will be undercover and responsible for a given geographical segment. Take a moment, turn to page seven of your materials, and you'll see your assignment."

Stephanie excitedly turned to page seven. She scanned the material briefly and made a face.

"A lawyer? I'm supposed to be a lawyer?"

Braxton laughed. "It will be a bit more tedious than flying off carriers, Lieutenant Commander, but yes. Your orders are to report to the United States Attorney's Office in Manhattan. You will be identified as Assistant United States Attorney Stephanie Shane from Main Justice in Washington. You will be given complete autonomy and the Bureau will be there to assist you. Your job will be simple. If there is an old man killed under suspicious circumstances in the New York metropolitan area in the next seven days, you will hear of it right away. Every bit of evidence will be forwarded to you. You will then forward it to me." Braxton hesitated. "Ms.

Shane—gentlemen—I don't have to tell you how important this is. We need to find that Sarin."

Assistant United States Attorney Stephanie Shane. She could do that.

"Yes, sir! she said briskly.

5

At 4:30 on a Friday evening, Pasquale Guiseppi De Marco, or "Patsy" to every fight fan in the tri-state area, left work to go visit his daughter in New York.

He shut out the lights in his gym in Paterson, New Jersey, checked the lock on the common door to the old abandoned silk factory next door, then walked to the corner of Main Street and Van Houten. The light from the dim February day was weak and giving up the ghost as the brown inter-city bus, number 30, pulled up. The driver said, "Hey, Patsy, who's lookin' good?"

Patsy climbed up the stairs, groaned and sat down. Old age, he supposed. "It ain't like the old days, Ed. A white kid named Jackson's the best I got." He fumbled in his wallet.

"Patsy, don't insult me. You never paid on this bus yet. Just keep me company."

So Patsy did as he was told, sitting quietly in the first row of the empty bus for the half hour it took to get down Route 3 through the Lincoln Tunnel into Manhattan. Nobody got on the bus the whole way except for an old lady who climbed on in Clifton and off in East Rutherford, and in between sat in the back and drew pictures on the steam of the window. After a while the driver got bored with all the quiet and looked over his shoulder.

"Patsy, you look like you're gonna die back there. Perk up and talk to me."

The old man woke from his trance. "Sorry, Ed. I was just thinking."

"Yeah? What are you thinkin' about that's so depressing?"

"I don't know. Ed, let me ask you something. You got any kids?"

"Sure, three. They're all gone now."

"Where?"

"All over, one's in Oregon, one's in Massachusetts. One lives in Wayne and comes over every time he needs money."

"I think that's what's got me down. My three are gone too."

The driver kept his eyes straight ahead. There was nothing to say. Everybody knew about Patsy's kids.

"Well, think of it this way, Patsy. Miguel and Tommy weren't really your kids, right? You were just like their trainer."

The old man bristled. "What the hell you mean, Ed? I was their trainer, their father, their everything. When I got them they were living on the street. I gave them a home. Sort of, anyway." The old man sat back and sighed. "I just thought they'd always be there."

The driver held up his hand. "Patsy, relax. You ever hear that saying? Don't wish too hard, you may get it. What would you think if all three were just laying on your couch? Besides, if you really get lonely you got all those pictures on your wall."

"That's the problem." Every picture on the gym walls captured a singular moment of triumph for a skinny kid with a hairless chest and headgear wrapped around a sweat-soaked face. Those blurred black-and-white photos recalled for Patsy the strange family he created, for those ten strange years.

"What can I say," the old trainer said at last. "The Italians are sentimental."

They left it at that while the empty bus cruised under the Hudson River into Manhattan. Once through the tunnel the bus was supposed to pull into Port Authority. Instead, Ed turned onto Forty-second Street, heading uptown.

"Ed, I don't want to tell you your business but you just missed the turn."

"To hell with the turn, Patsy. I follow too many orders in this job. Where you goin' anyway?"

The bus had now become the world's largest taxi. "Tell you the truth, Ed, I'm going to see Natala."

The driver's head jerked back. "No way!"

Patsy had heard it all before, too much for his taste. "Yes, Ed," he said wearily. "She's in town for a couple of days, a show at the Plaza Hotel."

"A show! You mean a *fashion* show?"

"I guess so." Patsy pulled a gold-embossed invitation out of his pocket. "This says I am cordially invited to attend the New York exhibition of the collection of the famous Jacob Misraeli. The collection will be displayed by world-renowned models such as Angela McAndrews, Meredith Beck, Dominique Dabuto and the incomparable Natala."

"Damn, Patsy, they just say *Natala*. They don't even say her last name."

"You think that makes me feel good they don't say her name? Which happens to be *my* name? Natala means 'Christmas,' Ed, the day she was born. Like my name means Passover, which is really Holy Thursday. Anyway, Ed, no it don't make me feel good."

"It sure would make me feel good. You got a daughter that's like the most beautiful girl on the planet."

"With no kids. And doing God knows what at night. And living in sin with John Bracca."

"Patsy! You givin' this girl a hard time 'cause she got no kids? She must make millions!"

Patsy snorted. "Millions ain't a grandson, Ed."

"You want a grandson, Patsy? Maybe you'll get one with John."

"Don't even joke about that."

"Why? John's a good looking guy. Successful, rich. What's your problem?"

"My problem is he's a damn mobster, and I don't want my daughter having babies with a damn mobster. And pardon my French!"

The bus driver sighed and stopped at a red light. He honked at a hooker who crossed the street at Fifty-third. She smiled, wiggled, and waved back.

"Patsy, Angelo's the mobster. John is his son."

Patsy folded his arms across his chest. "Same difference."

The brown bus was an oddity in front of the Plaza and the regular traffic gave it a wide berth. Even the limos seemed intimidated; a bus, after all, commands a certain respect.

Ed shut the engine off. "This is a nice place." The limos and taxis maneuvered around him, assuming he had some reason for being there. He was parked in a square dominated by a gold statue.

"Ed, thanks for taking me here. I hope you don't get into trouble."

"Maybe, who knows." The driver hesitated. "Patsy, do me a favor."

"What?"

"Bring me in with you."

Patsy squinted. "Why you want to do that? It's just dresses!"

"Patsy, you don't understand. I never saw one of these things in my life. And your daughter is not just some . . . some . . ."

"Some what?"

"Some regular person. She's in the papers every week. You get lonely, want to see your daughter, go to a magazine rack. She's . . ."

"On every cover. I know. Usually with something showing that shouldn't be."

"So will you do it?"

"What?"

"Get me in, maybe an autograph?"

Patsy sighed. "Okay, come on along, Ed."

Patsy and Ed drew as many stares when they walked in as any of the models might. Patsy wore a brown, corduroy jacket with a patchwork tie. Ed still had on his bus driver's uniform and looked as though his last name was Norton. A security guard came over fast.

"Can I help you?"

"Sure." Patsy fumbled for the invitation. "You know where seats A-eleven and A-twelve are?"

That answer didn't compute and the guard stared. "They're the best seats in the house, right under the runway. Let me see that." He examined the embossed invitation and the two tickets inside. "Okay, where did you clowns get these?" The man grabbed a small intercom hooked to his belt and spoke into it.

"I got them in the mail," Patsy explained, not getting it. "She sent me two, so I invited Ed. I don't know why two, maybe she thinks I'm lonely."

Another security guard and a woman in a crisp blue suit appeared magically from the rapidly growing crowd. Both carried hand-held intercoms.

"What's the problem?" the woman barked. She was clearly in charge.

The guard handed her the tickets. "They had these," the man said. Ed looked nervous.

"Patsy, I can leave if you want."

"Don't worry about it, Ed. These guys are just ushers I think."

The woman in blue was head of security for a multimillion dollar event. She wasn't used to being called an usher. Still, there was something in the man's voice that suggested caution.

"May I see some I.D.?"

"Sure," Ed said, fumbling in his wallet.

"I think she means me." Patsy handed her his driver's license.

The woman squinted at it. "Pasquale Guiseppe De Marco. Mr. De Marco, can you tell me where you got these . . ." And then she stopped talking and her eyes grew wide.

"What?" the guard said.

The woman turned to him. "Apologize to this man."

"What!"

"You heard me. Repeat after me. Mr. De Marco, I apologize for the inconvenience. I hope you and your guest enjoy your daughter's show."

"Hey," Patsy said, grabbing back his tickets. "Don't sweat it. Just show us the seats."

The ballroom of the Plaza was filling rapidly. There was an aura of tension and anticipation. The men were dressed in dark business suits with a sprinkling of tuxes. The women wore evening wear, black and strapless, and were universally dreading the comparisons their men would soon be quietly making.

Backstage was controlled pandemonium. The whole show would take no more than forty minutes and the next day the press would announce the success or failure of the entire collection. The great designer himself, an amiable, manic genius, had had two failures in a row. There were now many less millions behind him than three years before. One more dud and he'd be opening next in Baltimore.

There were eleven women in the show and each reclined queen-like on a deep padded chair surrounded by handlers. They sat with practiced serenity under the glare of high powered lights while they were fluffed and painted. They wore loose fitting casual clothes and smoked incessantly.

The elegant clothes soon to be displayed on the promenade hung in neat rows, carefully numbered and labeled. When the music started it would all happen fast, eleven women on the runway, each making four appearances. One trip out stage right, down to the end, a spin, back to the dressing room via stage left, two handlers to take the old off, two to put the new on, then back to the runway. The whole thing had to work with the precision of a pit stop at Indy.

The great designer sat in his dressing room alone, smoking cigarettes, drinking coffee and talking on the phone with his mother in Syracuse. He was close to a breakdown.

"Don't worry, it'll be fine," his mother told him.

The designer sighed. "It all comes down to her. And she *still* hates me."

"Hates you? How could she hate you? You're paying her how much for this show?"

"Don't ask. It'll make you sick. Forty minutes and she could walk out of here and buy a Bentley."

"So what's your problem, she should love you."

"Well, we had a little argument. Two shows ago, I was disappointed . . ."

"That was a terrible show, Jacob, and you know I adore you."

"Thank you, Mother."

"But go ahead. You were disappointed."

"Angry is a better word. And I said things to her I shouldn't have."

"That was a mistake. She's Italian, Jacob. I bet she has a terrible temper."

"Tell me about it."

"I was always happy you never ended up with an Italian gir . . . uh, person. They're too volatile."

He lit a new cigarette off the old. He poured more coffee and ate a donut. "Mother, I'm so fat it's disgusting."

"You're not but never mind. What about her?"

"Mother, I'm so stupid. I could be dead now. Her boyfriend is this . . . this *Mafia* person."

"Really!"

"Really. And she has these two brothers—well, not really broth-ers, but boys she was raised with—who were *professional fighters*!"

His mother laughed so hard she got the hiccups.

"I'm glad you think this is so funny, Mother. I'm here getting fat and having terrible shows and insulting girls who could have me . . . I don't know what people like that might do. And you're in Syracuse in your new house laughing at me."

"Jacob, don't be so dramatic. Wait, I have to drink some water . . . There, that's better. It's just the thought of you against those . . ."

"Thank you, Mother."

"I'm surprised you didn't try to date them."

"Mother, watch your mouth!" He drank more coffee. "I did meet one of the brothers. His name is Tommy Boyle if you can believe that. He's a police detective of some kind. God, would I love to see him in a uniform."

"Jacob?"

"Yes."

"You've got a show starting in an hour."

"Thank you, Mother, I didn't realize that."

"So I have a suggestion."

"What?"

"Get your mind out of the gutter, your hands out of your pants and go out and make peace with her."

He sighed. "Yes, Mother." Then he brightened. "Who knows, maybe she brought the nice Mr. Boyle tonight!"

6

Thomas Aquinas Boyle, the sort-of son of Pasquale Guiseppi De Marco, and the sort-of brother of Miguel Meza and Natala De Marco, was born in St. Thomas Aquinas Hospital in Paterson, New Jersey on May Day, 1970. His mother was an illegal Irish immigrant and the delivery was hard. She spent three days under sedation and during that time the nuns named the baby after the sainted Dominican whose visage dominated the east entryway of the hospital. When the woman finally woke she wasn't pleased.

"That's not what I would have called him. Now he'll just be Tommy Boyle like every third Harp in Dublin."

"Maybe not," said the nurse. "Call him by his middle name."

"Aquinas?"

"Well, maybe something shorter, a nickname."

"What in the world could be a nickname for Aquinas?"

The nurse thought hard. "How about Quincy. That sounds rich."

"Quincy? Who ever had the name Quincy?"

"Quincy Jones?" the nurse offered.

"And John Quincy Adams," the doctor boomed as he came in. "Glad to see you're up and about, Mrs. Boyle."

The woman shifted uncomfortably. "It's not quite *Mrs.* Boyle, I'm afraid. And who, may I ask, is Mr. Quincy Adams?"

"*John* Quincy Adams. Boston blue blood and sixth president of the United States. Quincy Boyle would be a fine name, ma'am."

"T. Quincy Boyle," the woman corrected. "It sounds much more refined."

"I agree," the doctor and nurse said together.

For the first twelve years of his life she told him his name was T. Quincy Boyle. The nuns called him that at school and the older boys mocked him with the name after school. He fought in response when he was eight but had despised the name long before that. It didn't matter. It was T. Quincy during class and a fight in the parking lot in the back of the church after class. Sometimes a lot of fights after class.

By the age of eleven an audience of Catholic kids formed after school on the grassy lawn between the parking lot and the church. They'd wait expectantly, at first a few, then, a window to the future, a lot. At 3:50, like clockwork, T. Quincy left the granite school and walked to the parking lot, listening to the noise build. He grew to love it, relish it, and after a time couldn't wait to greet it.

At first the boys who showed up to fight him were more or less his own age, but that changed in a hurry. When the older ones arrived he adjusted, developing cunning and speed, which at bottom was just common sense. It was suicide to grapple with a guy three years older and thirty pounds heavier, so T. Quincy adopted a more realistic strategy. He danced and baited until the taunts grew loud from the grass hill. Forgotten was the hated name and in its place was expectation, the sort a Spanish audience feels when the matador plays with the bull. Eventually, inevitably, the visitor grew frustrated and charged. T. Quincy would backpedal, brace and throw natural lefts, long-limbed and flashing. The first straightened the kid up and the next two dropped him, the bully no longer interested in mocking anyone's name. The kids on the grass cheered and went home.

Even after T. Quincy became Tommy Boyle, the daily fights continued, part of the fabric of South Paterson. No one cared anymore about his name, only whether some football player or gang guy from Clifton or Passaic had the guts to take his shot, try to put down the skinny kid from Paterson who now never lost. And every day after school someone came, enticed by the growing crowds on the grass, and the legend grew.

It might have lasted forever, Tommy Boyle and his mother in the refurbished attic of a house at 336 Atlantic Street. Like most things, all things, it didn't. One day he came back at five and saw a squad of blinking patrol cars parked in front of the house. He instinctually knew what it was all about.

"Mom!" he shouted and ran for the door.

L egend had it that Meza and Boyle arrived in juvenile hall on the same day, but that wasn't precisely true. Boyle arrived first, after his grandmother died, his last remaining relative, not because he did anything wrong, just because juvey was the only place in Paterson to put kids with no place to go. Meza arrived a week later for different reasons, after breaking the jaw of a shop teacher who invited him into his office, closed the door and reached between the boy's legs. It was a bad move for the shop teacher who denied everything from his hospital bed. The man had to write the denial because his jaw had been wired shut.

Boyle was sitting on his bed staring at the wall when a cop pushed Meza into the room. "Here's your roommate."

Boyle looked up briefly and then went back to his wall, which was just fine with Meza.

"Whatever," the cop said.

They might never have spoken if it hadn't been for the Berrigans. The Berrigans were fourteen and sixteen, had been raised in a shack on top of abandoned railroad tracks near Brandeis Field, and had just been expelled from the last school to take them in, a quasi-prison elegantly named School No. 9. As revenge the Berrigans hot-wired the school van, got drunk and robbed a bar. They were caught in thirty minutes and dropped in Paterson juvey.

It all came together in the rec room, on a Saturday night, when the dorms were empty except for the true detritus of the abandoned young. On this Saturday night all that was left were the Berrigans; Boyle and Meza, a couple of half-asleep cops, and a building full of empty rooms.

The Berrigans went after Boyle first. Tommy was half asleep watching a fuzzy black-and-white movie. When he got bored he shut off the television, turned around and there they were.

The older one, Vince, said, "Where you goin'?"

"Back to my room."

Vince smiled. "That's too far. Why don't you come back to *our* room?" The younger Berrigan, Mickey, laughed in a high-pitched voice, like a donkey braying.

Boyle didn't need anyone drawing him pictures. He was twelve years old, tall and skinny, with a baby face and no hair on his body except his head. Vince was sixteen, beefy and shaving daily.

"I don't think so," Boyle said.

Mickey brayed some more. Vince's jaw got hard.

"You don't think so!' Hey, we don't have to go no place. Here's just fine." Vince gestured to his brother.

Mickey moved forward and Boyle backed away until he felt the wall against his back. A table crashed. Boyle waited with relaxed hands until Mickey got close.

For all of Boyle's career, from the school grass to his last pro bout in Vegas, all anyone ever talked about was his fast hands, explosive pistons that worked a face the way a jackhammer works a tough corner of concrete. "I never taught him those hands," Patsy would later say. "You get them for free in the womb."

Mickey didn't scare Boyle, he was no bigger than the kids on the grass and a lot less athletic. When he charged, Boyle used the wall as a brace, firing the left four times off a planted right foot. He caught Mickey square in the eye with the first, broke his nose with the second, broke his jaw with the third and rendered him unconscious with the fourth. Mickey kept trying to fall forward, but the jackhammer jabs kept him up. The whole thing took no more than four seconds.

Then Boyle stepped aside and let Mickey fall, face first, bleeding on the tile. His brother went nuts.

"I'll kill you!" he screamed. Vince ran at Boyle, overturning tables. When the last table was gone he grabbed an empty Coke bottle and shattered it against the hard floor.

Now Boyle got concerned; Vince was an animal and a big one. He backed away and ran out of room fast, stumbling slightly against the overturned chair. Vincent saw the opening and charged. Boyle braced for the attack, blinked once and when he opened his eyes Vince was gone.

Later, when he thought about it, he could never figure out where Meza came from. One minute Vince was there, stalking him with the broken bottle in his hand, the next he was facedown, Meza on his back, slamming Vince's face repeatedly into the tile. The fight had all the grace of a great white tearing apart a dolphin.

"Stop it! Stop it right now," a voice barked.

Meza ignored the man, just kept banging Vince's head into the floor.

"Stop it!" the cop yelled again and ran across the room. He tackled Meza and dragged him off Vince. Vince slumped, bleeding, about fifteen feet from where Mickey was slumped, bleeding.

"Goddamn it," the cop said. He pushed Meza against the wall.

"You," the cop barked to Boyle, "on your ass, next to him."

When they took the Berrigans out Boyle and Meza laughed so hard they got the hiccups. Then the stretchers were gone, and the cop had the sudden pleasant realization that the Berrigans might be out of his life forever. He stood before the boys with his hands on his hips.

"Okay, you two, I got only one thing to say."

"What?" Boyle asked, whose hiccups were better than Meza's.

The cop held out a hand. "Great job."

At ten in the morning on the day after the Berrigans hit the ground they were ushered into the chambers of Municipal Court Judge Jacqueline B. Gardner, an independently wealthy widow who ran the juvenile department with the imperiousness of an Old World empress. She pointed to a chair.

"Sit down!"

They did, Boyle uncomfortable, Meza slouching. Judge Gardner looked at the file. Her eyebrows rose. "You beat up the Berrigans?"

"Yes, ma'am," Meza said, proud of it.

Boyle wasn't. "Do we have to go to jail?"

Judge Gardner shook her head. She was a slender woman of fifty, elegantly dressed. Her robe hung neatly on a hook near the door. "For defending yourself against the Berrigans? I don't think so."

She examined the file some more. "But what *are* we going to do with you?" She sucked on a pencil. "Do you have any family?"

"Nope," said Meza.

"My grandmother," said Boyle.

"Really?" The judge looked happy.

"But she's dead."

The judge rubbed her temples. "Well, we need to put you someplace. Have either of you been in foster homes? Not that there's any left in Paterson."

"About a thousand," Meza said.

"Right, okay, don't panic." She thought out loud. "Orphans, street kids, juvenile hall, no foster homes available. What? Come on. D... th... up. Th... H...g... Fighter. Fighter!" She screamed and the two kids flinched.

The judge punched her intercom. "Get Patsy in here immediately."

I t took an hour and when they dragged him in he wasn't happy. He complained before he hit the chair.

"Judge, forget it, before you even start, forget it."

"Patsy, please, just listen . . ."

"I can't. I'm full. You sent me seven kids already this year. Judge, you're a sweet lady but . . ."

"Mr. De Marco, be silent!"

Patsy glared at her set jaw. "Yes, ma'am," he mumbled. "But I'm tellin' you I . . ."

"Don't tell me anything yet, Mr. De Marco. Hear me out first."

He folded his arms across his chest. "I'm listening."

Better. The judge was used to getting her way, whether or not she was wearing her robes. "This time I am not asking for charity, Mr. De Marco," she said softly. "I am here to introduce you to two young fighters. Talented ones."

Patsy smirked. "Judge, I know your heart's in the right place. But you wouldn't know a fighter from a . . ."

The judge's eyes flattened. "From a what, Mr. De Marco?"

Patsy had to stand up for himself. "Well, from a damn petunia, Judge, that's just the way it is. And pardon my French!"

To his amazement Judge Gardner smiled. "Well, maybe you're right. How about we make a wager, a bet."

"What bet?"

"A simple one. You must have some test to decide if a boy has talent. Pick one of them and give him your test. If he passes, you take him. If not," the judge opened her hands, "I won't bother you for awhile."

Patsy scratched his head. This was too easy. He had a test no kid could pass. "That's it?"

Judge Gardner waved her hand graciously. "What else? Do you have such a test?"

"You bet your sweet . . . I mean, sure, it's my business."

"Proceed, Mr. De Marco."

He examined the two scrawny refugees. "Which one of you rug rats is better?"

The boys didn't answer.

"All right, I'll decide." He pointed to the tall one. "You."

The judge gestured to Boyle. "Young man, stand up."

Patsy looked him over. Skinny and scared, this would be easy.

"Okay, kid, we're going to play a game. It's real simple so you won't have to tax your brain."

Patsy held his hands twenty inches apart, then brought them together with a loud clap. The speed was breathtaking. One second the hands were apart, the next millisecond they were together. An old fighter's speed.

"You see that?"

Boyle had a blank look, a poker face. "Yeah."

"Good, now come here."

Boyle did, easing in, till he was about two, three feet away. Meza laughed quietly in the background, figuring it out.

"So here's the deal." Patsy spread his hands again and stuck his face between them. "No defense. Can you hit this face before I slap my hands?"

Meza answered for him. "No problem, pops!"

"Tough guys, right? We'll see." He turned to the judge. "Ready for that test?"

Judge Gardner smiled broadly. "The question, Mr. De Marco, is, are you?"

"Yeah, I think so." He turned back to Tommy. "Go ahead."

Boyle was nervous and let go a tentative left hand. The old fighter's hands slapped together.

"Not too good," the man said.

"I'm sorry. I don't want to hurt you."

Patsy laughed. The judge flew to her feet. "Young man, listen to me!" Boyle snapped to attention. "When Mr. De Marco tells you to hit him in the face you will do exactly as he tells you, no back talk, understand?"

"But . . ."

"Did you hear me?"

"Yes, ma'am." Boyle turned back, now terrified of the judge, who sounded a lot like his mother did sometimes. Patsy spread his hands again.

"Now go ahead, take your shot, I ain't got all day."

For years later when he was asked about it, the hundreds of times he was asked about it, he could never remember whether he got the sentence all the way out. All he remembered was one second he was looking at the kid's skinny face and the next looking at the ceiling. The judge had a better view and told the story better.

"Tommy was like a cobra," she said. "His left hand just snapped. Poor Patsy fell back, bleeding from the nose."

Meza described it in starker terms. "You don't stick your face in Tommy Boyle's left, man. You got to be nuts!"

For Patsy, the decision was made when his head bounced off the floor. No kid, and certainly no twelve year old, had ever come close to passing this test before. The judge's bailiff gave him smelling salts, cleaned his nose and helped him to his feet.

"Well?" the judge asked, keeping it cool, not gloating.

Patsy brushed himself off. "This other kid's as good as him?"

"You want to see?"

"Yeah." He gestured to Meza. "Just let me see you take a few cuts. You know, make believe you're punching."

Meza yawned. "Go to the zoo you want to see a monkey."

Nice kid. Yet this time the judge did not interfere, something in the boy's voice. "Well," she said, "at least I can tell you he beat up the other Berrigan."

Patsy's eyes came back to her slowly. "The Berrigans? You forgot to mention that."

The judge shrugged. "Anyway," she said, "we had a deal."

All that speed and youth. Plus there were two of them.

"Okay, they're in."

7

Alicia Kent arrived in New York at 4 P.M. on the afternoon Concorde. Her appointment with the killer she had selected for the old man was set for 7 P.M. near Central Park. It took forever to get there because there was some kind of fashion show at the Plaza which had the traffic screwed up. Plus some yutz had parked a bus on the corner of Central Park South and Fifth Avenue. She wanted to blow up the thing but first things first.

She met her contact a few blocks west of the stalled bus, under the statue of José Marti, the "George Washington" of Cuba. The car waiting for her was driven by a black male in his mid thirties, dressed in a dark suit, white button-down shirt and printed tie. He looked like a stockbroker, or a funeral director. He was every bit the latter, as the pale silver earring in his left ear indicated. He was stocky, broad in the shoulder and carried a squat Walther semiautomatic in a harness under his jacket.

She got in the front seat with him. "Okay, Carlos, you ready to go?"

"Always ready, baby."

Natala De Marco knew nothing about Alicia Kent's meeting with her father's killer four blocks away from the Plaza. She only knew she felt uncomfortable in the chaotic madness, but she always felt that way before she went on. The other girls—and some *were* girls, one was only fourteen—were sitting in the same stupid makeup chairs as she was, surrounded by the same anxious makeup artists. It took almost two hours for the eleven of them to be stripped, washed, coifed, painted and dressed, and she hated every minute of it.

They put her chair between her two best friends, an anorexic twenty year old named Elizabeth and a six-foot-three Nairobi beauty named Orlando. She sat down, threw her coat on the floor, and held out her hand. Orlando put a cigarette in it.

"What the hell's wrong with you, Nat?"

Natala lit a cigarette and puffed deeply while the attendants attacked her. Even tired, angry and without makeup, she had a radiant, natural beauty that was literally breathtaking. She was twenty-four years old now and her hair was black and thick, enveloping a pair of gray eyes so pale they were almost white. Her skin was lightly bronzed, like fine olive oil. Her mouth was Italian and full, naturally blood engorged and pouting. Her breasts and hips, counter to every fashion stereotype, were real, and Italian, and when she walked down a runway the whole package came together and made people stare. They paid her a fortune to wear their clothes and the people who paid her had made several fortunes in return.

She smoked rapidly, taking advantage of any gaps left by the hair and makeup guys. Orlando waited for her reply.

"What's wrong with me?" They tilted her backward and took her cigarette away from her. "I got a moron boyfriend and a moron brother. And I drank a quart of wine last night and my head hurts."

Elizabeth, the anorexic, laughed. "You're crazy."

"No, I've been crazy. Now I'm sane."

"Do you realize," Elizabeth said as they tilted her back too, "how quick I'd do either of them?"

"Appearances can be deceiving."

"Well, let me take a look and I'll tell you how it appears."

Orlando jumped to Natala's support. "Don't give this sweet thing a hard time. Just tell Orlando what's wrong, baby."

"John is a jerk who stays out whenever he wants and won't tell me anything. And Tommy, who's supposed to be smart, just keeps getting suspended over and over." She jerked her cigarette back from a handler who was trying to sneak it away.

"He's the cop?"

"Yeah. A homicide detective in Paterson when he's not getting suspended."

"Why does he get suspended?"

Natala sighed. "He hits people. Other cops mostly." Then before she could say more her worst nightmare was realized. Jacob was standing in front of her.

"Oh, God." She grabbed her pounding head.

"Natala," Jacob said in a whiny voice. "I'm here to apologize."

The show itself was ridiculous, over the top, but in the face of all reason was regarded as a great success. When the house lights dimmed, the runway exploded with alternating colored strobes. Giant speakers erupted with a deep repetitive bass. A male voice spoke gravely over the rumbling beat.

"God, this sucks," Elizabeth said.

The music in the giant speakers changed to an ear-splitting high-pitched wail followed by the detonation of an electronic drum. Blinding floodlights lit the stage and Elizabeth walked out, her eyes distant and uncaring, her hands on her waist, her hips snapping insolently with each deafening beat from the giant speakers. Every movement announced that she was special, unreachable, unattainable, and the clothes she wore were the same, unless the price was right.

The men looked at her with tight, frustrated lips. The women looked at her too and to their surprise smiled, feeling no more competition than a man would at seeing a professional athlete. True, I will never be her, but neither will anyone else he might meet.

The crowd warmed as Elizabeth pirouetted at the runway's edge. As soon as Elizabeth turned, Orlando began her strut downstage, moving with African abandon to the druid beat. The noise grew. Jacob pressed his hands together in silent prayer.

When Orlando spun a third emerged, her name announced above the din. It was getting raucous, as a good show should, and the crowd was now standing. Jacob saw a blessed confluence taking place, of cigarettes and cigars, of champagne, of women with bare shoulders and men with money, of darkness and floodlights, and ultimately, magnificently, of ear-splitting music and the most beautiful women on the planet, parading, whipping their hips in time to the beat, on display.

Oh, yes, and clothes of some sort.

By the time the tenth model made her turn the crowd was up.

The clothes had gotten skimpier, the music louder and the expectations higher. Only this time, after the girl swiveled and left, no
replacement emerged, nothing but the blue of the smoke in the
floodlights. Then the drums sounded, amplified to a painful repetitive rhythm. Faster and faster. Without pause.

The crowd rose as one, louder, trying to bury the repetitive beats
in sound.

"Ladies and gentlemen, the incomparable Natala!"

She strolled into a wall of noise. Her grin was wide and pure and
her black hair bounced with her hips to the beat of the music. She
was dressed in knee-high fake fur boots and an impossibly short
flowing skirt. Her black hair was topped with a peasant headdress
and she wore a spangled jacket. Her blouse was light colored, and
low, loose, and there was no question there were peasant breasts
underneath that blouse.

At the end of the runway she twirled twice and the short skirt
rose, revealing all of Natala De Marco that any man might see. Except John Bracca, who could see whatever he wanted. The crowd
was near delirium, as was Jacob, and there were still three more
rounds to go.

"This is unbelievable," Ed said.

"I never had any control over her," Patsy admitted. "She'd always
just show it to whoever she wanted."

"Patsy, you hear these screams. They're yelling for your daughter."

"This is really stupid. Plus that noise is hurtin' my ears."

Ed laughed. "Patsy, you got a free ride home on the bus tonight,
that's all I got to say."

"She offered me a limo. I told her 'No. I'd rather ride with Ed.' "

"Let me ask you, how come her brothers ain't here?"

"Migo's in L.A. Tommy's in Paterson. He . . . well, I heard he just
had another problem. He don't follow orders so good."

"Too bad."

"Yeah."

On her second trip out the girl saw him. She bent down and blew
a kiss. He had to laugh, he would see her backstage and she would
be as affectionate as she always was. If Miguel and Tommy missed
her shows, too bad, their loss.

He now had less than six hours to live.

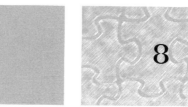

8

After Ed dropped him off, the old man stopped for a drink on the way home. It wasn't as easy as it once was because his choices in Paterson taverns were fast evaporating. One of the few that stood a chance of ending the night without a robbery was the Town Tavern. It stood squarely between police headquarters, fire headquarters, and the Paterson "campus" of Seton Hall University. The "campus" was a five-story brick building over a concrete slab, and, like the firehouse, scheduled to be demolished. The only real business anymore came from the cops, who always stopped to pick up containers at the start of each shift.

The Town Tavern, or "T" as it was known, was a throwback to a time long gone. The jukebox was stuffed with vinyl records of Big Band standards from the forties, and a record was replaced only when it got too warped to play. The bartender—an amiable rummy named Jimmy—had been back there a quarter century. He was fifty and looked seventy-five, the booze etching deep folds in his neck and face. The pain of ten thousand hangovers had hung lumps of flesh under his eyes that looked like brown satchels.

Patsy sat at the bar and Jimmy waddled over. There was a tradition to be observed. Jimmy looked into space, waiting, and put a white napkin down.

"Buy you one, Jim?"

A shrug. "Wouldn't mind."

Jimmy shuffled around and came back with a shot of Seagram's and a small draft for Patsy; a double shot for Jimmy. They sipped, Jimmy squinting, fighting to think through the fog. Patsy waited. Jimmy asked the same five questions every time.

"So how's the fight game, Patsy?"

"Good. Got some good young talent, Jim. Maybe Gloves material."

Nodding, struggling to remember question two. "The Golden Gloves. That's really something. Just like Miguel and Tommy. Who you think was better, Patsy?"

"Well, we'll never know Jim. They were both special."

"Yeah." Question three, back there in the haze someplace. Then a brightening. "You ever see Miguel?"

"He's in L.A., Jim." And had been for the six years Jimmy had been asking.

"No kidding. That's really something." Sip on the Seagram's, squint, brighten. "And Tommy, too? He in L.A.?"

"No, Jimmy, he's a homicide detective. Works right around the corner, at headquarters."

"No kidding. He should come in, Patsy. I'd love to say hello."

Love to and had, any number of times. "I'll tell him, Jim."

"Great." The Seagram's vanished and Patsy paid, then got up to leave. Jimmy shuffled down to the end of the bar where a well-dressed black man sat patiently. He wore a dark suit and sported a round, silver earring. Jimmy dropped the white napkin.

"What can I do you for?"

"Whatever my friend had," Carlos said. "And make it to go."

Patsy loved to look at the city at night from the top of Garrett Mountain. For all its inner cancer the city was a tarnished jewel to those few who knew it well. It was the first pure industrial city in the United States, founded in the late eighteenth century by Alexander Hamilton and something called the Society for Useful Manufacture. To this day it remains dominated by an improbable two hundred-year-old castle, built on an improbable mountain by a crazy, drunken Scotsman who was afraid of the farmers below. The Passaic River, once beautiful as well as wide, runs through its center, ending in the ridiculously improbable falls that first attracted Hamilton. The falls is, after Niagara, the largest on the East Coast.

In its early years the city prospered, its solid manufacturing base guaranteeing jobs and profits. Many of the most violent labor clashes of the early twentieth century took place in Paterson, a tribute not to the violence but to its place even then as a manufacturing hub.

Yet modern times were not kind to the city. Power plants elimi-nated the importance of the falls and rival industrial centers yanked away the city's monopoly on industry. By the 1940s it was known as the "Silk City," so called because all the mills had become silk mills. Then the Japanese silk beetle destroyed even that final industry after the war and there was nothing left. The former silk mills were empty husks, used if at all for warehouses. Just like the one next to Patsy's gym.

At the top of Garrett Mountain is a parking lot and viewing area with telescopes that cost a quarter. Patsy pulled in and sat quietly. It was a cold February night and the lights of Manhattan were clear twelve miles away. A dark Lincoln pulled up near him and he saw the driver and a woman emerge. She was viper-lean and tall. The man was dark-skinned and hidden in shadows. The black man stared at him for a moment, then took the woman's hand and led her to the edge of the precipice. They looked down and she tried to pull back. He grabbed her hair and yanked it, exposing her neck. There was something oddly dangerous about the sight and the old man felt a chill. He started his car, glanced once more at the strange pair on the bluffs and pulled out.

Alicia Kent saw Patsy's car pull away and was furious. She was cold, standing on the edge of a mountain in the darkness and had Carlos breathing heavily over her, the stench of alcohol on his breath, her hair in his fist. One day she would kill him, just not yet.

"He's leaving," she said, stealing a glance over his shoulder.

"So what?" He bit into her white neck.

"So we've got to move."

"Don't you think I'll get the job done?"

No, she thought. "Of course."

"So relax."

She squinted. Out of the corner of her eye she saw the red lights of Patsy's car moving away.

"I can't relax."

"All right, later then, let's go."

The killing occurred on the aptly named Cannonball Road, or at least was scheduled to. Patsy drove down the steep road slowly. He was a careful driver and avoided dangerous situations, which is why he never in his life drove a car into Manhattan. A loud moon glanced off the white crests of the rushing river as it raced over the falls. The river landed heavily on the rocks two hundred feet below and shattered against the long-dead power center built by a long dead entrepreneur.

Carlos got Patsy's car in his headlights about a mile down Cannonball Road. There was another mile and a half before the sharp bend where it would all happen. He rolled down the window. The deafening roar of the massive falls swept into the car.

"Hang on baby."

The big Lincoln accelerated and Patsy's car drew closer. The road dropped precipitously. Alicia felt a sense of vertigo as Carlos ignored the steep grade and accelerated to seventy. The front of the car dipped and her breasts pressed against the seat belt.

She should have been afraid. Instead, as always before a kill, her eyes were bright with concentration. Patsy's car filled the headlights and the road rushed down, the turn only a quarter of a mile away. At the bend was a harsh left signaled by a thin metal rail with reflective red circles. A blaring sign above the circles advised drivers to reduce speed to five miles per hour. Beyond the sign and the reflective circles was the void, and the horror of the falls.

Patsy blinked as the high beam filled his rearview mirror. What was this jerk doing, this was a dangerous road. At least three drunks a year missed the sharp turn and went careening through the guardrail. Some got lucky and just smashed into a tree or rock on the steep downslope leading to the river. Some didn't, and took a long horrifying death float, alive, down the last hundred feet of river to the crest of the immense cascade.

He slowed, the sharp bend rushing at him. The high beams from the oncoming car blinded him. He couldn't believe it. He accelerated to escape. It was too late.

The grating sound of metal on metal was drowned by the thunder of the river. Patsy ducked and the full-speed collision did not snap his neck as it should have. Instead it gave him the instant of life he needed to take his foot off the brake and slap the transmission stick to neutral. The maneuver saved him. The force of the Lincoln's weight was dissipated as the car rocketed forward toward the guardrail. Patsy spun the steering wheel and did a three-sixty on the windy road. He wound up facing Carlos, headlight to headlight.

"What the . . ." Carlos began.

"He seems to be still alive," Alicia said gently.

"Not for long." Carlos pressed the accelerator to the floor. Nothing happened. The Lincoln was stalled, silent.

Carlos screamed an angry curse and pounded the wheel. He tried the ignition again and the car lurched forward, still in gear. The engine remained silent.

Patsy watched the whole thing in his headlights with a smoothly running engine. He suddenly got it. Whatever the reason, and it probably had something to do with the mysterious, smelly boxes in the old factory, these crazy people were trying to kill him.

He didn't waste any more time. He gunned the engine and his little Toyota responded. He was going steeply uphill and his speed wasn't what he wanted. Nevertheless, it was enough.

Alicia Kent screamed. "Carlos, look out!"

Carlos had his head down screwing with the ignition when the Toyota rammed headlong into the Lincoln. Carlos' head slammed into the steering wheel, opening a large gash over his eye. His mouth sagged and he went for the Walther.

"Carlos, no!" Alicia Kent shouted. "No bullets."

Carlos swore, turning to argue. Then in the glare of his headlights he saw Patsy emerge from the car.

"Good, he's gettin' out. I'm gonna snap his neck. Then I'm throwin' him *and* his car into the damn water."

A broken neck was consistent with an unfortunate accident and didn't bother Alicia.

"Fine, just no bullets."

Patsy and Carlos met in the middle of the road, lit by two sets of dueling headlights. Carlos was bleeding profusely from the cut over his eye. Patsy squinted at him and remembered. The guy from the bar. Now he was sure.

"Why'd you do that?" Carlos muttered. "You drunk or what?"

Patsy didn't answer, just moved in closer. Carlos let him approach.

"C'mon over. That's right, old man, real close."

The guy looked strong but Patsy could tell right away he wasn't a fighter, just by the way he held his hands. If the guy wanted him close that was just fine.

"That's better," Carlos said when they were three feet apart. "Much better." He reached out.

Big mistake. Patsy slapped the hand aside and went right for the cut eye, opening it wide with two quick lefts. Carlos was completely unprepared for the assault and staggered backward. Patsy got further inside and worked the body hard. Carlos tried to respond but the blood from his eye was now falling in sheets over his face. One thing a corner man like Patsy knew about was cuts, how to close them, how to open them. He went for the eye again.

Carlos had had enough. His right hand went under his coat and came out with the Walther.

"Good-bye, old man. Time for a nice long swim."

He raised the gun and Patsy shut his eyes. He heard the gun go off and stiffened. He felt nothing and thought, "I guess that's what happens when you die."

Then he opened his eyes and saw the gun on the ground and Carlos next to it. A woman stood holding a blood-stained tire iron.

"I told you, 'no,'" she said softly, as though Carlos could hear her. But he couldn't because the back of his head was shattered. She picked up the Walther. Carlos groaned.

She turned to Patsy. "I'm sorry about that."

"Who are you? What do you want?"

She tried to look nervous, concerned, which was getting a lot easier as time went on. "I can't control him. I'm as frightened as you are. Can you help me?"

"I don't think he'll make it. You hit him pretty hard."

"I had to. It was the only way to stop him. You know about wounds?"

"Sure."

She gestured with the gun. "Take a look at him, will you? Then we'll put him in the car and I'll get out of your life forever. I'll be safe once I'm out of here."

Patsy knelt over Carlos and gently moved the man's head. The wound was worse than he thought. The tire iron had struck directly behind the ear. Carlos was breathing in shallow, labored bursts.

"It don't look good."

"Get him on his back. It may make him more comfortable."

"I don't know, he could swallow blood." Carlos was already weakly coughing blood.

"Just do it, okay?"

He shrugged and struggled with Carlos' inert form. It was hard work. He had him halfway turned when he saw the bright gleam of metal in the glare of the headlights. It was the last sight he would ever see. He twisted to avoid the blow but it was too late. He groaned and fell face forward on the oil-soaked road.

There was a lot to do and not a lot of time. It was late but she couldn't be sure someone wouldn't suddenly appear on this deserted road, maybe stop and offer to help. A couple of teenage neckers perhaps. Then she'd have three carloads of bodies to dispose of.

First things first. She put a pair of thin black gloves on and hauled Patsy back to the Toyota. She put him in the driver's seat, shut off the engine and took the keys.

Back to Carlos. She kicked him in the head with a pointed heel and he groaned, turning slowly onto his back. He opened his eyes.

"Don't worry, baby," she said, "I'll take care of you."

He nodded in gratitude, no longer remembering how he got in this spot to begin with. With her help, he staggered to his feet, disoriented, and didn't object when she put him in the passenger seat of Patsy's car.

She squeezed in next to Patsy, started the car, and turned it so it was again pointed down Cannonball Road. She drove to the flimsy metal guardrail and left the small car pressed against it, the engine running and transmission in neutral.

The Walther was a problem. Throwing it over the falls was one solution but too simple. She had a better idea.

She wiped off the gun and put it in Carlos' hand, squeezing his fingers around it. Then she went around the car and wrapped Patsy's hand around the gun as well. She pointed the Walther at Carlos and used Carlos's fingers to fire. Carlos jerked as the two rounds entered his throat. He slumped, blood flowing freely down his gorgeous white shirt.

Almost done. She grabbed Carlos' gin bottle from the Lincoln and poured it over both of them, then returned to her car. "Please God, start." She turned the key and the engine roared. "Thank you, God," she said. The inappropriateness of her prayers never entered her mind.

She buckled herself in tightly, raced the engine to seven thousand RPMs and popped it into drive. The Lincoln roared down the steep road. She kept her eyes focused on the twin taillights in front of her. Five feet from impact she shut her eyes, braced and spun the wheel. The big Lincoln hit the Toyota solidly, the Lincoln spinning left down Cannonball Road and the Toyota bursting through the guard rail into oblivion.

She got out of the car to watch. It was a magnificent sight. The Toyota flew through the guardrail and held a nose-up position in the moonlight all the way to the river, like a ski jumper. On landing, it sent waves of brackish water high around it, then settled into a sedate ride to the crest of the falls.

It went over surprisingly easily, without objection, once more taking to the air, majestically, the white spray acting as an escort. The falls were lit with floodlights funded by federal urban relief money and she got to watch the whole flight of the Toyota. The car seemed to sail through the air in slow motion till it crashed at the bottom between thick boulders. Red flames mixed with white water and then the whole mess sank beneath the waves.

She closed her eyes and felt pleasure surge through her. She needed to be with someone, someone who would fuel her passion, expand it, who would understand, someone with whom she could share. Not the perfect one she dreamed of, just someone for the moment.

"Ah, yes," she said aloud, her eyes still closed. "Gregor!"

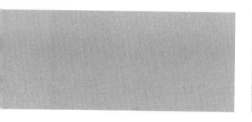

9

Thomas Aquinas Boyle should have been working the night Patsy died but instead he was suspended again. Natala found out about it a few hours before the show, which completely infuriated her and destroyed all the joy she had felt from Patsy's visit. She had called over to tell Tommy to come to the show and wound up talking to Sergeant Joseph Angelo, a buddy of hers from the old days.

"Sorry, Nat, he ain't here now and he won't be here later either."

"How come, Joey, is he sick?" Tommy was a pain but he was still her brother. If he was sick she'd call and fake being sympathetic.

"Probably, but not the way you mean. He's home again, this time for 30 days."

She rubbed her temples as the pain hit. "Are you kidding me, Joey?"

The sergeant's voice dropped. "You know, usually I'm on his side, especially when he popped that cop everybody knew was dirty. But this time he nailed a suspect, just dropped the guy."

"Jesus."

"Yeah. He's coming in tomorrow to pick up his check. I'll tell him you called."

The way Boyle saw it, he didn't hit a suspect, he hit a murderer, and one who dearly deserved it. But at the beginning of the shift there was no way to tell that, no way to get ready. Like every night, he rolled out of headquarters at midnight and for the first thirty minutes watched with disgust as Jack Ruffulo, his drunken partner, made him stop at four convenience stores so Jack could go grab vials of rum from shelves in back of the cash register. The Syrian and

Pakistani managers were used to it and paid no attention. Every time Jack got back in the car he dumped the latest vial into a large Coke, took a sip and groaned.

"You let me know when your hangover's gone, Jack, just in case I need some backup."

"Go to hell," his partner said amiably. "You want a drink, help yourself, otherwise just drive."

That he would. Boyle was not about to let Jack drive, shoot, or do anything else tonight. But Tommy Boyle didn't cause problems, just did his job, and everybody knew that.

"You know what's really wrong with you?" Jack said, when he'd drunk the fourth vial.

"No, Jack, tell me what's really wrong. Somebody like you, I should listen to." As he drove his head swiveled, watching the Hiroshima-like streets as vermin, or people, scurried in the dark, avoiding the headlights.

"You're too tight. You got to relax. You know, I figure that's why you're always getting suspended. Don't bang your head into the system, you know what I mean?"

"You think?" He tried to keep the sarcasm out of his voice.

"Absolutely. You probably just *need* a little. We *all* do."

Boyle turned the unmarked car around a corner, ignoring the open crack dealing outside a bombed-out brick building with no windows and a yellow city CONDEMNED sign on the front. Let vice sweep up the corner sometime next century. They were already late to the homicide scene.

"No, Jack, I don't know what you mean."

"Let me show you. Pull over."

"Forget it. We got a body waiting for us."

His partner's face flushed. "Hey, Boyle? I'm not asking. I'm tellin' you where I want to get off." He grinned. "So to speak."

Boyle sighed and pulled over to the corner. The Puerto Rican girl in the shadows came forward, exiting the shade of the unused, elevated railway under which she hid, not from the cops, just from the other creatures of the night. Jack walked to her and she held out her hand. They strolled hand in hand, sort of like the prom, until they were again in the shade of the El. The girl knelt on the concrete in front of him and it was all over fast. The girl coughed, spit and turned away. Jack zipped up. Boyle found himself oddly disoriented, repelled, watching anyway. If he complained, he knew what Jack would say: "So what if we're late, that body ain't goin' no place."

He grabbed Jack's Coke and drank deeply. "Ah," he said to the empty car. "Here's to Paterson's finest."

They were an hour late to the crime scene because of Jack's many detours and the beat cops were way past annoyed, now hopping from foot to foot to stay warm. The body was propped up against an unused set of railroad tracks that ran from Crooks Avenue through the guts of Paterson. Boyle walked gingerly over the parallel steel rails. Jack stayed in the car, squinting in the pale light left by broken streetlights a block away.

Boyle knelt beside the body. The girl was facedown, a pool of dark liquid spreading away from the metal track she was bludgeoned against. He used the flashlight and saw her right hand was balled into a fist. The left hand was open, the fingers splayed against the horror of impending death. The web of the left hand between thumb and index finger had the tattoo of a small bug. He looked closer.

"That's a beetle, I think," a voice said. He glanced over his shoulder and saw a cop he knew, a bright young kid, third year on the force and dying to get out of a uniform. The kid's name was Kevin something or other. Word was he practically had to be mugged to take his share of the bottle cut from the projects near Eastside. Boyle liked him. Kevin was one of the few people on the force who actually gave a damn what happened in this city.

"What do you got?"

Kevin crouched near him and pulled out a notepad. "Her stage name's Tracy Webster."

Tracy. Right. "I'm freezing, Kevin. Talk."

"She worked across the street." The cop pointed to the blinking lights of a now empty strip bar. The marquee still advertised their stock in trade: 24 GORGEOUS GIRLS. NUDE.

Only twenty-three now.

"What else?"

More flipping of the notepad. "Her shift's over at two, but tonight she leaves at one, like she's got someplace to go. She leaves alone. Guy at the door says 'you want me to walk you?' She says 'no, my car's right here.' " The cop pointed to a rusting green Datsun.

"Nice car."

"Yeah, beautiful. She walks across the street. The door guy watches her for awhile, then looks back inside."

"Okay."

"He don't hear nothin' for awhile. One time he says, that's about two minutes, three minutes."

"If you were any good, you'd know the song."

" 'Hanky Panky.' Madonna."

"Who's that?"

The cop rubbed a finger behind his ear. "Two minutes, forty-two seconds."

"Very good. What then?"

"A big scream."

Yes, just before the kill, when she knew she was going to die.

"So then the door guy tears himself away from the show?"

"That's what he says. And he sees nada. No girl, no nothing."

"Until?"

"Until he sees three guys running away from the tracks."

"Three?"

"Yeah," Kevin said. "That's why he didn't go help, he says. Too dangerous."

Boyle flashed his light at the girl again. No money gone, no jewelry gone, no rape, no drugs he could see. No three guys either.

"Three guys come here for no reason and kill her for no reason?"

"It don't make much sense to me."

"Where's the door guy?"

Kevin gestured to a warm patrol car. "He ain't happy he's still around. Also jumpy."

That he would be. Boyle took a pen and gently moved the girl's hair. One side of her face was untouched by bruises. He lit up her face with the light. He couldn't believe what he saw. He had to be wrong.

"Her bag still here?"

"Right here."

Boyle gingerly opened the small leather purse. The crime scene techs would scream about this but he had to know. He found her wallet intact, $112 in cash, lots of ones making the leather bulge, tips from the stage. He found the license where he expected, found the face on it he expected, found the name on it he expected.

"Mother of Christ," he growled. "Hey, Kevin?"

"Yes, sir."

"Take a look at her mouth. See if there's a gold tooth on the bottom, about halfway back."

"The techs don't like. . . ."

"Do it, Kevin!"

The cop took a pen and flashlight and gently opened the girl's mouth.

"Right on the money, Detective."

"And one more thing."

"Yes, sir?"

"Bring that lyin' door guy over here."

At noon Boyle was still working. His shift was technically over at eight, which was when Jack bailed, but it never occurred to him to stop. He knew what he had to do and at first tried to do it right, get the warrant to search, but it was Sunday morning and nobody gave a rat's ass about a stripper murder in Paterson. So he had to do what he had to do, break into her apartment, find what he wanted, then lay the whole thing out to the watch commander. The guy just stared at him.

"You're nuts, Boyle."

"Why do you say that?"

"Because it's a lot of 'if, maybe' nothing. What's your case? You know the girl? The door guy changes his story? You saw some stuff in an apartment you got no business in anyway! So what?"

"So we have a dead girl for no reason. And I know *exactly* who did it."

The man snorted. "We got a dead everything in this town, Boyle, and one more hooker don't mean nothin'. Go home and get some sleep. You hear me?"

"She wasn't a . . . never mind. I hear you."

"Good." Then the man's voice dropped. "By the way, you hear about the new bottle cut from the projects?"

The all important bottle cut. In Paterson, like most cities, crack cocaine is sold in small plastic vials called bottles. Five or ten dollars apiece, depending on size. A percentage of the gross on a daily basis went to a vice detective named Sanders who then shared it department-wide on the basis of seniority. The cut, the bottle cut. If you don't want it, fine, just say "no," and then spend your days watching your back.

"What about it?"

The man's voice dropped even further. "It's up ten percent." He laughed until a smoker's hack took over. "Price of poker just went up."

Thomas Aquinas Boyle smiled the smile he practiced a lot. "That's really great!"

IO

Boyle didn't go home like he was ordered to. Instead, he went west, arriving outside the Ridgewood mansion at three, as the sun sat high above Bergen County. It had been a short ride from Paterson across the Passaic River to the manicured lawns of Ridgewood. It's probably also a short ride from Gaza to Israel and the security at the border is about the same. Except in Bergen County the border guards are called cops, not IDF, and for the most part they're very nice. If you're black or Hispanic, and have legit reasons for crossing the river, no problem, just get out, spread them, and politely explain what that reason is.

Richard Preston had lived on both sides of the river—as a youth, on the Paterson side with Boyle and Meza, now, for the last four years, on the Bergen County side. He was a financial analyst, late of Drexel, now with the biggest white shoe house on the street. When he left Drexel, at the age of twenty-five, he was moderately strung out on amphetamines and had a net worth of $17 million. Now, five years later, his habit was double and his net worth half. He was heading in the wrong direction in lots of ways.

Boyle parked in front of a vast brick wall, watching quietly as a parade of partygoers festively walked past security guards standing stolidly next to a stone and metal gate. The well-dressed parents held laughing, small children by their hands. Occasionally one would grab a balloon available for the taking on the way in.

The house was a Georgian, about eight thousand square feet, with a half acre in the back. Boyle strolled in with the celebrants, didn't take a balloon, and soon found himself in the backyard, so far un-impeded by the stern men at the gate. He wore a rumpled raincoat, which was weird for a kid's party, but the gate guys only gave him a glance on the way in. The backyard was filled with screaming children, wrestling and running to keep warm against the late February chill. The adults were huddled under a large tent. Gas heaters kept everybody toasty warm inside.

A white coated waiter offered Boyle a tray of champagne glasses and he grabbed one, downed it, put it back on the tray, then grabbed another. The waiter gave him a look. Richard was across the pool, chatting with a twenty-five-year-old woman in a short wool dress. Richard's wife, Annette, drifted among the guests, and hovered over the children.

It was Annette who spotted him first. They had been high school classmates, all of them, even the girl on the tracks. Class of whatever. It had been only twelve years ago but it could have been thirty by the look of her.

"Tommy?"

"Yeah."

She hugged him impulsively. Her eyes were bright. "It's been so long."

"Too long."

Her head snapped back. "Tommy . . . you know . . . you know Richard and I got married. We've got two children now." She pointed to the yard.

"Congratulations."

"Thanks." She hesitated. "I heard you quit fighting."

"Yeah, a few years ago."

She looked him up and down, and her tongue involuntarily licked her lip. She couldn't care less what he did. "Miguel too, right?"

"Yeah, he's out in L.A. now. Kind of a . . . a businessman. He travels around a lot."

"Natala I know all about. I'm a big fan. You ever get to see her?"

"When she feels charitable."

She shivered slightly, maybe from the cold. Once she had been seventeen with black hair and large, youthful breasts. Now the black hair was prematurely streaked and her husband was talking to a young woman in a short wool dress, abandoning her to the care of a two year old and a five year old screaming in the yard. Once she had sat nose to nose with Boyle in a bar in Greenwich Village till three in the morning, drunk with youth and Scotch, and promised to suck him dry all the way back to Jersey. She was as good as her word before they got out of the tunnel. By the time they reached Franklin Lakes, she had done it twice more, washing it down with more Scotch. After all, he was seventeen. And so was she.

"And now you're a cop," she said.

"A homicide detective actually. It's sort of a step up."

She looked over at her husband. When she looked back she was already crying. "Please don't tell me that's why you're here. Because you're a cop?"

"I'm sorry, Annette."

She studied him and he could see the fear grab her. "Colleen called me this morning. Lisa?"

He let a beat go by, then took her face in his hands. He kissed her gently on the cheek, wiping away the tears.

"Sorry," he said again.

Richard was holding forth at the other end of the tented yard. He was twenty-nine, balding and paunchy, exactly as the door guy had said.

The color left Richard's face when he saw him. Boyle held out his hand.

"Hey, Rich, what's happening?"

More staring. "Tommy?"

Exactly like Annette. They could be husband and wife. "That's right. Long time, huh?"

Richard quickly downed his drink and gave it to a waiter, then grabbed Boyle by the shoulders. "Tommy Boyle! I can't believe it! You know how many times I thought of you the last ten years?"

"How many times, Rich?"

"Millions," he screamed. He pulled Boyle close, pounding him on the back. Boyle let himself be hugged, because it was a reunion and all. Annette looked on with a small, fake smile.

"I didn't even know Annette invited you."

"She didn't."

"Really?" Rich's smile quivered.

"Really," Boyle said easily.

"So . . ." Rich's face turned even paler. "I heard about it. You stopped fighting, then . . ."

"Came back."

"Right. And became a . . . a . . ."

"Cop's the word you're looking for, Rich, cop."

By the time Boyle got serious the two guys from the gate were flanking Rich protectively. Annette was watching, waiting. Several of the guests had sort of wandered over, the heat between the two men becoming obvious.

Boyle checked out the two guards with a professional interest. Both looked to be with private security firms, which usually meant former cops. Both were stocky, in their early forties and carried themselves arrogantly, with a sort of swaggering confidence. But Boyle could also see that while they crested two hundred pounds apiece—and therefore outweighed him by about forty pounds— both had gone to seed. The guts were prominent and the faces battered by the bottle. A lot of ex-cops looked like that. That's how they became ex-cops.

The leader seemed to be a guy named Paul, or "Pauli" as Rich called him. His mouth was cruel and his hands calloused. The hair was receding. His companion, equally beefy, equally dissolute, followed in Pauli's wake, awaiting orders with flickering eyes that didn't show a lot of light behind them.

Boyle wasn't concerned. These guys were big stiffs, not fighters, and the gulf between the two could never be crossed.

"You okay, Mr. Preston?" Pauli said.

"Sure." Rich's voice was hearty, like a top Wall Street salesman's should be. "This is an old classmate of mine. Tommy Boyle. He's here for Brandon's birthday. Tommy, say hello to Pauli Bello. He was a couple years ahead of us. Now he does my driving and security. You know, helps out."

Boyle said nothing, and never took his eyes off Richard. Pauli moved closer to his boss.

"Mr. Preston?"

"Yes?"

The man dropped his voice, like he was passing along a big secret. "This guy's packing, Mr. P. I can tell." Pauli then patted his own jacket.

"I know." Preston sighed and decided to drop the pretense. "Tommy, you're not here for Brandon's birthday party."

"No."

"What do you want?"

"Lisa, Rich. I'm here about Lisa."

Preston's mouth tightened. He took a step back and Pauli got it right away. He moved in front of his boss and gestured to his fellow thug to do the same. The partygoers started to notice the weird grouping: a guy with a beat-up topcoat, the two security guards, Rich looking real pale, Annette with a frozen, slightly hysterical smile.

"Colleen called Annette this morning," Rich said quickly. "It was a terrible thing."

Colleen had been a year behind them in high school. Lisa was her sister, several years behind, a young girl filled with beauty and promise, Boyle recalled. Now Lisa wasn't beautiful and wasn't anybody's sister.

"You didn't talk to Colleen, Rich?"

"I'm no good at that. Annette was real close to her."

"I guess you were closer to Lisa."

Pauli caught Richard Preston's panicked look. He knew his job. "Mr. P., I don't like this. You want this guy gone?"

All of a sudden that seemed like a great idea to Richard Preston. "Tommy, you're getting out of line. Not to mention spoiling my son's party. You've got no warrant and no right to be here."

"Sorry about your boy's party," Boyle said. "By the way, did you tell your son you killed Lisa? Did you tell Annette?"

Richard Preston flushed. "That does it." He gestured and Pauli and his buddy moved. Pauli grabbed Boyle's coat and yanked hard, like he was hungry to do it.

"Let's go, pal. You're out of here."

"You smashed her head, Rich," Boyle said, ignoring Pauli, ignoring Pauli's buddy, ignoring the beefy hand on his coat. "On a steel railroad track in the middle of Paterson."

"You're nuts, Tommy."

Pauli got louder now. "You ain't listenin', friend. I said let's go!"

"It's a no-brainer, Rich," Boyle told him. Annette's eyes were wider, expectant. "Rich, the girl's got phone records, letters, a diary! Christ, you left a tie over there." He looked to Annette. "Does he have a tie with red alligators on it?"

She laughed, maniacally.

"Okay, that's it." Pauli grabbed Boyle's arm and yanked. "Gino, grab his legs. Let's dump this stiff in the gutter."

Pauli's move was a big mistake. Fighters, even fighters who have been out of the ring for a few years, are a breed apart. For one thing all fighters learn the hard way how to both take and slip a punch, and have no fear of getting hit. Thus, a fighter looks at any dangerous situation, even a street fight, technically, almost in slow motion. Where are the guy's hands, what part is he leaving open. But most important, a fighter knows how to hit, just like a professional baseball player or golfer knows how to hit, the special skill that shifts the weight at the precise point of contact. The man in the street expends great effort for very little power. A trained boxer has effortless power.

Boyle moved first on Pauli, the leader. He pushed off and it only took three shots to drop him, one to the soft gut and two to the thick face. When Pauli fell heavily to the ground in pain, Gino stepped back, paralyzed by the sight. Richard Preston panicked.

"Call nine-one-one," he screamed. "This guy is nuts!"

Annette laughed at Preston's screams. "Tommy, are you allowed to shoot him?"

Boyle was inspecting his chafed knuckles. Damn, it hurt without gloves on. "Not just yet."

She moved nearer to her husband. "I'm going to take everything. Your kids, your money, everything."

"You bitch." He spit the words out. "You want to know why? Look in the mirror." Then he raised his hand to her.

That was another mistake. Boyle moved and the murderer fell, holding his soft gut and vomiting, his gags shrouded by the screams of the partygoers. Annette clapped over his prostrate form.

The partygoers screamed in panic. A boy, seven, whose party it was, cried softly and quietly, alone in the dark corner of the house.

They suspended him right away. He stopped in three days later to pick up his check and drop off his badge and gun. The commander's name was Ryan, another of the lost Irish. He was usually a friend to Boyle.

"You're nuts, Tommy," Ryan said sadly as he took the gun. "Now you got another thirty days watchin' soaps. Happy?"

"Look . . . this guy . . ."

"I told you to keep your hands to yourself!" Ryan barked. "No, you won't listen. You *never* listen. What the hell were you doin' in the man's house?"

"He killed her, Lieutenant."

"Who says?"

"I say. And now, forensics says. Forget the apartment, this yutz left more stuff around the crime scene than O. J."

"Well, that still don't mean you can beat him up." Ryan seemed distracted to Boyle, as though there was something more coming, something that made Ryan uncomfortable. "Look, Tommy, all I want is that you use your head. This is not some monkey from the projects. This is a white guy from Bergen. Besides, there's more."

Ah, Boyle thought, here it comes. "What?"

The man's voice dropped. "Well, for one thing, the bottles!"

The bottles again. Boyle breathed easier. If that's all it was, no problem. But Ryan's voice still had that distracted, nervous tone, as though he brought the bottles up to avoid something much more important.

"What about them?"

"You blew it, Tommy. Sanders says you can't collect a dime if you're on suspension. I tried to fight him and he says 'forget it, you're taking money out of my pocket.'"

Boyle had to laugh at that, the relief and irony combining. He never wanted Sanders' dirty money and now as punishment they were going to let him live clean for a month.

The laughter exasperated Ryan. "Tommy, I don't get it. Every time I give you cash you make a face. I never seen a guy so hard to give money to."

Boyle patted the commander on the shoulder. "Don't worry about it." He turned to leave.

"Wait!" the man said. His voice was crisp, almost military. Here comes the other shoe, Boyle thought. Departmental charges, probably. Then termination.

"What?"

Ryan coughed and wouldn't look Boyle in the face. "One more thing. I got some tough news for you. Tough for all of us. I wish to hell it wasn't me had to do it."

Now Boyle got real concerned. This was more than the suspension, or the bottle cut. More even than termination. "Go ahead, Ryan. Just lay it out."

"Patsy got killed last night," the man said simply.

Ryan had his head buried in his hands and there was no doubt he was crying. Boyle was stone white and the room was spinning. He grabbed for the door handle to steady himself.

"Patsy got what!?"

Ryan spoke into his hands, the words indistinct. "Coming down Cannonball Road. I guess he lost control, went through the rail." Ryan revealed his beet-red face. "Boyle, I'm so damn sorry. Hey, man, you okay?"

II

Nine hours after Patsy died Miguel Meza got a call. He was hungover. It was 6 A.M. L.A. time. The call woke him up and his voice was slurred.

"Hullo."

"Is this Mr. Meza?"

"Who wants to know?"

The voice was female and anxious. "Mr. Meza, Angelo Bracca told me to call you."

Meza rubbed his face but it didn't help. He had a disconnected feeling, the pain in his head separate from the now endemic nausea. He had learned to live with all of it, more or less.

"I'm listening."

"Mr. Meza . . ."

"Call me Miguel."

"Okay, Miguel. I've got a problem."

"Ma'am, it's very early in the morning." And I'm hurting.

"I realize that and I'm sorry."

"That's okay. Just tell me what your problem is."

"Certainly. My daughter was almost murdered last night."

Miguel's head went back on the pillow. He had hoped for something easy.

"Okay, just give me a moment." He rubbed his temples. "What happened?"

"My daughter's name is Christine Lee. She was raped and beaten last night by a group of drunken men who accused her of stealing drugs from them."

More rubbing. "The actress? She's like . . . what, Japanese or something?"

"Half-Chinese. Her late father was Chinese. My maiden name is Lo Cicero."

"You're a relative of Angelo's?"

"Exactly. I am Angelo Bracca's second cousin. He calls Christine a 'Chitalian.' "

That sounded like Angelo.

"Do you know who did it?"

"Yes, his name's Harrison Brent."

"I know that name."

"He's famous, at least in some circles. He's a director."

"Those ain't my circles, ma'am, sorry."

"I know, Mr. Meza . . . Miguel."

"I'm listenin', ma'am." Sort of, anyway. He was also in pain.

"I want you to come over to my house at noon."

"Noon?" He looked over at the clock. Damn, it was early.

"I'll tell you everything then."

"And then?"

"And then I'd like you to kill Mr. Brent by sundown. Painfully."

He figured that was coming. "Mrs. Lo Cicero?"

"Mrs. Lee."

"I'll make my calls. I'll check it out."

He called Angelo Bracca's man to get permission, which was how it was supposed to work. He tracked him down in New Orleans.

"Nick, this is Migo."

"Hey, Migo. Whattaya got?"

"I don't know. I just got a call from somebody says she's Angelo's cousin. Says her daughter got killed by some guy." At least he thought that's what she said.

"What's her name?"

"Lo Cicero. Her married name is Lee. Says her daughter's name is Christine."

"Angelo's got an uncle named Dominick Lo Cicero."

"Okay."

"What's she want?"

"She says I'm supposed to go over there by twelve. She wants the guy dead by tonight, quote unquote."

"Forget that! Don't go killin' nobody till I tell you."

"I get it, Nick, that's why I'm calling you."

"Okay. Just wait a second." Miguel could almost hear the wheels spinning.

"Go ahead over. I'll try to get Angelo quick."

"And if you can't?"

"Just don't go killin' nobody. You got that, Meza?"

"I got it, Nick."

Meza had a few hours to waste and used it to try to work off his hangover. He dressed in heavy sweats and ran a fast four miles, sweating hard as the witch's brew inside him burned and roiled. When he got back he stripped naked and snorted two lines. His body was tightly muscled, a little over five-foot-ten and still a solid welterweight at 147. Sometimes, if he'd been up for a few days, he looked thin, unless you felt his shoulders, or his chest, or his legs, and then you wouldn't think he was thin anymore.

He put on a pair of baggy shorts and went outside barefoot and bare-chested. In the backyard a heavy bag hung from a tree. He wrapped thick gauze around his hands and taped the ends with adhesive. A man next door looked over the adjoining fence.

"Hi, Miguel."

Meza ignored him and worked the bag, standing close and letting it bounce off his head and shoulders, delivering solid lefts, low, then rights, low. The bag swung easily on its metal chain. He hit the bag continually for ten minutes and the man watched with rapt attention. The twitching muscles and the viciousness of the punches were something few people get to see up close, something the man had never imagined. The big bag didn't just move, it danced, as it was supposed to, when hit by a professional.

After ten minutes, the endorphins were flowing, mixing nicely with the drugs, and Miguel Meza stepped back, breathing heavily, now exactly where he wanted to be. Meza had always been addicted to being high, which had always been his problem, and now he was expert at it, seeking out the ways and means, physically or chemically, to put his brain exactly where he wanted. Thirty seconds later, when he caught his breath, he turned to the man leaning on his fence.

"That looked great, Miguel."

Meza took the adhesive in his mouth, ripped it, and tore off the gauze. "Hey Bruce?"

The man muttered, "My name's Mark, not Bruce."

"You sure?"

"Miguel, don't talk like that."

"Listen, I got a job for you."

"What?"

Meza gestured toward the house. "There ain't nothin' in there. I'm about to starve!"

The man's face flushed with embarrassment. "Yeah?"

"Yeah. I got an appointment at twelve. I'm already late."

The man didn't say anything at first. He was flaccid and weak, wearing a ridiculous bathing suit, still wet from his pool. "Miguel?" he began.

"What?"

"If I take care of things . . . you know, go shopping . . . will you come over later?"

Meza laughed and threw the sweat-soaked gauze over the fence. The man caught it. The stench rose to his nose.

"In your dreams, Bruce," Miguel Meza said as he walked to the house.

12

It was hot and the sun was high when Meza left for the job. Solid white clouds dominated a blue sky. A dry wind from the desert ripped through the city as the weather changed suddenly. He opened the window of the car and let the air swiftly batter his head, clearing it, getting him ready for his client.

The woman's house was in Brentwood, north of Sunset, a mile and a half up a vigorous and windy road. It was an English Tudor and occupied what looked to be several acres. He announced himself to an intercom at the front gate, then drove to the flat, side parking area near the front door.

A quiet Filipino maid greeted him, bowed once and led him to the back of the house. The interior was cluttered with garish statuary and oddly mismatched furniture. None of it meant anything to him.

The woman was in the backyard, near the pool. She sat at a white, marble table under an umbrella. She wore a multicolored silk shift that covered her shoulders and fell to mid-thigh. Her face was lined with sun damage, creating the illusion of age. It was the sort of face that nature had destroyed only recently, and quickly, a cruel destruction that suddenly eliminated the stark, girlish beauty she had traded on for years. The body was still firm, only now encased from head to toe in wrinkled, brown leather. And although Meza didn't know it, or care, she was only forty-three.

There was also a girl of nineteen near the pool. She wore a large floppy hat and giant sunglasses. On the table next to her was a plastic container. Although Meza couldn't tell from this distance, the container held a high octane sunblock that would have shielded her from the meltdown at Chernobyl. The girl wanted no part of what had happened to her mother.

The woman held out her hand. "Thank you for coming. I'm Jo Ann Lee."

"Hi. Miguel Meza."

"Please have a seat. Would you like something to drink?"

"Yeah, I would."

She gestured for the Filipino maid. "Two Absolut, tonic, with a twist, tall." Now back to Meza. "Did I get that right?"

"Yeah, you did. Thanks."

They sipped and Meza watched the girl. She sat immobile, impassive, the floppy hat masking her face.

"Well, Mr. Meza, are you ready to talk business?"

He took his eyes away from the girl. "Sure."

"Excellent. What will it cost me to have Mr. Brent killed?"

He shrugged. It was a question he got asked a lot. "That ain't my call. You have to ask Nick. Plus"—he gestured across the pool—"let me ask you something. That ain't her, is it?"

"Of course. That's Christine."

Meza took a long sip of the vodka. "Lady, you got a problem."

"What problem? What are you talking about?"

"I'm talking about that girl. She ain't dead like you said. If she was dead maybe you got a point. But I can't kill nobody if she ain't dead."

"I didn't *say* she was dead. I said she was *almost murdered*. Besides, can you see what they did to her?"

"I can see enough. Unless she's a dummy, she's alive."

"I mean can you see her bruises?"

"Not from here."

"Then let's get closer."

They walked around the pool to where the girl now lay facedown on a lounge chair. She was wearing a black bikini cut high at the bottom and low at the top. She was slim and her skin naturally olive.

"Christine, say hello to Miguel Meza."

The girl twisted and looked up. Her legs were smooth. Dark yellow and blue blotches covered her thighs. Her bare stomach was discolored. Her hair was black and fell to the middle of her back. Meza felt an odd anger rise and he didn't know anything yet.

"Hello." She waved a limp hand in his general direction.

"Mr. Meza is the man I told you about."

"The hit man, you mean."

The woman's face darkened. "Christine, watch your mouth!"

Christine laughed and had to grab her face. "Ouch."

Meza found himself staring at her. The girl intrigued him and he didn't know why. He didn't blame her for mouthing off at her mother though. He moved closer to her.

"Take off the hat," he said.

"Take off your own damn hat," she said easily. Then she turned back onto her stomach.

Attitude. Okay. Meza grabbed her long hair and yanked, then flipped the hat off. "Hey, stop it!" she screamed. He ignored that, ignored the impulse to smack her on the ass, and just threw her glasses into the pool. Now she really screamed, twisting and cursing. Her eyes were swollen slightly and her cheekbones bruised. Her lips, large and round under normal circumstances, now looked tender and blood engorged. Thin streaks of red ran across her chest and stomach. The sight again gave him an emotional, angry rush that was new to him. He tried to hide it and be cool.

"Yeah, I'd say she got it. Looks like they tried to save her face, maybe just slap her around."

"Show him the rest," her mother ordered.

"Like hell I will."

Her mother sighed. "She'll show it on a screen but not here."

"I kind of get the picture to tell you the truth."

"I want this man to see it all," the mother barked. "They may have tried to save your face but that's all they saved."

"Mother!"

"Shut up. If you weren't partying with scum like Brent, none of this would have happened. Now show Mr. Meza what he needs to see or I swear I'll instruct him to look for himself."

The girl hesitated, then obediently stood up. She knew her mother wasn't kidding and she now had *no* doubt what Meza would do. The bra left first. Her breasts were small and firm, and had the same bright red stripes across them. Then she turned, lay face down on the lounge chair and pulled the bikini bottom to her knees. Miguel Meza recognized the black swelling around the kidneys and the angry welts from the back of her knees to her shoulders. The kidney bruise was the same thing fighters got. Except this girl wasn't a fighter.

"The stripes are from an electric cord," her mother explained.

"First they beat her with fists wrapped in a towel. Then they whipped her until she passed out. When she woke up she was face-down, her hands were tied and they were all taking turns. You know why? They say she stole things from them. Need I go further?"

"No." He handed the bathing suit to her. "Here, put this on."

"You mean the show's all done?"

He didn't blame her for that one. "Yes. The show's all done."

13

When the murders were finished Alicia Kent dumped the Lincoln and went directly to the airport. She departed into the gathering dawn and in six hours was back in London. Gregor Portov's flat was three blocks from the Council's manor house, in an old and very fashionable building. She called from the lobby and he told her to come up, don't worry, the door will be open.

The sight when she entered didn't surprise her. Portov was dressed in a long satin dressing gown that billowed around his beefy frame. He sat cross-legged on the floor, Indian-style, holding a glass of champagne in his right hand and an enormous Cohiba cigar in his left.

The room was heavily shrouded and she had to strain to see. Then she heard the small whimpering. The naked young girl was slight and looked to be in her late teens. Portov's labored breathing was harsh.

Ah. If only Portov could be the one she wanted, the one she craved. But he wasn't, just as Magnus had never been.

"Having fun?"

Portov laughed and poured more champagne. "Not as much as I intend to have."

Alicia went to the girl and lifted her face. She had dark, curly hair and fawn brown eyes. Her face was wet with tears.

"I want you to do something for me," she said gently.

The girl looked up, expectant.

"Go into the bedroom. Close the door and just relax. It will all be fine."

The girl smiled with gratitude, kissed Alicia on the cheek and rushed away, naked. Alicia turned to Portov.

"Well," he said.

"It's all done."

"You mean Carlos has once again performed?"

"Not exactly. The job is done but Carlos he is no down."

Portov knew what that meant. "How unfortunate for Carlos."

"Yes."

He rose and looked out the window. "With the old man dead I won't have to explain anything to the Council. As you know, Yomoto's death was controversial. Just tell me I have nothing more to worry about."

She poured herself some champagne. He watched her with admiration. She sipped and let the alcohol burn through her. "That's correct. The warehouse is secure and the contaminated Sarin is being dumped. It's now your job to get me a pure version."

"Don't worry. Josef Alexeyev is making the arrangements."

Alicia smiled. Alexeyev was the ruthless head of the Moscow branch of the Russian *Mafiya*, and the closest thing Portov had to a soulmate. Alexeyev would not let them down.

"Now about the killing?" Portov pressed. "The whole thing looked like an accident? I don't have to worry about Angelo and his nonsense?"

"Correct." She drank deeply. "It was very stressful."

"I'm not surprised. Is there anything I can help you with? Anything you need?"

She considered that while she sipped on the champagne. Today she would sleep. This evening she would meet with her professor. Then to Paris to meet their banker. Then to Los Angeles to tie down her part of the deal. There was lots to do but now she needed to relax. "Just one thing for now."

"Yes?"

"That young girl in the bedroom? She seemed to be crying."

"As well she should have been."

"Then with your permission, Gregor, I'd like to go in and really give her something to cry about."

Gregor Portov's eyes grew wide. Then he laughed in a deep, hearty voice.

———

Alicia Kent met her professor at ten that evening in a quiet club near the river. Professor James Ashforth possessed all the affectations one might expect in a physicist with a world-class, if rapidly declining, reputation. He was unctuous, watery-eyed, liked long weekends at a country home about to be seized for back taxes, and poured a steady stream of milk and bourbon down his throat from earliest morning until midnight.

Alicia Kent had identified him years before. He had been an expert witness for the firm on six different occasions on important matters in Europe. Now she needed him on the most important matter of all.

"Professor, nice to see you again." She extended a hand.

"Delighted to see you also." He kissed her hand, then sat down. His eyes darted about, hunting for the waiter. "Shall we have something first?" He snapped his fingers.

"Of course," she said gaily. "This is a celebration after all."

"Really? Of what?"

"The excellent work you've done for us. That matter in the Mediterranean, for example."

"Ah, the tanker spill."

"Precisely. Our client was facing substantial damages. Your testimony about the beneficial effects of hydrocarbons on Mediterranean sea life was first rate."

"Well, it's not that well known, I'll grant you that." He drank deeply from his milk and bourbon.

"So, if you'll permit me," Alicia said, "I have a token of our appreciation." She handed him a small satchel.

He unzipped it and saw bundles of blue and green pound notes, ten thousand strong. There was also a brown paper package. He closed the satchel.

"How very kind."

"Now don't forget to declare it," Alicia said smiling.

"Of course."

They drank some more, chit-chatted about London life and then Alicia Kent got to the point: she wanted to become educated in the strange metals Portov wanted to trade for the Sarin.

"We have a matter I need information about. It should be right up your alley."

"Yes?"

"Do you know anything about substances called dual-use metals? Zirconium, beryllium or titanium might be examples?"

His jaw widened. "Nuclear or non nuclear?"

She smiled. It was exactly the question she wanted. "Both."

Professor Ashforth leaned back and adopted his most didactic air.

"There are many so-called dual-use metals, all highly restricted. They are important for commercial detonations as well as the weapons industry."

"They're explosives?"

"Not really explosives, more facilitators of explosions. Some cause explosions of even modest size to take on much greater intensity."

"Like in cluster bombs."

He smiled. "Zirconium, you've done your homework."

"Somewhat."

"You're right. Zirconium increases dramatically the intensity of the charge. Zirconium-treated cluster bombs can actually melt holes in tanks."

"Yes." Her voice had gotten soft. "Now the nuclear application."

"Nuclear grade metals are very important for secret nuclear powers. Let's imagine the only bomb you have is a Fat Boy–sized weapon, the sort that was dropped on Japan, a pop gun of a nuclear weapon."

"I think it killed a hundred and fifty thousand people."

"And would again if dropped on London or New York. But if that's all you've got, a tiny nuclear weapon, you need a heat facilitator."

"And that's where these metals come in?"

"That's where *nuclear* grade metals come in."

She sat back, thinking it over. "*That's* why they're heavily restricted."

"More restricted than plutonium. Plutonium at least is a byproduct of nuclear reactors. These are not."

Her mind raced. The possibilities were endless. Libya with its huge oil reserves, Iran, Iraq, North Korea, Bangladesh. *That* is why Alexeyev wanted these metals in trade for the pure Sarin!

She was lost in thought longer than she should have been. When she looked back up, he was staring at her quizzically.

"So tell me, beautiful Alicia, why do you care so much about strange nuclear grade metals?"

She waved the question away. "An overseas client with an import export problem."

"Ah, I see."

He smiled in disbelief. It was the wrong gesture. She immediately realized he knew way too much. It was a pity, he had been so reliable. "Professor, let me ask you something. Do you think we can continue this chat in your flat?"

He almost choked on his milk and bourbon. "Of course."

She smiled. Her semiautomatic was in her purse. Good-bye Professor. "Fine, let's go."

At seven the next morning, six hours after she left Professor Ashforth's naked dead body on his bed, Alicia Kent and Gregor Portov flew from London to Orly for the meeting with their banker. He wasn't really a "banker," simply a middleman, a conduit between buyer and seller. The meeting took place at his two thousand-acre estate about fifteen minutes from the airport, an hour from Paris. They were driven there in a Bentley by a handsome Iranian with a light silk suit and black sweater. The man was a killer and carried an Israeli Uzi in a harness underneath the seat and a small semiautomatic underneath his left breast. Alicia made a mental note. Someday she would come back for this man. Perhaps *he* was the one she could be happy with, the one who would make her whole.

The Iranian drove at 160 kilometers per hour over rain-slicked roads to the estate. As always, she was astounded by the sight of the place as they cruised along the mile-long approach road. The main house had been built in the seventeenth century and had passed from Jewish hands to the Luftwaffe during World War II. Its 263 rooms included 55 bedroom suites. The palace, which is what it was, sat majestically on a hill looking out over a two hundred-acre lake stuffed with trout.

The German who owned the estate had purchased it in the seventies, during the heady days of the oil embargo. He enjoyed the irony of the acquisition and poured $20 million into renovation and furnishings. Now, every inch of the house was stuffed with a garish nineteenth-century French antique. The man particularly liked enormous solid silver renditions of tigers.

Alicia warmly embraced the young English woman who greeted them, the middleman's consort, a lovely woman who had much a quiet deal.

"Kathleen, so nice to see you again."

"And you, my dear, as well."

"Mr. Portov, always a pleasure."

Gregor nodded, uninterested in any deals, only his own. "Is he here?"

"Yes, he'll just be a moment. Is there anything you'd like to see while we wait?"

Alicia brightened. "Are there new additions?"

"Well, one you might enjoy. Come with me."

They walked up to the second floor to a bathroom the size of a small house. A sunken tub that looked like a swimming pool dominated the room. Next to the tub, two life-sized marble nymphs, naked, pointed fingers toward one another. From their arms hung towels.

"These nymphs are the most expensive item in the house."

Alicia squinted. "How so? I'm sure they're expensive but compared to the . . ." She gestured to the solid silver tigers, complete with a solid silver antelope in their jaws.

"Not because of their value," Kathleen explained. "Because of what we had to do to get them here." She pointed to the wall. "The nymphs would not fit in the window. There was only one way to get them in."

"Which was?"

"Tear down the side of the house, of course. Then Klaus rebuilt it afterwards."

Alicia and Gregor exchanged a knowing look. They had come to the right spot.

The actual deal took place at an enormous dining room table. The German arrived and commented on the weather in Paris, then sat at the head of the table. The table extended for thirty feet and was solid black onyx. Portov and Alicia sat across from each other. Kathleen served them, occasionally smiling at Alicia. The German ate with his fingers: mixed grill and beer. Piles of sausage were set in the middle of the table. Alicia and Portov, because they were guests, got the first grab. All she could think of was how luxurious the George V would feel this evening and what five-star restaurant she would make Portov take her to in Paris.

After an hour the German gestured to the drawing room.

"We should discuss our business."

Once around the marble drawing room table the conversation proceeded with the same maddening indirection. The German would only refer to the nuclear metals as "fabric," perhaps out of respect for the lovely drapes surrounding the room. The Sarin became a "beverage."

"So tell me, assuming that funds are not a problem, where will you obtain my fabric and beverage requirements?"

Portov took the lead. "We have two principal sources."

"The former Soviet Union? Your partner Alexeyev?"

"For the . . . the beverages, yes. We have another source for the . . . for the fabric."

The German looked up quizzically. "Sarajevo? Belgrade? Banja Luka?"

"No, a city much more decadent. Los Angeles."

Klaus blinked in confusion. "Los Angeles? I do not want to make a film."

Alicia Kent jumped in. "Trust us. Los Angeles is perfect. Southern California was once the defense capital of the United States. Now its defense plants are struggling. We have identified an excellent source of fabric."

The German bit on a sausage that was mostly pure gristle. "By fabric do you mean the very *best* fabric?"

Alicia knew he meant "nuclear-grade." "Of course."

"There are severe time constraints," the German warned. "Do you need to know the identity of our buyers?"

For the Sarin, he meant. She desperately wanted to know, but also knew the German's fierce sense of secrecy, his stock in trade. Perhaps she could draw him out discreetly.

"It's not necessary, of course. I'm just curious what outside terrorist group would be this well financed and committed."

The German laughed heartily. "Ah, lovely viper, who said anything about an *outside* terrorist group?"

14

Christine told Meza that the famous director lived in Broad Beach on the coast north of Malibu, a haven for wealthy celebrities, a hundred beach shacks pressed shoulder to shoulder against the sand. The shacks were very small in the 1950s but are definitely not very small today.

Immediately after Brent bought his beach bungalow he tore it down to replace it with a bizarre multi-storied mansion. The proposed construction violated every building code and coastal regulation on the books but Brent greased a subsequently-indicted Coastal Commission chairman named Nathanson and before you could say "fifty grand worth of art" the bungalow was gone, the approval given and the palace under construction.

Christine and Meza drove over in her open Jeep, then sat parked on the PCH, high above the house. "It's actually five stories," she explained, pointing. "The two stories above ground you can see. Then there's an underground tennis court and two stories of underground parking." She shrugged. "It was considered a construction marvel at the time, with the ocean coming in and all."

"He's there now?"

"I'm sure of it."

"Why?"

"He's always there unless he's working."

"Who's with him?"

"His bodyguard. They always come back together to do some lines. That's what happened last night. They ran out of white and blamed me."

Meza only cared about one thing. "What's he like?"

"The bodyguard? A Samoan guy. He weighs about three hundred pounds. He tried to rape me once."

"What'd you do, beat him up?"

"No, just screamed. Back then I was a meal ticket."

"No more?"

She laughed. "No more."

They drove down to the beach a half mile south of Brent's place and walked out onto the sand. A rock jetty jutted into the ocean, a favorite roost of feasting sea birds, half-dressed scuba divers and kids smoking pot. Meza wandered out to the end of the jetty, looking as out of place as it was possible to look out of place. The sun was drifting down the horizon, catching the tips of white sailboats and sending long shadows back to the shore. He turned to her, enjoying the moment in a way he really didn't get. She had pulled up her shirt and was smiling.

"What's so funny?"

"The drawings. I still have them all over me."

The drawings. She had been ashamed of the marks covering her body so he had taken a black felt pen and drew pictures on them. A black-and-blue circle on her abdomen became a beetle. Another on the inside of her right thigh, a butterfly. He joined the horizontal red lines with vertical black lines and made her play tic-tac-toe with him, best of seven. At the end she was giggling, then laughing, which she hadn't done for awhile.

"You forgot some," she told him, and lifted her bra to show him. Not exactly a shy one, Meza thought, which he liked.

"Don't worry, I'll draw some more on you later."

"You promise?"

"I promise." He pointed. "But first things first."

The house was dark when they got there except for a pale light near the kitchen. The sun had dipped under the water, leaving in its wake a red glow that faded as the earth turned. There were two cars in the driveway, a gold-bronze Bentley and a red Porsche Carrera.

"You *sure* he's there now?"

"I guarantee it. I called and told him I was coming to apologize. He loves that."

"Just him and the Samoan?"

"Probably. Sometimes they bring a girl back to party." She shrugged. "That's how I met him."

He hoped that wasn't the case. A girl would be an innocent witness and he didn't want to go there. Then a more mercenary thought occurred to him.

"If he comes back to do blow, that means he's got a stash?"

"Not last night. He will now for sure."

Now he was very interested. There was a lot more here than the five grand Nick promised him, and *nobody* would care if he helped himself.

"What about cash and jewelry, all that kind of stuff?"

"There's a safe behind a wall. I don't know the combination."

"Is it free-standing?"

"What does that mean?"

"I mean, can you pick it up and take it away?"

"Sure, I saw the Samoan do that."

Meza rubbed the stubble on his face. He was wearing a dark suit and a dark shirt. His impossibly tangled bright red hair was tied in a ponytail. He had sunglasses on and the 9 mm was tucked underneath his jacket.

The gun was a problem. He didn't want to bring it into the house because he didn't want to use it. But all the fighting talent in the world wouldn't make up for the 150 pounds he was giving up to the Samoan. He took the gun out, looked at it wistfully and knew right away what he had to do. He just wasn't ready to kill two people as revenge for a beating, no matter how lovely the victim. He dropped the gun in the sand.

"Let's go."

The door was opened by a monster of a man. He stood over six-foot-six and easily weighed the three hundred pounds Christine had estimated. There was no doubt it was all muscle. Meza looked like a small child next to the giant.

"Who's that?" the man barked.

"A friend of mine," she said quickly. "I asked him to drive me out. I can't . . . can't drive so good today."

The Samoan grabbed her and pushed her into the house, then stopped Meza with a finger to his chest. He patted him down, and when he found nothing, pushed him roughly in front of him.

Harrison Brent sat at a kitchen table fumbling with packages wrapped in brown paper. Christine stood before him, her hands behind her, looking crestfallen. She was talking, as Meza told her to do, begging forgiveness.

Brent had his eyes down, ignoring her, letting her grovel. The wait gave Meza an opportunity to wander around. There was a balcony off the living room with a metal railing. He leaned over the railing and saw a fifty-foot drop to a tennis court, the one that had required the expert greasing of the Coastal Commission chairman. The court was still under construction. In the dim, developing moonlight he could see tools, broken concrete, a small utility vehicle and a jack hammer.

He went back inside. The Samoan was concocting something from his homeland. A large iron skillet bubbled quietly on the stove, filled with roiling vegetables and seafood in a hearty broth. It looked like it had been simmering a long time.

Meza gestured to Christine and she stopped talking. Brent looked up with surprise.

"That's it? That's all you got to say?"

"Yeah, I think so," Meza said.

Meza reached in his back pocket and took out a pair of leather gloves. They had the tightness and consistency of golf gloves, although much thicker. Brent's confused eyes turned to him.

"What's this geek doing?"

Meza put on the gloves and wandered over to the stove. "Smells good."

The Samoan grunted. Meza grabbed a large fork and stirred, then turned the handle so that it was near his left hand. The handle was red with heat but Meza did not feel it through the glove.

"Who said you could do that?" the Samoan growled.

Christine backed up, standing apart from both Brent and the Samoan. Both men were staring at Meza with puzzlement drifting toward anger. Meza sniffed at the food one last time. "Man, it's a shame to lose this."

The Samoan's eyes narrowed. "Okay, move away! Now!"

"Before dinner? How rude." Meza grabbed the skillet with his left hand, stirred the contents and laid the fork down. The Samoan moved, which was exactly what Meza wanted. When he felt the

Samoan's hand grab his right shoulder, he turned and flung the boiling contents in the man's face.

The Samoan screamed. Brent jumped to his feet. "Are you nuts?"

The Samoan howled in a low-toned, guttural way as his hands, also burning, tried to rake the scalding vegetables off his face. Meza swung the empty iron skillet like a baseball bat and caught the Samoan dead in the throat. The man fell, gagging, and a table-top shattered. Shards of glass cut into the Samoan's arms and the arteries spurted. He struggled to force breath through his crushed windpipe.

Meza always got crazy during a fight when the adrenaline surged. He brought the heavy iron skillet down hard three times, more than he wanted. Yet it took all three for the giant to finally crumble. When he did, he lay still, his breathing staggered. Meza glanced at him briefly, a little contemptuous at a pro who'd let this happen. He put the empty skillet back on the stove, turned off the heat and took off his gloves.

Brent sat at the table rigid with fear. "Who are you? What do you want?"

"Stand up," Meza ordered.

Brent did as he was told. "Please, if you're here to rob me, just tell me."

"Great idea. What do you got here?"

Christine answered for him. "He's got everything, cash, coke, even some jewels."

"That right?"

Brent was too scared to argue. "I got some stuff."

"Show me."

It took thirty minutes to assemble the cache on the kitchen table. The now open free-standing safe revealed rings, gold chains, an emerald bracelet and four rolls of Krugerands. The cash was bundled in hundred dollar bills, twenty-five to a stack, wrapped in crisp Bank of America money wrappers. From the underground parking garage came the bags of cocaine, seven of them, encased in coarse brown paper. Meza took a kitchen knife and slit one down the middle. White powder splattered on the slate table. Meza took one of Brent's credit cards, formed a phalanx of thin lines and helped himself.

In the refrigerator he found large tins of caviar smuggled from

Iran. The tins were wrapped in crude string and covered with Farsi lettering.

Meza opened up the caviar, poured himself a glass of ice-cold vodka from a bottle in the freezer and ate the caviar with a finger. Brent was aghast. "That's twenty five grand of caviar!"

"And it's good too." Meza put Christine on his lap and fed her with a soup spoon. "This is fun," she said and hugged him.

When the caviar was gone, Meza did a quick inventory of Brent's holdings and realized he had over a hundred large in cash and who knew how much in the jewelry and drugs. He jammed the whole mess in a large shopping bag. Nick wouldn't care.

"Okay," he said to the director softly, "play time."

The blood left Brent's face. "What do you mean? I gave you everything."

"Not quite."

"What more do you want?"

Meza gestured to Christine. "Show him."

She cocked her head. "Show him?"

"Absolutely. The man's entitled to know what it's all for."

Christine stared at the director with hate but did as Meza told her. First the jacket, then the white T-shirt. She stood in the moonlight in tight jeans, boots and God's blessings. Then she unbuckled the belt, snapped the button and yanked the jeans down. It took a lot of effort to get them to her ankles.

"All the way?"

"Every bit of it," Meza ordered. "You want to shortchange the guy?"

She sat in a chair and pulled off the boots and jeans, then the thin panties. Brent stood motionless. She stood naked, her arms high over her head and turned slowly for him. The bruises and stripes might have been decorated but there was no doubt what they were.

"I had no idea," he said softly. "I didn't know what they were doing."

"Right." She grabbed her clothes.

"Anyway," Meza said, "it's time to pay for the show."

The man backed away until he hit the wall. "Don't hurt me. You can keep the stuff in the bag, all of it."

"I know that. That ain't what we're talkin' about."

Brent turned to Christine and the tears flowed. "Baby, help me. Please!"

She was quietly getting dressed. She didn't answer.

Meza walked onto the balcony and sniffed the salt air. It was a beautiful night, the moonglow dancing off the sand.

"Come here," he ordered.

"No," the man pleaded, now openly sobbing, "you're going to throw me over the edge."

"No I ain't. C'mere."

The famous director walked over. Meza pointed and Brent stared over the edge. It was fifty feet to the bottom. The man collapsed against the rail, wailing.

"I know what you're going to do. Please don't."

"You think I'm going to throw you down there?"

"Yes! Yes, I do!"

"You're wrong."

The man looked up with hope. "You're not?"

"Absolutely not. I want to see you jump."

Brent's face froze. Christine watched with tight lips, her clothes still in her hand.

"I can't, I won't."

Meza's eyes were black as coal. "You're gonna hurt for what you did. Maybe I give you a break. You get to stand on the railing, then jump off, whenever you're ready."

"I'll die!"

"You should die but you won't." Then he looked over the edge again. "You know, if you miss that jackhammer and the broken concrete, you can land on that flat part."

"I'll break my legs."

"I think so but maybe you get lucky and it's just the ankles. It's all how you do it." As Christine looked at Meza she saw someone new, someone frightening. "Look, this is the best I can do. Go to the other side, grab the bars, hang and drop. That'll save you what, three, four feet." Meza stared at him with pure hate. "Whatever comes down, I live with. You land okay, it's all over."

"And if I don't jump, you'll throw me off?"

Meza's hands came together with a loud clap. "You got that right. Believe me you don't want that. Let gravity and all that broken stuff do the job. It's like what you call a win-win for both of us."

Brent had been in a lot of negotiations in his life and prided himself on knowing his adversary. Now he looked into eyes that showed not an ounce of mercy, just black resolve darkened by hate. He couldn't believe it, he had only one choice, to jump off his own balcony, the one he so carefully planned with his high-priced architect. He slammed his palm against his forehead and decided to end this nightmare.

"I've made up my mind. I'm going to jump."

Meza was actually disappointed but clapped him on the back anyway. "You are one smart guy. No wonder she went for you." He whistled, rocking on his heels.

"Let me ask you just one thing before I . . . do it. Who are you? Who do you work for?"

"Fair enough. I work for Angelo Bracca."

Brent backed against the railing in shock. "Angelo Bracca! The mob guy? What the hell does he have to do with . . ."

Meza just shook his head. "It don't matter whether you knew or didn't know. She's half-Italian. You went and gang-raped a nineteen-year-old girl who's one of Angelo's relatives."

The man blinked once, screamed, hopped onto the railing and leaped into the black void. He didn't aim like he should have and fell like a leaf in the wind, flailing, toward the broken concrete far below. He hit the jackhammer first, then spun with enormous force into the concrete. He lay twisting and groaning, fighting for the breath to scream from the pain. It would take almost a year in various hospitals to repair the damage. The plastic surgery alone would cost a million dollars. Three years later the director, hopelessly addicted to pain killers and all but blacklisted in the business, would shoot himself in the head on this same tennis court, by then beautifully completed, the day the bank acquired the property at a foreclosure sale.

Meza watched the splatter with professional interest, and a lot more anger than he usually brought to a job. Christine came over, shaking, her clothes still in her hand.

"Happy now?"

She shook her head. "It doesn't make me feel better. I thought it would but it doesn't." Then she looked at him. "Miguel, you scare me. You wanted to kill him."

She was right, but she didn't have to know that. He kissed her on the top of the head. "You got too much imagination. Matter of fact, I'm goin' right now to check him out, make sure he ain't dead. Those were Nick's orders. Do me a favor, sweet stuff. Go call nine-one-one."

She shivered. This was a man she had never seen before. "Okay, but I have to call my mom first."

"Sure. Do it."

It took thirty minutes and when she came back her face was drawn. Meza was again on the balcony, puffing on one of Brent's cigars, listening to the man's screams mix with the roar of the sea. He was happy to hear the moans.

"Miguel?" Her voice was tentative. She was more frightened than she had been during the rape.

He turned. "Hey. I checked him out. He ain't happy but he's breathin'! You talk to your mother?"

"Yes . . . Miguel, my mom says Nick's been trying to get you. I'm so sorry!"

"Don't worry about it. It's probably nothing."

"No, it is. Nick said that guy you told me about? The trainer?"

"Patsy?"

"Yeah. He was in an accident, a car crash of some kind."

She saw the light go out of his eyes and with it the naked brutality that had so frightened her. He seemed to fold, slumping against the railing where Brent had met his fate. He tried to speak, to ask a question, but the words got caught in his throat. Christine ran to him and held him, squeezing him hard, hoping to wrap him in warmth. He was still trying unsuccessfully to speak.

"Miguel, I'm so sorry!"

Boyle walked slowly with the line of mourners to the slab where Patsy lay cold and dead. The corpse, remarkably intact after its trip over the falls, was dressed in a dark suit and red neck-piece, the white of the shirt matching the paleness of his skin. He was dead, no doubt about it, and forget the muscle still seeming to swell in his forearms. A fighter's forearms, the fists attached to them now flaccid, empty of power. Dead as death, no doubt about it, Boyle thought, the same place we all go.

Boyle watched with detached interest as the line of fighters inched forward. There were about sixty of them, ranging in age from eighteen to fifty, all sharing an awkward, shuffling gait and a tendency to trail an insistent forefinger underneath crisp white shirts. These were men and boys unused to ties or lines. Their athleticism was endemic, a pantherlike flip of the head, a shuffling of the shoulders like a thoroughbred at the gate. The younger ones struggled with suits too large for lean, trained bodies. They ran dark hands through hair cut short to intimidate. One wiry flyweight had the number sixteen cut into his left temple and the number seventeen cut into his right, the last a testament to his last knockout.

The slab where Patsy was sleeping was more of a pedestal, the Catholic white lace drifting around the dead man's head like a halo. The casket was set high above the floor of the gym, in the ring, the ropes taken down. The mourners climbed up one side of the ring, circled the casket, blessed themselves, and climbed down the other side. Most of them had walked that ring many times before.

On the walls were reflections of over forty years of training young fighters for the Golden Gloves, the finest amateur boxing tournament in the world. The photos were black-and-whites, starting in 1953 when Patsy had his first finalist, a bantamweight named

Angotti, and finishing in 1998 with Julio Flores. Flores was pictured with his arms held high and Patsy next to him, the Madison Square Garden crowd on its feet behind them. There was also a picture of Tommy Boyle, in the same pose, with a welterweight named Hector Lopez at his feet. There were lots of pictures of a teenage Miguel Meza, just none as a champion.

Boyle walked away from the casket toward the crude bar set up in the abandoned factory next door. There were over three hundred people milling around the beaten wood and metal structure that shared a common door with the gym. Patsy had used it for years to store a half century of junk and memories. Now the common door had been opened and bottles lined on a makeshift bar. Mourners of every ethnicity were helping themselves. The makeshift warehouse was oddly vacant, with a lot of packing boxes strewn around, as though the place had been emptied in a hurry. Boyle grabbed a Dewar's and walked over to where five fighters were mingling.

"Anybody see Miguel or Nat?"

A middleweight named Morales gestured. "Over there."

He saw Meza at the other end of the long warehouse corridor. He had his arm around a stunning Eurasian girl with long dark hair.

"Long time," Boyle said when he walked over.

Meza turned and blinked. "Yeah, long time, man." They both hesitated an instant and then shook hands, breaking it off pretty quick, slightly embarrassed. They never talked a lot to each other. They didn't need to.

"Christine, this is Tommy Boyle."

She held out a hand. "Miguel told me all about you." Boyle saw the fading discoloration on her face.

"I hope he didn't do that."

She smiled. "Someone else did. I met Miguel when he was brought in to . . . to . . ."

"I get it," Boyle said. "I take it the guy is gone?"

Meza waved the question away and lit a cigarette. "You got too much imagination. Incidentally you seen her yet?"

Boyle knew who he meant. "No. Is she here?"

"She will be. You ready for that?"

Boyle grabbed a cigarette and poured another Dewar's. "I'm never ready for that, Migo."

———————

When she got there her eyes flashed with the anger of the bereaved and vindictive. Boyle leaned against an abandoned packing case, watching her approach, trying not to flinch at her incandescent beauty, now handed away for free to a scum named John Bracca. Whatever protective emotions bubbled up were useless and he squelched them. She walked directly to him and stopped an inch from his nose. Her voice was harsh.

"I need to talk to you."

"That's it? How about, 'Hello, Tommy, how are you?' "

"I know how you are. Suspended again." She looked around. "Where's Migo?"

He pointed. Meza was across the room, introducing Christine around.

She turned back to Boyle. "What have you heard?"

"Not much. There was a carjacking, a fight, a gunshot, an accident. That's all I know."

"I don't believe it."

"Why not?"

"Lots of reasons. Dad . . . Patsy came to see me that night in New York. I didn't notice at the time but now I remember what was bothering me. He was afraid of something. I could tell from his voice."

"New York?"

"At the Plaza. I was doing a show."

"I see, a show. I wasn't invited. Was John there?"

She sighed. "You were not invited because you're a pain in the ass. As for John, he can come anytime he wants. I'm living with him, Tommy, get used to it. You're my brother, not my goddamn father."

"I didn't say I was your father. That job's too hard. How is John anyway?"

She snorted. "He's a bigger jerk than you sometimes."

"I'm sorry. What happened, too many dinners on Mulberry Street? Too much coke after the shows?"

"Tommy, get a life. My father's lying dead next door."

He flinched at that. "Mine, too."

Her head cocked to the side, softened. "I know."

Three days later, after the funeral, when everyone hugged and left, Meza took charge.

"Okay, children, enough tears. It's time to find a bar. What's open?"

Boyle stopped arguing with Natala long enough to answer. "The 'T.' It's open twenty-four hours a day."

Jimmy was behind the bar, as always looking befuddled. He watched them walk in through glazed eyes.

"Hey, Tommy, how's it going?" He held out a hand. "My name is Jimmy. I know Patsy."

Boyle had met Jimmy about five hundred times but shook his hand anyway.

"Jimmy, you know Migo, don't you, Miguel Meza?"

"Never had the pleasure, no. But I remember when you fought. God, was you a good fighter."

"We're going to sit here for a little while, Jimmy, have a few drinks and remember Patsy."

Jimmy squinted. "What do you mean, 'remember Patsy'?"

"I don't know if you heard. Patsy was in an accident."

"An accident, what kind of accident?"

"A bad one. There was a car crash on Cannonball Road. He went over the falls."

Jimmy was visibly upset. "Over the falls!" He shook his head and something like a tear rolled down his cracked face. "Me and Patsy go back . . . I don't know . . ."

"A long time, I know."

Jimmy raised his eyes. "When did it happen?"

"Tuesday night," Natala said.

"Tuesday night?" The old rummy scratched his head. "Why Tuesday night Patsy was in here."

The stunned silence that followed would have surprised anybody in the bar, if there was anybody in the bar. Natala recovered first.

"In *here*," she screamed. "Patsy was at my show on Tuesday night! *When*, Jimmy, *when* was he in here?"

"It was real late, midnight. He sat right there, right where you are. It was just like always, he had a beer, a shot back, and I had one too."

Boyle was listening closely. Natala didn't have to say anything. Patsy had not been drunk at the Plaza and would barely have had time to get back to Paterson by midnight. But the car was covered with spilled alcohol and "smelled like a brewery" in the words of one cop.

"Think hard, Jimmy. What time exactly?"

"Right about midnight, I'd say. Just before the graveyard guys come in for containers, you know?"

Boyle knew. His shift was the graveyard shift, midnight to 8 A.M., and Jack Ruffulo always stopped at the "T" to tide him over till his first Pakistani convenience store.

"So Patsy left just before the shift change?"

"That's right. Patsy went out that door, a minute or two later his friend went out, and about five minutes after that the shift came in."

Natala's head snapped. "What friend?"

"I guess it was his friend. The guy was sitting right there not sayin' much. Then when Patsy leaves, the guy says, 'I'll take the same thing as my friend had, to go.' "

"What did his friend look like, Jimmy?"

Jimmy tried to bring Carlos back. It was a foggy exercise, but guys like Carlos didn't wander in too often.

"Let's see, he kind of looked like a fighter, maybe that's how Patsy knew him. He was big in the shoulders and dressed nice. Shirt and tie, you know what I mean? He looked like he was black or Puerto Rican or whatever, probably Puerto Rican because he had that curly black hair. And he had an earring, a real bright silver one."

Boyle didn't meet Natala's accusing stare. He was thinking of all the fighters Patsy trained, and which ones might be that age, that look. Boyle knew precisely all of Patsy's fighters, and now he also knew who Patsy's friend was.

"Midnight," Natala said, her face tense with concentration. "That's about an hour before the accident. What does that mean? Who was that guy?"

Her eyes were fixed on Boyle. His face was rigid. "I don't believe it," he said finally.

"What? What don't you believe?"

"The guy with the earring? That Jimmy just described?"

"Yeah?"

"I already saw him in the morgue. That's the guy that went over the falls with Patsy."

16

Even Boyle couldn't argue with Natala after Jimmy told them about Patsy's last night. He listened to her wail in his face for a full ten minutes before he held up his hands, begging her to shut up, promising he'd check it out further. At nine the next morning, exactly as she ordered, he walked through the front door of police headquarters in downtown Paterson, the same way he had a thousand times before. Only now he was on suspension and Joey D'Amico knew that.

"Hey, Boyle, you ain't supposed to be here." The sergeant's voice dropped to a half whisper, and he shifted behind the desk. "You hear about the new bottle cuts?"

The topic of the month. God bless Sanders.

"Yeah, I did. I'm not here officially. I stopped by yesterday real quick. Now I need to spend some time to check some things out."

"Like what?"

"Just some things about Patsy."

The desk man shook his head sadly. "Yeah, I heard. A nasty way to go, coming down Cannonball Road. What the hell was he doin' with that guy anyway?"

"I really don't know. Anyway, I need to see Hayward again. Is he around?"

The desk sergeant gestured. "Back in the freezer, white as the stiffs. Help yourself."

Dr. Oscar Hayward was a ghoul, there was no other word for it. He had long, bony fingers and a high-pitched nasal laugh that erupted involuntarily and almost always inappropriately. He was as pale as death and loved what he did for a living, which was forensic pathology, or more simply, autopsies of crime victims. After the cutting he testified in court about the cause and manner of death.

Boyle had always gotten along with the ghoul, finding him perversely honest and even thoroughly interesting. For his part, the good doctor regarded Boyle as one of the four homicide detectives who didn't openly mock him.

Boyle walked into the frozen room to find Oscar standing with rat eyes over a cadaver. The stiff was a forty-year-old man who had been found in the Passaic River the night before. He was naked and pale, his musculature covered by a healthy layer of fat and the white bloating of death and river water. Oscar ran his hands lovingly over the man's chest.

"Hello again," Boyle said as he got nearer. He had visited Oscar briefly the day before, to get a good look at Carlos' remains.

Oscar continued his delicate stroking. "This beauty goes on the table at eleven o'clock. Oh, what a mess he'll make with all that fat. But trust me, Detective, I'm going to find something."

"Why do you say that?"

"You see this bruise here?" He pointed to a dark coloration above the man's breastbone.

"Yeah?"

"I say that came from a fist. I also say when I get inside I'll find more than river water." The manic laugh came and went so quickly Hayward almost got the hiccups.

"Well, if anybody can find it, you can, Oscar. Let me ask you something before you get started."

"Sure."

"Did you do Patsy De Marco yet?"

"Of course." He waved his hands in a slashing motion over the cadaver's form. "Right after the guy he went over the falls with."

"You do a report?"

"Autopsy report, medical examiner report, the whole thing."

"You got a copy, right?"

"Back in the office."

Anything to get away from the freezing cold and the sight of the bloated cadaver. "Any chance I can take a look at it?" Boyle gestured to the cadaver. "Before you get started, I mean."

Oscar looked vaguely disappointed. "Can it wait till after? You can watch if you want."

Boyle was only willing to go so far with Oscar. "Maybe next time. You can give me ten, can't you?"

"Detective, no problem."

B oyle sat in the chair across the gunmetal gray desk from the coroner. He read the report closely.

"I don't know if I get this. Are you calling this a car crash?"

"No way. Two people go over the falls. One of them has gunshot wounds in the neck. There's alcohol in and around the bodies. Definitely not an accident."

"So you're declaring it a homicide?"

"With the guy with the bullets in his throat, yes. Justifiable, of course."

"I meant Patsy."

"With him, no."

"What's his cause of death?"

"Falling down a slope about two hundred feet, landing in the water, going over the falls another two hundred feet and drowning. He actually looked damn good, all things considered."

"Did the car get searched?"

"What was left of it."

"What did you find?"

Oscar shrugged. "About what you'd expect. Lots of blood from the guy that got shot. Booze all around which accounted for the smell. The usual."

"Did you take blood?"

"Sure, from both of them."

"And?"

"The black guy had a BAL of point two-one. He must have put away a quart before he died."

"And Patsy?"

The ghoul consulted his report. "This is weird. It says point zero-four."

"That's not much."

Oscar scratched his head. "That's right. Probably a couple of drinks not long before death."

That made sense. Patsy never got drunk and even if he did would never drive down Cannonball Road. Patsy's blood alcohol level was perfectly consistent with a drink with Jimmy after seeing his daughter at the Plaza.

"Any drugs?"

"In him, sure."

"Who's him?"

"The black guy. We got solid readings of cocaine and Percodan. Plus the elevated BAL. This guy was flying."

"Who was he?"

Oscar shrugged. "Unclear. We sent his prints to the FBI lab to get checked. You wouldn't believe the buzz that caused."

"Try me."

"Let's just say it attracted some serious people."

"Who?"

Oscar consulted his notes. "This is all off the record, right?"

"Of course."

"Okay, listen. I have to send the originals of all ME reports to somebody named Stephanie Shane in New York." He showed him a copy of a memo from the captain. "She gets the original. We keep one copy only. And nobody sees copies either, so forget you saw this."

"Who is she?"

"DOJ."

"An agent?"

"FBI, AUSA, I don't know."

Boyle stared at the memo, then at Oscar's weird report. The whole thing made no sense. The FBI? Why the FBI? "You know something, Oscar, Patsy was pretty careful about drinking."

"Yeah?" He shrugged. "Maybe. But I did the autopsy and I got to tell you, Patsy was smelling pretty bad. I don't know how we got that point zero-four on the BAL. It wouldn't be the first time we blew it."

"You think he was drunk?"

"I guess. What else was he doing driving out there so that scumbag could get him? There's only one car so maybe the other carjacker gets away. Anyway, you tell me. What else?"

What else indeed.

———

Paterson is the oldest industrial city in the United States and in the eighteenth century was one of the most prosperous. Now it is the opposite of prosperous and a city of very few taxpayers. All the money followed the white man out of town long ago and the notion of a tax on local income is a joke, unless you count the bottle cut. Whatever federal money flows in is there to support the police department and little else. As long as the cops keep the bodies on the right side of the river everybody's happy, and beyond that nobody cares what else happens in Paterson.

So, it isn't every day that a Paterson car accident gets the attention of a federal agent in New York City. The black guy was a celebrity, and Patsy's murder had drawn flies. Boyle decided to find out why.

In New York or Los Angeles, there are two hundred-person departments set up to identify criminals and crime victims. In Paterson, the department is one woman, an extraordinarily sullen yet buxom half-Italian, half-Puerto Rican computer operator named Sonya Cortez. She and Boyle had been on the edge of something forever, one push, an extra beer, and they'd be over the top. Thus far, to the amazement of everyone, they had managed to keep their hands to themselves.

When he walked into the gray windowless room, Sonya was typing at an ancient Wang computer. Boyle sat on the edge of her desk. She said nothing, just kept typing.

He enjoyed the wait. It gave him time to admire her face, a smooth olive mixture of Mediterranean and Caribbean blood. There was no doubt about it, he liked women way too much for his own good.

"Do I have to sit here till I fall down?"

She never looked up. "Detective Boyle, you don't have to sit there, you don't have to sit nowhere near that place. You don't mean nothin' to me, you know what I mean? Matter of fact, you don't mean nothin' to no one. You got fired."

"Suspended. There's a difference."

"What did you do, go smack around some suspect? You got no sense."

"He was a murderer. *Is* a murderer."

She looked up. "He's rich, Boyle. How come you don't be smart?"

He shrugged and smiled. Sonya was as mad at him as Natala. But she eventually sighed and went back to her typing. "That's why it's good we keep things like they are. You got no sense."

"Does that mean you won't help me out?"

"Yeah, I know how you want help. Use your hand for that, Doyle, instead of smacking people."

"Nice talk, Sonya. And from a good Catholic girl."

She chuckled, as though wondering how good a Catholic girl she was.

"Anyway," he continued, "I do need help on a name."

"Who?"

"The guy who went over the falls with Patsy."

Her demeanor changed instantly. "Oh, God, I'm so sorry, Tommy. You know that, right?"

"I do know and thanks. I told Nat I'd look into it. What can you tell me?"

"You talkin' about the black guy, right?"

"That's right."

She got up and closed the door. "You heard about the rules on this? There was this memo."

"I know. Oscar says his originals go to some fed in New York."

She nodded. "I never seen nothin' like it. We send one copy to the chief, one to New York, and that's it."

He'd figure out the reason for the weird rules later. Right now he needed information. "Let me ask you straight out. Who was this guy?"

She never hesitated. She'd give him anything he wanted if it had to do with Patsy's death. She typed on the ancient computer, then squinted at the screen.

"Name, Carlos Cardena. Birthplace, Jackson Heights, January 4, 1955. First conviction, assault and battery, March 19, 1968."

"Thirteen years old?"

"That's what it says."

"What else?"

"March of 1972, another assault. July of 1974, suspicion of homicide, dealt to involuntary manslaughter, two and a half years. 1978, suspicion of homicide, dealt to voluntary manslaughter, three and a half years."

"I see a theme here."

"1981, cocaine bust, suspicion of three homicides."

"How can you *suspect* three homicides?"

She shrugged. "Deal to the drug charge. 1985, another drug charge, another suspected homicide."

"Another deal?"

"You got it."

In Boyle's world there was only one way a guy skated this much.

"Sonya, was this guy an informant?"

"My computer don't tell me that."

"How many times was he arrested since 1968?"

Sonya pushed more buttons. "Twenty-six times."

"How many convictions?"

More clicking. "Three."

"And his total time in prison was, what, three, four years?"

"Yeah."

Now he was convinced. Carlos had a sponsor. That *had* to be the reason the feds were so interested.

Boyle stood up. "What's the name of that fed in New York?"

Sonya consulted her memo. "Assistant U.S. Attorney Stephanie Shane."

An AUSA. A damn lawyer. Well, whatever. "Thanks, Sonya, I'll see you."

She looked uninterested until he started to leave, then she grabbed his arm. "Hey, Boyle?"

"Yeah?"

"Don't lose that number."

He squinted. "Of the fed?"

She grinned. "No."

Boyle's last stop at the Paterson Police Department was to see Detective Sergeant Mark Sanders. Sanders was the head of Vice, a bigot, a misogynist and the man in charge of the bottle cuts from the projects. Boyle despised him, and at least three of his suspensions were the result of fights with Sanders. Sanders was on the phone as Boyle walked in.

"I don't care what your orders are. My people are not going into those buildings. You got that?"

Boyle could hear only one side of the conversation and watched as Sanders' face got red, his temples bulging. "Because they can get killed in there, you hear what I'm sayin'? The people in there ain't human! They're animals!"

Then silence. It gave Boyle time to hate the man even more, which he hadn't thought possible. "That's right, they belong in cages. But castrate them first, so they can't reproduce no more." Then Sanders slammed down the phone.

He was still flushed when he saw Boyle. "What do you want?"

Boyle didn't answer. They could suspend him a hundred times and he'd never take a word of static from Sanders.

"Sorry." Sanders waved his hand apologetically. "I'm just out of it today. They want me to send a car into the projects every time they got an overdose. I got no time for that, you know what I mean?"

"Sure, Sanders, you're absolutely right."

The man relaxed, although his eyes still flickered, suspicious. "Boyle, maybe you and me ought to chill a while. How about you sit down."

Boyle sat down on a hard wooden chair. Sanders kicked the door shut, pulled out a bottle and two glasses, and poured them each one. He lit a cigarette and threw the pack across the desk. Boyle accepted the drink, accepted the cigarette and eased into his very familiar role, the good guy, the ex-fighter, a cop who'd stand up for other cops. Plus he was male, white, rugged and could drink, smoke and fight with the best of them. It was an easy role to fake most of the time.

"Thanks," he said, sipping and smoking.

Sanders took a sip and shivered with pleasure. "*That's* my problem. It feels so good I gotta have another." And he did.

Sanders slammed the glass on the desk and looked at Boyle with sad eyes. "Listen, I know why you're here, but there's nothing I can do." He opened his hands in a gesture of sympathy. He was a good-looking guy with close cropped blond hair. He wore conservative clothes, a blue button-down shirt and a patterned tie. His face was youthful except for the bags under the eyes caused by the booze. They looked incongruous there, emphasizing that they had not been part of the man's face to start with.

"Why do you think I'm here?"

"The bottle cut!" Sanders leaned forward. "Look, don't blame me on this. I really want all our stuff behind us. I'm your buddy now, right?"

"Absolutely, Sanders. You'd kill for me. Give me your sister to play with. Even give me my share of the bottle cut while I'm on suspension."

Sanders raised his hands high. "The first two, Boyle, no problem. Who you want dead and what time you want my sister on her knees, but the third, the bottle cut, my hands are tied."

Boyle sighed. "I understand. There's rules."

"Exactly! Just because the animals don't have rules don't mean white people don't."

"That's like poetry, Sanders."

Sanders smiled and drank some more. "Boyle, you're a good man. What can I do for you that don't involve money? I could work on that suspension if you want. Why did you drop that guy anyway?"

"He had a bad attitude."

Sanders pointed his cigarette at Boyle. "That, I understand."

"Anyway, there *is* something you can do for me. Something that doesn't involve money."

"Talk to me, sweetness."

"You know the guy who brought up Miguel and me. Nat's dad?"

Sanders hung his head. "A sad thing, Patsy. He's like the last of a kind you know? He could've left, just like the rest of us, but no, he stays. And what does it get him? Jacked and dead."

"You're right, Sanders. Anyway, Nat's all upset and she wants me to look into it."

"Like how?"

"She wants some mementos, you know? Just find out how it went down, what the investigation shows."

"You know there's a huge zip on that."

"Hey, man, that's why I'm talking to you."

Sanders grinned. This was the world he knew, trading favors. "The guy was like a father to you, right?"

"To all of us, me, Migo, Nat. He had a lot of friends in this city."

Sanders shivered as the booze grabbed him tight. "Greatest fight in history, between you and Meza. I screamed till I was hoarse." He sighed. "And then Meza goes and blows it all."

Boyle kept his face fixed. "Well, that's in the past. Can you help me now?"

Sanders flipped the cigarette at a wall, then walked to a metal filing cabinet. He grabbed a bunch of tan folders, then threw them on a table. "We're not having this conversation, right?"

"Never happened."

"Okay, here's how it shakes, and I'm only going to say it once."

"Once is just fine."

"We did everything possible on this deal, because everybody liked Patsy, understand? I don't mean me, personally, I mean Robbery, Homicide."

"Yeah."

"We did serology, even though we got no serology lab. We did prints, even though the print guy is a defective. We had two detectives on it from the start to check it out. And the other dead guy, the one that got shot, we sent his stuff all over the world. With me?"

"Right next to you, Sanders."

The man pursed his lips and stared at the material in the folders. "Then one day, let's just say things changed. We get orders from someplace else."

"Like New York, maybe?"

"Exactly. And I don't care how you know that. The broad's name is Shane and it's all weird. She's an AUSA out of Manhattan, Southern District of New York. Now tell me what that's about? Anyway, she tells us we don't do nothin' till she says it's okay. We say stuff it. Then she goes up top. All of a sudden we get shot out of the saddle. Got it?"

"Every bit of it. We do like we're told."

"Exactly."

"So what do we get told?"

"Everything's buttoned. Everything goes to her. We shut down, she takes over. That's it, no questions."

"That's a lot of heat for a car crash."

"You think?" he said sarcastically. "It's a lot of heat for a car anything."

"So where's that leave me?"

"Dumb and worthless unless you can get that AUSA to tell you why she's so interested."

He got that. "That's next. First tell me what *you* know."

Sanders fidgeted. They had never really been friends, not even now, and there was no trust in his world. "That's all you want?"

Boyle flipped open his interview notebook and snapped his pen. "I don't complain on the bottle cut, you tell me everything, the lady in New York don't know we talked and me and Miguel owe you one."

Sanders finished the whiskey in his glass and shivered, maybe from the booze, maybe from the thought of Meza. One way friend, one way not. "No problem, Boyle."

17

Meza wanted to stay in Paterson to help Boyle but Nick said no. Christine knew him well enough to correctly interpret his sullen silence as borne of anger and frustration. She waited until they were off the ground before turning to him.

"You want to talk about it?"

"What?" He signaled for a beer.

"Whatever's bothering you."

"There's nothing bothering me. Funerals are depressing."

"That's it?"

"Sure, what else?"

"I don't know. Incidentally, I liked Natala a lot. Tommy too."

"Yeah." He got his beer, drank it fast and looked out the window.

"So what's the story? Were they ever an item?"

"Tommy and Nat?" He snorted at the thought of it. "They fight every time they see each other. She thinks Tommy is the older brother from hell. If Boyle had his way, she'd be in a convent. That's probably why she wound up with John."

"What about you and her?"

"What do you mean?"

"I mean did you two ever . . ." She made a circle with her left hand and put the index finger of her right through it repeatedly.

"Jesus, what a sick question! Is that all you think about?"

"Does that mean no?"

The plane banked left, cruising over the massive island below, heading to the faraway coast. He didn't answer at first.

"Nat and me understand each other," he said finally. "We don't get in each other's way. And she knows I'm a phone call away, *anything* she needs. It's always been like that."

"She thinks her father was murdered, doesn't she?"

He sipped his beer and nodded.

"Is she right?"

"I don't know."

"What do you mean you don't know! Miguel Meza, you know more about this than anybody!"

"What, carjackings and murders?"

"Yes!"

He had to laugh at that one.

"Anyway," she continued, "we should've stayed and helped her."

"Tommy's there. Besides, I asked and Nick said 'no.' I got a job in L.A."

"What kind of job?"

"I don't know, some collection thing."

"Migo!"

"It's nothing, some gambling debt. It's just a first call."

"So can't it wait? Isn't Natala more important?"

"That's what I thought. That's what Nick thought at first."

"And?"

"And then he called back, said he checked it out, and it didn't work. Said I had to get back to L.A. and finish the job."

She flounced against the seat cushion. "Just tell me the truth, what do you *really* think?"

He sighed. "I think Patsy got hit."

"Why do you think that?"

"Lots of reasons. Number one, the black guy's got to be a cleaner . . . a professional. Tommy will find that out in a hurry."

"You're kidding!"

"No. Plus the way the hit went down."

"How?"

"The whole thing. Who got shot, when? It's a hit. Where they were sitting? It's a hit. How they went over the falls? It's a hit. Plus it's a bad hit."

"What's a bad hit?"

"One that . . ." he thought about it ". . . one that doesn't go like it should. One that maybe had somebody else involved."

"Who?"

He shrugged. "Who knows."

She was as excited as she could ever remember. "Migo, we have to go back and help her! She *needs* you."

"I can't, I got a job to do."

"The collection, you mean."

"Yeah, first call."

"I'm coming."

He snorted. "Unless you mean it the nasty way, you're crazy."

"Don't be a pig. I'm coming and that means I'm going with you on the job."

He rubbed his temples with both hands. "Why? Just tell me why?"

"Because," she said, her jaw set, "Natala is now a friend of mine. When we finish Nick's job we're getting right back on a plane to go help her." She paused. "Besides, you just said you're always there for her. *Anything* she needs, you said."

The plane hit turbulence and bounced. "Damn," he muttered.

Boyle first tried to meet Stephanie Shane on a Thursday, late in the afternoon, as the day was ending and the employees at the U.S. Attorney's office in Manhattan were looking for the quickest way out. He begged the receptionist for a chance.

"I just need to talk to her for a couple of minutes. Tell her it's about the murder in Paterson."

The receptionist spoke into the phone. "He says it's about some case in Paterson."

She looked up. "What's the name again?"

"Boyle. Paterson Police Department." He would have flashed a badge if he had one.

She held her hand over the phone while she whispered the message, then shrugged in resignation. She seemed to want to help.

"Tell her I'll sit here forever. And if she won't see me today, I'll be back tomorrow. Same seat."

"She'll have you thrown out. There are a hundred FBI agents on this floor."

"Then I'll *really* get suspicious."

More mumbling into the receiver.

"She only has ten minutes to give you."

Maybe. "I'll take it."

The door buzzed and a lock disengaged. "Walk to the green line. Somebody will be there for you."

"Thanks."

Assistant United States Attorney Stephanie Shane didn't look anything like Doyle remarked. She had a pale, innocent face surrounded by light, close-cropped curled hair. The hair and face made her look too young to be a lawyer. Yet there were also contradictions, parts that aged her. Her suit was dark, rumpled and entirely out of date, as though she just grabbed it off the rack at a flea market. And then there were the eyes, piercing green, but ringed with dark circles.

He decided Stephanie Shane was working too hard. And he also decided she was beautiful.

Boyle held out his hand. His voice was formal, no nonsense. "Good afternoon. Detective Thomas Boyle. Paterson P.D."

Stephanie took the hand. "Detective? They still call you that?"

"Of course. Why wouldn't they?"

She shrugged. "Lots of reasons. Anyway, Detective, if you are a detective, you've got ten minutes. But first, how did you get my name?"

"It wasn't hard. You got every cop in Paterson scared to death."

"Not scared enough, it seems."

"You're not doing bad. But I have a question. How did you know about me?"

"What about you?"

"My . . . my *status* with the department."

"What status?"

He pointed a finger at her. "*That's* what I mean. How'd you get to be so smart?"

She deflected the question with a brief flick of her fingers. She now had eleven agents full time on the De Marco hit. She actually *did* know everything those agents knew. And it was all stored in that magnificent, detail-charged memory. "We stay up to date." She consulted her watch. "About seven minutes left."

Again, maybe. "I'll go fast. Why is the federal government interested in Patsy De Marco's death?"

"It's classified."

"What is?"

"Why we're interested."

"Why's it classified?"

"That's classified too."

This was getting boring. He decided the circles definitely made her look older.

"You should get more sleep."

"What!?"

"Never mind. Look, if you know all about me, you know why I'm interested."

"I do and I'm sorry. I understand Patsy De Marco was your in structor or trainer or whatever they call it."

"They call it father and that's what he was. To all three of us."

"I know. Two boys and a girl."

"You know *everything*!"

"Not really." She checked her watch. "Four minutes." A sigh. "Two boys, neither of whom turned out very well. One a corrupt cop in Paterson."

"Corrupt!"

"You mean you're not on Sanders' list?"

He coughed. "If I wasn't, I'd get a bullet in my back."

"That's what all the dirty cops say. What about your multiple suspensions, the most recent for excessive violence on a citizen? Did they force you to do that too?"

"I have an explanation."

"I'm sure. Three minutes. The other two kids, no better. Meza, a hired killer in L.A. for anyone who'll pay his bill, usually Angelo Bracca, but he's not particular."

"He has an explanation too."

"And then the lovely Natala. Born on Christmas Day and the apple of her father's eye. Dropped out of college after sixty days and now a party girl fashion model who likes late nights and lots of wine."

"Princeton was sort of like the Citadel for her. Just not her thing."

"No, but John Bracca was."

He tapped a pencil distractedly on her desk. "Now that one I really don't have an explanation for."

She let him know when he ran out of time and then relented. "I'll give you five more minutes, even though it's a waste of time."

He spoke fast. "Natala asked me to look into Patsy's death. She's convinced it's not how it looks."

"She should be."

"Pardon?"

"Never mind, go on."

"So I did what she wanted, I checked it out, and it turns out she was right."

"Because?"

"Because the black guy's a known hitter named Carlos Cardena. He followed Patsy out of a bar near the PPD. A half hour later they both go over the falls with a lot of bullets, blood and alcohol everyplace except inside Patsy." He opened his hands. "Hey, I do this for a living. The old man got set up. Also, there's a guy missing."

"Who?"

"Where's the other car? How did good old Carlos *get* to Cannonball Road?"

The plain fact was there were a lot of strange deaths in the short time she had been in New York. She had an encyclopedic knowledge of all of them. Yet there was no doubt in her mind anymore that Patsy was special. The lack of a motive. The strange lives of Patsy's kids. The Bracca organization right on the periphery. For now, though, she wanted to play devil's advocate, find out what Boyle's take on this was.

She spread her hands in answer to the question of the one car, like it was a no-brainer.

"Easy. De Marco parks his car at the bar because he doesn't want to drive into the city. Then he comes back later and drinks. When he leaves around midnight Carlos jumps in De Marco's car, pulls a gun, forces him to drive to the river. They fight for the gun, shots are fired and the car goes into the river. Splish, splash. What's wrong with that?"

"Forget for a sec why Carlos is driving Patsy to the falls. The way you tell it, Carlos' car should be back at the bar. What'd he do, take a bus to Paterson? Or maybe he *lives* in Paterson."

She tried to squelch a smile. "Once upon a time people did."

"Yeah, right after the war with Germany."

Stephanie laughed involuntarily and leaned back, studying him, a handsome Irish guy that still had the easy athleticism of a fighter. And the easy arrogance. She'd give him a few more minutes, then shut him down fast.

"Say you're right. There's two cars. So what?"

"So if there's *two* cars, then someone drove the *other* one away, the one that's not at the bottom of the Passaic River and not in the parking lot at the 'T'. So, now you have two killers. Tell me, what are two professionals doing hitting some old man in Paterson? Plus, Carlos has to be expensive."

"Why do you say that?"

He pointed to the computer. "Run his sheet and you'll know."

Stephanie knew all about Carlos' sheet, just like she knew everything about all the potential cases. "Maybe Patsy just ran into a bad crowd."

"I'd say that's a safe bet."

"What I mean is, it could be anything. The fight game can be rough."

"Really? I didn't know that."

She smiled involuntarily. "I forgot," she said. "You *do* know something about that."

"So do you. And I bet you also know that Patsy was small time, like a little league coach for Christ's sake. Training amateurs for the Golden Gloves. Nobody hires some Carlos to button a trainer for the Gloves."

"Sometimes amateurs become pros. You did."

He smirked. "Not much of one."

"You didn't cooperate. De Marco wouldn't let you. No cooperation, no dates."

His eyes widened. "Is there anything you don't know?"

"Yes," she said cautiously. She hesitated, then decided to speak the truth. "I still don't know exactly why he died."

They talked longer than ten minutes that night. By the time they were done it was dark. Three times the secretary had come in to remind her of a phony appointment and three times she waved the man away. Now the hallway was empty. She checked her watch.

"I really have to go."

"Fine, I'll walk you down."

"That's not necessary or permitted."

"Then I'll buy you a drink."

"That's also not necessary."

"Someplace public. Nobody could ever criticize you."

"They could and would."

"Okay, what time tomorrow?"

Her eyes flattened. "You're kidding."

"No, I'll be sitting out there at nine A.M. We just started."

She rubbed her temples. "One drink and you go home to Pator don?"

"Absolutely. It's only twelve miles away."

"Where?"

"Just east of here across the George Washington Bridge, or through the tunnel, whatever you want."

Her hands went back to her temples. "I meant where do you want to . . . you knew what I meant."

"O'Malley's. Near NBC and Rockefeller Center."

"Why?"

"It has cold Guinness."

That was better than the beer at the Officer's Club. "What time?"

"Thirty minutes."

"And then you're gone forever?"

He crossed his fingers. "I promise."

18

I've never seen a hit man go out on a collection job," Christine told him. "You should be proud I'm interested in your work."

He wasn't proud at all, he was angry, although he tried to hide it while he got dressed and checked the square Walther he was going to carry. He turned to her with dark eyes. "Let me explain something," he said slowly. "There's business and there's social. You get to hang with me on the social, not the business."

Christine never liked it when her men got attitude. She dropped her hands on her hips. "Who made that rule, not me."

His voice rose. "That's the rule that's been around since God made man and God made woman."

"Really? One of the Ten Commandments, maybe?"

"Don't get a mouth on you now. Look, we had fun, but don't mess with me when I'm trying to work."

"I'm coming."

"Congratulations."

"That will cost you," she said. "Tonight."

They were now nose to nose and their voices were loud. "Listen, little girl. Forget it! You know those marks on your butt? I can do better!"

"If you don't let me come . . ." She stopped. "If you don't let me go along . . ."

"Don't say it."

"Every one of those outfits you bought will be burned. No, more than burned."

"You'll be standing for the next month!"

"And I'll send my mother that sick note you left me."

He was shocked. "That was confidential!"

"And it can stay that way. Do you want my mother to send that thing to Angelo?"

"You're a goddamn blackmailer, you know that?"

"Don't curse, I hate that in men. Just tell me what time we're leaving."

They arrived at the downtown L.A. building at noon. It was fifty-five stories and commanded a great view of the ground zero devastation to the south and east. Bradford Easton's office was on the forty-seventh floor.

"What's he do?" she asked, as they rode the high speed elevator.

He stopped sulking long enough to look at notes written in pencil on the back of an envelope. "He's a senior partner at the law firm of Jenkins and Dorman. He does 'complex commercial workouts.' "

"Whatever that means."

"It means gyms, you know, with weights? Where you go to work out?"

"I don't think so."

"Whatever, he owes us money."

The elevator opened onto an elegant anteroom. Dark wood paneling with pictures of sailing vessels and hunting dogs dominated two sides of the vast space. The far wall was a single sheet of glass with the city spread out far below. A no-nonsense receptionist in a tight gray bun sat behind a curved, brass desk. She was surrounded by high-tech equipment, red and green blinking buttons.

"May I help you?"

"Yeah," Meza said, "how do I call Mars? Just kidding. I'm looking for Bradford Easton." He peered around the corner.

She looked at the long red hair tucked in a ponytail, the two-day growth of beard, the dark foreboding suit with the black shirt. He also had now topped off the ensemble with his favorite black bolero, sitting astride his head, circled with silver dollars. The question didn't compute, nor did the man.

"Do you have an appointment?"

"Lady, I'm not here to get my nails done. I just want directions."

"Sir, you may not go back there without an appointment."

Meza sighed and reached over the oval desk. There was a floor scheme with the names of the twenty-eight lawyers who were officed on the forty-seventh floor.

"Sir, hand that back to me immediately!"

Meza twisted the floor scheme around, trying to make sense of it. "Here he is, in the corner. But what corner?" He twisted the paper around some more. "God I hate these goddamn places."

"Stop cursing!" Christine ordered. "I told you I hate that."

The woman behind the desk turned purple. "Sir, I must insist . . . oh, hello Mr. Vaughn."

A distinguished-looking man got off the elevator, nodded pleasantly at Christine and Meza and stood in front of the door. "Beam me in, Marcia," he commanded. His voice was deep and warm.

"Nice voice," Christine said, waving. The man waved back, the receptionist pressed a button, an electronic buzz answered, and the door swept open. The man started to walk through.

"Excuse me," Christine said quickly. The man held the open door and turned.

"Yes?"

"Can you help us with this map?"

The nice Mr. Vaughn led them through the labyrinth of lawyer offices.

"I'd never have found him," Meza admitted. "He could have hid in here forever."

"It is somewhat confusing," the man agreed. "Are you clients of Brad's?" He checked out Christine as he asked the question. She was wearing black leather pants, thigh-high boots and an orange halter top. Her grin was wide and she was chewing gum.

"Who's Brad? Oh, Easton, right. He's sort of a client I guess you'd say."

"Really? How so? Insurance?"

"No . . . let's just say it's between the two of us."

Mr. Vaughn stopped. "You're here to collect a gambling debt, aren't you? He's been gambling again."

"I don't want to get into it. Maybe just point me."

The man didn't move, which made Meza jumpy. Unless this guy showed him the way, he'd starve to death in this maze.

"Well, isn't this something," the man said finally. "Brad Easton. Mr. Respectability. Getting a visit from a . . . what are you? A mob soldier? A made man, isn't that what they call you types?"

"No, I ain't made. Even when the books are open you got to be Italian on your father's side. Full blooded Italian, no shit."

"And you're not?"

"No, I don't even know who he was. Puerto Rican I think." He gestured to Christine. "She's not even full blooded and she's Angelo's cousin."

Mr. Vaughn's jaw was set. "But you're still some sort of employee of what's known as the *mob*!"

"Just Angelo Bracca's crew." Meza shifted nervously. "Not all the time, but a lot of the time. I try to stay independent, you know? Be my own boss? Unless Angelo really wants something."

The man just stared at the two of them, Meza's words seeming to come from another planet. Then he sighed and made a decision. "Let's just go find Brad. This may be just the thing he needs."

Bradford Easton was finishing his speech and felt great. The conference room was filled with cigarette smoking Japanese executives surrounding a long, walnut table, each representing the creditors of a medical supply company that had fallen on hard times. The defunct company was about to sink under the waves owing about $240 million to a consortium of Japanese banks. Tonight the men at the table would vote on counsel to represent them in the bankruptcy proceedings. There were twelve firms competing for the business.

The winning firm would collect a cool $20 million in fees over a three-year period. At least fifteen associates would be kept busy full-time. The firm would bill the associates at two hundred dollars per hour. It demanded two thousand hours a year in billable time from each one, grossing four hundred thousand dollars minimum per head. It paid the kids seventy-five thousand dollars a year. Buy wholesale, sell retail, Brad always said.

Meza and Christine walked in and stood in the corner. Stuck to Meza's hip was the Walther, square and squat, and he adjusted it.

Bradford Easton stopped in mid-sentence. The room turned to

Meza, who had Christine and her leather pants now draped on his shoulder.

"Uh, the coffee's over there," Easton said. "We could all use a refill. And please take off that hat when you're in our offices."

Meza's gaze followed where the man pointed.

"He thinks you're here to get him coffee," Christine explained.

Meza kept it cool, not wanting to offend. The guy was a good customer, after all. He just owed Angelo money.

"Hey, Brad? I'm not the coffee guy."

Easton stiffened. "Then who the hell are you?"

"I work for Nick out of New Orleans."

The blood left Easton's face. Out in the hall, Mr. Vaughn leaned against the wall and stared into the conference room.

"Wait in my office," Easton ordered. "I'll be in to see you in one moment. Just let me finish here."

"I'd like to do that, Brad, I really would. But it ain't possible. One, I got no idea if you'd show. Two, I'd get lost anyway."

Easton glanced toward the glass wall and saw his partner staring at him. He had to get this over fast.

"What do you want?"

Meza shrugged. "Not much." He reached into his jacket.

"No!" Easton screamed. He backed to the wall. Meza watched him blankly, his hand still in his jacket.

"Brad, what are you doing?"

"He thinks you're going to shoot him," Christine explained.

Meza sighed and held out both empty hands. "Brad, you been watching way too many movies. Relax. Your Jap friends are getting pissed."

"I don't think you should call them Japs," Christine chided. "And that was close to cursing. Maybe 'pissed' is okay, just crude." The men at the table murmured, waved their cigarettes and were talking rapidly to one another in Japanese.

Meza's hand went under his coat again and this time came out with a sheaf of paper. He dropped the papers in front of Easton.

"You still live at Thirteen-thirty Georgina, Brad?"

"What!"

Meza sighed. He hated the paper stuff. "Thirteen-thirty Georgina Avenue. Beautiful Santa Monica. That still your address?"

"Yes, but . . ."

"Good." Meza gestured to a chair. "Just park it and sign these." Bradford Easton, still in a twilight zone between shock and disbelief, sat down. He examined the documents through blurred eyes.

"This is a note and deed of trust," he yelled. Then he grabbed the papers. "This is a mortgage on my house!"

"Now you got it, Brad."

"This is outrageous!"

"Not at all. Look here. You got a year to pay us off. A hundred large, twelve payments plus interest. Regular interest, nothing fancy, we ain't pigs with guys like you. You're a helluva good customer. We want you back!"

"And if I don't you foreclose? You take my house?"

"Not me, some lawyer Nick's got. I don't know nothin' about that. Except this is completely legit, Brad."

Easton grabbed the pen and scribbled his name on both documents. He pushed them back at Miguel.

"Here, now get out of here! You'll have your blood money in thirty days!"

"Blood money? Brad, you just like the ponies way too much. And to be truthful, Brad, you ain't that good." Meza examined the signatures. "Anyway, there's more."

"What?"

"We got to get this notarized."

Christine came close and kissed Meza. "Then we have to go back and help Nat."

19

When Portov and Alicia left their German banker in his enormous estate they first spent one very passionate night in Paris filled with champagne, fine food and whatever Portov wanted from Alicia. The next morning they finalized the plans and headed in opposite directions. Portov flew nonstop to Moscow to arrange transfer of the pure Sarin canisters already collected by his ruthless partner, Josef Alexeyev. Alicia flew west, to Los Angeles, to arrange the shipment of beryllium that her late professor had educated her so much about.

"I'm only concerned about one thing," Alicia said, before they separated at the airport.

"What?"

"Magnus."

She waited while he thought hard. Braxton had already told them everything about Purcell. "That problem will have to be addressed quickly." She waited some more. "But he probably can't hurt us any more than he has right away. And my dealings in Russia are delicate and must have priority."

"I understand."

"Give me a week. Then I'll rid you of Purcell."

"Yes, sir."

Several thousand miles northeast of the Paris hotel where Alicia and Portov grappled, the Ural Mountains slice Mother Russia in two, extending in an unbroken line from the icebound Kera Sea to the north to the landlocked Aral and Caspian Seas in the south. Yuri Rudenko knew the Urals represented much more important psychological than physical barriers. To the west of the Urals lay Moscow, the throne of Russian society, as well as Munich, Paris, London, New York—in short, civilization. To the east was Sverdlovsk, Novosibirsk, the Central Siberian Plain and the yellow hoards of Mongolia. Rudenko was now definitely east of the Urals.

Rudenko didn't have it as bad as some on this side. As the official representative of the Minister of Audits and Controls, he traveled in high style, which meant a government Fiat and an alcoholic engineer to drive him wherever he needed to go—to the oil fields, to the power plants, to the Institute of Physics for the Motherland, to the vast storage facilities for now unneeded enriched uranium, even to abandoned military installations where chemical weapons were crudely stored. These small privileges only marginally made up for the fact that he was cold, incredibly hungover in a way he had never experienced in his fifty-five years, and terrified at the thought of reporting to his superiors in Moscow the depressing oil production figures the drunken engineer was providing between burps.

The minister would be furious. If Rudenko did not come up with better figures than these, it was entirely possible there would be a new special assistant to the Minister of Audits and Control and Rudenko would be back shuffling accounts at the *Vsesoyuzniye Obyedineniya* for the importation of woolen fabrics. Although it was as head of *V/O Exportlyon* that he first caught the minister's eye, there wasn't much good to be said about woolen fabric. And there was nothing whatsoever about woolen fabric that could any longer satisfy Ingrid.

That's what it all came down to, Ingrid. Ten years before, she had come to him like a breath of western air across the Gulf of Finland. He had been in Leningrad at the time, a clerk in *Sovincentre*, providing administrative services to Finnish exporters, learning everything about woolen fabrics. Ingrid was a secretary to a Finnish exporter named Horst Arklund of Arklund Woolens—he could never look at that label without remember their first passion. He was stricken by her immediately: hair the color of dried wheat; breasts the size of the Scandinavian peninsula; a backside that spread forever like the steppes of the Kazakh Uplands. There was more of Ingrid than any one man had a right to keep for himself.

Within days he had asked her to return to Moscow with him and to his amazement she accepted: the Finns had little appreciation of her Rubenesque beauty and she was between suitors at the time.

There was no objection from what was then the Soviet side—Finland is, after all, connected to the Russian mainland and, were it not for a few ill-advised treaties in the 1940s, would always have been part of the family of modern socialism. Ingrid even learned some Russian in preparation for her Leningrad trip. They settled into placid house-keeping together.

The halcyon days did not last. Ingrid retained unfortunate bour-geois leanings that rose to the surface the first time she had to stand in a two-hour line to buy cosmetics.

"Mud," she screamed at him. "Mud! And two hours in line."

There had been no roaming over her immense form that night or for two weeks thereafter, and Rudenko quickly learned the only way to bliss was through the black market. Or, after a few promotions, the currency-controlled shops. Ingrid was the greatest spur to am-bition a man could have.

All this was prologue to a frozen ride in an aged Fiat with the drunken Alexei Michnev next to him. At the beginning, Rudenko thought the man was just being polite when he offered warm wheat vodka with herring sandwiches; it was, after all, a Russian staple. But Rudenko quickly realized what he was up against when he saw that Michnev liked to drink his vodka—he preferred Sibirskaya—de-canted and drunk from wine glasses. For the ride to the oil fields Michnev simply put a stopper in the decanter and brought the wine glasses along. After the first hard night, Michnev filled the decanter with brine from salted cucumbers for an hour or two before refilling it with the hair of the dog. Between vodka bouts Michnev drank sweet wines from the Crimea, washed down with *Leningradskoye* beer, or *peevo*. Rudenko, although he mostly just sipped along to be polite, was now on the back end of a three-day hangover. No wonder it was called the Russian curse.

Rudenko's headache got no better when Michnev's government-Fiat rounded a curve and entered the oil fields. The sight stunned him. He quickly snapped open his briefcase and grabbed the pre-vious year's audited quantity report on local oil production. This field was supposed to be one of the most productive in the Caucuses, yet half the rigs were empty and the others operating at half speed. His voice was sharp.

"What is the meaning of this?"

Michnev sipped before he spoke. "This was once the finest field in the motherland. But during the Brezhnev years," he shrugged before continuing, "the demands of the Poles, the Hungarians, even the Fascist Germans were too much. Each year our quota increased. For the last ten years we met our quotas only by water injection methods. Do you know what that means?"

Rudenko shook his head.

"So why do they send you? How can you audit if you do not know what you're looking at? It means we are not harvesting our oil. It means we are forcing petroleum out at a great cost. The figures you see on that paper"—he waved a hand at Rudenko's journal— "they are like the reports of our annual income." He laughed heartily at his own joke. "A myth!"

Rudenko didn't laugh. There was no possibility of returning to Moscow with a report that disclosed that the entire preserve on the most fertile petroleum plain east of the Urals was a fraud. "What can we do?" He said it softly. Michnev had to strain.

"What? What did you say?"

Rudenko screamed. "What can we do? What can I say about this?" He pounded the paper.

Michnev smiled and reached for the decanter. "You will audit us and report a full field, with my signature, just as your predecessors have always reported." He took a long sip. "But before you leave with my signature you will leave me a great deal of this."

He held up the bottle and laughed, his yellow teeth clacking as he did so. The government driver stopped at the first idle platform. The workers on the few remaining rigs were mingling, ambling slowly toward a makeshift bar in the rear of the desolate range. As they did, Rudenko thought of the famous underground story making the Moscow rounds for years, the one about the tank crew in Czechoslovakia in the early 1980s. It seems the crew drove into a town, sold the tank to the local bartender for a case of vodka and were found drunk under a tree three days later. The bartender cut up the tank and sold it for a fortune on the black market as scrap metal. They caught him a week later trying to sneak into Yugoslavia. The army shot everybody as quickly as possible and the story had still got around. The Russian curse, no doubt about it. The workers had all left the motionless rigs. It was two o'clock in the afternoon.

A week later Rudenko arrived back in Moscow. The plane landed in late afternoon, bouncing down from ten thousand feet on the leading edge of gusting winter winds. Rudenko suffered mightily from the turbulence, which he feared, and from the tenth day of what he called his Michnev hangover, which no amount of aspirin or tumblers of vodka seemed to cure. More importantly, he now faced the formidable task of facing not only Ingrid, but his superiors as well. Every quantity report he had examined was a fraud, from the oil fields to the chemical weapons storehouses, particularly the reports of canisters of some strange chemical called Sarin. There were at least one hundred canisters missing from last year's audit and he had the photos to prove it. Neither his boss nor his wife would be pleased.

Rudenko took a taxi to Moscow, a gross extravagance at twenty kopecks per kilometer, but one he felt he needed. He got out at the metro station and checked his bags at a public locker. Then he went to the escalators, dropped a five kopeck piece into a rusted slot and walked to the platform. He ignored the station map because he really didn't care where the train would take him. When the train roared to a stop in front of him he piled in with the mob. He sat facing the window. For the next two hours he rolled in and out of stations and around and through Moscow neighborhoods in the late part of a bleak winter day that perfectly matched his mood.

Eventually, he decided that while there wasn't much he could do to make the minister happy, he could at least try with his wife. He thought of a present for her and was again wracked with envy for those lucky enough to have access to the *Beryozka*, or hard currency shops. He passed them daily in the International Trade Center on the *Krasnopresnenskaya* Embankment, and stared with undisguised fury at the foreigners and gangsters passing freely within the shops, never having to stand in line, easily purchasing the finest delicacies Russia could offer. Once he thought he might rise high enough in the bureaucracy to gain access to a hard currency shop in Bolshaya Gruzinskaya, where diplomats with D-series coupons could always shop. But it never happened, a failure Ingrid never let him forget.

The only thing left to him were the department stores, and at Rudenko's level that meant GUM. The very thought of it depressed him. He imagined its cavernous innards: three enormous complexes built on two levels a short walk from what used to be called Red

Square. Even if he could find something for Ingrid at GUM, the lines were too much. There would be at least three separate queues to stand on: one to buy the merchandise, one to wrap the merchandise and obtain a receipt, one at the cash desk. And what would he buy her? A raincoat? A fur hat? If the size was wrong he'd have to go back and exchange it. Three more lines. Six for a hat. He didn't have the strength.

He exited the train and went home with nothing for her.

The great privilege of his modestly rising position was a private apartment, a two-room flat which shared a bathroom with only two other families. The rent was good and the local DEZ—the housing maintenance officer—was moderately efficient. The thought of the DEZ made him think of the rent book and he fumbled in his coat for it. He checked the stamps on the left-hand side and realized that his payment had been due at the *Sherkassa*—the state bank—that afternoon. Another reason for Ingrid to scream at him.

The private apartment meant nothing to her. She constantly complained of the cold, and even with the gas-fired, unvented space heater running nonstop in the winter, she still complained. When Rudenko finally got the DEZ to turn up the gas, she claimed it was too hot, and the sight of her enormous frame leaping up to yank open a window to let in the freezing Moscow night was the stuff of nightmares. Because of her fits and starts between extreme heat and extreme cold, Ingrid was constantly sick, and used potato vodka as a year-round cure. Rudenko didn't mind the vodka but had no use for the *gorcheechniks*—the mustard plasters—which Ingrid thickly applied over her ample chest. Between the mustard plaster and the complaining, even Rudenko's marital ardor had recently cooled.

He paused outside the apartment to imagine the Ingrid he would find inside: unhappy, complaining, covered with mustard plaster, filled with potato vodka, angry. He fumbled for his key and realized he had left it in his bags, which, in his fogged state, was back in a locker at the train station. Ingrid would now have new reason for rage. He knocked feebly.

The door opened immediately and Rudenko squinted. Dimly, near the metal table, he saw two candles lit. He had no idea where she might have gotten candles, and thought at first there was a death. Then came the smells, strange confused smells that overlapped and fought for dominance. There also seemed to be a sweet, sickly smell of perfume that was even odder than the mustard plaster. Then he smelled the food.

He could identify the food instantly: the hot *shchee*, or cabbage soup, which he loved highly salted and cooked in a meat broth; the sliced beef covered with stroganoff sauce; the *bleeny* or unsweetened pancakes; and above all the *piroshkee*, pies filled to the brim with chopped meat and boiled cabbage. He even detected one of his favorite vegetables, a spiced and pickled mushroom mixed with lentils.

The onslaught of smells left him staring into the dark. Then Ingrid spoke and her voice was delicate. He was so surprised that the painful, unconscious twitches he had recently developed—his head kept diving down toward his right shoulder and back again at twenty-second intervals—stopped for a moment.

"Will you stand out there all night?" She said it teasingly.

"Ingrid. I don't . . ."

"Come in, please." She reached into the hall for his hand and pulled him close. As she did the light hit her and Rudenko gasped with shock. She was naked. Her entire, formidable, mountainous, billowing form was naked to the world. She pulled him in.

"Come in quickly. The food can wait."

She made love to him in a way Rudenko thought was probably illegal. Then she bathed him, drying him with warm towels hung over the space heater. She brought him to the table wrapped in a robe and toasted him with sips of potato vodka between courses. The blustery day outside had turned black, and Rudenko realized this whole, fantastic event was happening at four in the afternoon. After dinner she left him with a cigar and Pravda while she swept away the dishes. Then she sat beside him, dressed in a flowing night-gown that could only have come from the West.

"Ingrid . . ." he began.

She put a finger to his lips. "Don't. Are you happy? Is there anything you need?"

"Ingrid . . ."

"There's something I must tell you. Something that happened while you were gone."

"Yes, my sweet?"

"A representative of the minister came."

Rudenko stiffened. The minister! They knew! He could never explain all the phony quantity reports, or the oil fields, or the missing 3urlu. "Came where?"

"Why here, of course."

"Did he say anything? Why did he come?"

"Oh, yes, he said something. He said very nice things about you."

"He did?"

"Yes. He said you are a hero. Your work on corruption in the oil fields and chemical storage facilities has reached the highest circles. You are to be promoted!"

Promoted. So that was the cause of all this. Promoted. No more trips to the Kazakh Uplands for reports on quantities of strange chemicals. No more freezing, bouncing flights in World War II aircraft into the Putoran Mountains on the Upper Siberian Range for timber reports. No more winter trips to the ice clogged shores of the Kara Sea for reports on gas exploration beneath the Arctic Ocean. From now on, winters in warm Moscow flats. Could it be true?

"What else did he say?"

Ingrid moved closer. Her hand ran up his leg. "He said you will now be responsible for rooting out corruption in our country, to help us all against the gangsters. He left papers for you to sign."

That confused Rudenko. "Papers?"

"Yes, just bureaucratic nonsense. A throwback to the old Soviet days I suppose. Here, let me get you more *bleeny* and vodka."

He let her serve him and forgot some of his confusion. And when she kissed his ear and whispered, "I'm so proud of you," he forgot all of it.

By eight that evening they had drunk the vodka, eaten the food and made love again on the floor, which Rudenko was certain had never happened before. He was pleasantly near sleep. She came out of the bedroom with something in her hand.

"Here are the papers the minister's man left. You might as well sign them now so you won't forget."

"Just leave them on the table. I'll get to them in the morning." His eyelids drooped.

"Yuri, don't be silly," she snapped. Her voice was sharp, more like the Ingrid he knew. "You know you'll only lose them like you lose everything else. Now sit up!"

Yuri's eyes opened and he sat up. "Fine, let me see them."

"See what I mean? I told you, they're just papers. Don't waste time! Here." She handed him a pen.

"I need my glasses."

"To sign your name? Yuri, don't talk nonsense. Here, where my finger is."

The papers were a blur. He signed where she pointed. When he finished, she took the page away and put another down, pointing again.

"So many?"

"It's the bureaucracy. Sign."

It seemed he signed fifteen times. Each time she carefully took the signature page away and clipped it to other pages. At the end there were more than a dozen neat stacks of papers.

He looked up expecting approval. "All done?"

She ignored him. He got up, found his glasses and stood next to her.

"Wait. Those aren't personnel forms. They're audited quantity reports on chemical weapons!"

"Yes," a voice said in perfectly accented American English. "That's exactly what they are."

Rudenko spun. A *man* was walking out of his bedroom! He was white-haired and stocky and wore an expensive foreign suit. His hair was slicked back and there was jewelry on his fingers. A gold watch gleamed in the light from the candles.

"Who are you? And what did you just say? What language is that?"

"I apologize," Portov said switching back to Russian. "Sometimes I forget I'm speaking English."

Rudenko's confusion only grew when a second man emerged. "I demand to know who you people are," Rudenko screamed. The second man was younger and carried a cellular phone. "Ingrid, I demand an explanation!"

They all ignored him. The younger man had hooded eyes and wavy brown hair. He wore a business suit with a no-nonsense blue tie over a white shirt. The man examined the documents, then snapped open the cellular phone.

"They're all signed," he said into the phone. "You may release the shipment of potatoes."

The younger man turned to Portov, "Satisfied?"

"Yes, half now and half on receipt in our Turkish warehouse."

"True. Just remember I need that beryllium shipment desperately."

Portov nodded. "We need the Sarin just as quickly. There's a deadline."

Ingrid sat down and lit a cigarette. Rudenko felt weak and nauseous.

"May I ask again," he said, his voice slightly cracked. "Who are you and what do you want?" Ingrid smoked quietly.

The younger man stacked the signed documents inside his briefcase, then closed it. He glanced at Portov.

Portov filled a glass with Rudenko's vodka. "My name is Gregor Portov," he said finally.

"You are not Russian."

"You're right, I was born in Brooklyn of Russian émigré parents. Do I have an accent?"

"Not really. You're an American?" Rudenko had never met an American.

"Yes."

"And him?"

"His name is Josef Alexeyev."

Rudenko stiffened in fear. He *knew* he had recognized the man.

"The *Mafiya*," he said quietly.

Portov laughed heartily. "It has become a Russian word, now." He drank more vodka. "Yuri, trust me, he's nothing. You have to come to Brooklyn if you want to see some real mobsters."

Alexeyev was talking rapidly into the cell phone. *"Da,"* he said finally.

"We're through here," he said to Portov in English.

"Fine. You know how to reach me?"

"Yes."

Portov finished his vodka and gestured. The badly frightened Rudenko was standing rigidly.

"Ingrid," he said weakly.

"Don't worry, you fool, these are the men from the minister's office. They'll be gone shortly and we'll be rich."

"Yes," Alexeyev said quietly. "Don't worry."

His hand emerged from under his coat with a 9 mm Luger in it. There was a silencer in his jacket pocket that he didn't even bother with. Rudenko held up his hands and backed up. Alexeyev fired twice and Rudenko grabbed his chest, the blood spilling between his fingers. Ingrid screamed and Alexeyev fired again, just to make sure. The man fell backward and lay still.

Ingrid's screams were high pitched. She knelt beside her fallen husband.

Alexeyev went back to arranging his briefcase. "Your turn."

"I prefer a Beretta," Portov said. He grabbed the kneeling woman by the hair and fired twice into the back of her head. The room became quiet. The bodies were huddled together, the smoke from the guns mixing with the candle and swirling.

"I will call you on Tuesday," Alexeyev said. "After we file these audited quantity reports we can ship the Sarin. It will never be missed. I expect you to deliver the beryllium in seven days. Do I have your word?"

"Of course."

They shook hands. Portov took a last look at the bodies and noticed the meat-filled pie had been left uneaten. He grabbed a handful and stuffed it in his mouth.

"Not bad," he said, licking his fingers on the way out.

20

As soon as Boyle left her office, Stephanie Shane thought a bit about just shining him on, missing their encounter altogether. Yet there was still information to be gained. She needed some advice so she called Cameron Braxton in Washington. He came on the line immediately, his voice jovial.

"Stephanie! My favorite naval officer. What do you have for me?"

She had already faxed him a complete report on the De Marco murder, as well as any others in the area that looked suspicious. FBI agents had now swept the Paterson warehouse and found no canisters inside. She wanted to keep the place under surveillance but they told her to forget it, they're probably watching us by now.

"A couple of things. Carlos, the man who died with Patsy De Marco, must have been under some sort of protection for years. But no federal agency has him down as an informant. If he has friends, they're from the outside."

"The Council!" Braxton said. "I don't care what the CIA thinks."

"Well, if you're right about that then De Marco is the old man we've been looking for. Which means the Sarin is somewhere in the New York area."

Braxton's voice boomed. "Stephanie, you're a miracle worker! Can you find it?"

"You let me keep my agents, I'll find it.'

"You got it. Anything else?"

Stephanie hesitated. She really didn't know how to explain the next part.

"I met with one of De Marco's children."

"Who? Natala?"

"No, Boyle."

"Ah," Braxton said. "The dirty cop."

"I guess that's right. He seemed normal to me but who knows." Plus the background memos should have warned her: Irish charm, Intelligence ahilerh Ishi

"Don't bu fooled by appearances, young lady. He's on suspension right now for brutalizing a suspect."

She stiffened. Young lady? She had four hundred hours in carrier landings in F-14s and could still run a three-hour marathon. Young lady?

"I know." Her voice had flattened. Braxton's tone kind of annoyed her, like Duncan did sometimes.

"Good. Stephanie, we value you so very much. You're not planning on meeting this rogue cop again, are you?"

She decided to make her own rules on this one. "No, of course not," she lied.

"Excellent. Well, keep me posted. If that Sarin is in New York we'll find it."

"Very good, sir."

Cameron Braxton hung up the phone and stared at the wall. "No!" he screamed to the weak light outside the window. The city was quieting down with a deep blue glow. Thousands of bureaucrats were escaping like rats, before the deep blue turned to black and the enemies they feared most emerged.

"No!" he screamed again.

He had done everything perfectly, just as ordered. He had ceaselessly, tirelessly trumpeted the Council's existence and was therefore the natural choice to head up the Sarin team. There had been hundreds of experienced agents offered to him for the all-important New York theater, men and women both, agents who had been to Beirut, Cairo, Tel Aviv. Rumania after the Ceaucescu execution. Beijing after Tian'amen Square. Moscow after the aborted revolution. He had rejected them all.

There was only one agent who fully met his needs, a twenty-nine-year-old woman with no serious intelligence credentials whatsoever. If it weren't for an overprotective, high-placed father the girl would be flying planes in the Pacific with her other jock friends. She was perfect! The navy demanded one of its own because it was their man who had run Purcell to ground. Great! Give them the daughter of an admiral!

He screamed again at the ceiling. The witch had not only figured out the De Marco murder, but had found the warehouse and met with Boyle. The Council did not like mistakes and definitely did not forgive mistakes. The instructions from his handler had been very clear. Keep Boyle out of it, keep the Bracca organization out of it, and above all, keep Meza out of it.

There was no way to make a call from his office. He grabbed his briefcase and bolted out the door.

T he Georgetown tavern was full. Cameron Braxton glanced around to make sure he was not recognized, then walked up to the bar. The barmaid was young and fresh, with a sassy attitude that mocked his wealth, his power.

"What can I do for you, sir?"

Even the "sir" was mocking. "One grappa, please. Castillo de Gabbiano."

The girl's eyes flickered. "I don't think we have that. Do you have a second choice?"

"Yes," he said. "The Candolini. And if that's not available I have another choice."

"Yes, sir," she said. The noise in the bar was deafening. "What's your third choice?"

"I'll have celery."

She never blinked. "I think we have celery in the back. Would you like to go look?"

"Yes."

He inched his way through the crowd to a storeroom in the rear of the raucous tavern. Once inside, the door closed harshly behind him. He waited.

She came in five minutes later. Her smile was fresh and pure, as befits a young woman, and the plaid uniform skirt the bar required was high. Her legs were taunting and bare, the flashing of red meat outside the bars of a caged animal. She had been chosen well.

"What do you have?"

He told her the whole story. At the end she was incredulous.

"You put someone competent in New York?"

"There was no way to know that. She was completely inexperienced."

"I'll mention that to them, that you thought this one inexperienced." The barmaid walked around the empty storeroom, astounded at the news. "She met Boyle?"

"Yes, but just once. I've ordered her not to meet him again."

Her voice was sarcastic. "Did you give the same orders to Boyle?"

"No, there was no way I could . . ."

The girl slapped him, the crack bouncing off the concrete walls. His head whipped to the side.

"You are a fool. I will have to report this."

"No," he pleaded. "Don't."

"You are pathetic." She sighed. "Today you are too important to kill. I don't know about tomorrow."

"Just tell me what to do."

"That's easy. Your little friend in New York. She will have to go."

Braxton stiffened. "She's an officer in the U.S. Navy."

"An ex-officer, once Portov hears of this. Plus you have bigger problems. Did you know she's secretly meeting with John Bracca?"

Braxton almost fainted. "What?"

"Inexperienced and incompetent!" She shook her head in exasperation. "You idiot! Bracca is under surveillance by one of our best people. He's been meeting with Shane in a small Spanish restaurant in Greenwich Village every night since De Marco died. He leaves messages for her on a machine in her apartment. And you didn't know a thing about it!"

Braxton's head was swimming. "Why . . . why would John Bracca contact the government? He knows nothing of . . . of the . . ."

"The Council? Of course not. But he's far from an idiot. He knows Patsy was murdered. And he doesn't want Angelo blamed for it."

All the blood was gone from Braxton's face. He was a dead man, he knew that, unless this problem was solved fast. "What do you want me to do?"

"Nothing right now. You'll only make things worse. Go back and make believe you're doing your job, keep screaming about the Council like you always do, nobody listens to you anyway. Come in on Tuesday and you'll get instructions."

He felt like a small child and answered like one. "Yes, ma'am."

21

Stephanie Shane was still smarting with irritation when she hung up the phone with Braxton. She stormed out of her office and went right to her meeting with Boyle. The bar was filled when she arrived. It was an old, wood-laden Irish bar that attracted a good crowd, the NBC types from Rockefeller Center mostly. Boyle had discovered it years ago, invited in by an NBC news reporter doing a feature on homicides in the tri-state area outside Manhattan. It turned out Paterson was a pretty good place to start.

She sat down next to him and ordered a pint of Newcastle. The dim light hid the stress in her face and made her look even more beautiful, which Boyle hadn't thought possible.

"Don't say it," she said.

"What?"

"That part about how I need sleep."

"I was actually going to say you look . . . better."

She sipped on the Newcastle. "It's makeup," she admitted. "I never wear it except in emergencies. I looked in the mirror after you left and saw a raccoon looking back."

"It wasn't that bad," he lied.

She sighed. "The work is addictive. Nobody forces me to put in these hours, it just gets in my blood."

"Why?"

She deflected the question. "The 'why' is my business. We're here for me to ask questions."

"Just give me a couple."

"Fine, make it fast."

"How old are you?"

She laughed and again he liked the way that looked.

"I was born twenty-nine years ago, like you."

"Where?"

She had her biography all worked out. After the DOB it was all a lie. "New York."

"We practically grew up together."

Stephanie shook her head. "You were born illegitimately at St. Thomas Aquinas Hospital in Paterson. Father unknown. Mother, Elizabeth Boyle, illegal Irish immigrant, age thirty-six. She dies in a freak electrical accident in her own house. You're taken in by her mother, Mary Elizabeth Boyle, aged eighty-seven, who heroically hangs in there for six months. Then you wind up with Meza in juvenile hall."

He wasn't surprised by this exhibition anymore. For some reason she had done her homework well. "Illegitimate? They still use that word?"

She softened slightly. "No, and I shouldn't."

"Where'd you go to school?"

"Columbia undergrad, Princeton law school."

"Hey, Bracca went to Columbia. You ever run into him?"

Stephanie choked on the Newcastle and he had to pat her on the back. "Sorry, it's smoky in here. No."

Then she ruffled her hair. The half-gone Newcastle had calmed her. Her shoulders lost their rigidity.

"You know," he said, noticing the change. "You should relax more, trust me. You're wrapped a little tight, you know what I mean?"

"How sweet of you to say so," she said, the sarcasm dripping. "I relax just fine."

"You ever take a vacation?"

"Sure."

"What, an afternoon at the museum?"

More shifting. "Different things." She kept the different things to herself. Flying an F-14 into a fat moon at Mach-2 off the African coast. A frosty ten-miler through the woods at 5:30 pace. The ballistics range. Glacier skiing. Not many drinks with ex-fighters though, she realized, or with anyone.

"I read a lot."

"You got any friends?"

She coughed. "Let's change the subject. What's Natala up to these days?"

What Natala was doing these days was using her father's key to get into the gym in Paterson. The lock was rusted, almost impossible to work in the dark. There was an outside light which was no less rusted, but at least worked. She flipped it on, finally got the lock open and went inside.

She went right for Patsy's crude office. His desk drawer was jammed shut and she dug at it with her fingers. Three professionally manicured nails cracked simultaneously. She screamed with a ferocity that might have awakened Patsy.

She hopped around the office on one foot, sucking her fingers to ease the pain. After a decent interval of cursing she went back to the desk with a screwdriver. When the drawer finally snapped open she started rifling the one drawer that Patsy always kept to himself, the one she always suspected had something special in it.

She searched slowly, like an archeologist. On top was her mother's obituary, then a dozen photographs of the interior of a storage facility. The photos meant nothing to her and she flipped through them quickly. Pictures of boxes and crates were all she could make out, plus a bunch of metal cylinders in one of the open crates.

She set the clipping and pictures aside and went back to the drawer. The second layer contained letters yellowed with age. The handwriting was smeared as if from a fountain pen. She read them— love letters from a lady in Newark in 1958. A woman who later on became a judge. She smiled . . . Judge Gardner! Patsy's secret life, four years before he met her mother. No wonder the judge hovered over him all those years.

The third layer contained photos she'd never seen before, although they all seemed familiar to her. They were taken years before, when the boys were in their teens. In some, Miguel and Tommy were getting ready for a fight, naked from the waist up, their hands taped. In others she was with them, wrapping her arms around their sweaty necks, congratulating them. Then there was one on the night of her junior prom. She was dressed in a sophisticated black gown that left her shoulders bare and her hair high. She was sixteen years old and her breasts were full, half-exposed to the world. Her legs were muscled and ended in black heels.

John Bracca stood next to her, beyond handsome, an eighteen-year-old, olive-skinned, curly haired, full-lipped answer to every teenage girl's dream. She precisely remembered the evening, remembered his beautiful black tux, remembered with ice-cold clarity the ease with which he had taken off her pretty dress after the dance. It was everything she had hoped and planned for. She stared at the picture for a long time.

Eventually she laid her memories aside and went back to the odd photographs of the wood crates. Why would Patsy keep such things in his secret drawer? They showed nothing more than the interior of a shipping department, occasionally with the figure of a man drifting about. All were taken at night, some from a distance showing the front door of a dark building, some from inside.

Yet, there was something oddly familiar about the blurred photos. It was frustrating, like trying to remember the name of a long-dead actor from an old black-and-white movie. She felt a tickling at the base of the brain. Where the hell were these photos taken?

The room was so quiet she never noticed the darkness sweep through the crusted windows high above. Except for the light in Patsy's office the rest of the gym was black. So when the sound came, it was doubly frightening, a scurrying, harsh sound that caused her to scream and twist. She looked for the face of a human and saw nothing. Then she saw the brown creature skating across the dark wood floor like an ice dancer. Its long tail, like the tail of all wharf rats, flicked from side to side as it ran.

The shock of the rat made her realize how alone she was. It also focused her attention. The rat ran across the floor toward a half-open door and then through it. That's when she realized where the pictures were taken.

She ran through the door after the rat. Inside the old silk mill the darkness was palpable. She felt with her hands. There was nothing, not even a light switch.

"This certainly sucks," she said to no one.

"What are you doing here?" a quiet voice asked.

She screamed and jumped backward. "Who are you? Who said that?" Her voice bounced off the walls.

"What are you doing here?" the voice asked again.

She felt rather than saw his presence growing closer. Her hand reached out and she felt a face. She screamed again.

"Who are you? What are you doing here?"

A flashlight snapped, a single beam of white light in the midst of total darkness. She was pinned to the wall with the light blasting into her eyes. "My name is Natala," she said. "Natala De Marco."

"You're lying."

"No, it's true." His hand moved slowly over her. She closed her eyes and remained immobile. She could take some groping, she couldn't handle death.

"What are you doing here," the voice asked once again.

"My father ran the gym next door. I'm just getting his things."

"Liar," the voice said again. The voice had an odd accent, not Hispanic, more like European.

"It's true, I swear."

The man's hand moved some more. She heard his breathing harden.

"I'm getting out of here," she said.

The crack of the flashlight across the back of her head stunned her. She fell backward against the wall. She felt blood mix with her thick hair.

"Who is here with you?" the voice asked. He was now pressed against her.

"No one."

"Are you sure?" the voice said. "If you're lying, I'll kill you."

"I'm not lying."

He pressed harder. She could feel every part of him.

"Stop that!" Her voice was tentative.

"Shut up." She stiffened, wondering whether she could run. She felt cold metal against her throat. She relaxed, tried to regulate her breathing and picked a spot on the far black wall to focus her gaze.

"Don't move," the voice said.

"Okay."

The man stepped back. His flashlight trailed slowly over her body. "Take off your clothes."

"No."

The knife again caressed her white throat. "Do what I say."

She was not about to be both raped and killed. She would make her stand now. "You're making a mistake."

"What mistake?" the voice asked.

"I've been sent here by somebody. If I don't return, you'll be in trouble."

"Who sent you, the bogeyman?"

"No," she said. "John Bracca."

The silence was immediate. Then the knife left her throat. She heard the man curse just before the heavy flashlight crashed again against the side of her head, much harder than before. She saw lights, then darkness, and she crumbled against the packing boxes.

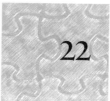

22

I want to know it all," Stephanie Shane said. They were still sitting on the stools at O'Malley's. It had gotten late and the Irish bar was crushed with refugees from the NBC building. They had to shout to be heard.

"You already know everything."

"I know some things. But I want to hear it from you, everything you know or think you know."

The Newcastles and Guinnesses were rolling and Boyle found himself willing to tell her anything. Stephanie had turned to face him, which caused her skirt to rise, about the only thing that could make that skirt look better. And to make sure she heard him over the din, she was forced to put her lips close to his ear. It was nice all around.

"Ask me anything, I don't mind."

"Let's stay with Natala. How does a smart girl like her quit Princeton after all of sixty days?"

"Well," Boyle said. "At least she tried."

That she had. It had all been arranged by Judge Jacqueline Gardner, who hovered over Patsy and his brood like a protective hen. But it was one thing to get Natala a scholarship to Princeton and quite another to get her to like it. She was only there three days and feeling very bitchy when a strapping young man invited her to a "club dance."

"There's a 'member-guest' next week," the guy explained. "I'm playing with another 'two' so we ought to do well."

"You're playing with a what?"

"With Jenkins. He's a 'two,' a two *handicap*. We both are. That's why we ought to do *well*." The man took an imaginary golf swing.

"You want to go to a stupid golf dance?"

Now the guy got defensive. "God, you're rude. It's not a *golf* dance. On Saturday night, after the tournament, there's an awards ceremony. It's quite formal, black tie."

"Did you just say 'quite formal'?"

"And maybe we'll win." He took her hand. "I'd love to have you at my side if we do."

That was the beginning of the end of Princeton for her. The guy won and they gave him a crystal plate with a depiction of the first green etched in it. Then a twelve-piece band in white tails played show tunes. He danced her to the patio, hidden under a moon-filled night, thirty feet above a brick walkway.

"Isn't this beautiful," he whispered, his hand drifting along her bare back.

She wanted to jump face down to the bricks below. "Beautiful."

"I told you it would be like this. You didn't believe me."

"Yeah. Who could have figured it." Her mind escaped and she thought of other men. Boyle was then twenty-two and fiercely handsome, winding down his career with bouts in Las Vegas, still a string-bean welterweight with the speed of a wasp. Miguel was full-time with the Braccas in Los Angeles. And John? Well, John was in New York, attending Columbia, and near, available.

Then a fourth man entered her consciousness, her date. The champagne and glory of victory in the member-guest had emboldened him. She found herself backed into a corner with the man's mouth fastened on hers. She allowed the kiss and resisted only when she felt him push against her, insistent. His hand roamed up the front of her body and grabbed her breast like a melon.

"Ow!"

"You love it," he breathed, swollen with victory and collegiate passion.

"Are you crazy?"

He moved closer. His hands found the zipper in back of her white dress. She felt it move.

"Stop it, jerk!"

"Make me," he said, and nuzzled his face in her neck. She let him nuzzle, no harm in that, then felt his teeth, driving deeply into her soft very gorgeous skin.

"Ow!" she screamed. She slammed her palms against his chest. "What are you, a vampire?"

"I love it when you call me names," he said. "Do it more."

"I'll do more than call you names if you bite me again."

"What will you do?"

"Beat the shit out of you, jerk." Her neck was actually bleeding and her breasts hurt and she hated the band and could care less about his ridiculous tournament. She got very lonesome for Patsy and John and her brothers.

"You think you can do that?" He was strong and athletic, as befits a "two," and he moved in again.

"Hurt me again and you'll see."

"Like this?" His left hand moved under her pretty party dress. He squeezed and this time it hurt even more than her neck and breasts.

"You like that?" he asked in a husky voice.

"Yeah, I love it." She retreated one step to the wall behind her. That at least got the guy's hand out of her crotch. Then she planted her right foot like Meza had taught her, fired the closed left like Meza taught her, and kept her head back, protected, pushing off the wall so the weight shifted naturally. "It's all timing," Migo always said. "Get your butt into it, girl." When she opened her eyes her date was gone.

It took ten minutes to wake him up. By that time his white shirt was splattered with red blood from his broken nose. An elegant woman in her late fifties stood next to Natala.

"What happened?"

"We had an argument."

The woman looked at her and sighed. "You mean you did this?"

"Yes. I'm sorry."

"Oh, don't be." The woman gestured. "That's my son."

"I'm *really* sorry."

"You're sorry he's my son?"

"No, that I had to hit him."

The woman understood. "He was fresh to you?"

"Fresh? He grabbed everything!"

More sighing. "He's so weak. Just like his father. Getting beaten up by a girl!"

"Well," Natala said, "I had some pretty good lessons."

The woman smiled. "So it appears. How old are you?"

"Nineteen."

"And extraordinarily beautiful. But you know that, don't you?"

Natala knew it just fine, but she shrugged anyway.

"Of course you do. May I give you some advice? One woman to another?"

"Sure."

"I was once young and beautiful. I had my pick of men, as will you." She gestured to her fallen son. "My mother pushed me toward the rich ones, his father for one. Don't make that same mistake. Understand?"

She actually did. "I think so."

"Seek strength. Avoid weakness. Money . . . the money comes to the strong anyway. And even if it doesn't you'll be better off. Now do you understand?"

She thought of her bloody date, then of Boyle, and John Bracca, and Miguel Meza. Those were the men this woman was talking about.

"Yes I do," she said. "I understand exactly."

Stephanie Shane liked that story, liked the way Natala had handled herself and wondered if she'd have done the same. But she'd never find out, because no man had ever had the temerity to grope an admiral's daughter. Her rare dates at Annapolis, if they could be called that, always ended with a correct nod at her barracks. She was actually dying for one of these guys to kiss her, but there was something off-putting about one midshipman kissing another. There was even a rule about it, although a rule breached fairly easily when convenient. With Stephanie, it was never convenient. At graduation, everyone threw their caps in the air. All white. How appropriate, she thought.

There was never a doubt she'd wind up at flight school in Pensacola, even Duncan couldn't stop that, and she wondered whether that might change things, whether the vast imbalance between men and women at Pensacola might finally start working in her favor. On the first day in flight school all the rookies met their flight instructors. Hers was a captain with nice features and close-cropped sandy hair, a crack pilot only four years older than her. She was delighted when she realized the man had no idea who she was.

"The training is intense," Captain Adam Hollis told her. "Are you sure you're ready for this?"

"Very sure, sir."

"Well, I'll try my best to get you through all this but I can't really promise anything. There's a rigorous physical you know. We get a lot of washouts after the physical."

"Yes, sir, I do know." She had known about the physical since she was twelve.

The man opened his hands. Nice hands, Stephanie thought. "You may *think* you know. But here things are much more rigorous than Annapolis, missy. Next month we take you to the track." He smirked. "You think you can do four miles in thirty-four minutes? I don't want to be embarrassed here."

She blinked in confusion. "Sir?"

"That's right. No messing around in Pensacola, missy. Four miles in thirty-four minutes or you're on the first plane out. If you don't think you can handle it, make it easy on all of us. Tell me now."

Stephanie hadn't been in serious training since she failed in the Olympic trials. She now regarded herself as a "recreational runner." That meant her four-mile speed workouts had dramatically slowed, all the way down to eighteen minutes flat. She usually coupled the speed workout with a three-mile warmup and three-mile cooldown at a leisurely 6:30 pace. Now this guy was asking whether she could possibly slog around a track at an 8:30 pace. It more than annoyed her; she could walk it that fast reading the paper.

"I'll do my best not to embarrass you, sir. You know, really work hard." She hesitated. "When's the test?"

"One month from tomorrow."

"You know what might really help?"

"What?"

"If you would take me out a few times, maybe give me some pointers? I'm sure it would help my time."

"Good attitude! And I'll do better than that." He leaned forward. "I'll take you and push you, get you to the outside of the envelope, just like in the aircraft. By the time I'm done, you'll be running flat eight's out there."

"Eight minute miles! You really think?"

"Absolutely, miss!"

It turned out that Captain Hollis had a moderately decent sense of humor. He came out wearing a pair of ridiculous shorts and a too-tight T-shirt. Stephanie wore a pair of sweat pants that could be pushed off with a strong pull. She decided not to wear her U.S. Olympic trials T-shirt.

Captain Hollis made her sit on the grass while he delivered his lecture. She bit the inside of her cheeks to keep from laughing. He told her about form, breathing, pacing the run and nutrition and there wasn't a single thing he said that was right. Finally it was time to run.

She let him lead for six revolutions around the track, about a mile and a half. Captain Hollis was breaking into a nice sweat. Stephanie felt like she was walking out to get the milk.

"How we doing back there, missy?"

That was one too many "missy's" for her. She ripped off the sweat pants and tossed them on the grass infield. Underneath was a set of heavily muscled runner's legs and the same thin shorts she had worn for the trials.

"Sir, is it okay if I try to pick it up for a few laps? You know, just to see if I can do it?"

"That's the spirit, missy, just don't overdo it."

She broke past him and ran the next lap in under a minute, cruising the mile in a flat 4:45. Captain Hollis got lapped three times before he stopped, and to his credit collapsed laughing by the side of the track. When she came by again he stood and pointed.

"Two more laps! Open it up, missy."

"Yes, sir!"

She always had a great finishing kick and now put the pedal down to show off for him. Her heels rose so high they clipped her round, taut bottom with each long stride, then lightly brushed the ground before rising again. He was transfixed, amazed at the sight of a world class runner doing her thing. It was a different animal, like a world class fighter, and those who see it for the first time can only stare.

When she finished she came back and stood before him, this time seriously puffing, her hands closed around the hem of her shorts. He had his hands on his hips.

"Ensign Shane?"

"Yes, sir."

"You have just seriously embarrassed a superior officer. I have several choices."

"Yes, sir."

"One is to make your life miserable for the remainder of your time at Pensacola. Two is to do what your father should have done long ago."

"That would be Duncan, sir. On occasion he threatened that."

Captain Hollis squinted at that. Then his face stiffened. "Duncan? Your father's name is Duncan?" His voice now rose. "Admiral Duncan Shane!"

"Yes, sir."

He put his hands to his temples and tried unsuccessfully to rub the sudden pain away. "I had the chance to read the bios they sent us. I could have. They were just sitting there. They even told us it would be a good idea."

Stephanie had grinned at him. "Don't worry about it, sir, could happen to anyone. Matter of fact, happens all the time."

He left her then still shaking his head. He did make her life miserable, but also taught her to fly jets, and by the eighth week she came to like the intensity he brought to his job. It wasn't the first time a young female flier had come to admire a superior officer and it wouldn't be the last. However, it was a very real first time for Stephanie and, against all good common sense, against all the rules, she decided to go for it. She picked an April night. They had just finished two dozen night touch-and-go's off the runway and parked the trainer at a rear hangar, near a grass field. Stephanie took off her helmet and shook her hair free. Not a perfect look but plenty good.

Adam Hollis hopped off the wing. The hangar was empty and would be until the mechanics came in the morning. The night was right for it, just drifting in over the grass field beyond the runway. The only question was how to ask.

"Well," he said. "Are you excited?"

Her jaw just dropped. How could he know! "What . . . what do you mean?"

He laughed. "Don't try to fake it. It's not every day you get to bust that cherry."

She had blushed deep purple. "What!"

"Your solo. Maiden voyage? Next Tuesday?"

Her pulse descended from 190 to 120. It would take a while to return to its normal 54. "Right. I'm very excited." She hesitated, then decided to jump off the building.

"Hey, Captain?"

"Yes?"

"There's . . . uh . . . there's something I want to ask you."

"Sure, that's what I'm here for. Ask away, don't be shy."

To her big surprise she wasn't shy. But then again she never was when she had her mind made up.

"It's sort of personal. Do you mind if we go in there? I'd feel more comfortable." Her head bobbed toward the empty hangar.

Captain Adam Hollis glanced at the hangar and then slowly back to her. He held her eyes and they never wavered. Neither of them spoke for a full minute.

"Are you sure?" he said finally. His voice was husky.

She reached out slowly and took his hand. He didn't pull it away.

"Yes, sir. I'm *very* sure."

She shook her head to clear away the memory. Captain Hollis had been very necessary once upon a time. But now she had a serious job to do.

"Okay, enough about Natala. Let's move on to you and Meza. The way I get it, De Marco discovered you early, trained you as fighters with the blessing of Angelo Bracca, and when the time was right, turned all three of you over to the mob."

Boyle blinked, disbelieving. "What possible planet did that come from?"

"Come on. Are you denying that Meza works for the mob?"

"No."

"Or that Natala is living with John Bracca?"

"Trust me, not my first choice."

"Do you deny it?"

"No."

"Shall I go on? Do you deny that Patsy staged fights between you and Meza as amateurs so that the mob could take the gambling action?"

He coughed. It was impossible that she could know this much. "One fight."

"And we've already covered Sanders' pad. So tell me, given all this am I to believe De Marco was a wonderful man, sort of a saint?"

He bristled. "That's exactly what he was. If it wasn't for Patsy we'd have been on the street."

"Mr. Boyle, please, I'm not stupid. Miguel Meza was disqualified from the Golden Gloves for drug use, just after he beat a fighter named Lopez and just before he was scheduled to fight you in the finals. Angelo Bracca knew all about it and made a fortune. Now tell me that Patsy De Marco was a saint."

She could tell that question angered him. His face darkened when he turned on the stool to face her.

"You think you're so smart. But you don't know anything."

23

The hardest part was the living arrangements that were immensely more complicated than the training. Patsy told the judge he'd take them in for two weeks, until someone could find a place for them, but that was a joke and everyone knew it. Nobody wanted them, nobody even sort of wanted them, and Patsy's initial two-week commitment turned into two months, then two years, finally forever, and nobody said much about it. There was only one extra bedroom, where Natala slept more or less innocently, so the two boys were jammed into the living room, one on the couch, one on the floor. After about six months it seemed normal. There were too many people in too small a space and not a hell of a lot anybody could do about it.

Patsy watched them grow and knew right away what he had. By the time they were fifteen he realized he had to find a way to protect them. They were street smart, and tough, but still kids, and the sharks ate kids.

But no matter how he tried to shield them, to establish rules, to make them study, go to bed, eat three meals, run quiet hooded miles in the dawn cold, the word still got out. Perversely, the more secretive he got the more the legend grew. When he finally let them train in the ring the sessions drew fans. Yet there was one rule he held on to till the end: he would never let them fight each other until the finals of the Gloves.

Patsy's heart was in the right place but the law of unintended consequences was stronger. The "no fight" rule wasn't a shield for the boys, it was blood in the water for the mob. By the time they were seventeen, and eligible for the Gloves, the debate over who was better had been raging for two years in every factory and gin mill in Paterson. The firemen, for reasons no one understood, were convinced Boyle was better. The cops, for equally unknown reasons, were Meza backers. Angelo Bracca was back in town from Brooklyn after visiting his cousin on his mother's side when he first heard of it.

He had stopped at Paul's, a nice place on Crooks Avenue with a lady bartender with a great butt, just to taste a little grappa after dinner. Two men, still in uniform, were bellowing at each other.

"I'm tellin' you," the fireman shouted, "Boyle's so quick it's scary. I saw him the other day, he was using some pro's head like a speed bag. That pro was twenty-two years old!"

Eddie Dutchess had been a cop for a long time and didn't need advice from any fireman on anything. "You been suckin' too much smoke. Meza has guts. He just walks in and punches, the head, the body, it don't matter to him. He don't try to make it look pretty, he just makes sure the guy bleeds."

"Boyle's a way better fighter, nothing but speed," the fireman countered. "He's been up against pros for two years now."

"So's Meza. Besides, just because Boyle's a pretty fighter don't mean he'll be too pretty when Meza gets done. And another thing: whenever your kid's not fighting he's got his nose in a book. You never see Meza with a book."

"Boyle likes books so he can't fight?"

"Goddamn right. When you were seventeen, you read any books?"

The fireman was on a slippery slope. "I don't remember."

They both had to laugh at that. "Anyway," the cop said, not giving up, "you want to give 'em a test on books, I grant you, Boyle wins. You put them in a ring, he don't."

The fireman shrugged. "I don't care about books. Hell, it's probably *Playboy*, which is great. These seventeen year olds, they get horny, all they want to do is fight."

"It ain't *Playboy*. I saw it. If it was *Playboy* I'd know it. It's a thick book with no pictures by some Jewish guy."

"What Jewish guy? What are you talking about?"

The cop squinted. "Just give me a second."

"You hearing this," he shouted to the bar. "These cops just make it up!"

The firemen roared, the laughter almost drowning out the argument. "No, I'm telling you, I saw it. Stein or something."

"Yeah. Or something."

"No, that ain't right. *Steinberg*. That's it. No wait, that's close though."

"Whatever, we know you're just making it up."

"Stein*beck*, that's it. I'm sure of it."

"Well," the fireman said, figuring he had to yield the point, "so he was reading some book, don't mean he can't fight." He sipped and looked up. "Oh, hi, Mr. Bracca."

Angelo was staring. "What are you clowns talking about?"

O nce Angelo got it he was over to Patsy's gym in an hour. "Patsy, what's happening," he bellowed. Patsy was watching a black pro work the heavy bag. Periodically he would stop the fighter to suggest something, an adjustment. Cover with the right when the left gets thrown. Remember, the right is just a long jab; and when you throw it, you have to keep the left up; then when you throw the left the right covers. Get it?

He wanted to stay with his young fighter. He didn't want to talk to Angelo Bracca, now or ever.

"Patsy, let me introduce you to my boy John."

Patsy shook hands. The kid was a good-looking teenager, about Tommy's height and weight, with a pure olive face and deep-set brown eyes. When he shook Patsy's hand he looked straight at him. A proud boy. "Nice looking kid. He ever fight?"

"No, John's a lover. Ain't that what you told me?"

John Bracca shrugged. He was seventeen years old and didn't listen to the old man on anything these days.

"So what can I do for you?"

Angelo looked offended. "What's wrong, I can't come down here and just watch your fighters?"

"You never done it yet."

"So I'm overdue. I got a question for you."

"What?"

"I heard you got two kids here you're training for the Gloves?"

The old trainer stiffened. "I got lots of kids want to be in the Gloves. Most of them won't come close."

Angelo waved his hand. "I ain't talkin' about lots of kids. I'm talkin' about your two best kids."

Patsy coughed. "I got a couple here and there. You never know till they get in the ring. It's a tough tournament."

Angelo shook his head "You're lyin', Patsy, There's two kids everybody's talkin' about."

John interrupted. "He means Miguel and Tommy."

Patsy's eyes darted, but there was no exit. "What about them?"

Angelo grabbed a few boxing gloves, started juggling them. "Nothing. I just heard they're good."

"Maybe. I took them in when they were twelve. They just fight to stay in shape.

Angelo laughed heartily. "Good one, Patsy. Tell me, they gonna win the Gloves this year?"

"No way. To win they got to go through the preliminaries, win all those, then get into the semis, win that, then fight in the Garden. They won't get that far but even if they did, there's this Puerto Rican kid out of the Bronx who's unbeatable. Same class, welterweight, one-forty-seven."

Angelo Bracca's eyes narrowed. "Who's the Puerto Rican kid?"

"Kid named Hector Lopez. Supposed to be the next Ray Robinson. Nobody touches him, he's fighting pros now for practice."

"So are your kids from what I've heard."

Patsy didn't answer. Angelo knew too much.

"Once again," Patsy said finally, "what can I do for you?"

"Nothing much. When's the Gloves?"

"About four months."

"They ever fight each other?" Angelo asked innocently.

Patsy tried to keep his voice calm. "Sure all the time. You know, sparring."

Angelo laughed so hard he choked on the smoke. "Patsy, you crack me up. I heard they're the greatest action in town. It's one of those things everybody's got an opinion on. Which kid you think is better?"

"We'll find out in the Gloves if they get that far."

"So make that the rematch."

Patsy's feet shifted and belied his nervousness. "What does that mean?"

Angelo Bracca gestured to the metal bleacher seats. "I figure we could jam about what, four or five hundred people in here?"

"I couldn't say, Angelo."

"We could charge ten bucks to get in, then take all the action. We set the line. The firemen go one way, the cops another. We take a percentage for ourselves."

Patsy was now beyond fury, and beyond judgment. "Forget it, I won't let those kids fight each other."

Angelo squinted. "You won't do what?" His face flushed. "Why don't you think real good about that again? And then you tell me what you're not going to do."

Patsy never flinched. He hated Angelo Bracca and everything about him. Plus these kids were now far more than his fighters. They were his sons, or as close to sons as he would ever get. "Angelo, these kids ain't gonna fight."

"They ain't?" Angelo lit a cigar and flicked the ashes on the ground. "Let me explain something to you."

"What?"

"I'm announcing this fight tomorrow. You get in my way . . ." he pointed to the ashes, ". . . this rat trap is gonna look like that. And one more thing. You won't have to worry about the Gloves because there's gonna be a couple of accidents. Do I make myself clear?"

Patsy said nothing. Angelo patted him on the shoulder. "It'll be great. Let's go, John."

24

Angelo set the fight for April 17 at 9 P.M. At 8:30 Boyle and Meza were in the dressing room listening to the screaming from above. Five hundred cops, firemen and barflies jammed into a small gym can make a lot of noise. The boys involuntarily looked up with interest and, although they'd never admit it, anxiety. At 8:55 one of the cops opened the door.

"Okay, let's go."

Both were in prime fighter's shape, young and lean, the muscles dancing and cut in their arms, chest and legs. Boyle was by far the taller of the two, impossibly skinny at 6'2" and 147, with a long reach and all that speed. His curly black hair was cut close to the scalp, surrounding emerald green Irish eyes. Meza was more compact at 5'10", with tangled red hair and dead black eyes that held no mercy at all. When they walked into the ring and dropped the robes the crowd went nuts. And when Natala, in her best party dress and heels, walked around with a placard that said Round One, the men, well oiled from the pre-fight bars, screamed till they choked.

Patsy tried to shout the crowd down through a crude microphone. "You are now about to see a bout between two seventeen-year-old amateur welterweights, you hear that, *amateurs*! The fight will be *three rounds*, just like in the Golden Gloves. These are *kids*, not professionals. Understand that?"

The men loudly booed.

Patsy shouted through the noise. "I said these fighters are amateurs, kids! Anybody got a problem with that, let me hear 'em now!"

It was the wrong question. The deep-throated roar had Natala putting her hands over her ears and wincing. Patsy was defeated; now he just wanted to get it done.

"All right, let's go."

The bell shocked everyone and the two fighters sort of wandered blinking from their corners, standing bewildered in the center of the ring. Then Meza's eyes flattened and he charged. Boyle immediately backed into a corner, fighting off the ropes, struggling to create space. Meza's head was down and he worked Boyle's midsection savagely, ripping and tearing like a predator in the wild. Boyle had to drop his hands to protect the belly and when he did Meza left his feet, catching Boyle square on the side of the head gear with a sweeping hook. Boyle's head snapped and his mouthguard flew in a lazy arc over the ropes and into the now screaming crowd. Boyle grabbed and tried to hold on but a second hook dropped him to his knees. He stayed there for an eight count to catch his breath. The cops were up as one and bellowing.

Back in his corner, Boyle watched groggily as Natala walked around the ring holding a placard with a big "2" on it. Patsy was the ref tonight and a fireman was in Boyle's corner, a cop in Meza's. The fireman held out a cup. "Spit here."

Boyle spit and it came out red. The fireman grabbed a sponge, Tommy held his head back and the man squeezed. Cold blessed water fell on his face and into his mouth. He didn't swallow it, just swished it around and spit again. More red. No one had ever hit him like Miguel Meza had just hit him. He had no idea *anyone* could get hit that hard.

"Listen, Boyle, you're strolling around like it's the goddamn prom. We gotta lot of money on you, man!" The fireman jammed a new mouthguard into his face. "You gotta stay away from that guy."

Boyle looked up, stunned. What a jerk. "How about I squirt water in your face and you go fight him?"

The fireman couldn't be insulted. "I'm just tellin' you the truth. You let him get close, he'll kill you."

Boyle got up, bouncing on the balls of his feet, shaking his head to clear the fog. "That I get."

The bell sounded, the firemen were moping, the cops were howling and Miguel Meza sprang from his corner like he'd been let off a leash. Boyle again came out tentatively, watched Meza charge recklessly again, then skipped lightly backward, his footwork as precise as a dancer's. Meza stopped in half-swing, stumbled slightly, let his hands down, and met the three fastest lefts he would ever see in his career, all thrown from a fully braced right foot, all hitting square.

Meza's head jerked from the shots and he staggered, stunned, catching flashing lefts all the way to the ropes, where he tried to make his stand, and where Boyle worked his face like a speed bag, snapping the headgear side to side. At two minutes Meza ducked, then slumped, toppling sideways. Boyle repaid his brother for the first round with a nasty hook on the way down. Patsy was only to six when the bell sounded. Two cops with wide, disbelieving eyes helped Meza off his knees and the firemen went nuts.

For years later they said round three was the greatest two minutes of welterweight fighting anyone could remember outside of an old clip of a Sugar Ray Robinson fight. If the number of people who later claimed to have seen round three was even remotely close to accurate they could have filled the Garden. The round started with Meza charging again, bloodied but undefeated, the only way he knew how to live or fight. Boyle flashed more lefts that this time Meza slipped, getting past the maddening jabs to crowd Boyle in a corner. Once there he pounded to the body, only to see Boyle fight his way out of trouble and slide down the line of ropes, firing the jab like a protective machine gun. With one minute left, the two fighters were drenched and exhausted, standing in the middle of the ring, hands down, panting, motionless for a heartbeat. And then what became the legend began.

"One minute," Patsy announced and every man in the gym was on his feet screaming. Both fighters braced and hit, and neither moved an inch from the center of the ring. They stood rock-still and pounded, no defense, no strategy, just hitting, Meza working the body and hooking to the head; Boyle firing jabs and combinations at the speed of light. The deep throated roar of five hundred beer-soaked voices rattled off the metal roof and walls in a single, undistinguished ocean of noise, and there wasn't a man in the gym who could even follow the speed of the punches. With fifteen seconds to go both fighters staggered the other and they both stepped back, furious at the surrender, then stepped up again. At the final bell they were still swinging and Patsy had to jump in, taking a few shots to the head as he tried to end it. It took the help of the corners to pull them apart and get them back on their stools. Natala ran from the crowd and hugged both of them, even Boyle, who annoyed her even then.

John Bracca turned to his father.

"It's a draw. There's no way to call that. We get to collect from both sides. You want me to go tell him?"

"No," Angelo said. "You tell that crazy old man it's a draw, he'll gìm il ìn rìm ìì 'em Jìnt tn watch me throw up."

John was right on the money. Patsy called it a draw and everyone sort of half-cheered, half-booed, and everybody lost money. Back in the dressing room, Meza and Boyle sat naked and sweat-soaked on wood benches across from each other and tore off tape with their teeth. Natala sat next to Meza with her chin in her hands and didn't care what her brothers wore. Outside was pandemonium, only slightly muffled by the dressing room door.

Meza spoke first, without looking at Boyle. "You okay?"

"Yeah." Meza was the more marked of the two because Boyle's jabs always went for the head. Boyle hurt more, because he had taken all of Meza's shots to the body.

Boyle waited a beat. "Nice shot there in the first."

"Yeah, you too." Without looking up, Meza held out his hand in a fist. Boyle tapped it with his own fist.

"Man," Meza said, "that was great!"

John Bracca stood quietly outside the gym watching his father count his money. Angelo had made over a hundred grand from a bunch of cops, firemen and their buddies, five hundred men betting an average of two hundred dollars apiece. He sighed.

"This is the easiest money I ever made in my life. Now, if only I knew how to bet the Gloves," he said sadly.

"Why, what's the problem?"

Angelo gestured toward the gym. "There's three fighters could win this thing. Those two kids in there, who knows who's better. Then this kid out of the Bronx they say is the best of all. How the hell do I bet that?"

"Three's too many," John agreed. "We have to drop one out."

Angelo snorted. "How do I do that? Shoot one?"

"No." John hesitated. "What if one got disqualified?"

"That'd be great. Who? And how?"

"After every amateur fight, they have to take a drug test. They piss in a bottle."

"So what do I do, spike the bottle? Who'll believe that? These kids are heroes. You hear those cheers?"

John Bracca shook his head. "Meza's been buying for two and a half years."

Angelo's eyes grew wide. "You ain't serious!"

"Dead serious. Pills and blow for two and a half years. Trust me."

Angelo got real interested real fast. "If I only have two to worry about, instead of three, it's easy. How about the other kid, Boyle, is he buyin' too?"

"No way. He's the straightest kid in Paterson."

More thinking. "There's still a risk. What if Meza cleans up his act?"

"It's possible. We have to make sure."

"You mean spike it."

"Spike it or him. Believe me, no one will be surprised."

Angelo shuddered a little. "Man, the apple didn't fall too far from the tree."

"No, Pop, it sure didn't."

When Angelo left, John hung around until Meza came out. He had known both of them for years, Meza he sort of got along with, Boyle not at all. Patsy saw him, looked once with suspicion, then continued on.

"Hey, Miguel, nice job," John said.

"Thanks."

"What're you doin' now?"

Meza shrugged. "Nothing."

"How about we go over to my Uncle Paul's and eat. You know the place?"

"Sure."

"Great."

Moska's sat on a lonely bluff near the Passaic River. It was named after a restaurant in New Orleans that was rumored to have been founded by Al Capone's personal chef, after the fall. This Moska's was founded by John Bracca's Uncle Paul, Angelo's brother. The waitresses knew John and treated him with respect. As for his friend, the taut kid with the thick neck and tangled, red hair, they treated him with wariness, and didn't know why.

Miguel Meza always ate like he was in a race. After the third bowl of pasta, even John was amazed. "How do you stay in shape eating like that?"

Meza just shrugged. "The more I eat, the skinnier I get. You ought to see Tommy eat."

John Bracca gestured and two red wines appeared.

"Listen, you think you guys are ready for the Gloves?"

"Sure." Meza kept eating. "Me and Tommy are going to walk through the sectionals, no problem. By the time we get to Madison Square Garden there'll be four welterweights left and two will be Tommy and me. I *guarantee* it."

"What about this kid from the Bronx. What's his name, Ruiz?"

"Lopez. Nasty, way nasty. He'll be there too."

"And the fourth?"

"Could be anybody, nobody to worry about."

John nodded. It was just like Angelo had said.

Around eleven the place quieted. John had already thought carefully about how to play it. "You know, this Gloves thing is real popular. Fifteen thousand fans for the finals. They even televise it."

"Yeah, I heard."

"Can I tell you a secret?"

"Sure."

"My father likes to bet these fights."

Meza drank the red wine in one long pull. "Good. Tell him to bet on me."

"I already told him that. You or Boyle. He asked me, 'are you sure?' I told him, 'absolutely.' "

"You told him right. Except I'm better."

John took a sip, thinking it through. "So give me your opinion. Who makes it to the finals? You and Tommy? Lopez?"

Meza sat back and considered the question professionally, like a T.V. commentator. "The way I figure it, it's the three of us plus a nobody in the semis. The odds are me or Tommy picks up Lopez in the semis. Lopez gets beat and we get each other in the finals."

"You think Boyle can beat Lopez?"

"Tommy can beat anybody except me."

John read it almost the same way. So did Angelo. Except neither cops, firemen or the Braccas knew who would win between these two brothers.

"I have to ask you one more question."

"What?"

"What about the drug tests?"

Meza stiffened. "I'm clean."

John Bracca shook his head. "Migo, I'm your friend, believe me. But I know how it is, it's fun to get a buzz. You get yourself some toot, maybe some bud, then you get some babe with you . . ."

Meza was nodding his head involuntarily.

"And my father can't afford to take chances. He bets a bundle on you, and you get disqualified, what happens?"

"I won't get disqualified."

"Why's that? I know you're playin' around, Migo."

The kid looked embarrassed and went back to the wine. "Not for a couple months. I can turn it on and off. Trust me, it's off till this is over. No problem."

That was important information. If true, it meant Meza would pass the test.

"That's great! So there's only one more thing and I hope you don't take offense."

"I ain't gonna take no offense."

"Let's say some guy comes up to you. He's friendly, tellin' you how good you are, you know what I mean? Then he says, 'Hey Miguel, I got an idea. How about I just slip you some cash, some-place quiet, and you just happen not to beat Lopez in the semis.' That changes the odds a lot. Instead of three guys to worry about, there's only two."

Meza looked up, interested.

"You understand what I'm saying?" John Bracca prayed Meza would take the cash, make the spike unnecessary.

"I don't know. How much money's this guy offering?"

"It could be a lot. The money that's bet on these fights, it'd be worth his while. Let's say, I don't know, twenty-five thousand, thirty-five thousand."

"No way!"

"Absolutely." John Bracca spoke quietly. "So you think that'd tempt you? We have to know."

Meza shook his head. "No, I was just curious. You know Patsy's sign in the gym?"

"What sign?"

"Above the lockers. It says 'The Gloves, the Games, the Dough.' You know what that means?"

He did. "The Golden Gloves, the Olympics and then . . ."

"And then the big bucks. Why throw that away for twenty-five, thirty-five grand?"

Why indeed. John Bracca was deeply disappointed. He hid it and spread his hands expansively. "Exactly what I told my father you'd say." He leaned forward. "So tell me. How does this drug testing work?"

25

S tephanie Shane had a smirk on her face when Boyle finished. "You must think I'm stupid. Am I supposed to believe any of that?"

"It's true."

"So Patsy was a model father. You're completely misunderstood, sort of forced to beat up suspects and get suspended. And Miguel Meza didn't deserve to get disqualified. It was all evil John Bracca's fault."

He shrugged. "It's the truth."

She checked her watch. "Okay, I'm getting tired. Let's just end this with you. You're a cop. Or rather you were a cop."

"I am . . . was . . . a homicide detective."

"Why?"

"Why? Simple. I was through fighting and needed a job."

"I don't believe that," she said softly. "We've checked it out. You could have done much more."

"Like what?"

"Anything. Everybody we talked to said you were smart. Your records from high school show you were smart. Nobody could figure out why you just came back and started walking a beat."

"It was actually driving a car. You walk a beat in Paterson you really do get killed."

"So why?"

"I told you."

Stephanie shook her head. "I don't buy it. I think you're working for the Braccas like Meza."

Boyle gestured to the bartender. "Let me have one of those." The bartender gave him a cigarette. "Just once in a while," he explained.

"Like when you can't answer a question."

He blew out the smoke. "That makes no sense. Me and the Braccas? I *hate* the Braccas worse than Patsy did."

"It makes a lot of sense. You're fighting in Las Vegas and Natala drops out of Princeton to live with John Bracca in New York. Three months later you retire and come back to Paterson. Sure you hate John Bracca because you're jealous of him but there's nothing you can do. So you become a cop, sort of like joining the army, especially when your in-laws can make you a great deal."

"That's quite a theory. You make extra money as a shrink?"

"It's the way I read it, Tommy."

"Well, you read it wrong."

"So tell me. Why?"

He spun on the stool to face her. His face was very close and she had to admit it looked very nice.

"I became a cop for reasons you'll never understand. I fought professionally for seven years and loved it. Then it was over. What do I do then? Learn about computers? Accounting? Maybe go to law school? You think that's the same rush?"

Stephanie Shane understood exactly what he meant. "No, I don't."

"Plus, if I do my job, I'm doing good, trust me. You think killers should get away with it?"

His passion was intoxicating, and he was right in her face. "No."

"Take yourself," he continued. "You're a lawyer and I hope you're happy at it. But say you really wanted to play the violin or be an astronaut. You think you'd be happy sittin' at some desk?"

She found herself staring into those unblinking green eyes. This was a man who understood, even if Duncan never would. "No," she said. "I don't."

It was 10 P.M. when they realized they were both starving. "Listen," she said. "I didn't plan on this lasting so long. We've got to eat."

"Okay, where's the nearest deli?"

"No, I mean really eat. Don't worry, it's on the U.S. government. There's a great Italian place across from Carnegie Hall. You'll love it."

Boyle decided to be polite. "I love Italian restaurants in New York."

The meal turned out to be surprisingly good and it was almost

1 A.M. when they left. They walked up Sixth Avenue toward the park. Several attractive ladies, nicely dressed, smiled pleasantly at Boyle. They seemed to be circling the block. And they say New Yorkers aren't friendly.

When they got to Central Park South, Stephanie checked her watch.

"Look at the time!"

"Yeah, it's late."

"Where's your car?"

Boyle looked sheepish. "My car?"

"Yes, please tell me you drove over here."

"No, I took the bus. It drops you right off in Port Authority." He waved at the brightly lit city. "It costs a fortune to park in New York."

She squeezed the bridge of her nose. "Did you check to see what time the buses stop running?"

"Uh, not really."

She pointed to a phone. "Check it out." She prayed this would not turn into a disaster.

"We may have a problem," Boyle said when he got back.

"No bus?"

"That's what they said. Last one was midnight."

"So how do you expect to get home? I'm sure there's no trains going back either. Does Paterson even have a train station?"

"Yeah, but it burned down."

She ignored the pain drifting across her eyebrows. "What, may I ask, are you planning to do?"

"I can get a room," he said brightly.

"Okay, that works."

He grabbed his wallet and checked. "Ninety-six bucks. Where can I get a place that'd leave me a few dollars left over for the bus in the morning? It doesn't have to be the Pierre."

"For ninety-six dollars you couldn't sleep in the gutter in front of the Pierre."

"Very funny. What about that place in back of St. Patrick's Cathedral where the priests used to live? How much could that cost?"

"The Helmsley Palace? For ninety-six dollars you could certainly get breakfast. I doubt you could get lunch. The room would be another four hundred or so."

"Well," he said, "it's not your problem. I'll figure something out."

The pain over one eyebrow had now crossed over to the other eyebrow. "All right, you can stay at my place. You sleep on the couch and you stay as neat as a pin. I'll drop you at Port Authority in the morning."

"You don't have to do that."

"I only wish that were true."

The navy had put her in a nice co-op on the Upper East Side. It was a one bedroom flat with copies of signed oils on the walls. The furniture was art nouveau and functional. The couch where he was supposed to sleep looked like it was about four feet long.

"I'll have to scrunch up on this thing."

"Not as much as you would in the gutter in front of the Pierre."

She brought out some pillows and blankets and set them on the couch. "There's some rules."

"You don't have to tell me. That door"—he pointed to her bedroom—"is like the Berlin Wall. I go near there I get shot."

"That isn't what I was going to say but that's true too."

"Okay, what then?"

She gestured around the room. "See how neat this is? That's how I like it. Before you go to sleep, go in there and take a nice shower. I don't want to wake up smelling man all over my living room. Then fold your clothes neatly on that chair. There's an extra toothbrush in the bathroom."

"I have to take a shower to sleep on your couch? I don't have any diseases."

"That's probably true," she said gallantly. "Nevertheless, I'd prefer it."

"Okay."

She looked slightly embarrassed. "I assume you're wearing . . . like . . ."

"You mean underwear?"

"I was thinking of the word 'boxers.' "

"Boxers is exactly what I'm wearing, with snails on them."

"Snails?"

"Maybe sea horses. They were on sale at a scuba shop."

"Great. Wear them."

"You mean you don't want me sleeping in the . . ."

"That's exactly what I mean."

It took him forty-five minutes to get it all right for her. By the end he was not only showered, but had also shaved with the razor she used for her legs. His clothes were folded neatly on the chair and his hair was slicked back. She came out for the inspection. He stood in the light from the bathroom, quiet, elegant in his boxers. It turned out they were sea horses, not snails.

"Satisfied?"

She walked toward him. She was dressed in a pale, silk robe that reached her knees. "Wow," she said softly, and involuntarily.

"What? I did everything you said."

"Come here," she said. "Stand in the light."

He stood before her and felt no embarrassment. After all he had appeared in roughly the same outfit in front of fifteen thousand screaming people in Madison Square Garden. Take away the sea horses and give him a mouthguard and it would all be the same.

"What's wrong?"

Now that she could clearly see him she was even more amazed. She had seen her share of men in boxers in her life, in every barracks and ready room in Pensacola. Yet those men, fit as they were, bore no resemblance to what she was looking at now. He was hairless, except for a thin line of fuzz that ran down his chest and disappeared in his sea horse boxers. His bare chest was as chiseled as a rock formation. His arms were lean cascades of muscle, starting at the shoulder and descending in concentric circles to a pair of powerful forearms. His hands, which she had noticed in the bar, were thick and primitively strong. His stomach was simply six parallel bands. She had never seen anything like him.

And the legs were even more striking. His thighs had a muscle group that started at the knees and danced its way up to disappear inside his shorts. His calves were thick and round and every bit as intimidating as his thighs. And none of it seemed contrived or preciously sculpted. It was just the way a top fighter looked.

She couldn't watch or think any farther. "It's time for me to go to bed," she said firmly.

26

Gregor Portov finished his grisly business with Josef Alexeyev and reentered the United States easily, straightforwardly and without any inconvenience. The replacement Sarin had been easy to obtain once the unfortunate Rudenko met his fate. He strolled out of Rudenko's flat, spent a few days in Vilnius, the capital of Lithuania, then left Moscow on an Interflot flight to Paris. He ate well, drank wonderful Bordeaux and spent the night in a hotel owned by a member of the Dubai royal family. The next day, refreshed and with a plan now firmly in mind, he took the train from Paris underneath the channel to Waterloo Station in downtown London. Then, after another lovely night's sleep, he flew the daytime Concorde into JFK.

The flight was only three hours and he was quickly through customs and into a dark limo at curbside. An hour later he was pacing in a park-view room at the Ritz-Carlton, waiting with apprehension for the call from Angelo Bracca.

At 7 P.M. the phone rang. "Mr. Portov?"

"Yes."

"My name is Nick, Nick Franzetti."

"How do you do, Mr. Franzetti."

"Nick. Angelo asked me to pick you up."

"I'll be ready in ten minutes."

Nick was exactly what Portov expected, a stocky man in his fifties dressed in a dark suit and matching pullover sweater. There was a bulge underneath the left side of his jacket that Portov figured was the perfect size for a Beretta. He asked out of professional curiosity.

"Yeah, a nine millimeter," Nick told him. "I got a permit for it."

"Great."

Nick took him to Greenwich Village, to a restaurant called Santorio's on Mulberry Street. Angelo Bracca sat at his usual table, his back to the wall. He was sipping an espresso with a clear glass of grappa next to it. Portov was exposed, and without guards, and he immediately knew he had made a mistake.

"Hello, Angelo. And before you say anything, I know we have a problem."

Angelo Bracca looked up with sleepy eyes. "You walk in here and the first thing you talk about is a problem? But I'm not ready to talk about *your* problem. First, I'm gonna eat. *Then* we discuss business."

"Look, I flew in from Europe especially for this meeting. We can't let this . . ."

Angelo's palm slammed on the table. "Hey, me and Nick drove over from Jersey especially for this meeting," he said, mimicking Portov. "I said first I'm gonna eat!"

Portov did not just spit in the man's face like he wanted to. "Sure, Angelo."

What followed was a long, tedious, typical Angelo Bracca meal: salad, pasta, more salad, beef, more pasta, Chianti by the bucket, iced sherbet to cleanse the palate, espresso and grappa. "Or sambuco or anisette, if you like," Angelo offered. "But grappa's good for the digestion." Then he belched.

Portov was not a delicate man, but Angelo Bracca simply disgusted him. He couldn't wait for the day when he would no longer have to pander to petty local thugs like the Braccas.

Angelo lit a cigar, biting off the tip and spitting it out. "Okay, now I'll talk to you. Tell me one good reason I shouldn't shoot you like a dog."

Portov realized that threat might be real. There was a risk coming here without support and now he felt a jolt of concern. "I'll give you lots of reasons, Angelo." He talked fast for ten minutes. Angelo puffed on the cigar, never once interrupting. When he finished there was quiet for a moment.

"Let's go over this slow, make sure I got it."

"All right."

"You asked me for a favor, get you some old factory in my part of Jersey where you can store some stuff. I don't ask no questions even though I know it's drugs. Nick, you ask any questions?"

"No, Mr. Bracca."

"Right. So Nick takes care of things and we give you the keys. The place is all yours. Have a party. Am I right?"

"You did a fine job and we moved the . . . the material in."

"Yeah, I did a fine job." Bracca's eyes narrowed. "I did a fine job and then you did an even better job on me!"

Portov sighed with exasperation. This was so tedious he could scream. "Nobody did a job on you, Angelo. We just had problems with the warehouse."

"Problems! What problems? You wanted someplace out of New York, low key. You ever been to Paterson? It's like a city got run over by a truck."

"The city was fine. But the old man broke into the warehouse three times. Our cameras caught him opening boxes and examining shipping documents. He threatened my people. He even changed the locks!"

Angelo looked vaguely amused. "Patsy changed the locks?"

Portov lost judgment at the memory. His voice was bitter. "Exactly! A decrepit old coot running a rat-infested hole almost blew our entire operation!"

Angelo blew smoke at the ceiling. He didn't say anything at first, which Nick knew was dangerous, even if Portov didn't.

"I told your people real plain," Angelo said, again very softly, "don't touch Patsy De Marco. But you didn't listen and now you're in deep shit. And I don't mean just from me."

"What does that mean?"

Angelo leaned forward. "Patsy's kids. One's worse than the other. Meza's a professional! He works for us! Every time I can get him, which is gettin' harder all the time. Let's just say he's got real busy he's so good."

Portov laughed out loud. One contract killer in Los Angeles against the forces of the Council. How absurd. "I'm terrified."

"You should be, you just don't know it. Boyle's just as bad. He's a homicide detective in Paterson."

"So he'll get to investigate the old man's death. Who cares."

Angelo took a big breath. "Plus, there's my son!"

Portov knew that was the real problem. He tried to adopt a conciliatory tone. "Believe me, I understand the relationship of the girl and your son. That was unfortunate."

Sparks flew from Angelo's eyes. "Unfortunate! You hit the father of the girl my son is in love with? Are you nuts?"

"Wait, Angelo, you're making a mistake." When caught, he always said, admit nothing, deny everything, demand proof. "We didn't hit Mr. De Marco. We had nothing to do with it. I just meant it was a shame your son was so close to the man."

Angelo Bracca's eyes narrowed. "What'd he say, Nick?"

"Mr. Bracca, I'm not sure I heard right."

"I just said you've made a mistake. I swear we had nothing to do with the old man's death."

Angelo Bracca never moved. "Nick," he said quietly.

Nick was a heavy man who ate too much. Sometimes people took him for granted, which was a mistake.

"Mr. Portov," he said.

"Yes."

"Mr. Bracca is not listening to this conversation." Angelo was staring with fixed, thin lips. "Underneath the table is that Beretta I told you about. It's pointed at your gut."

Portov stiffened but Nick held up his left hand. The right was hidden under the table.

"You insulted Angelo," Nick said. "In exactly thirty seconds he will tell me to shoot you."

Portov knew the drill and folded. There'd be time to settle accounts later.

"Tell Mr. Bracca he didn't hear right and . . ."

"He heard right," Nick said and there was a loud click.

"Then tell Mr. Bracca I apologize," Portov said wearily. The exchange had given him time to think. "I know who did it." He slammed his glass down in mock frustration but went too far. The glass shattered and he cursed, licking the blood off.

Angelo smiled. "He knows who did it. How nice. Nick, you must've heard wrong. You always get too excited."

"Sorry, Mr. Bracca."

"Now, Greg baby, listen to me."

Greg baby. "Yes."

"We can still make a lot of money together. You know all these Russians over here and I know how it works back in Jersey. But we ain't gonna make no money if you lie to me."

"I understand."

"Good." A girl came over, put a new glass in front of Portov, filled it with wine, even took care of his cut.

"Now drink up and when you're done take a deep breath and tell me who did it."

By this time Braxton had revealed everything he knew about Purcell's betrayal of the Council. The fat man would now die, the only question was how. To kill him immediately might unnecessarily expose Braxton. But if Angelo Bracca did it, as revenge for the murder of Patsy, no one would link Purcell's death to the Council. Besides, as he always told Alicia, tell as much of the truth as you can, it's easier to remember.

"All right, Angelo, it was the fat man and the woman who works for him. Here's what I know." He told Angelo exactly how it came down, only with Purcell ordering it to happen. At the end Angelo turned to Nick.

"You know what to do?"

"Yeah, I do, Mr. Bracca."

Back to Portov. "And as for you, Greg, you don't know it but I just done you a huge favor."

"Yeah? What?"

Bracca's voice dropped. "If Patsy's boys thought it was you, they'd hunt you down like a dog. Boyle's bad enough but Meza would never let up till you was in the ground. He'd make it a lifetime crusade. And when he found you, there wouldn't be enough left to bury, I don't care how many Russians you got working for you. Am I lyin' Nick?"

"Mr. Portov, there's nobody I hate enough to wish those two on. That's why we sent Meza out to the coast till we could figure things out."

Portov started to smirk, then stopped, because neither Nick nor Angelo was smiling. If he laughed at Angelo he'd be back with Nick pointing a gun at him. So he just shut up and played along. He grabbed the wine and drank deeply. "Okay," he said, in what he hoped was a calm voice. "Do you have the information you need?"

Angelo's face was set, purposeful. He had never liked Purcell and now it was time to settle accounts. "Yeah, we do. Let's go, Nick."

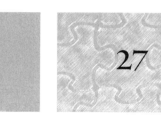

27

Magnus Purcell had never been this terrified, not even when he woke up hungover and sorrowful the morning after he betrayed the Council. The bellowed, profanity-laced accusation from Angelo Bracca had come roaring over the phone two hours before. Now he ushered Angelo and Nick wordlessly into a secret conference room he maintained in the New York headquarters of his international law firm. It was circular and green-marbled, modeled on the Medici burial crypt in Florence, an ironically suitable place for this particular meeting. Very few people other than Magnus and Alicia Kent knew of its existence.

Angelo walked in wearing a gray, sharkskin suit with a silver tie and white shirt. His shoes were gleaming black. His white hair was pushed back, gelled, and his every movement announced a graceful and pitiless power. Nick had a similar look, right down to the gelled hair, and looked to Angelo for direction. Angelo didn't look to anybody for direction.

Once the door was locked Angelo spoke right away. "You're dead, fat man. The only question is when."

Magnus squirmed, his three-hundred-fifty-pound, perfectly-coifed frame shifting uncomfortably in the chair. He had no idea Portov had accused him. And he still naively believed the Council did not know he betrayed them.

"Mr. Bracca, you made your wishes perfectly clear. But your accusations on the phone are just wrong. I promise I had *nothing* to do with Mr. De Marco's death."

Angelo said nothing. He just lit a cigar, poured a Scotch and spoke to Nick. "Our accusations are wrong the man says. Damn. We just made a trip for nothing. *Nobody* killed Patsy. He died of old age."

He turned back to Magnus. "I told you in plain English don't touch the old man. His daughter is living with my son. I *told* you that. I told *everybody* that."

Magnus' head bobbed like a toy dog. "And I didn't. We never would."

Magnus' denials just infuriated Angelo. "Don't lie to me. You killed him. I say *you*,"—he jammed a finger in Purcell's chest—"got together with that scary witch that works for you and killed Patsy De Marco. Now tell me I'm wrong."

Nick shifted. Magnus knew the signs. It was like a large cat stretching from a deep sleep.

"Mr. Bracca!"

"Mr. Bracca nothing. I know she did it and I know you ordered it. She don't do nothin' without your okay."

Magnus was outraged that he had to protect her, but he had no choice. "I promise you she didn't have anything to do with this either, Mr. Bracca." As the words left his mouth his deep hatred for Alicia Kent grew and flowered.

"Where is she now? How come she ain't here?"

Magnus didn't have time to think up a good lie. "She's in Los Angeles," he said quickly.

"Los Angeles," Bracca said slowly. "Now what the hell is she doing in Los goddamn Angeles?"

"Just some firm business. Honestly."

"Oh, man, this is rich. What firm business?"

Magnus thought so hard beads of sweat broke out on his brow. "A real estate case. It's about to go to trial."

"Nick," Angelo said, "shoot him."

Nick reached into his coat and Magnus was absolutely sure he would do it.

"I'm telling the truth!"

"That hag would need a phone book to find the courthouse. She's a hitter, that's all. Nick, don't make me say it twice."

Magnus turned pale and stood up, his arms extended. "Wait!"

"Last chance," Angelo said softly. "You don't use her for court-rooms and if you say that again Nick will shoot you in the eyeball."

Magnus collapsed. "All right."

"What's she doin' out there?"

The argument had given Magnus time to think.

"You're right, the real estate matter is just a ruse."

"That's right. Nick, what's a 'ruse'?"

"Like a scam, Mr. Bracca."

"Yes," Magnus said. "We have a very secret deal there. Each day a young bond trader on the Pacific Exchange makes trades. Records need to be . . . well . . ."

"Changed?"

"Yes, Mr. Bracca. On every bond trade there's a winner and a loser. The records need to be, well, arranged so that . . ."

"You get all the wins."

"Yes. A certain pension fund has been less successful."

"How much?"

"About a half billion in gross trades. But our upside is much less, only forty-five million over two years."

Angelo Bracca laughed with real mirth this time. "Nick, put your gun away. *Now* he's tellin' the truth."

Nick pressed. "What *exactly* is she doing there?"

"The trader is getting sloppy and has a drug problem. It's only a matter of days before a formal investigation begins."

"And?"

Magnus looked uncomfortable. "And . . . well, we can't let him . . ."

"Talk," Angelo said. "She's out there to waste the bond guy?"

Magnus shrugged. He did not correct him.

"Nick?"

"Yeah?"

"Who we got out there can check out this story?"

"You know, Meza."

Angelo stabbed the air with his cigar. "He's *perfect*."

"We can't tell him about the Patsy part though."

"Right. Just tell him to check out that hitter . . . what's her name?"

"Alicia Kent."

"Yeah. I want to know *everything* she's doin' there. And at the end of the week I better see one real cold dead bond guy."

"Don't forget that real estate thing," Nick reminded him.

"Well, I ain't gonna hold him to that. I already know that's a . . . what's the word, Nick?"

"Ruse, Mr. Bracca."

"Yeah, ruse."

Angelo moved close to Purcell. His breath was pungent with cigar smoke. "First off, the only reason I ain't killing you now is because you just got a new partner on this bond scam, understand?"

"Yes, of course."

"And if you're lying to me, you're one seriously dead fat man. Meza will do it himself. Right after we tell him you killed Patsy. You got no clue how long Meza will take before you beg him to kill you."

"Gentlemen," Magnus said, his arms wide and the sweat pouring from his face, "you really have no cause for concern."

28

Stephanie Shane got no sleep the night Boyle lay on her couch. At 4 A.M. she got out of bed and went to the window. The sleeping, unsuspecting city spread out before her. She shook her hair and let it fall free. In an hour she would begin work anew, still with no sleep. No wonder she had circles under her eyes.

She was about to wander into the living room when she remembered she was not alone. At the risk of scandal, she opened the door and stealthily walked toward the couch. He was lying on his back, on top of the covers, an arm thrown over those beautiful light green eyes. The dense muscles in his chest and abdomen were highlighted by the faint moon sliding into the room. Then he moved his arms, saw her and sat up.

"I'm sorry," she said. "I didn't mean to disturb you."

He rubbed the sleep away. "That's okay."

"I just wanted to tell you I'm kind of an early riser."

"What time is it now?"

She checked her watch. "Four-thirty. I'll be getting ready soon."

"I'd like to tell you one thing before . . ."

"No."

"It's nothing bad, I just wanted to say that . . ."

"I said, no!" She had no idea why she was being so rude to him. Maybe the fact that the two of them were eight feet apart, in her apartment, in the moonlight, wearing very little that might be called decent.

"All right. I'll take off when you do."

"What will you do today?"

"I have to find John. He'll know where Natala is. Then,"—he spread his arms—"I'll come back and see you."

"No," she said quickly. "We're done. No more."

"Look, we're both after the same thing, to find out why Patsy died. I still don't know why you're so interested, but I'll find out."

"No!"

He stood up and walked insolently over to her. She didn't walk away. When he was six inches from her and his bare chest and green eyes right there, he lifted up her chin slightly.

"No," she said, and this time her voice was so weak she could barely hear it.

He kissed her gently on the cheek and she didn't recoil, hit him, or have any other appropriate reaction.

"Let me explain something. If Patsy was home tonight eating pasta, and we met on a train, I'd still come back and see you."

She took a step back, then another. "I have to get dressed."

Natala De Marco woke up dazed, lying on a slate floor in the dark. Her head and face ached. She felt dried blood sticking to her thick, dark hair.

She sat up and the room spun. Her jacket dangled from one arm and her T-shirt hung in strips. Her breasts hurt as much as her head. She ran a finger gingerly over them and felt teeth marks on her left nipple. Somebody had been having quite a party.

She reached down with apprehension and touched her waist. The belt around her jeans was opened, as was the button and zipper. Her hand crept in the dark under her jeans and between her legs. She sighed with relief. Nothing.

The guy had been planning an even bigger party before something changed his mind. Maybe the name Bracca was enough to make him think twice. Whatever, she was happy it stopped where it did.

She began to remember how she got here, following the brown rat into the darkening old factory, the man appearing from the shadows, the struggle. The dirt-encrusted window that in daylight sent insistent sunlight and dust into the room was now invisible. It was deep night and she had been unconscious for hours.

She felt her way to the door. On the other side, the gym was black except for a single bulb burning in Patsy's office. It was an eerie light, which only heightened her fears. She was in a dark gym, next to a dark abandoned factory, with one working light, and had nothing going for her but pain and questions.

She turned on every light in the gym, locked the common door to the makeshift warehouse and started to calm. "Chill, girl," she said out loud, "it could be a lot worse."

She hunted for aspirin through Patsy's drawers. What she found was a bottle of Seagrams. She got a soiled glass from the filthy fighters' bathroom and filled it half up with the whiskey. She put her feet on the desk and toasted the empty gym.

"Here's to you, Patsy," she said, and then drank it all in a series of long gulps.

Her mood improved so much she poured another, about the same size. After all, she was Patsy's daughter, born on Christmas Day! Some daughters get millions in the will; she got beaten up in an old silk mill and a half bottle of cheap Canadian whiskey. Some bequests were better than others and she laughed at her own quiet joke.

By the third glass, she had lost judgment. She picked up the phone and dialed. The phone rang ten times before he picked it up. "Hullo."

"Hi."

There was a long silence. "Is this some kind of joke?"

"Probably." She twirled the glass. "I need to talk to you. Any chance of that?"

"Nat, it's three A.M. Where are you?"

"I'm in Patsy's gym?"

A beat went by. "What?"

"That's where I am. I'm sitting in his office and I'm drinking his whiskey. I just got beat up and my head hurts. The guy that beat me up tried to bite off one of my breasts. You remember those, don't you?"

She heard a long sigh. "Listen, I can tell you've been drinking. I want you to stay right there."

"There's more."

"What?"

"Patsy didn't die in his sleep, didn't die in any accident, and didn't die in a carjacking." She started crying. "Somebody killed him!"

His voice softened. "Nat, baby, I know that."

"You do?"

"Yeah, baby, I do."

"Hey, John?"

"Yeah?"

"I want to come talk to you about it. Maybe you can help." She finished the glass and poured another, wiping away tears with the ripped shards of her T-shirt. "After all, sweets, you're the Mafia, right? What better guy to know who killed somebody?" Her voice was getting seriously slurred.

"You can't drive."

She hiccupped. "Sure I can."

John Bracca had a man there in ten minutes. He was dark-suited and humorless. He yanked her to her feet, checked her efficiently for injuries, loaded her into the back of a black car with darkened windows and drove down Route 80 over the George Washington Bridge to Manhattan. The pale pre-dawn blended with the fading lights of the New York skyline. When they exited the bridge the driver cut onto the Henry Hudson and headed downtown. John Bracca was not the sort of scion who lived in Jersey for old times' sake. He had a four-thousand-square-foot apartment two blocks from the park on Sixty-fifth. Some of it was paid for by his profits as an investor and some of it wasn't. From the time the man arrived in the warehouse till the time he yanked her out of the car he never spoke.

The doorman knew her well and nodded as she was led past by the arm. She never resisted the man in the dark suit. John's men followed orders, she knew that.

She rode alone to the twenty-seventh floor and debated whether to use her key. She decided it would be more dramatic if she knocked.

John Bracca opened the door and stared.

"May I come in?"

He stood aside. She entered the room, walked immediately over to the bar and poured herself a drink.

"Make me one."

"Sure, sweets."

John had much better whiskey than Patsy and it went down her throat easily. She leaned against the bar and looked at him.

"Do you have any idea who did it?" he asked softly.

She was still dressed in high-heeled boots and tight jeans held together by a thick belt. Her thin jacket covered the ripped white cotton T-shirt. One breast was exposed. Dried blood crusted against her left nipple. Her face was pale and her thick hair mottled with sweat and blood.

"What do you care?"

He shook his head in exasperation. "Don't start. Just tell me what happened?"

She told him everything she remembered, sipping the whiskey as she talked. He listened with his arms folded across his chest. His face darkened.

"You should never have gone into the warehouse alone."

"I didn't. The rat went in with me."

He grinned at that and walked to the bar. He was dressed in a pair of long cotton pajama bottoms. His chest was bare. Even half dressed and half asleep he was gorgeous to her and always had been. Whether it was the shoulders or the dense, black curly hair, the dark Italian skin or even white teeth she never knew or cared. Maybe the whole package. John was the only man who had ever gotten to her, completely gotten to her, right from the very beginning.

He grabbed her and kissed her hard in a way he hadn't for a long time. He was clearly angry at her and it showed in the kiss, which she loved. It reminded her of the first time she decided to disobey her father and go out with him, the night of Tommy Boyle's glorious victory over Hector Lopez in the finals of the Golden Gloves.

She was embarrassed that night because she felt like a kid. She was fifteen years old, had lied to her father and brothers, was out with a seventeen-year-old boy who looked like a dream and was being taken to dinner at Moska's. She was supposed to be going straight home with a girlfriend.

John Bracca was the perfect gentleman, then and always after. He escorted her in like a princess and introduced her to all his relatives. Angelo was there, leapt to his feet and kissed her hand.

"Natala De Marco. You're as beautiful as they say."

"Thank you, Mr. Bracca."

"Listen, I'm glad you came here with my son. Are you hungry?"

"A little."

"What would you like?"

"Can I get some pizza?"

He gestured and the waiters went sprinting. "You mind if I talk to John a second?"

"Sure. Go ahead."

Angelo put his hand on John's shoulder, leading him gently away. When they turned a corner he spun on his son. "Are you nuts?"

John flinched. "What?"

Angelo's face was bright red. "What! That's jailbait you got there. Plus her father will be in here with a shotgun. I don't want to get killed so you can go get a little girl."

"That won't happen."

"You bet your ass it won't."

John was getting as angry as his father. "Look, Pop, you're insulting me and insulting her. I wanted to get to know her for a long time, and I wanted her to meet you. After we eat I'll drive her right home and talk to her father."

"Talk to her father! You *are* nuts."

"You're wrong. I *need* to talk to her father. It's the right thing to do."

"He's gonna shoot you. Right between the eyes. And you *deserve* it!"

"You don't understand. I want to tell him exactly how I feel. I'm glad Boyle beat Lopez. And I'm glad Nat is celebrating with me."

"Patsy's gonna love that. How come his daughter ain't celebrating with him?"

"Because she's with me."

Angelo rubbed the pain from his temples, then looked at his son in disbelief. "John, she is twelve years old."

"Fifteen."

"Same difference."

"No. She's old enough to decide who to eat with. I have *never* treated her with disrespect." He paused. "I never will."

Angelo still wasn't satisfied. "Her brothers are gonna just rip you up. Which one you want to go outside with, Miguel or Tommy?"

John Bracca shrugged. He wasn't afraid of anything. Or anyone. And never would be. "I know what you're saying but you got it wrong."

Angelo just shook his head, defeated. "I give up. I still say you're nuts but it's your funeral." Then he thought some more. "Incidentally, thanks on that Boyle bet. He dropped Lopez like a bad habit. We made a bundle."

"You're welcome."

His father sighed. "Just be careful."

She had been daydreaming, remembering the two of them giggling at Moska's as John told her about his fatherly chat. But that was then and this was now and now was a lot different. John Bracca broke the kiss that felt so good and picked up a pack of cigarettes off the bar. He lit one and placed it in her mouth, gently. Damn, she thought, he even does that good.

"Stay with me, Nat. There's no reason to go."

She blew out the smoke. "No."

"Why?"

"Same reasons. You got too many secrets."

She meant the time he had been spending with Stephanie Shane, and the lies he had to tell her about that. He hated to lie to her. And until now, he never had. "They're not secrets. It's just business."

"Right. What is it, construction jobs on the turnpike? The unions on the docks?"

That remark angered him. "There's nothing about me or my family you didn't know going in."

"Time's change," she said weakly.

"Or maybe a certain brother has been bad-mouthing me again?"

"No," she said. "Not again. Anyway, I stopped listening to Tommy long ago." She was more than a little drunk and stumbled against the bar. "Did you kill Patsy?"

"What!"

"Okay, did Angelo?"

"You're insulting me again. Do you really think Angelo would harm the father of the girl I was . . . was . . ."

"Screwing?" She slurped at her whiskey.

"Stop it! Living with. In love with."

"So who killed him? Cock robin?"

"Cock robin got killed, he didn't kill anybody."

"Somebody killed Patsy."

"I know. I'm asking questions."

"Of who?"

It was still too dangerous for her to know he was cooperating with the government, a family first for sure. "I can't discuss that right now."

She smirked. "More secrets." She finished her cigarette and tossed her torn T-shirt into the middle of the room. She was now nude from the waist up. John Bracca laughed.

"What's so funny?" She drank some more and hiccupped.

"You. Here you are with the two most beautiful . . . what can I call them . . ."

"Tits. Call them what they are." The pain and anger had definitely had an effect on her language, which was usually moderately clean. Patsy had let her know early and often how he felt about that. "I had to let some air on the left one though, where that raccoon bit."

"And I'm supposed to be a vicious mobster? What do you think a real mobster would do if he saw you like this?"

She burped. "Bite the other one, put teeth marks on both of them."

"Okay," he said, moving forward.

"Forget it, your biting days are over." She lit a new cigarette off the old and coughed.

"You are going to be so miserable later. I assume you're sleeping here?"

Hic. "Yes, alone."

She put her head in her hand. He grabbed her arm.

"Time for bed, baby."

Suddenly there was a crash, then a series of bangs. "What's that?" He let her go.

"The door. Somebody's banging on the door."

"At six in the morning?" He reached underneath the couch where two Glock 9 mms were carefully hidden. He grabbed one, snapped the release and went to the door.

"Who's there?"

"Open up," a voice said.

Bracca released the latch and stood back. The door flew open and Bracca dropped to one knee, the Glock on his forearm pointing.

A man walked through the door. He looked at Bracca, then at Natala. Natala was standing stiffly at attention, still naked from the waist up.

"Hey," Boyle said. "You guys having a party?"

29

Long before Alicia Kent was a killer she was a child, with horrific nightmares that began at the age of four. They were always the same. She'd be alone, the dark form would be at the door, and she'd start to scream. Her mother was visible in the other room, drinking with a man and laughing. Yet no matter how loud she screamed her mother never heard, and when she looked over, the black form was closer.

She entered the Sandra Wickett Special School for Girls in San Diego at the age of six, soon after she had pushed a girl off a thirty-foot pier into the roiling sea. The girl had a lovely brooch that Alicia wanted and wouldn't give up. The girl's father leapt screaming into the foam at the base of the pilings and when he dragged his sobbing daughter to the beach vowed to sue everyone from the district superintendent to the janitor. The next day Alicia sat with her mother in the office of a kindly principal named Jefferson Jones.

"Look, Mrs. Kent, we really do think this is for the best. Alicia is a troubled girl and the Sandra Wickett School is equipped for that."

"Why's she troubled? She's only six."

"Yes, but the danger signs are there. She is a very slow learner. Plus she is physical with the other children and extremely disruptive in class."

"Physical? She's a girl! What kind of wimps you got there?"

"We don't tolerate violence among the students. Plus there was the incident with the Rosen girl on the pier."

"That's a bad rap. Alicia says she fell by accident."

The man spread his hands. "Mrs. Kent, there were at least thirty witnesses, including four teachers."

"Well, anyway, I can't send her to no special school. I don't have that kind of money."

"Mrs. Kent, please don't worry about that. This is a district issue and a district expense."

"Really?" Her mother grinned. "In that case send her anywhere you want."

The Sandra Wickett School had sixty girls with severe behavioral problems from all over the district. The noble goal was to intervene early, provide counseling and pharmaceuticals, and return them to regular schools by the eighth grade.

For the first three years Alicia was sullen, barely speaking to the shrinks they sent her to, still suffering mightily from ceaseless, crushing headaches that blurred her vision and left her nauseous. In the fourth year, as she turned ten, they sent her to a new counselor, a young woman barely out of school named Dr. Juliet Adams. Alicia liked her and the two became inseparable. After two months Dr. Adams sat down with Alicia.

"I'm going to send you home, Alicia."

The girl was shocked. "Why?"

"Because this is not the place for you. You should be in a regular school. You're very smart, did you know that?"

"I get horrible grades."

"Yes, but I've tested your intelligence. Twice, because I thought there must be some mistake. You tested higher than any girl in the history of this school, Alicia."

She refused to meet her gaze. "I don't care. I just want to stay here with you."

The doctor put her hand on Alicia's shoulder. "I know you don't. You don't care about anything. It's like there's a crust on your heart. Alicia, you're holding everything in. That's what's causing the headaches and nightmares."

The girl almost cried, but didn't because she never did. "So, you want to kick me out?"

"No, Alicia. I'll still see you like always. I just want you in a normal environment." She handed her a package. "Look, I brought you a present."

Alicia opened it. It was a stuffed animal, a fish. She started to laugh and then shut it down quick. "What's this?"

"I call him 'Squid.' Do you know you have no animals, no dolls, no nothing at all?"

Alicia shrugged. "I don't care about that stuff."

The woman smiled and smoothed the girl's hair. "I know that, angel. Look, do me a favor and go home for six months. Take Squid. Try to open your heart to your family and the kids at school. They won't hurt you Alicia, I promise. Will you do that for me?"

She thought about it for a long time before answering. Dr. Adams had never been wrong yet.

"Okay."

Alicia's mother was not at all thrilled to have her daughter back, but there wasn't a lot she could do about it. For her part Alicia just tried to stay out of the way and make an effort to get along. By that time Alicia's father had completely lost interest and her mother had taken up with an amiable ex-marine named Elmer. Like Dr. Adams suggested, Alicia tried to be nice to all of them, and quickly agreed when her mother suggested she join her dad and Elmer on a nice fishing trip to the Tetons.

"Sure, Mom, that sounds like fun."

"Great idea," Elmer said.

The three of them took off from San Diego on a Thursday morning in late June, just after school ended. Alicia wore white shorts, a T-shirt and sandals, her long legs bare. They planned to get to Salt Lake by noon, drive to Idaho, fish till they were awash in trout, then fly back on Sunday.

The men drank beer on the plane and Alicia watched their personalities change. They laughed more and their voices grew loud. She didn't care. She sat by the window and looked at the beautiful mountains they passed over. The clouds were pale and puffy and sat like cigar smoke ringing the tips of the Sierras, still snowcapped, even as summer loomed.

It was dark when they reached the lodge. The men drank more beer at the airport bar before picking up the rental car and joked about getting out of jail—meaning out of Utah, a dry state—when they drove away. Once across the border into Idaho they stopped at a fake Indian antique store and bought a case of cold Coors. Then they continued the ride.

The fishing lodge had three bedrooms and a deck overlooking the roaring Snake River. A full moon sat fat and proud over the surging water, highlighting the sharp light sprinting from the water as it caught the rocks. Alicia walked out on the deck and looked at the magical sight. It was gorgeous, and for the first time in a long time her headache eased.

Her father had fallen asleep on the ride in and seemed to trip on the walk to the lodge. Elmer made a joke about old age but her father didn't say anything back. An hour later, Alicia went in to kiss him good night and found him fully dressed, snoring loudly. The sight vaguely disturbed her. She turned quickly and went back out onto the deck.

Elmer sat in a wood chair drinking a beer, his eyes filled with broken red lines. "Hey," he said as she walked out.

"Hi."

"Your dad asleep?"

"Yeah, he looked tired."

"Well, I guess I got to be your dad tonight."

"Okay."

He carried her suitcases in and helped her unpack. He seemed to look at each item carefully before handing it to her. When he got to her nightgown he set it out on the bed. It was cotton, had ducks on it, and barely reached past her bottom. Then he reached into her suitcase and pulled out a light dress.

"What's this pretty thing?"

"That's just in case." The dress was new, thin and silk, white, hardly longer than the nightgown.

"Really?"

"Yeah, if we go someplace nice, you know?"

"You'll look very grown up." He licked salt off his upper lip.

"Yeah. My mom bought shoes too. I think my sandals look better."

"Let's take a look."

She held the dress up. "What do you think?"

"It's hard to tell. Why don't you try it on." His voice had changed, become huskier.

Alicia squinted. "Try it on?"

"Yeah. Put the dress on, bring your shoes, and come show me. I'll be on the deck." He said it in a commanding way, like the shrinks did sometimes.

"Yes, sir."

———————

She felt stupid when she walked out. The breeze was stern off the Snake and blew the thin dress high. She had to hold her black shoes in one hand and hold the short dress down with the other. It was hard and she wasn't even close to successful.

Elmer was a beefy man and for some reason had changed into a bathing suit and T-shirt. The shirt clung tightly to his soft belly and ended six inches above the shorts. The bathing suit wrapped snugly around his thick hips and thighs. There were four beer cans on the round table next to him. Three were empty, one he sipped. There had been none the last time she was out on the deck.

"You sure do drink those fast," she said.

"Yeah." He turned to her. "So that's the pretty dress?" His voice sounded different, like he was real tired, or talking with his mouth full.

"Yup." She held up the black shoes. The wind whipped over the deck.

"C'mere," he said.

"What?"

"Said c'mere. Can't see so good from here."

She walked closer, hesitant, confused. But like Dr. Adams said, trust people sometimes.

"Like this?"

"Yeah." He stared at her dress and twirled his finger. "Turn around."

She did as he asked, a complete three-sixty.

"No, not that," he barked. "Turn and look at the river. Stay like that."

Her anxiety grew but she did as he ordered. The moon, previously an arc light in the night sky, was shrouded by passing clouds. It created an eerie, picketed light that came and went like a strobe. The wind freshened and her hands flew to her sides.

"Don't do that," the man commanded. She could hear the clank of the beer can against his teeth and a rustle of clothes being moved, or adjusted. She also heard a harsh, nasal breathing, like when somebody's running real hard.

Her hands remained at her sides. She didn't dare turn. "I have to."

Alicia heard a chair scrape. Then she felt his hands on her arms.

"Hold your arms like this." He moved her arms wide.

"But my dress! The black shoes!"

"Drop the goddamn shoes," the voice said. "And forget the goddamn dress."

That's when Alicia knew that Dr. Adams was wrong.

She stood as Elmer said, her arms wide, holding her shoes tightly. Tears of rage formed as she felt the night wind off the river blow her dress high. He can see *everything*, just *everything*.

"Hey look, can't I . . ."

"Shut up," the voice said, and it didn't sound like Elmer at all.

Then she felt the hands.

"C'mon, sit on my lap," the voice said.

"No," she screamed. She tried to turn but the strong, beefy hands held her. She pulled again and heard the fabric rip.

"My dress!"

"Forget the goddamn dress." He pulled her on his lap and that's when she felt it against her bare leg. And she knew exactly what it was.

"No," Alicia screamed, hard and young into the abyss of river noise.

At 4 A.M. she was still awake, sitting on her bed clutching the stuffed animal to her chest, rocking. Her dress was torn and soiled. Between her legs a dried pink mucous flowed like the river near the deck, an unholy marriage of red blood and white semen. Her head hurt because Elmer had slammed it into the deck and there were bruises on her chest. She had been talking to the animal for hours. "We have to stay awake. We can't go to sleep or we'll get nightmares again."

Just before dawn Alicia felt something change. It had been growing within her for hours, and she had fought against it, knowing instinctually the horror that would be hers if she let it take over. Yet despite her resistance it continued to grow, encrusted in a hard shell, like a spore, and she knew exactly what it was.

By dawn she was too tired to fight. She heard her father emerge, stumbling to a bathroom, heard his groaning, heard the flush. The sounds disgusted her, and the thing grew some more.

When her father's door slammed it was all over. She lay back on her pillow and to her amazement felt a sense of peace. She tossed the stuffed fish to the floor, then inspected the torn dress dispassionately. It was a sodden mess. She pulled it off and used it to clean the mess between her legs. Dr. Adams had lied, and the toy that once meant everything was now a reminder of that lie. Everyone had lied to her. She threw the hunk of fabric on top of the toy.

She would sleep all day. No one would bother her now, not even the dark shape of her nightmares, because now the shape had taken her, body and soul. Her mind, lit by embers of a fantasy of revenge, was calm. She vowed she would never suffer again. Others would.

She said nothing about the rape for two years, until she turned fourteen. Then, more out of curiosity than any other emotion, she decided to tell her mother.

It was after midnight and her mother had just returned from an evening with Elmer. "I need to talk to you," Alicia said, looking up from her book.

"What?" Her mother's voice was slurred. "Tell me in the morning."

"It's about Elmer."

"What about him?"

"It's something you should know."

Her mother lit a cigarette. "I'm listening."

"You remember a couple of years ago when Dad and me and Elmer went fishing?"

Her mother stiffened. She remembered just fine. "No, I don't."

"It was in Idaho, along the Snake River. We went in June just after school ended."

"Yeah?"

"I need to tell you what happened."

Her mother's voice thickened even more. "I don't care what happened! I don't want you sayin' bad things about Elmer!"

"It's *important*!"

"Well, if it's so important, you should've told me back then."

"What's the difference? I'm telling you now." Alicia spoke fast. At the end, her mother was stone faced.

"Well?"

Her mother's hand flashed and there was a loud crack. Alicia's head whipped to the side.

"What the hell was that for?"

"You whore," her mother hissed. "You're nothing but a little slut."

"I'm a slut? I'm a slut? I get raped and you call me a slut?"

"Get out of here," her mother screamed. "Get out of my room!"

The next day Alicia dressed quickly and left the house before her mother woke up. By then she was a sophomore at Thomas Jefferson High School, a moderately upscale public high school in San Diego. It had good students and bad students, white kids and brown kids. And like any public school on the border of Mexico, it had gangs.

The gang guys had always been polite to Alicia and she had no problem with them. They met every morning a half hour before school started, huddled in a circle, dressed in baggy jeans and colored caps. Colors meant gang affiliation, which translated into who got shot when in the drivebys. But all that happened at night in the barrios. During the day Thomas Jefferson was still a pretty safe place to be.

Her one friend among the gang guys was a fifteen year old named Rudy Diaz. Rudy was sitting casually with his friends, a red bandanna around his head, smoking a cigarette. Alicia touched him gently on the shoulder.

Rudy turned. "Hey."

"Hey. Can you talk?"

The other guys looked over with curiosity. Alicia waved at them. "Hi."

They nodded, cool, uncaring. It was enough permission for Rudy. "Sure. Here?"

"Maybe over there? I have a favor to ask."

They walked to a picnic table. "What's up?"

"I need a gun."

Rudy laughed. "You need a what?"

"I'm serious. I need a gun. Can you get me one?"

"What do you need a gun for?"

"Does it matter?"

Rudy shrugged. "What are you gonna do with it?"

"Take care of some business."

"What business?"

Alicia told him the truth. Rudy was stone faced through the whole thing. "She hit you?"

"Right here." Alicia showed him the corner of her lip, which was still slightly swollen.

"Bitch!" Rudy hissed.

That she was. "So, can you help me?"

Rudy sighed. "You ever use a gun? You don't know what you're doing. You know you only pull it out to use it. And you only use it to kill."

"I know. I want you to show me how."

Rudy laughed. "You want lots of stuff."

"Will you help me?"

Some thinking now. "What's in it for me?"

She was ready for that too. "Whatever you want."

Rudy Diaz shrugged. "I don't want nothin'. I was just wondering."

"Well?"

He looked back toward his friends, who were now ignoring him. "Can you get out tonight?"

"Sure."

"Meet me here at ten. I'll see what I can do."

She arrived fifteen minutes early. Rudy was a few minutes late because he circled the block to check for cops. There was no one around.

They sat at the same picnic table. Rudy opened a small cloth bag. "Is that it?"

"Yeah." He turned the bag upside down. A squat weapon clunked heavily onto the table. Alicia stared at it with fascination.

"It's a cheap gun, a thirty-two. You load it like this." Rudy popped the chamber, loaded the weapon, then closed the chamber. "See?"

"Yeah."

He did it twice more for her. "Now you try it."

She fumbled around but Rudy was encouraging. "Yeah, that's it." After a few tries, she got it right. She turned to Rudy.

"Hey, watch it!" His screams were loud and he dove under the table.

"What?"

He came up slowly. "Point it over there."

She did as she was told. "Sorry."

"I told you, don't point that thing at nobody unless you're gonna use it. And *never* point it at *me*!"

"Okay, sorry."

"All right, let's go practice." He put her in his car and they drove to the ocean. He parked on a deserted bluff high above the water. There was a pathway leading along the cliff into darkness. The waves crashed and they had to raise their voices to be heard.

"The only thing you can hit up here is a fish."

She took the gun with both hands and pointed it at the open ocean, like Rudy taught her. She fired and the gun jumped in her hands. The sound was muffled by the roar of the sea against the boulders far below. She emptied one magazine and then another. Rudy made her reload the gun and fire. After a half hour she felt comfortable.

"It's not as hard as I thought."

"No, it ain't."

She fired the last of the bullets and held the gun toward the sky. She snapped the magazine and made sure the gun was empty.

"Hey, Rudy?"

"Yeah."

"I promised you something, you remember?"

He shrugged.

"I really hate to owe people. I want to pay you."

Her tone kind of stunned him. "I guess it'd be okay."

"Great. Just lie back and we'll get this done fast."

She thought about the right way to do it with the same attention to detail she later brought to all her kills. She couldn't go in and just blast away while the two of them were in bed together. No, that road led straight back to lawyers, shrinks, social workers, juvenile hall and a whole lot of aggravation. Besides, her mother was simply pathetic, not evil. Elmer would do fine.

She started out being nice to him. When he came over, she'd smile, give him a big hello, ask about his day, kiss him on the cheek. At first he was taken aback, then interested, finally relaxed. The Snake River problem was now long behind him.

After a month Elmer got into it and came over before her mother even got there, at first a few minutes early, then a lot more early. Alicia made sure Elmer saw her in short summer dresses that exposed a lot of bare leg when she spun. Once, when she heard Elmer's car in the driveway, she jumped out of her clothes and into the shower, then emerged in a towel. "Oh, my God," she squealed, dropping the towel, then grabbing it inefficiently. "I'm so sorry. I had no idea you were here." Then she smiled at Elmer's gaping look and scampered away.

With the inevitability of the rising sun, she one day found herself next to him on the couch. He was on his eighth beer. She had on a one-piece yellow satin shift that wasn't even moderately decent when she crossed her legs. Elmer patted her bare leg.

"You been workin' hard now? Studying and all that?"

"Sure," she said. His hand moved along her bare skin. She didn't pull away.

"That's good, that's good." More patting and the hand moved again. "You been smokin'? Foolin' around with boys?"

Alicia held her breath, causing a slight blush. "Sometimes."

"Yeah, that's what you little girls do."

Her smile was sly. "But those boys are too young. They don't know *anything*."

Elmer's breathing took on that same concentrated cadence she remembered so well from the deck on the Snake.

"Maybe you ought to try somebody knows a little more." His hand was all the way up her leg, his fingers groping at her panties.

"Wait," Alicia said. "Not here!"

Elmer took his hand out and mumbled a disappointed curse.

"But I know a place," Alicia said quickly.

"Yeah, where?"

"It's real private, near Point Loma. You and me could be . . . well, alone."

"You want that?"

"Oh, yes, sir. That's exactly what I want."

She scheduled the execution for midnight, a dark, romantic time that seemed nicely traced to the dark, romantic time in the Tetons. Elmer took her mother to his apartment and got her drunk and snoring by eleven. Then he went into the kitchen, poured a large shot of Early Times, no ice, washed it down with the remains of a Budweiser, and went out the door.

It was a moonless night. The cliffside parking lot was empty except for a bicycle tossed carelessly against seaside shrubs. He offered to drive the girl, but she refused, and he was glad. The less time in his car, the less chance of some jerk charging him with some stuff he'd have to explain.

He found the path where she told him, next to her bicycle. He walked down it and the street disappeared, no streetlights, no moon, no traffic, no nothing. The stark blackness excited him, and he freely entertained the fantasy of taking the young girl with the crashing surf in the background. The Early Times bit into his brain as he thought of her short dress and bare legs. It gave him a nice jolt.

The path was strewn with rock outcroppings that forced him closer to the edge. The dirt track rose and fell with the terrain. Soon, the ocean roar, still loud, lessened, and he rose higher along the bluffs.

At the crest the trail narrowed and he had to walk sideways. The lonesome pine she told him to look for was dead ahead. The night wind from the black sea freshened and blew harshly against his back. The sea noise was of a crashing, ominous sort.

He heard a rustle and looked in the direction of the sound. Suddenly, he was blinded by a harsh light. The light bit into his face and spread down the hundred feet to the crashing surf bouncing against the rocks below.

"Hey, shut that thing off." He raised his hand to fend off the glare. The narrowness of the path made it impossible to back away.

"Don't move," a girl's voice said. He recognized it.

"Alicia? Alicia, is that you?"

"Why did you do it?"

Her voice was so strange. It caused more confusion.

"Do what? What are you talking about?"

"Why did you do it?" she asked again, a monotone, repetitive question.

He decided to play dumb. "I don't . . . I really don't know what you mean."

It was hard to balance himself on the precipice and at the same time hold up a hand to block the light. Plus there were bugs up here, because suddenly he felt a sharp, stinging sensation, like a small animal biting against his leg. He twisted with the pain, then reached down to rub it. He felt warm liquid.

"Jesus!"

The sting bit into his right leg. This time he knew it wasn't a bug. When he held up his hands in the glare from her flashlight they were both soaked with blood.

"Oh, my God." He felt faint and struggled to avoid falling.

"Why did you do it?" she asked a third time, in the same maddening monotone.

He had once been a marine, and knew he'd been shot. He had to answer quickly. "I didn't plan it, honest. It just happened."

"Just happened? Like this?"

Now the sting hit his arm. He spun, grasping at the blood spurting from his shoulder.

"Why did you do it?" the voice asked again.

He panicked and sweat filled his face. "I had to," he screamed.

He heard bright laughter. "You had to?"

"Yes, I had to. You were there, you looked . . . you looked so good, your father was . . . asleep, I just had to. I was drunk."

"Are you religious? You know, like a Catholic or something?"

"No, not really." He swatted again at the bright light. It didn't go away.

"So you don't think you'll go to hell?"

"What are you talking about?"

"I thought you'd want to pray."

This time the bee stung him under his ribs, and he realized with horror what she was going to do. His shirt was dripping. He dropped to his knees, sickened and faint. "Please don't," he begged.

"Hey, that's exactly what I said."

He felt more bee stings and this time it was too much. The ledge was too narrow. He grabbed a bush and squeezed. The search light remained trained on him, so she could watch it all. The bush came off in his hands and he rolled to the left, nearer oblivion. The last sound he heard was her casual, "Bye Elmer," just before he left the ledge, his arms and legs windmilling.

He landed heavily on the sand, not the rocks, and to his horror didn't die. He lay there, paralyzed, bleeding from his wounds. The waves came in and he screamed with the pain of the salt. He stayed like that, howling uselessly into the roar of the night sea, until the rising tide gently carried him from that hell to the one awaiting him.

ngelo Bracca left Magnus Purcell's secret conference room and told Nick to get Meza involved right away. But Nick was used to dealing with Miguel Meza and figured it would be best to wait until the following morning.

When the phone rang, however, Meza didn't have a hangover, and hadn't had one for the seven days he had been with Christine, which made seven days out of the past six years he didn't have one. Out of habit he clenched his teeth against the pain before opening his eyes. When all he felt was the cool breeze of morning through the open window he said, "Hmm," once to himself and answered the phone.

The ringing phone woke Christine up, who was lying naked on top of a thin white sheet. She stretched like a cat and looked at his groin, the predator seeking out the morning meal.

"Wait a second," he hissed, before she could spring.

She shrugged. She could wait one second. She'd use the time to engage in what passed for foreplay in her warped mind, sliding a bit of oil onto her magic button. "Don't trouble yourself," she had told him the night before. "You don't do it right anyway."

She now milked him like a cow twice a day, sitting astride him and rocking back and forth to the sound of blaring, guitar-driven heavy metal. When he finally told her to turn the goddamn thing down she looked at him darkly, pushed him back on the bed, and sat astride him with a set of earphones on, twisting and dancing to the barrage of noise inside her brain.

"Jesus," he complained when that one was over. "I'm no better than one of those damn vibrators."

She sighed. "Men just don't get it. With vibrators you're always looking for batteries."

He got the phone on the third ring. "Hullo."

"Miguel, Nick. You okay?" The question was a legitimate one. A lot of times when Nick called in the morning Miguel was not okay.

"You wouldn't believe it, Nick."

"Good. Hey, Angelo says thanks on that collection thing. You got paid okay?"

More than okay once you added in the extras he picked up from the Brent job. "Yeah. Tell Angelo thanks."

"I will. You ready for something else?"

"Sure." He glanced warily at Christine, who had finished her foreplay and was starting to move.

"It's sort of a weird thing."

"What's that mean?"

"Don't worry, we just need information."

"About what?"

"Not 'what,' 'who.' Someone out there we need checked out. She's a cleaner."

"She?"

"Yeah."

"She works for Angelo?"

"No, somebody Angelo does business with. They told us a story about what she's doin' and we want to make sure it's real."

"What's the story?"

"She's supposed to cap somebody this week."

Meza was quiet. This was stranger than Nick was letting on. "Who gets it?"

"Nobody important. Some guy that sells stocks or something."

"Damn, Nick, I don't want to watch that."

"What, like you're a virgin?"

"I pick my spots, Nick. You know that. Plus I want to get back and figure out that Patsy thing."

"I know you do. Look, give me a couple days, I got nobody else out there can cover this. Check her out and let me know what she's doing. Then it's first class back on Angelo. Your girlfriend too."

He sighed. "Nick, if I don't like it, I'm bailing."

"No problem. You can even stop it if you want."

"Yeah?"

"Absolutely. Angelo doesn't care, he just wants to know."

"And who pays for stopping it?"

"Angelo, no problem."

He felt Christine's hand on his leg. He had to talk fast.

"And the cleaner? What do I do with her?"

"That's up to you. Fairer than that I cannot be."

He couldn't think of an objection. He could check it out and tell Angelo, or he could check it out and stop it. Either way he got paid and still got to go back. "I'll need information."

"An hour, I'll call you then."

He hung up the phone, so deep in thought he forgot the main rule of the jungle, watch for meat eaters. One minute she wasn't there and the next she was baring her teeth in a fake grin.

"You through with your phone call?" She liked to appear polite.

"Yeah, I am, but don't get too interested. I got a problem."

She straddled him, nuzzling his neck, getting ready for another ride. "You *used* to have problems, now you got no more problems."

"You'll notice it in a second."

She looked down. "Oh my God! What happened?"

"What happened? The skin's almost gone. You can't just scrape at it like you're takin' the paint off a house. If you touch it now, I'll scream it hurts so bad."

"Baby, you're right, it's all raw and red. You have to take better care of that guy."

"Me!"

"Hell, yeah, it's yours, not mine."

"Our bodies, ourselves," he said, and had no idea where that came from.

"What?"

"Never mind. We have to give him . . . it a rest through."

"Don't call him 'it,' and that's not a problem."

"No?

"Absolutely not," she said brightly. "We can work around him while he's resting."

His eyes narrowed. "What's that mean?"

"Nothing. You don't even have to move."

"I don't?"

"Nope." She moved north. He saw what was coming.

"Christine!" The light disappeared.

"Relax. Don't move, don't talk." She grabbed the headboard of the bed with both hands.

"Just enjoy yourself."

When she was done she hopped off like she was jumping off a horse.

"Now *that* was nice. You want some coffee?"

"Please."

"Okay." She grabbed for her discarded panties. "Incidentally what was that call about?"

"A job," he said, grabbing a cigarette and wiping his lips.

"What kind of job?"

"It don't matter."

She stopped. "What?"

It was hopeless. "Another job from Nick."

"Great! We can go together again."

"Not on this one."

She laughed merrily and kissed where he had dabbed. "That's why I love you, you're so funny."

Nick called back in an hour with the information.

"Here's the address." He rattled off the number and street where Alicia would be staying. "It's in Bel Air. You know where that is?"

"I'll find it."

"Good, don't get made, keep me posted."

"You got it."

31

A fter Portov's very unpleasant lunch with Angelo Bracca he immediately called Alicia Kent in Los Angeles.

"I hope you're sitting down. I have a lot to tell you."

"I am. Go ahead."

"The good news is everything went great in Russia."

The pure-grade Sarin. One problem solved. Two to go.

"Has delivery been made?"

"Josef Alexeyev is arranging everything," Portov said. "He's already got it. But he wants his stuff right away. So who's working with you on the fabric acquisition project?"

Nuclear grade-beryllium. The second leg.

"Roberta, I think."

"Good choice. I was never fond of the man you used on the East Coast."

Nor was Alicia. "Well, we won't have to worry about Carlos anymore."

"True enough. Anything else at your end?"

"Yes." She paused, reflecting. "I got a call from Purcell. Right out of the blue."

"Really? That's strange."

"Yes. Very strange. He hasn't wanted me working with him for years. But now he wants me to resolve a problem out here involving . . ."

"A bond trader?"

Alicia relaxed. "How could you possibly know that?"

Portov told her about his meeting with Angelo Bracca and Angelo Bracca's separate meeting with Purcell. He also told her about the later call from Nick, telling him about the bond trader, and that one of his men was going to be monitoring Alicia, making sure the man died. "That guy Meza. You know him."

"That's very bad news," Alicia said. "I've tried to tell you Meza is much more dangerous than you realize."

Portov sighed. "Forget Meza. He's one guy and no match for you. This bond trader, there's money to be made?"

"That's the deal I told you about in Paris. There's a *ton* of money involved." She didn't have to say anything more. He remembered, and also remembered that the Council knew nothing of the deal.

"Then I suggest you follow Mr. Purcell's instructions, Alicia," he said. "The bond trader must go."

"Yes, sir."

Alicia Kent was in a tense mood when Roberta arrived. She gestured briskly to a chair.

"What do you have for me?" she barked.

Roberta Alvarez was a muscular Argentine who was almost as ruthless as Alicia herself. They had been working together for three years now. Roberta was thirty-two years old, over six feet tall and 140 pounds, and liked to dress in black denim pants with high-heeled boots. She topped the ensemble today with a red vest and a cowboy hat. A bright silver buckle danced at her waist.

Alicia's quirky moods always annoyed Roberta. She tried to stay cool, a coolness that hid a deep resentment. But for what she got paid, it was worth it to try to keep Alicia happy.

"I don't know why you're so mad. I did everything exactly like you said. Things are set up perfect."

Alicia relaxed slightly. Roberta had never let her down yet.

"I'm not mad, just concerned. Promise me this thing will go off without a problem."

"Of course it will. We're meeting him tonight in Long Beach." She laughed. "He's in love."

Alicia squinted. "He's selling us restricted metals because he's in love with you?"

"Not me. A girl named Jamaica. Very high maintenance. He needs money bad."

"He's a shipping manager?"

"Yeah."

Alicia went to the bar. She dropped ice cubes into a glass and filled it to the top with single malt Scotch. She handed the glass to Roberta, then made one for herself. When Alicia concentrated her eyes became black, staring, letting out no light.

Roberta got nervous. "What?"

Alicia woke from her trance. "Listen carefully. I just talked to Gregor. You *can't* mess this up, understand?"

Roberta again swallowed an angry retort. "I'm not gonna mess up nothin'. Why are you so jumpy?"

"Lots of reasons. The Carlos thing, for one. You heard about that?"

"You mean the Carlos who ain't here no more?"

"Yes. It was a sloppy hit that just keeps getting worse. Angelo Bracca knows I did it."

"And Angelo is after you?"

"In a way, yes. So is Magnus. That's why this deal has to work fast. *No* problems."

Roberta gestured and Alicia Kent sat next to her. Why in the world had she ever used Carlos when Roberta was available? Roberta had been trained in the Argentine special forces before immigrating to the United States at the age of twenty-six. She had followed that with three years in a private security firm specializing in international business kidnapping. It was there she had met Alicia. Roberta put a hand protectively around Alicia's shoulder. It was a fake act of compassion, like everything Roberta did.

"Don't worry, I won't let evil Magnus get you."

They became strangely quiet. Alicia's hand traced Roberta's jaw line. "I need you here tonight," she said. Her voice was husky.

"Of course." Roberta smiled. "Besides, I have a present for you later."

They talked for an hour, not about the deals, just talk. Then there was a soft knock. Alicia instinctually lurched for her bag but Roberta stopped her with a touch. "Don't worry. It's just your present a bit early."

Roberta opened the door to a young man who could not have been more than nineteen. He was dressed in a blue oxford button-down shirt, white pants and a blue blazer. He was about six feet tall and extremely slim. His hair was close-cropped and his eyes light blue. His face was pale, the lips effeminate. Roberta led him by the hand to Alicia. He stood quietly in front of her.

"This is Peter Lynch," Roberta explained. "Peter, say hi to my my friend, Mary."

"Hello, Mary." The boy's voice was tentative. He had a youngster's face and Alicia was sure he had not even begun to shave.

"How pretty. What's Peter's story?"

"Peter is from Indiana," Roberta explained. "He's a sophomore at UCLA and a member of the gymnastics team. Full scholarship, I believe, isn't that right, Peter?"

"Yes."

"How nice."

"Sort of nice. Peter developed a problem. It seems Indiana is different from L.A. Soon after Peter arrived his new girlfriend introduced him to cocaine. Now, our young man just isn't the same without about two hundred dollars a day going up his nose."

"Peter," Alicia scolded. "Such a nasty habit. And for a gymnast too!"

The boy was mortified as Roberta continued the tale. "Peter's credit line became, shall we say . . . overextended."

"How much does he owe and to whom?"

"He now owes a Hispanic gentleman from East Los Angeles just over sixty thousand dollars. He used to owe a lot more."

Alicia got it. "You're protecting him?"

"Now I am. Once I was hired to kill him."

Alicia smiled. "I see." She stood up and stroked the boy's chest. "He is magnificent. Do you really find much use for him?"

"Sure. Arabs mostly, some Asians."

Men. Of course that's what she'd use him for.

"You charge high fees?"

"Five or ten grand a night. And there's no rules. Just deliver him back alive."

Alicia's eyes hardened. "Well, let's try out young Peter. Has he had his evening pick-me-up?"

"Just before he arrived."

"Then let's begin."

licia Kent and Roberta finished with their UCLA gymnast about 6 P.M., as the sun faded into the green of the Bel Air hills. Then they let him go to his car, red-faced and embarrassed.

"That was fun," Alicia said. "We have to bring him back."

"That won't be hard. I only gave him a gram and a half. He'll be hungry by Thursday night."

Alicia checked the time. "What time is the meeting?"

"Eight."

"Let's go."

It took an hour to get there. Alicia used the time to get a complete debriefing.

"How old is he?"

"Fifty-six."

"Race?"

"Caucasian. Sort of mongrel white I guess you'd say."

"How long with the company?"

"Thirty-two years. First in sales, now in shipping. Graduated from . . ."

Alicia held up her hand. "Just answer my questions."

Roberta bit the nasty response before it came out. She despised how this woman ordered her around. "Sorry. Thirty-two years."

"Schooling?"

"Two years at Cal State Long Beach and then the job at Pacific Aeronautics."

"Married?"

"To a school teacher in a public school outside Long Beach."

"How long?"

Roberta thought for a second. "Twenty-one years. Maybe more."

"Children?"

"Four. Nineteen, fifteen, thirteen and eleven. Two boys, two girls."

"What kind of money's he make?"

Roberta turned onto the 405, heading south. The traffic meandered like a slow moving tidal inlet. "He did okay when he was in sales. He made vice president in 1982. Back then Pacific could sell what it wanted to the military. Those were the Reagen years."

"Party time?"

"Exactly. A lot of money to pass around, and lots of booze and babes to help it get spent."

"They never caught him?"

"Caught him for what? He didn't do anything wrong. If you were in sales, you hustled. The generals love hunting lodges, golf courses . . ."

"Women?"

Roberta smiled. "Sure."

"He got to like that too?"

"He got to love it," Roberta said. "He sampled the girls before he delivered and he drank before he showered. Let that go on for a few years and see what you get."

Alicia was quiet, thinking about it. Those perks would be hard to give up. "Different times now?"

"Way different. No fat generals looking to get laid. No prime contractors looking to select a sub if they get to play Augusta National. Our boy's numbers went way down. That's why he's in shipping now."

"Everybody's numbers went down."

"His went down more. In 1991 he hooked up his computer so it played solitaire. All day he stared at the computer and played solitaire with it."

"No world-class hookers, no coke, no parties, just solitaire on the computer?"

Roberta nodded. "Exactly."

"How long did that last?"

"About three years."

"And then?"

"Then he got fired from sales and demoted to shipping. He tried to straighten out, even went to a shrink who gave him pills. Only our boy mixed the pills with the booze."

Ah, Alicia thought. Perfect. "The women?"

"He couldn't give them up," Roberta said. "Except now he had to pay retail. It turns out even in a recession the price of pussy stays high."

"I see where this is heading."

Roberta lit a cigarette and turned on her blinker. Not exactly where you think, Alicia, she thought, but close enough for now. "Right into the gutter. He paid a lot of women a lot of money before cutting a deal with Jamaica. Now he's in love. For the last six months he paid for her apartment in Torrance."

"Cost?"

"Twelve hundred a month. Plus he picks up utilities, food and lets her use a credit card with a thousand dollar limit."

Alicia smiled. Men were so easy. "And the booze? He still likes that?"

"Day and night."

Alicia never needed help with math, particularly when it involved money.

"Between everything, it's costing him three grand a month to party."

"Sounds right."

"How much does he make?"

"Eighty-four thousand before taxes."

"Eighty-four thousand gross," Alicia said. "He's in a forty percent tax bracket. That's about fifty-three thousand net after taxes. Jamaica and all the rest cost him three grand a month, that's thirty-six grand a year. Leaves him seventeen thousand net. Unless he's living in an igloo with a dog, he's going broke."

Roberta nodded. "Our P.I. says he had a hundred and forty thousand in savings in 1989. Now he has twenty-seven thousand in the bank. He'll be broke in four months."

"And the school teacher at home?"

"She don't know anything. She retired to raise the kids. She'll believe any line he gives her."

Alicia reached for the champagne bottle under her seat. "Roberta, you're beautiful."

For now, Roberta thought. For now. "Thank you."

"Our friend needs a supplemental source of income."

"Like a junkie needs junk."

Alicia sipped the champagne. "What's our pigeon's name?"

"Arnold Messer. He told Jamaica his name is John Doe, so that's what I call him."

"How devious of Arnold." She shivered, getting ready to enjoy the evening. When she had sex with Portov she was acting. But abusive acts with a strange boy or girl she'd never see again required no act at all.

"Hey, Roberta?"

"Yes."

"When we're done in Long Beach, I want Peter back."

She sighed silently, still patient. "Sure."

They arrived in Long Beach as the sun dipped into the grimy Pacific outside the harbor. The Greek and Turkish merchant seamen had long since left their boats for the dockside brothels. The bars near the wharfs were full. Roberta parked the car outside a bar called Fantasy Island.

"This is where Jamaica works?"

"Yeah."

"Let's go meet her."

Inside was about what Alicia Kent expected. There was a stage, backlit, crowded with naked women. There were men, sitting uselessly, letting women grind against them. It was an even trade, the male financial dominance against the female sexual dominance, both sides simultaneously degraded by the oddity of it all.

Alicia Kent turned abruptly to Roberta.

"What now?"

"Now we find out whether John Doe is ready to deal." They sat at a table, two women, and tried not to pay too much attention to the look of the men upon them.

Eventually Jamaica took the stage. She was Caribbean and had large breasts and a round, brown bottom. She took off all her clothes and the men hooted. When she was done, she came over to the table where Alicia and Roberta sat.

"Is your name Adrienne?" the girl asked.

"Absolutely," Alicia said.

"I have some news for you."

"Yes?"

"He's waiting for you, has been all day."

Roberta shut up and let Alicia talk. Her turn would come, just not yet. "Where is he?"

"He's at his apartment. But he says the money's not good enough. He told me to give you this."

Roberta stiffened. Alicia lit a cigarette and read the note slowly. The message was a threat to back out unless the money improved. She blew out the smoke slowly and put the note in her pocket.

"Give him a message for me. Tell him if he doesn't show in one hour, the deal's off. Tomorrow a memorandum will be delivered to his employer explaining his treachery. This handwritten note"—she held it up—"will be attached." What a moron, Alicia thought, a handwritten note.

The girl squinted. "Treachery?"

"He'll get it."

"You want me to tell him that? He'll be really pissed."

"One hour," Alicia said. "And tell him even if his company doesn't get him, we will. He's way too dangerous to keep around." She thought of Professor Ashforth in London, and the old man in Paterson. Yeah, same thing.

The girl's eyes widened. "Okay."

As Alicia expected, Arnold Messer, aka John Doe, arrived forty-five minutes later. His face was drawn. He had a paunch and wore a white, short-sleeved shirt. His thick glasses sat upon a pair of lumps under his eyes.

"Hi," he said extending his hand. "My name is John Doe."

"Nice to meet you, John," Alicia said. "I'm Adrienne and this is my friend, Belinda."

John Doe's smile fluttered as he tried to convey a confident manner. "You girls look good. Tonight's amateur night. You ought to compete."

"What a sweet compliment," Alicia said. "What do you think, Belinda?"

"I think it's a great idea, Adrienne. Maybe after we finish with John here."

Alicia sighed. "She's just all business. Anyway, I guess that's what we should do now."

Arnold Messer's face was beaten by life. He looked around warily. "It's a weird place to do business."

"It's a weird world, John," Alicia agreed.

They spent the next half hour going through the details. The shipping documents would show a phony buyer—a company named Guajira Mining—purchasing *conventional* beryllium for copper mining in Nigeria. The actual shipment of *nuclear-grade* beryllium would leave LAX for Peru and be transferred to a charter flight bound for Barbados. The plane would then refuel and fly across the Atlantic to Lagos, Nigeria, for final delivery to Josef Alexeyev. Half the cash would be paid to John Doe when the charter left Lima and half when it left Barbados. Only when he got paid would he call his contacts and authorize the flight to depart each airport.

"See, that wasn't so hard," Alicia said.

John Doe's head nodded dumbly in reply. "I'll make sure the shipping documents show conventional beryllium. We won't have a problem."

"Excellent."

When they had it all worked out, John Doe left, fading into the crush of males in business suits at the bar. Alicia was pensive, figuring out all the possible holes in the deal. Roberta was pensive too, but for different reasons, for a different agenda.

"It's a big risk," Alicia said finally.

Roberta listened carefully. "You mean whether this guy will deliver?"

"Whether he'll deliver, whether he'll turn on us, anything."

Roberta wasn't worried. Not about this. "Don't panic, baby, there's a lot of money here."

"And a lot of time to be dead if I'm wrong." She sighed and lit a cigarette, oblivious to the chaos around her. "Damn! I need somebody watching him now!"

"How about the girl?"

Alicia's head swiveled. "Jamaica?"

"Yeah."

"Not bad. Is she still here?"

"Sure." Roberta gestured toward the stage on which the women danced. "She controls this guy is what I see."

"Bring her over."

Jamaica came right away. Alicia spoke to her for fifteen minutes, slowly, telling her everything she needed to know and nothing more.

"I get a thousand a week?"

"That's right. Cash money." Alicia gestured to Roberta, who put some bills on the table.

"Here's five hundred as a down payment. Belinda will get you the other five when you check in with her. If you *once* fail to check in or don't tell us *everything*, you don't get paid."

"Don't worry. I just tell you what he's doing?"

"What he's doing, who he's talking to, everything. Belinda will call you every two hours."

Jamaica smiled. "You got a deal." Then she was gone.

Alicia felt better. Now she'd be able to keep track of the guy. Plus when it came time to get rid of loose ends, Jamaica would be right there.

"Hey, Roberta?"

"Yeah?"

"We're done for the night."

"Okay."

"I want Peter back. Now!"

Yes, massah, Roberta thought.

33

Natala de Marco had never felt so bad in her life. It was 8 A.M. and she hadn't slept in twenty-four hours. She now had a screaming headache from the half bottle of Seagram's she consumed in Pasty's office and her breast hurt more than her head. She could handle the exhaustion and the pain. What she couldn't handle was her stupid brother and her stupid boyfriend now suddenly deciding to become buddies.

Boyle and Bracca usually got into more arguments than Boyle and Natala did, which was hard. This time, maybe because they were both angry at her, they had found common ground. They sat at the table, drank Scotch, and talked about Patsy's murder. Natala had been ignored for hours, which was hours more than she ever got ignored.

"I would appreciate it," she said finally, "if you two clowns would stop playing around and figure out what we're going to do." She sat in a chair, topless, dabbing alcohol on the teeth marks. Neither one of these slugs was offering to help.

"Just a minute," John Bracca said. Then they ignored her for another half hour. Boyle told Bracca everything about his meetings at the Paterson police department and his evening with the mysterious AUSA, Stephanie Shane. He decided to leave out the part about where he spent the night until Natala squinted.

"You went back to Paterson and then came back here in the morning?"

He coughed. "No, I found a place over here, you know."

"That's not important," John said quickly. His face had gotten taut when Boyle talked about his meeting with Stephanie. "I want to know exactly who the government thinks killed Patsy."

"You won't believe it."

"Try me," John Bracca said evenly.

"She thinks Angelo did it."

Natala looked up from her dabbing. "What?"

Boyle shrugged. "She thinks we're all tied into the Krasna organization. You're sort of like Sharon Stone in *Casino*."

John stood up. Everything he had done to this point had been worthless. Shane *still* thought it was Angelo.

"Anyway," Boyle continued, "this might not be a bad time to go visit her." He gestured to his sister. "You'll have to put a shirt on though, much as I'm sure you'd love to flash those beauties."

She never looked up. "Hey, Tommy, screw you."

A licia Kent lay naked on the bed, sweat-soaked, for a moment sated, sipping a glass of ice cold rosé champagne. Roberta escorted the sobbing gymnast to the door, then gave him brusque instructions. Next to Alicia was a simple bedside phone with three outside lines. The third number was known only to Portov and Magnus.

Alicia picked up the phone on the third ring. "Hello, Gregor."

The voice on the other end laughed and she stiffened. "Magnus?"

"Good evening," the man said easily.

She could feel her concentration rise. Two calls from Magnus was very unusual these days.

"Well, this is certainly interesting. What do you want now?"

"Want?" Magnus said slowly. "Quite a bit, my little viper, quite a bit."

Roberta sat next to her on the bed. Alicia pushed her roughly away. Roberta let herself be pushed. For now.

"What? Tell me?"

"Alicia," Magnus continued, "do you remember we once had a long discussion about honesty? And trust?"

That was a long time ago, when he got her into the Council. "Sure, Magnus."

"And you remember what I told you would happen if you ever betrayed me?"

She leaned back on the pillow. She didn't need this. "I remember all your threats, Magnus. They started to bore me a long time ago."

The man's voice thickened. "Bore you? You must have thought I was kidding, perhaps just engaging in hyperbole."

"No, Magnus, just that your threats were meaningless. And right now you're putting me to sleep. So if you have something to say, spit it out."

"When was it, my dear, that you decided to lie about me to the Braccas?"

"I don't know what you're talking about. I haven't spoken to Angelo in ages. And I never talk about you."

"Don't lie to me, Alicia."

"I'm not lying."

"I repeat, when did you tell Angelo Bracca that I ordered the old man's murder?"

She stiffened. So Magnus *knew* the lie that Angelo had been told. But Magnus thought *she* had lied to Angelo, not Portov. That meant he was still guessing.

"Magnus, I'm sorry. You're not making any sense."

"No sense?" Purcell's voice was barely-contained fury. The stress, the booze, the threats, they were slowly destroying him. "Well maybe the Council will make sense of it when they learn of it all. Everything, including our broker friend."

"No!" she said quickly. "The broker is *my*, I mean *our* separate deal."

"*Our* separate deal?" He laughed. "Once it was, before you betrayed me. Now it's going to be mine alone. So if you don't want everything in a fax to the Council tonight you'll meet me at LAX. I'm catching the next plane out."

Alicia considered it. Yes, there was danger, also opportunity.

"I'm working with Roberta. What about her?"

"I want her there, too, where I can watch both of you. I'll tell you what I want then."

Now she knew she had to meet him. "All right. I agree."

"But Alicia, even if you do everything I say?"

"Yes?"

"You are underestimating me, I promise."

He said it to frighten her. Instead she just smirked, and felt an icy calm, which was actually pleasant.

"Never you, Magnus."

Magnus Purcell arrived in Los Angeles from New York on the first redeye. He could find The city sparkled beneath him, ten million lights on a flat desert floor, ringed by the blackness of ocean and mountain. A staggeringly beautiful sight from the air, less so from the ground in the smog of the day, or, more ominously, in the night corners hidden among the sparkling lights.

He left the terminal with no baggage except a nondescript briefcase, then eased his massive bulk into the back of a black car waiting. The driver asked where he wanted to go in a heavy accent. Magnus stared in shock. The accent was Russian!

"Did Portov send you?"

"What?"

"You were sent by Portov, right? I must tell you that killing me will do you no good."

The man squinted. "I'm sorry but English . . ." Then he brightened. "I was physicist in Sverdlosk. And Jew." His hands swept the air again. "I get out, now drive limos, cars, cabs sometimes."

The whole thing was too strange to be true. "Are there many of you here? Russians, I mean?"

More of the fluttering hand. "All drivers here Russian. Where you from?"

"New York."

The man laughed. "All Indians there."

"What?"

"You know, Indians." The man twirled a finger around his head. "What you call it . . . the white thing?"

"A turban?"

"Yes, yes." The man pointed to his forehead. "With dot in head."

Sikhs. "Yes, that's right."

"So where?" the man asked. There were horns honking behind them.

"The Hilton," Magnus said. "Just the Hilton."

The driver frowned. "Long time to get here. Short ride."

Magnus took out a crisp hundred and threw it on the front seat. "Say a Russian prayer for me."

The man grinned. "Da, da."

Alicia Kent and Roberta waited for Magnus in Room 2307 of the Airport Hilton. Alicia was at her most focused and cautious. The anonymity of the giant hotel meant it could also be unsafe. Maybe Magnus would send someone in his place. Maybe the door would be opened by Miguel Meza on a mission of death. The bodies of two women, without identification, would be found by the maid the next morning, bullets expertly entered into the backs of their heads. And nobody, but nobody, would care.

Alicia told Roberta enough to keep her on edge, not enough to make her knowledgeable.

"I want you armed," she told Roberta. "Just in case something strange happens."

Roberta was always armed. And always ready. "You got it."

"Dress like you're working. But don't draw attention to yourself."

More orders. Like she didn't know what she was doing. "Okay."

Roberta wore black jeans and high-topped black athletic shoes. A combat knife was taped in a sheath along her legs, disappearing into the shoes. On top, she wore a white T-shirt and a loose-fitting beige jacket. The harness for the ever-present Browning .38 was stitched into the jacket. It sat neat and available against her left breast. Over her shoulder was a stylish bag containing a Ruger P-90, a .45 caliber semiautomatic. The bag was made of light brown leather.

Magnus was due to arrive just after midnight. Alicia inspected the room, turned out most of the lights and placed a bottle of Grand Marnier on the table. She had purchased it from a liquor store miles away, not from the hotel. She set two glasses next to it, then sat in an upholstered chair and crossed her legs.

When the insistent knock came, she glanced at Roberta, who sat facing the door with her hand wrapped around the P-90 in her purse. If Magnus entered, she would rise, set the purse aside and greet him. If it wasn't Magnus, she would fire through the bottom of the soft leather bag.

There was no need to fire. The giant man burst through the unlocked door, ignoring the two women. He walked to the table, inspected the brandy and poured a glass half-full. He drank it easily and poured another. He didn't offer her any.

Alicia waited. After he had drunk the second glass, he wiped his mouth with the back of his hand. Then he stood, walked to her and yanked her by the hair, exposing her neck. She sat quietly, calm.

"You will suffer for this," he whispered. "I promise you."

Alicia still said nothing. Roberta shifted expectantly. When Magnus yanked Alicia's hair back further, she made a small noise and Roberta rose.

"Okay, that's enough." Roberta was up and had the Browning .38 in her hand.

"No," Alicia shouted. She needed information from Magnus, not a confrontation. "She doesn't understand. I need her. *We* need her."

Magnus let go of Alicia's hair and walked to Roberta. He pressed his stomach hard against the gun and smiled.

"Roberta," Alicia said. "Listen to me carefully. Put the gun down very slowly."

Roberta turned to her and never saw the backhanded slap that whipped her head to the side. Then the man grabbed her gun and slapped her twice more. The gun fell to the floor. Magnus picked it up.

Roberta stayed on her feet, staring at Magnus with professional cool. But slightly below the cool there was purpose replacing resentment. She could kill Magnus easily, even without her gun. She could kill both of them in fact. Not yet.

Magnus was breathing heavily, his face red and spotted with white blotches. The pump that was sending the blood through his body was having a hard time of it, and not getting to all the important places. Roberta saw Alicia's signal, right hand outstretched, palm down. She moved closer to Magnus and held her chin up, to give him a better shot. As she expected, he swung again, this time with fist closed. She spun her face to deflect the force of the blow, a slipped punch that Boyle and Meza would have admired. She groaned as if she'd been killed and fell faceforward with her leather bag underneath her. Magnus turned back to Alicia.

"You didn't have to do that," she said.

Magnus had the Browning in his hand and played with it. "You made a serious mistake. I had nothing to do with the old man's death and you know it!" She saw that he was drunk, which meant his judgment was shot. Just like when he betrayed the Council.

"You're the one making a mistake. You're paranoid. I'm sorry, Magnus, but no one is betraying you."

He sighed, letting the breath go out slowly. "We're all sorry."

The room got quiet. Her mood had passed from careful concentration to calm resolve. Alicia didn't know it yet, but so had Roberta's.

"Can I ask you something?"

"Of course," Magnus said, enjoying his brandy and his gun.

"Have you told the Council about the bond broker?"

"Not yet. I'm flying to London in two hours."

"But you told Angelo Bracca?"

"Yes, but he doesn't believe me. He assigned one of his people to make sure the broker dies. I believe you know the man."

Alicia again made a small gesture and Roberta lay still. "What's his name?"

"I don't remember."

Alicia pressed. "Goddamnit, what's his name? I have to know who's following me."

"He's the son of a man you killed."

"Could you be more specific?"

"De Marco."

She silently cursed. "Meza? Does the name Meza ring a bell?" She prayed that Portov had been wrong.

"It doesn't matter, Alicia. You won't have to worry about it."

That wasn't true but it no longer mattered. She was now convinced she had all the information he had to give. She deflected her gaze toward Roberta, who was awake, and waiting.

"I'm sorry, Alicia," her mentor said again.

To her surprise, Alicia felt the same. They had once understood each other, and worked well together. He was once the most important man in her life, for whom she would have done anything, and for a brief time she thought he was the one that would make her whole. He wasn't, just as none of them ever were.

"Me too," she said simply.

Her casualness unnerved him. His hand shook slightly as he raised the gun. Roberta was up and watching.

"What about her?"

Magnus had his back to Roberta. "You know the answer to that. There must be no witnesses."

"Really?" a voice said.

Magnus turned slowly, in control, the Browning still in his hand. Roberta stood with her feet spread, the leather bag covering her breasts.

"I don't think that will be much protection."

Roberta never moved, just stared.

"Do it," Alicia said.

The bag shifted. Magnus' laugh was deep. "Please don't hit me with your purse," he begged.

The Ruger exploded. A dozen .45-caliber bullets ripped from a high speed semiautomatic weapon into Magnus' fat chest, each no more than a quarter-inch from the others, the whole thing taking 2.6 seconds. Magnus' heart burst with the first round and the eleven brethren were just for show. It took a surprisingly long time for the fat man to fall, and when he did, he fell forward. Newtonian physics at work, Alicia supposed.

Alicia walked up to the body and kicked the very dead Magnus repeatedly in the head. "You pig. You were going to kill me. You pig!"

Kill *us*, Roberta wanted to say, but didn't. She put a gentle hand on Alicia's arm. "Shh. Pigs die like this. Don't worry about it."

Alicia stepped back from Magnus, stone dead on the floor. The bitterness in her throat surprised her. "Scream in hell, fat man. Say hello to Elmer for me."

34

After they killed Magnus, Alicia and Roberta exited the Hilton efficiently and very anonymously. Alicia's hands were rock still as she slipped the Mexican valet a few bucks. The man spoke no English and sprinted away from Alicia's car to help with the mobs of Japanese tourists entering and leaving the hotel. Nobody remembered them at all.

At three in the morning they were back at the Bel Air house. Alicia wandered out onto the rear balcony and found the door unlocked. She didn't like that at all.

"Did you leave this open?"

"I don't know, maybe."

"How could you be so stupid!" Alicia slammed the door, locked it and grabbed the gun from her bag.

Stupid? Roberta thought. Stupid? "Hey," she said, "all that's out there is a bunch of golfers. Don't worry about it."

Alicia pointed to the bar. "Don't mouth at me! I'm inspecting this place and taking a bath. Bring up some ice."

"Sure, Alicia, no problem. Anything you say."

A half hour later, Alicia emerged from the tub. Roberta sat waiting for her, still in her black jeans and a halter top, her shoulders wide and muscled. Alicia grabbed a short, satin dressing gown and sat next to her.

"I want you to listen to me very closely. We are in danger, do you realize that?"

Roberta shrugged. "I'm always in danger. And I'm always careful after a hit."

Alicia grabbed the woman's face so they were nose to nose. "You're not listening to me, goddamn it. This is Meza that's after me."

Roberta yanked her face away. She barely squelched the desire to destroy her then and there. But that would do her no good.

"So what? Meza's one guy. What do you know about him? What's to scary?"

Alicia stood up, pacing, staring out at the now black golf course. It was hard to make people understand. It had been impossible with Portov so far.

"Okay, let me try. We use killers all the time. Carlos, you, and a lot more. You're all professionals, the best we can find, and mostly get the job done. Sometimes not perfectly, like Carlos."

She turned back to Roberta. "I've wanted to use Meza for years. For a time I was *obsessed* with him. I *studied* him. I know more about Meza than almost anyone alive."

Roberta was listening, but still didn't get it. "Okay. So what did you find out?"

"I found out that . . . that he's almost a ghost."

Now Roberta laughed out loud. "What?"

"Yes, a malicious, sadistic ghost. His intelligence and craft are almost supernatural. He *knows* what his enemy is planning before the victim even knows. He can kill with anything, his hands very easily, knives, guns of all kinds, even ordinary items." She paused. "And he's killed a lot, more than anyone knows."

Roberta shrugged. "So have we. Matter of fact just a few hours ago."

Alicia shook her head. "That was different. It was simple." She paused, thinking, remembering. "Meza was only on the wrong side of me once," she said quietly. "That was enough."

"Yeah? What happened that was so scary?"

"We had a customer who had a very beautiful, young wife. Very vain and half his age, also very expensive. Our customer wanted control of a competitor's very successful business. He needed the owner to sell cheaply. The man refused. So we kidnaped the owner's twelve-year-old son."

"That'll get his attention."

"Yes. The owner was Italian and called Angelo. Angelo called Meza." She sighed. "We gave the man a deadline to sell. It passed. So we acted."

"You killed the kid?"

Alicia shook her head. "No. The boy had a distinctive birthmark on the back of his left hand. We had the hand surgically removed. Without anesthesia. And videotaped the horror of the boy's screams."

Roberta shuddered. This was like old Argentina! "Nice. Then a new deadline for the right hand. After Daddy gets the tape and the severed hand?"

"Yes." Even Alicia hadn't liked that play. But once made there was no turning back. "There were four operatives involved, not me, it wasn't my deal. The four were the surgeon and three kidnappers. Plus the customer, of course, and the wife, so six all together. Meza figured out who the customer was right away. He just *knew*. Just *knew*."

"And?"

"And then one day the customer came home. The house was quiet. He called out to his lovely young wife and three lovely little children. Nothing."

"Meza killed them?"

Alicia shook her head. "No. The customer found all four in the garage. The wife had been expertly disfigured. There wasn't an inch of her face that wasn't cut to pieces. The children had watched. And had . . ."

"Been mutilated? The left hand?"

"No," Alicia said slowly. "Only the wife. The face destroyed and *both* hands gone. The kids unharmed. Except for numbers written on their hands. And a note that said this was the order the kids' hands would be severed if the boy wasn't returned immediately."

Roberta didn't say anything for a long time. Neither of them did.

"The kidnaped boy . . . returned?"

"Yes, within an hour. The customer was left alive, to live with it all. The surgeon, the three operatives, all went into hiding. It took Meza thirty days to find them all, one by one."

"Dead?"

"Very. The operatives were given professional courtesy, a single bullet to the brain. The surgeon was not so lucky. Meza hung him."

"What?"

"Yes. In a rather nasty way. He stood the man naked on a block of ice with a wire around his neck. Then Meza sat in a chair and pointed a heat lamp at the ice. He watched while the ice melted and the wire tightened. It took three hours. Meza never said a word. The surgeon's begging was recorded and left there."

"I see," Roberta said slowly. "I think I'm getting the picture. Now what exactly does this ghost want with you?"

"Angelo hired him to make sure I wipe this broker."

Roberta opened her hands. "Alicia, I say do whatever Angelo wants. No questions asked."

"I agree. But how do I do that and still do Long Beach?"

Roberta had thought about that. It actually worked perfectly. "The only way I figure it will work is if we split up. I know Long Beach so I do that. You do the broker because that's what this ghost wants you to do."

Alicia liked that. It made sense. "Not bad. I need that stuff on a plane in the next twenty-four hours. You understand?"

Jesus, what a bitch, Roberta thought. Of course she understood. "Trust me, I can handle it. Let's go over to my house and grab my truck. We'll come back and sleep here in case Portov calls. Tomorrow we go our separate ways and do what we got to do."

Alicia shook her head in agreement. She usually didn't like changes in plans but had to admit this one made sense. Both deals get done, Portov's happy, Angelo's happy, and she gets all the juice from the bond deal. Plus, most important, Meza goes away. Roberta moved closer to her on the couch and touched her bare leg.

"Not now," Alicia snapped.

"Later?"

"After the broker's gone, after the beryllium is delivered, there'll be plenty of time."

Roberta gave her a fake grin. "I can't wait."

The women were gone for ten minutes and the house was quiet when Christine turned to Meza. There were tears in her eyes. "They're lying, right? You never did that."

Meza didn't answer. "Forget about that. Let's get out of this closet. I'm sweating to death." He glanced toward the light in the kitchen. "I can't believe I forgot to lock the damn door."

They walked out of the closet and into the bedroom. The

room was dark. Meza flipped on a light. "They're gone, no doubt about it."

Christine buried her face in her hands. She was crying hard. And scared. Meza sat on the bed next to her.

"Please, please tell me they lied."

He reached for her and pulled her close. She was stiff at first and then melted into him.

"It didn't happen that way," he said. "They wanted to do the kids but I said no." He paused, knowing he had left that garage with four people tied to chairs, and Angelo's men and the father inside. But they knew if they touched the kids he would have turned. Plus, he spoke for Angelo. "I won't lie though. I did the doctor. And the three other guys." He breathed hard. "The wife was the one who wanted the kid's hand cut. I got everybody into the garage. The boy's father did it all to her after I left."

She spoke into his shoulder. "I don't care about her. She deserved it."

He pushed her away and wiped the tears away. "Listen, let's forget that. I need you. You want to help me?"

"Really? You want me to?"

He knew it was a mistake but he had no choice. "Really. We got to stay here and watch for them to come back."

"Here?"

"Not in the house, just nearby. I have to follow the hitter tomorrow. We need to stake the place tonight." He grabbed her face. "And you do *exactly* what I tell you."

She forced a grin through the strength of his hands. "You love me, admit it."

"Yeah, you get killed, I'm back to the guy across the fence watching me work out."

She wrapped her arms around his neck and squeezed so hard it hurt her. "You love me, I can tell. You're just trying to be cool."

"Forget that. Just listen to me for once. Every single thing I tell you, you do. Just like I say."

"Hey, Migo?"

"Yeah?"

"They'll be gone for awhile."

"Yeah?"

She snapped a button on her blouse. There was serious purpose in her eyes. This was not for fun. It was for closure on the horror of the story she had heard. "They already rumpled the bed. They'll never be able to tell."

oyle, Natala and John Bracca arrived at the U.S. Attorney's
office in Foley Square at nine. They had to negotiate the same
phalanx of secretaries, agents and metal detectors as Boyle
had the first time, except now, once past it all, they were ushered in
quickly. She was standing at the door of her office, hands on her
hips, not at all pleased to see him.

"I thought I told you not to come back."

"You did. And I told you I would. Plus I brought some friends
who want to meet you."

When she didn't respond he walked past her into her office. A
man sat quietly in a straight-backed government chair, sipping
coffee.

"Hi," Boyle said, extending his hand.

"Hello," the man in the chair said.

There was a moment of awkwardness while everybody stared at
one another. Stephanie recovered first.

"I'll say it again. What are you people doing in my office?"

"We're here to talk to you about Patsy De Marco's murder,"
Boyle said. "This is his daughter, Natala. The guy over there is John
Bracca."

Bracca barely nodded at her. Her eyes flicked across his face and
then away, as though slightly embarrassed. Boyle watched the
exchange.

The man in the chair did not get introduced. John gestured to
him. "Maybe this gentleman should tell us who he is."

"Don't answer that," Stephanie snapped.

The man shrugged. "Stephanie, it's time we all put our cards on
the table."

M y name is Special Agent James Keller," the man began. "I am an FBI agent assigned to the Organized Crime Task Force, U.S. Department of Justice."

Boyle poured himself some coffee. "We got an expert on that here."

Natala rolled her eyes. "He's a defective. Just ignore him."

"Three years ago," Keller continued, "we began following a criminal named Gregor Portov, an American of Russian descent who works with a Russian national named Josef Alexeyev. Alexeyev is the head of the main branch of what the Russians call the *Mafiya*. He is responsible for twelve murders in Moscow and six in Lithuania that we know of."

"What does this have to do with my father?"

"Quite a bit. Eighteen months ago Portov and Alexeyev decided to establish closer relationships with American groups."

"Let me guess what that means," Boyle muttered.

"You're correct. They made a deal with a family in North Jersey."

"Say it all," John Bracca ordered.

"All right. Portov's partner is Angelo Bracca. In lots of deals."

The blood drained from Natala's face. John Bracca just stared at the agent, his expression revealing nothing.

Stephanie felt the whole thing spinning out of control. Although Braxton wasn't in the room this was Braxton's agent and Braxton's theory. "I think you've said enough."

"No!" John's voice was flat. "Say it all."

"Portov and Bracca have been involved in drug importation and money laundering together. Plus some smuggling."

"Of what?"

"That's . . . unclear."

"They killed Patsy because they were smuggling?"

"Sort of."

"Not a word more!" Stephanie ordered.

Boyle leaned forward. "Patsy found out what they were storing at the old silk mill, right? That's why they killed him?"

Keller shrugged. "Maybe. Or maybe he stumbled into enough to scare them." He bowed in Natala's direction. "I'm sorry."

John Bracca's eyes were blazing. "My father would never permit that," he said, speaking as much to Natala as the agent.

Natala turned to him and the crack of her slap was loud. John didn't move, just took another one, and the screamed curses that went with the slaps. She hit him five times before Boyle gently pulled her away. John's face was bright red and his lip puffed.

"I'm afraid I agree with this girl, Mr. Bracca," Keller said simply. "Angelo arranged for the space. We know that."

Bracca turned to Boyle. "Don't say anything, just answer one question. Can you take care of her for the next few hours?"

"A hell of a lot better than you, Bracca."

"Good. My apartment's yours. Stay with her for the rest of the day."

"It'll be a lot longer than that before you see her, Bracca."

"I know of one problem you might want to consider," Stephanie said. "He has only ninety-six dollars."

"Less actually. I had to take a cab this morning."

John Bracca took a wad of bills and jammed them in Boyle's hand. "Don't say a word. Just take care of her today."

"Where are you going?"

His eyes had a faraway look. "Paterson."

The South Paterson Athletic Club is a two-story wood frame building with a simple sign that doesn't reveal anything. It was built in the 1920s and hasn't changed much since. The only athletic activity that had taken place over the last eighty years was the tossing of dice and the shuffling of decks. But to Angelo it was home.

Angelo sat with Nick in a booth when John walked in. About twenty members of Angelo's crew milled around playing cards and smoking cigars. They looked up when John entered and nodded with respect. When Angelo saw his son he jumped up, wrapped his arms around him and kissed him on both cheeks.

"John, sit down. Bring him some coffee."

John sat down silently. His father knew right away something was wrong.

"All right, take a sip of your coffee, take a deep breath and tell me."

"You're not going to like what I have to say."

His father spread his hands. "There ain't nothin' in this world you could say would bother me."

"I'm working with the government."

The silence crashed into the room like a train. John's words had filtered through the air and the gunmen just stared open mouthed, like Angelo and Nick.

"What?"

"That's right. With an AUSA who's investigating Patsy De Marco's death."

Angelo slumped. No one in the room moved. "Jesus, John."

His son leaned forward. "Patsy called me a week before he died. He wanted protection because of the warehouse. I told him, don't worry, my father would never harm you. A week later he's murdered."

"John," Angelo began.

"Wait. I told the government it wasn't you, couldn't be you, and I'm workin' my ass off to prove that. But now I find out you're working with Russians and were smuggling in there. So tell me. Did you order Patsy De Marco hit?"

Nick coughed hard, like something got caught in his throat. His father looked old and his voice cracked when he spoke.

"You think I'd have that old man hit? With my son living with his daughter?"

"With your son in love with his daughter. I need to hear you say it, Pop."

"I swear on your grandmother's grave, John, I didn't do it."

"Somebody did."

"That," his father said, "is correct."

"I want to know who."

Angelo turned involuntarily to Nick, who was studying his fingernails. Now back to his son. "John, it's complicated. I'm trying to get a read on it. Right now it's none of your affair."

His son's eyes flashed and Angelo wanted to yank the words back. John had the same temper as Angelo. "It's none of my what?"

Angelo felt like a rat in a maze. "John, I . . ."

His son leaned over the table. "Look, I don't want to be disrespectful. But I demand to know everything you know, who did it, why and what you're doing about it."

None of the schemes flashing through Angelo's brain made sense. Sometimes you just got to open up. His son, maybe above all people, had a right to know.

"Nick," he said. "Take John for a walk, away from the mikes. Tell him everything."

John Bracca made one phone call before heading home and got back to his apartment an hour after dark. Boyle was sitting on the couch drinking a beer. Natala was curled in a chair wearing one of his shirts and that was all. Her feet were under her and she was sleeping peacefully. She looked more beautiful than on any runway.

"Hi," John said. He tossed his coat on the floor.

Boyle never even looked up. "How was Paterson? Get any nice ziti?"

"I met with my father. Here's what I know." John repeated it all, how and why Patsy died, and who did it. "A guy named Magnus Purcell ordered it. He's working with a woman who was the real killer."

"Really? That's Angelo's story, huh? So where's this mysterious Russian now? Where's the woman? Where's this Purcell guy?"

"My father doesn't know where the Russian is, Tommy. The woman is in Los Angeles. She's supposed to be there on business that has nothing to do with Patsy. Angelo doesn't believe it."

"So, what's he doing about it? Playing dice at the SPAC?"

"Angelo has Miguel checking her out. Only Meza doesn't know yet that the woman killed Patsy."

Natala had woken. She refused to look at Bracca but heard it all. "I'm going out there," she said.

John sighed. "I knew you'd say that. I tried to call Miguel, no answer, just a machine. Look, it's a five-hour flight to Los Angeles and we pick up three hours on the way. There's a nonstop United out of JFK at eight in the morning and four-thirty in the afternoon. I say let's get some sleep tonight and take the morning flight out."

Her look at him was venomous. "I say you shut up and go back to Daddy."

Boyle decided to get while the getting was good. "Can somebody get me a lift back to Jersey while you guys do this arguing thing?"

"No," John Bracca said. "I'm staying here. You're going with her."

"With ninety-six dollars? Well, now eighty-four dollars."

"Boyle, don't insult me. All that's taken care of."

Natala walked to her brother and got right in his face. "Will you come with me? I don't want this scum's money. I've got plenty."

Boyle took her face in his hands and kissed the top of her head. "Of course."

36

Stephanie Shane had been stunned when the weird trio of Bracca, Boyle and Natala De Marco appeared in her office. She was still in a state of shock when they left. Keller, the agent Braxton sent to help her, laughed.

"Let me guess. No appointment?"

Stephanie returned to earth. "Good guess. Now what do we do?"

Keller shrugged. "I say we keep an eye on Angelo Bracca. He's the brains there. I'm not concerned about these three. Boyle especially don't look too swift."

Stephanie coughed a little at that one. "Whatever you say." Let the FBI chase Angelo forever. She believed John. Angelo Bracca did not kill Patsy De Marco. "Will you call Braxton and report all this?"

"Sure."

Special Agent James Keller left Stephanie Shane's office and smiled amiably at the other agents and attorneys he passed in the hall. He walked into his office, closed the door and called Braxton, just as he promised he would do. He called on a line both private and scrambled. Braxton picked up before the first ring ended. "What?" he said abruptly.

"Bracca, Boyle and the girl were just here. They met with Shane."

There was a silence. "Bracca?"

"You got it."

"I pray you don't mean Angelo Bracca."

"No, John, but it's worse than Angelo. John's smart."

"I know he is. I know all about John." Braxton sat back and thought it through. John Bracca had the ability to discover everything Angelo knew or suspected. More importantly, between John Bracca and Shane, they had the ability to put the whole thing together.

"Has John been out to see Angelo?"

"He's heading there now."

Braxton slammed a fist onto his desk. "We waited too long!"

"You're right. But we still got time to clean this up. What do you want me to do?"

The days of just tailing John Bracca were over. Now it was time to act. If they did it right the whole mess would look like a typical mob brawl, Patsy's death, Bracca's death, all of it. Angelo would go nuts, have his people shoot everything that moved, which would then *really* look like a mob brawl.

"Tell Gregor everything you know. And tell him I think John Bracca should go tonight."

"You got it."

Around 10 P.M. John Bracca left Boyle and Natala at his apartment and drove aimlessly around Manhattan hunting for the tail he was sure was there. As Angelo's son, John had been followed since he was old enough to walk, pros and amateurs alike, and he knew what to look for. But this guy, whoever it was, was good, more than professional, which made the whole thing more than dangerous.

Finally he left Manhattan altogether and drove out to JFK. He parked, walked to a pay phone in the American terminal and called the private line in Stephanie's office. A mechanical recording tied to a beeper answered.

"Hi, it's me, I'm at the airport. I'm sure I'm still being followed and I think they'll try something soon. Meet me in Spain at noon. Important."

Before he left the airport, he checked the monitor for the American arrivals. A Chicago flight was unloading in ten minutes and he went to greet it. The gate was chaotic as hundreds of departing passengers lugging carry-on luggage slammed into limo drivers with signs and relatives holding up children. When the crowd was thickest he mingled easily with it and was transported by the river of people toward the baggage carousels.

At the cab stand he was tapped by a Lebanese with an outlaw car. John said nothing, just pointed to the curb. The man scurried away and returned with a nondescript Mercury. John Bracca slid quietly into the backseat. He would leave his car in the lot, let them watch that.

"Where to?"

"Central Park South. In front of the Plaza."

"Fifty, okay?"

"Fine."

He put on a pair of sunglasses even though it was now 11 P.M. The outlaw driver knew when to shut up. He pointed the Mercury toward Manhattan and drove.

At the Plaza, Bracca paid the driver and was gone like a thief in the night. He entered the hotel by the front entrance and intermingled with twenty partygoers in tuxes. The doorman held the door open and said "Good evening" over and over. The doorman's eyes were glazed and saw no one.

Bracca strolled nonchalantly through the hotel, staring sightlessly at jewelry and clothes exhibits. Periodically he turned slowly around, taking careful note of the faces, making sure there were no repeats.

At the end of the corridor a set of stairs led to a downstairs bar. He walked down the stairs, around the bar, in and out of the men's room, then back up the stairs. Halfway up he stopped and waited. No one followed. He took off the sunglasses.

At the top of the steps was the Oak Room, crowded and noisy. He sat at the far end of the bar and ordered a beer. He had a full view of the room.

He inspected every face that came in. No one connected.

Then he froze.

The young woman was dressed in a beige business suit and heels. She had fashionable reddish-brown hair. Her eyes were bright and enthusiastic as she entered the room. She caught his look and smiled. He had seen the same eyes, the same girl, the same smile, among the Chicago crowd at the American terminal.

She moved through the crowd to him.

"Hi," she said.

"Hello."

"Place is hopping tonight."

"Yes." He had no time for games. "I saw you at the airport."

"Me?" She ruffled her hair and laughed. "No, I live here. I wish I was getting out though. Someplace tropical."

He stiffened at the lie. "Must be someone else."

"Yeah, somebody lucky." She reached into her purse. "Mind if I smoke?"

"Go ahead."

She lit the cigarette and sucked. The bartender came over. "Another, sir?"

"No, I'm fine."

"And the lady?"

She hesitated and glanced at him. "Please," he said, "on me."

"I'll have a glass of champagne."

She sipped, smoked her cigarette, and shifted in her seat, the silence making her uncomfortable. "You staying in the hotel?"

His eyes were locked on her. "No, just stopping by."

"That's great. What's your name?"

"John."

She smirked. "Yeah, right. I'm Mary."

His voice was flat. "Don't lie. You were following me."

She laughed again. "John, how much of that you been drinkin'? I'm just looking to have fun. You want to have fun tonight?"

He relaxed. He had found the tail. "Sure. I love to have fun."

She glanced around warily. "Keep your voice down, John. Is two hundred okay?"

"Sounds fine. Where?"

"If you're not in the hotel I got a place nearby. But it's extra for the room."

"No problem."

"And if you have a good time, a tip's okay. Maybe fifty?"

"Of course."

She grinned. "Let's go."

They jumped into a cab in back of the Plaza. She directed the driver crosstown, then downtown. At Ninth and Forty-ninth the cab pulled up in front of a beaten hotel called the Hamilton Arms. There were metal bars on the windows at street level.

"It's sixty-five an hour for the room," she explained. "Cash. Plus the cab."

"Right." He paid the cabby and handed her a hundred dollar bill for the room. "I don't want to be seen going in."

"I understand. Just go around back by the fire door. I'll pay and come get you."

The rear of the Hamilton Arms was pitch black. He waited next to a metal door, absolutely sure she'd show up. Ten minutes later the door opened. He followed her up the dark, institutional stairs to a bedroom on the third floor. It had yellow walls, a bed, a bathroom and a grimy window. He looked out the window to the street below.

"You want me to undress?"

"What?"

"Undress? I need to get paid first, though, you know how it is."

He threw two hundreds on the bed, then went back to studying the street.

"Thanks." He heard rustling. "This okay?"

He turned. She was standing naked, smiling at him. She had thin breasts and a slightly protruding belly with a dark black bush between her legs. There was a mark that looked like a small snake on the inside of her right thigh, as though it had been cut there.

She put her hands on her hips. "Well, don't just stand there. Come and help yourself."

He didn't move, and didn't say anything.

"God, you're so serious. This is supposed to be fun!"

"Who sent you?" he asked quietly.

"What?" Her smile became confused, her mouth quivering.

"You heard me." He walked over and grabbed her purse. There was a serious Smith & Wesson Lady Smith inside.

"Hey, what the hell are you doing?"

"Who told you to get me here?"

"I don't know what you're . . ."

He hit her backhanded, splitting her lip, and she fell heavily to the ground.

"You bastard! You dirty bastard!"

"One more time," he said. When she looked up she saw he was holding his own gun, a Walther 9 mm with a silencer screwed onto the end.

"Get up," he ordered.

She did, holding her bleeding lip, staring at him with hate. "You filthy bastard!"

"Who told you to get me here? What time are they coming?"

"I don't know what you're talking about! Get out of here. Take your money with you."

He moved his thumb and there was a loud click. She just stood there, naked, her lip spilling blood. The Lady Smith .38 was on the bed, next to her purse.

"One more time, baby. One last time."

The woman never flinched. "Too late, Bracca," and she dove for the gun.

He fired twice and the quiet bullets made small holes between her breasts. She was dead before she hit the floor.

He rifled her purse again. Then the phone rang loudly, startling him. They were on their way for sure. He bolted through the door and down the grimy hall. Just before the fire door closed behind him he heard the elevator sound a dull tone.

He didn't wait to see who got off.

John Bracca sat in the back of the cab trying to calm down and think clearly. It was hard, his heart was pounding and he was confused. Okay, one thing at a time: Spain at noon. The cab driver with the turban was yawning, meandering around the low thirties.

"Greenwich Village," he said at last. "There's a Spanish place called El Cortijo, right across from St. Anthony's, about a block off Bleeker. You know it?"

"What?"

"Never mind, I'll direct you." Spain at noon. "I need to be at the El Cortijo at midnight. Can you make it?"

"What?"

"Just make a right."

He was almost an hour late, the chill of the kill swirling within him. The bartender was young, her skin flawless and fair. She smiled easily.

"May I help you?"

"Yes, a whiskey, please."

"What kind?"

He was barely listening. What kind of whiskey? What about the gun? The bullets? Any possibility of a trace? What if they were monitoring his calls to Stephanie? Maybe that's how they found him.

"I'm sorry. What did you say?"

She laughed easily. "What kind of whiskey? We have a lot."

"Anything, a Scotch."

"What kind of . . . never mind, I'll choose."

As she walked away she gave a small swivel, intentional and inviting. John stared dead ahead, serious, confused, purposeful.

When the drink came he downed it, and put the empty glass down. The girl refilled it, not quite sure if she had ever seen anyone this handsome up close. "You here alone?"

"Waiting for someone."

"Yeah, who?"

"Nobody, a friend."

Her attitude was flirtatious. "You married?"

"What?"

Another laugh. She tossed the hair out of her eyes. "A simple question. You married?"

He was seriously paranoid and his eyes flattened. If they monitored his calls they'd know he was coming here. She could be another plant. "You ask a lot of questions."

"Just being friendly." She gestured and sighed. "Anyway, your date's here."

Bracca spun around, reaching under his coat involuntarily.

"Hi," the voice said. "What's the emergency?"

He relaxed and took his hand out.

"You got my message?"

"Of course. I was here an hour ago. I thought you wouldn't show."

"We got problems. It turns out I was being followed."

"Are you sure? Did you ever find out who it is?"

"Who it *was*."

There was a silence. "You killed him?"

"Her."

"John!"

"I know." He downed the rest of his whiskey. "Plus this one behind the bar's been asking a lot of questions. It's making me nervous."

"John, relax! Where did you do it?"

"Some hotel room."

"Anybody see you?"

"No." He hesitated. "I left Natala and Boyle at my place."

"I understand. I'll take you back there now. Just try to relax."

"Okay." He tried to regulate his breathing. "I need to figure out how they got on to us."

"Don't worry about it now," Stephanie Shane said softly. "We'll talk about it in the car."

He paid the check and they left. The girl behind the bar smiled as she watched them leave. John Bracca didn't know it but once again his worst fears were real. The lovely El Cortijo bartender was the same girl who days before entranced and slapped Cameron Draxton in a Georgetown bar. As soon as the door closed her studied smile left and she picked up the phone. Her voice was bitter.

"They just left. She's taking him back to his place. He says Boyle and Natala are there. Oh, one more thing. Juliet's dead. He killed her!" She listened for a moment. "No problem, just make sure they all go together."

37

John Bracca and Stephanie Shane left the El Cortijo immediately and drove in silence to Bracca's apartment. They arrived just after 2:00 A.M. Boyle and Natala were still awake. Boyle looked up quizzically at the sight of Stephanie.

"Are we going to have a party?"

Bracca ignored him and went behind the bar, tumbling some ice into a glass. "Anybody else?"

Nobody answered and he poured a long one over the ice, then drank deeply. "Now what?"

"Now we tell each other the truth," Stephanie said. "Each one of us has somewhat different information than the others. Let's go slowly and talk in turn. At the end, I want every one of us to know everything." She gestured. "You first, Natala."

She didn't want to say anything to John Bracca but they made her do it. It took a good hour to go around the table. At the end, Natala had a quizzical look as she considered the one and only lover she had ever had.

"You're an informant for the federal government?"

"No!"

She smirked. "Sounds like one to me. How did Angelo take that?"

"He was thrilled."

Natala walked to him and touched his face. He had to wince at the touch. Her voice was soft. "I don't care about Angelo. I believe you." She paused. "And I want to come home."

Boyle just stared at the ceiling in disgust. Just when he thought Natala was done with Bracca. But first things first. "Hey, I feel a tear coming on. Will somebody please explain why it's so hard to just arrest this woman in Los Angeles?"

"I hope it's not hard at all," Stephanie said. "The lead guy on this is Cameron Braxton, out of Washington. I'll tell him everything as soon as I get home. I'm sure he'll have agents all over L.A. right away."

"Don't forget Miguel," Hugh said. "If I was this woman I'd pray the FBI got to me first."

"Well," said Stephanie, who really did know everything, "on that one I think you're right."

An hour later, just after 3 A.M., Gregor Portov arrived at John Bracca's apartment with three Russian gunmen. He walked in, smiled at the doorman and introduced himself as a messenger from Angelo. He held a package high.

The doorman stared impassively. "You can't go up there. Just leave it with me."

"I understand," Portov said quickly. "I just need to know you're going to get it to him right away. Apartment eight-seventy-three, right?"

The doorman didn't answer, just hit a button. John's voice came over the intercom.

"Mr. Bracca, I have a man down here with a package from your father. Is it okay if I bring it up?"

"Sure," the disembodied voice said.

The doorman hung up and reached for the package. "I'll see he gets it right away," the dead man said.

"Oh, don't bother yourself," Portov said and fired.

Fifteen minutes later there was a knock on Bracca's door. Bracca shouted at the knock, "Yeah?"

"I got that package for you, Mr. Bracca," the voice said from beyond the door.

Natala hopped up. "I'll get it."

She was halfway there when Boyle had a small primordial twitch at the base of his brain. "Nat," he said, and started to rise.

He was too late. When she took the latch off the door exploded as if in slow motion. Natala fell back heavily and Portov and three Russians entered the room. The first showed his gun and Boyle went for it. The second had a small cylindrical metal pipe and brought it down hard on the side of Boyle's head. He staggered to his knees and the first one brought a knee up hard into his chest. He tried to slip the blow but was again too slow. He fell back choking. When he looked up there were two guns pointed in his face.

"Don't talk, just listen," Portov said. "Pick up the girl and walk over to that wall. Join your two friends." The gun clicked. "This ain't a boxing match, Boyle. Use your head. I will shoot you. Understand?"

Boyle understood just fine. He did as he was told.

Portov ordered them all to stand against the far wall. The three gunmen closed the broken door and stood facing them, each holding a semiautomatic. There was a small couch between Portov and his captives that wouldn't provide any protection whatsoever.

Stephanie Shane remained still, driven by a combination of fear, which she had been trained to deal with, and concentration. Her eyes swept the room. She had seen enough photos of Portov to know who he was, the question was what was he doing here? Her mind swiftly ran through the possibilities, as if she were piloting an aircraft that had suddenly lost an engine. Only this time nothing on her mental checklist made sense. There was no way Portov should know they were all here.

Portov's men conducted a cursory search of the apartment, then returned. Bracca moved protectively in front of Natala.

"Do you have any idea what my father will do to you when he finds out about this?"

Portov shook his head wearily. "I am bored to tears hearing of the dangers of fat Italians from broken little towns in Jersey. Let me put it to you simply. We do not care what the Angelo Braccas of the world think or do."

"He'll have you killed!" John Bracca shouted. Out of rage and frustration he kicked the couch hard. It moved forward about four inches. Then he took the glass he was holding and threw it to the floor. It shattered in back of the couch.

Boyle's gaze involuntarily followed the exploding glass, like it was supposed to, and he immediately saw why John Bracca was engaging in such uncharacteristic histrionics. When the couch moved it revealed the two Glock 9 mms Bracca kept there, now easily accessible, now surrounded by the broken shards.

The last of Portov's men finished searching the apartment. The lead soldier, a tall, lean Russian, nodded briefly and Portov turned to the four captives huddled against the wall.

"Let's keep this simple. I'm not here to harm you, I just need information."

Bracca leaned forward against the couch. The handguns were next to his leg. "What information?"

"John, I want to know everything. What you know, what you think you know and, more importantly, who you've told."

John spread his hands expansively. "That's easy. You're an arms smuggler. You're working with a woman named Kent who's on the West Coast. You lied to my father about the contents of the warehouse. One of his men is following the woman now."

Portov listened carefully. "Who? Who's following her?"

John kept it vague. "A man on the coast."

Boyle yawned. "I hate to interrupt you guys, but I have to get back to Jersey. I don't know what the hell you're talking about."

Portov turned to him. "You're right, you don't know anything about this. You just had to stick your nose where it didn't belong." Now to Natala. "Like your father."

Natala refused to give him the satisfaction of reacting.

Stephanie's voice was sharp. "You're making a serious mistake. I'm a federal prosecutor. There will be agents swarming all over this apartment soon."

As Stephanie spoke, Portov walked in back of Bracca's bar and poured a large vodka, warm, into a water glass. He laughed heartily.

"Ms. Shane, you wouldn't know how to prosecute a parking ticket."

Stephanie visibly flinched. Boyle squinted. "What does that mean?"

"You mean she didn't tell you? After you slept with her last night?"

Stephanie blushed and Natala looked over quizzically. But Boyle was only interested in answers. "In my dreams, but what are you talking about? She's a lawyer with the Justice Department."

"Really? What law school did she go to?"

"Princeton. Columbia undergraduate and Princeton law school." He turned to Stephanie. "Isn't that right?"

Stephanie didn't say anything. Portov smiled and sipped some more. "That might be possible except for one little thing."

"What?"

"Princeton doesn't have a law school."

The room got rock quiet after that. There was soft music playing in the background that suddenly seemed very loud.

"It's odd. You figure Ivy League and all, they'd have one. But no, they think it makes them special, like a restaurant with no phone." He turned to Stephanie and waved expansively. "You really should have checked that out before inventing a bio. A *real* federal agent would never be that stupid." Another sip. "But let's not waste time. Why don't you tell them who you are?"

The tall, lean Russian raised his semiautomatic. Stephanie was too shocked to do anything but fall back on training. When captured in enemy territory, give them the basics and shut up.

"My name is Lieutenant Commander Stephanie Shane," she said in a monotone. "U.S. Naval Intelligence. I'm assigned by the secretary of the navy to a confidential unit specializing in counter-terrorism and counter-intelligence. My serial number is . . ."

Boyle was furious. "I can't believe this! I'm gonna get killed because of some game." He swung open-handed. The blow caught Stephanie by surprise and she fell backward against the wall. Her lip bled freely. He swung twice more, cursing, and Stephanie's face snapped to the right, then to the left. She finally fell hard to her knees and crumbled.

Portov laughed so hard he choked on his vodka. "Nice shot! Do it again."

"My pleasure." Boyle dropped to one knee and yanked her by the hair. Her eyes were wide, the blood on her lip thick. He leaned down and gently kissed the swollen skin. "Don't move."

Boyle screamed another expletive and raised his left hand to strike. Portov's men leaned forward with anticipation.

Then the right hand came up, and Boyle fired, like a cop was trained, rapidly, three times in succession, the right hand now resting on the left like a tripod.

The ill-shaven man near the door got the first one and slammed back into the door. Portov's lean assistant screamed and fired a semi-automatic burst while Boyle flipped the second Glock to Bracca. John grabbed it and opened up at the third Russian, who twisted and crashed a table as he fell. Two down, two left, one with a vodka glass in his hand and one firing on automatic. Natala was open-mouthed and exposed and the Russian opened on her a split second after Bracca jumped in front of her. He took four of the bullets meant for her, a dozen others scraping the wall. As he groaned and fell he dragged her down by the hair, then lay heavily in a bloody ball on top of her.

Boyle knelt behind the couch like a cop should and emptied the magazine. Both Russians were prone on the floor firing back. From the hallway came a loud shriek and then the sound of a faraway siren. The intercom barked. "What's going on up there!?"

Portov couldn't believe it. He was trapped and had no choice that he liked. He couldn't get behind the couch without going through Boyle, a trained homicide detective. And any delay would reveal the dead doorman on the first floor to the battalion of cops on the way.

"We're out of here. Move!"

The Russians opened up on the couch on full automatic as they backed to the door. Bracca was rigid over Natala, choking, bleeding freely. At the doorway Portov fired a final burst and was gone.

The room was filled with smoke and screams. Boyle pulled Stephanie to her feet and held her face with both hands.

"Look, I'm sorry, it was all I could think of. I hope you're not . . ."

Her face was bright red from the slaps. "I'll deal with *you* later. Let's help John."

Natala sat with John's head in her lap, wooden, impassive. She was covered with her lover's blood.

Stephanie gently pulled her away and opened John's shirt. "He's lost a lot."

That he had, but John Bracca was now in very good hands. Every cop knows how to save a shot-up partner and every military pilot knows how to save the life of a downed comrade. Within minutes, Boyle and Stephanie had crude tourniquets around every major pumping artery. They used rags and shirts and twisted them tightly. They never spoke a word as they worked. The bleeding stopped.

Stephanie lay back against the wall, exhausted. From the hall came the sound of police and paramedics.

"Is he going to die?" Natala asked.

Boyle reached for her head and pulled it to his shoulder. "No way, baby. You go to the hospital with him now. I'll call you later."

She nodded and the death quiet of the room was shattered by

stretchers and paramedics and equipment. The medics substituted real tourniquets for the crude ones and soon had John on a gurney with an IV in his arm. Boyle collapsed against the wall and watched the commotion. Stephanie sat down next to him.

"So you're not a lawyer," he said. "Anything else you didn't tell me?"

She started to answer but the exertion caused her to wince with pain. "Ow, that hurts! Look, how could I know that Princeton thing, Braxton just told me to pick good schools. I even ran it by him. Why he didn't pick that up, I'll never know." She worked her jaw back and forth gingerly. "Damn, you slap hard. Anyway, we'll discuss it all on the plane."

"What plane?"

"I'm going to Los Angeles right away. And you're coming with me whether you like it or not." She hesitated, then coughed. "And one more thing."

"What?"

"When I was lying there on the ground, and you got the gun . . ."

"Yeah?"

She dipped her head to his shoulder. He could actually feel the wet, warm blood flowing freely from her lip. "I liked the way you kissed me. A lot."

38

Miguel Meza and Christine woke up at 4 A.M. after a short nap on Alicia Kent's bed overlooking the tenth green of the Bel-Air Country Club. They hadn't meant to fall asleep, it just happened. Meza couldn't believe it.

"This is the most amazing thing I've ever done."

"That old thing? I can do that whenever you want. I'm not a prude, you know."

He did know. "I'm not talking about that, I'm talking about sleeping in her bed. We're supposed to be tailing this woman, not sleeping in her goddamn bed."

Christine was moderately chastened. "Okay, you're probably right." She looked around. "I'll put the mattress and sheets back on, you pick up the lamps and sweep up the broken glass. Then we should get out of here."

"Thank you."

There is no real way to remain inconspicuous on the Bel-Air streets, which have a lot of private cops and no sidewalks, so they went out the back entrance and hid on the golf course. The women returned at five in the morning and the lights inside the house went out thirty minutes later. Miguel and Christine then fell asleep on the famous tenth green under a declining moon. It was romantic in a warped sort of way. Meza took off his jacket and let Christine use it for a pillow.

"What'll you use?" she asked.

"No need for modesty now." He pulled off his pants.

"Now we're talkin'!"

They were awakened two hours later by a loud thump nearby. It turned out to be a pretty good two-iron off the tenth tee.

"Damn, these people start early."

"I think he going to smack it again and then stick it in the hole." She grinned. "Like you do." She rubbed her bottom and made a fake grimace.

Meza grabbed his pants. "Let's get out of here."

They left the green and set up surveillance on a knoll under a copse of elegant oaks that shielded them from view. Almost immediately they saw movement. The women were awakening, opening windows, wandering around. At 7:45 they strolled onto the rear veranda drinking coffee. One was tall and elegant, with large glasses. The other was just as tall but muscular, young, with the easy, natural movements of an athlete. He immediately realized he had a problem.

"Oh man!" he said.

"What?"

"We only got one car. Damn!" He pounded the ground.

Christine blinked in confusion. "What's the problem?"

Meza didn't answer. He was just royally screwed and it was all because of this girl, who was now seriously confusing him. The two women would leave in separate cars and he'd have to choose one to follow. There was no way to be sure, not really, that he would pick Alicia Kent. Plus he had to find a way to get Christine home. Maybe she'd take a bus.

"I'll just have to guess, hope I get lucky. I got a fifty-fifty chance is all." He studied the pair on the balcony. "Okay, here goes. I say the one in jeans is the cleaner."

"Maybe they're both . . . what would you call them, hit babes?"

"Why not? Anyway, the one with the glasses don't look so dangerous. She's like a teacher."

"Well," Christine said, "looks can be deceiving. But we *really* need another car, right?"

Meza was paying no attention. "Time to roll the dice. It's got to be the big one."

"Give me twenty minutes."

"She just looks the part. Damn, I hate to guess."

She returned in fifteen. "It's a blue LeBaron. Believe me, not my first choice. I was hoping for a BMW maybe."

Meza was staring at the balcony, finalizing his decision. It took a
few beats for the information to register.

"What's a blue LeBaron?"

"It's a Chrysler, silly. I thought they went bankrupt. They
should've, the car's so ugly."

He turned wide-eyed to her, disbelieving. "You got a car?"

Her grin was so broad she almost stopped chewing the gum. "Are
you proud of me?"

"Where the hell did you get a car?" he screeched.

"You're so loud! Just listen. It's easy around here. I go to the
valet and say, 'I'm not going to play with that mope anymore, he's
too critical.' "

"Who?"

"Who? Listen! So the guy fake smiles, he don't know who I am,
but he don't want to admit it, you know?"

"Yeah?"

"So I say, 'Bring that bastard's car around, he can ride home with
his buddies. Matter of fact, if he wants some tonight he can get that
from his buddies too.' Like I'm real mad, you know?"

Meza's mouth was open and he again understood he really had
no clue about her.

"Then the guy says, 'Mrs. Martinson?' just hoping he's right."

"Mrs. Martinson?"

"Right. And I go, 'Well I sure hope so. Either that or I been
suckin' the wrong guy the last five years.' That was pretty crude, I
admit. Anyway, the guy goes running for the car."

"And he gives you the keys?"

"Yeah, even opens the door. Cute guy. It's parked around the
block. This Martinson must be cheap though, stupid LeBaron." She
sighed and looked up. "Would you stop staring! And close your
mouth!"

At 8:30 Roberta and Alicia walked out to the wide driveway. They
hadn't had much sleep but right now neither one cared. Roberta
wore her work clothes: tight black jeans, a black T-shirt, boots and
an oversized brown leather jacket. She carried a canvas satchel over
her shoulder with the Browning in it. Alicia Kent wore an elegant

beige business suit, beautifully tailored, with high heels and a shoulder-briefcase made of soft, tan leather. Inside was an elegant, silver-plated Colt.

Alicia pressed a button on an electric key and a beep sounded unlocking the door of a large, silver S 600 Mercedes. Roberta threw her jacket and satchel into the back seat of a Range Rover with blacked out windows and beefed-up suspension.

"Check in every four hours on the answering machine here," Alicia ordered. "We meet on this spot, forty-eight hours from now, noon on Thursday."

Maybe, Roberta thought. We'll see. "You got it."

"So," Christine said, as they watched Roberta get into the Range Rover. "Which one you gonna follow?"

"I'm taking the one in the truck. She's *got* to be the hitter. Man, that babe's got bigger shoulders than me."

"She's also got a great bod. Try to keep it in your pants."

"Don't worry." He checked his weapon. "Look, I got something to tell you and don't give me any mouth about this. Drive home in that stolen car and I'll call you later."

Her face was innocent. "Sure, Migo, no problem."

If he had known her longer her tone would have alerted him. "Good. How do I get hold of you?"

Still innocent. "Just call me at the house. Or leave a message on the machine."

"Okay. I have to go now." His voice got firm. "I got one rule for you. Go home and wait for me to call. This is not any kind of game. This is dangerous."

"I promise. I got one rule for you, too."

"What?"

She kissed him hard, then blatantly patted his groin. "Bring my best friend home alive and perky."

39

Stephanie Shane felt strangely calm when she left John Bracca's apartment after the shootout. She knew she was only alive because of Boyle, even as angry as he still was at her because of all the lies. She had seen a lot of men in dangerous situations, women too, and some people you wanted in your foxhole and some you didn't. Boyle was a homicide detective in a city of daily homicides, and had seen death and guns of a quantity and variety to rival any soldier. She didn't know where it was going, but wherever it was going, she was quietly glad to have Tommy Boyle next to her.

Not that Boyle was perfect. There was, for example, the pain in her jaw and the discoloration in her cheekbones. Even though he had hit her open-handed, the slaps still came from a man who knew only one way to hit. In the cab back to her apartment he vaguely suggested she was partly at fault. Now that was rich!

"My fault! Pardon me?"

"You *are*, a little. I tried to put you under the couch with the first slap, but no, you had to be macho and stay up. I thought I'd have to throw a punch!"

She couldn't believe it. Duncan would just love this guy.

"You slap me in the face four times and . . ."

"Three. Plus maybe you deserve it anyway, Miss Liar!"

"Are you nuts!?"

"Well you are! You lied to me about *everything*!"

She was so upset she almost choked.

They argued like hens all the way from John Bracca's apartment to hers. Once there she slammed the bedroom door behind her and called Braxton at home. He again came on the line immediately, with no sleep fog in his voice.

"Stephanie, what's happening? I heard there's been some trouble."

Her harsh laugh had no humor. "Some trouble? I guess you could say that. They tried to kill us."

Braxton's voice boomed. "That's incredible! Was anybody hurt?"

"Yes, John Bracca was shot."

A hesitation. "He's dead?"

There was an odd, hopeful inflection in Braxton's voice and she squinted at it. "Not yet. He's in surgery. He looks bad."

"That's terrible. Who did it? A rival mob?"

The question exasperated her. "Of course not. John Bracca was working with me. It was Portov. I saw the whole thing."

Braxton feigned surprise. "That's amazing. Who else was there?"

"Natala, Boyle and me."

Braxton cursed silently. All three could have been taken out. "Was anybody else hurt?"

"Just two Russians that Boyle and John shot. They're way gone." Then there was her face, but she didn't want to get into a long explanation about that.

She heard a choking sound. Another odd sound. "Two . . . two Russians were killed?"

"Yeah, real dead. Do you have the flu? You sound terrible."

"No . . . no, I'm fine."

"Good. Mr. Braxton?"

"Please, Cameron."

"Okay. Cameron, I have a question about this."

Braxton's heart skipped. "What question?"

"They knew exactly where we were and when we'd be all together. Very few people knew that."

Braxton stiffened. "What are you saying?"

"I'm saying that agent you sent me knew everything." Stephanie was nervous accusing an FBI agent. But it was getting hard to know who to trust. "You know who I mean, Jim Keller. He knew *everything*."

Braxton breathed easier. Keller was expendable. "That's a very serious accusation."

"Yes, it is."

"Maybe it's best we take him off this."

"I think that's a *great* idea."

"Consider it done." Braxton made a note. "Where are you going next?"

"I'm going out to L.A. with Boyle."

Braxton sat back in shock. "What?"

"That's right. I'm going to call my base and try to catch a ride out this afternoon. If there's no room I'll ask to fly something. But if I fly I need to sleep for a few hours first."

Braxton was near panic. "Are you sure? What about the Sarin in New York? What about Patsy's killer?"

"Trust me. The answers to both of those questions are in L.A."

"And Boyle? A corrupt cop? Are you sure it's wise to take him with you?"

"Oh, yes," Stephanie said, "I'm very sure that's wise."

She finished her calls and went back to the living room. Boyle was lying on the couch, his arm over his eyes, catching a quick nap. She watched him breathe, with interest and more than a bit of excitement. It was time.

He stirred when he heard her. "Hi. You finished with your calls?"

"Yeah, I called my base. We can get a ride out this afternoon." She sat on the edge of the couch, far enough away to maintain decorum, close enough to keep things interesting.

"Your base? You really *are* in the navy."

She shrugged and grinned. "Are you still mad at me?"

"We'll see. Can you dress up in a little sailor suit for me?"

"Pig!"

He had taken a nasty scrape on the side of the head during the gunfight and it was still lightly bleeding. She examined it closely. "You really should clean that off. Plus,"—she gestured to the clothes he had worn for forty-eight hours now—"to tell you the truth, detective, you're getting a bit ripe."

"Sorry, it's hard to stay neat *when people are lying to you!*"

"God. Give it a rest. Boyle, it's time to get out of those clothes."

Men are so easy, and among men in general, Detective Thomas Boyle was a lot easier than most. She brought out a large towel and told him to strip and wrap the towel around him. She promised she'd turn her back, which she did, then watched the whole thing in the clear reflection from the window.

"Like this?" he asked.

She turned slowly and saw him standing there, shifting from foot to foot. The towel was around his waist and his fighter's body rose above it. She had once travelled to Florence with Duncan and saw famous statues glorifying a young male's naked body. She was excited by the sight then and excited by it now. Maybe one good hard yank on the towel. No, not yet.

Stephanie inspected the clothes on the floor. "I'll throw these in the washer while you take a bath." She squinted. "Hey, where's the snails?"

"The what?"

"The snails." She searched again and they weren't there. "Boyle, I said *everything*!"

"You mean including the . . ."

"That's exactly what I mean. The snails are *definitely* ready for the wash."

It was hard for him to yank off the boxers and at the same time keep the towel in place and he wasn't completely successful. This time she didn't bother to turn away. Once the towel slipped and he turned his back to her. It was the final piece of the puzzle for her. Well, not the final piece, she thought. Let's say *almost* the final piece.

He threw the boxers on the floor. "There."

She moved the clothes around with her foot. "I wish I had a shovel."

"That's very nice."

She laughed merrily. "Only kidding. Go on in and take your bath. Use a lot of soap please."

He did as she said and she resisted the urge to pat him as he walked past her. When she heard the water running she dumped his disgusting clothes into the machine and put it on a very long cycle. The snails were sea horses, and cute, but in the future she'd buy his boxers and they wouldn't come from a scuba shop. Those reveries took just long enough for the water to fill the tub.

Stephanie went back into the living room and listened for the sounds of splashing water. The door was closed and he had probably turned the lock. No matter, that lock hadn't worked in this government-issue apartment since the first day she had moved in.

She gave him another ten minutes to get relaxed. The switch for the bathroom light was on her side of the door, which was either fortunate or unfortunate for Boyle, depending on how you looked at it. When she was ready she flicked it, plunging the bathroom into darkness, except for the light of the New York night streaming into the room.

She turned the knob and it opened easily. He sat in the bathtub, wide-eyed, surrounded by bubbles. How rude, he had found her expensive bubble bath. Well, good, she thought.

He stared, his mouth open, while she pulled the thin T-shirt over her head and threw it on the ground. There was nothing underneath but beautiful skin and he was so focused on that he didn't notice her unbuckling the large belt on her jeans. The jeans opened and she pulled them down, letting them puddle at her ankles before stepping free. There was only one thing left and the flimsy material slid down her strong legs and soon joined the jeans.

She stood near the tub with her hands on her hips. She was so proud of herself, he realized, just like Natala.

"Aren't you going to invite me in?" She felt utterly shameless, and loved it.

"Turn around. I'll decide then."

"No problem." She held her hands high and turned slowly and he saw a world-class runner's legs disappear into a round, taut . . . well, whatever.

"Do you approve?" She looked like Betty Grable in the war photos, hands now on her hips, showing it to him.

"No, it's too flabby. Go away."

"Really? We'll see." She stepped gracefully into the tub, then lowered herself on top of him, letting the warm, sudsy water surround them both. She could feel every part of him.

"Now we're even. You're a liar, too."

"Baths do that to me. It has nothing to do with you."

Her lips moved near his ear. "Detective Boyle, you're a big, fat liar."

His fingers dug deeply into her hips. His voice was as cracked as hers. "I'll be gentle with your face, liar," he said. "But that's all."

Stephanie's head drifted to his shoulder, half under the sudsy waves. She could already feel strong hands becoming more demanding. She started to bite hard on that strong shoulder.

"Good."

40

licia Kent waited for twenty minutes after Roberta left, then drove down the windy Bel-Air streets toward Sunset. She forgot about Meza stalking her and focused on the task at hand, Bernie the broker. She had lied through her teeth when Roberta asked if there was money in that deal. There wasn't money in that deal, there was a fortune in that deal, and with Magnus gone, and with the Council knowing nothing about it, a fortune that could be hers alone.

It was Magnus who first found Bernie, then a no-name operating out of a boiler room in New Jersey, cold-calling retirees and selling newly issued securities sure to rise. The stocks were rising, that was true, but only because a thousand salesmen in the hangar-sized boiler room were pitching the same stock eighteen hours a day, seven days a week, to other retirees. The old folks were the buyers; the sellers were Magnus and the insiders. The insiders received a few million shares at fifty cents in the initial public offering—IPO in the trade— then dribbled them out on the climb. At the end it was all like a baseball hit into the seats: an exhilarating rise, a momentary stop at the twelve-dollar apogee as the last sucker bought the last of the IPO shares, then a sickening drop to bankruptcy. "Pump and dump" Bernie called it, and the old folks never knew what hit them.

Bernie was the best of the boiler room guys and came to Magnus' attention early. He moved him from Jersey to Manhattan, where the action really was. That's where Bernie discovered Drexel.

Bernie moved out to Drexel's Beverly Hills office in the late eighties, becoming an expert high-yield bond trader, sitting at the left hand of the X-desk, the great man's desk. He was there every morning at four, wired, and Mike thought he was the best.

After the meltdown Magnus got him out without harm and moved him to a safe harbor in downtown L.A., trading on the Chicago Board via the Pacific exchange. Bernie had more experience than any of the locals and soon became chief bond trader. He was thirty-one years old and in his glory.

The scam Magnus now had working was satanically simple. Each evening, after the exchanges closed, Bernie would take to the computer, reconciling $3 million in bond trades made that day. If bonds went up, Magnus' account would get the lion's share of the benefit. If not, twenty-four select institutional accounts had a bad day.

Even Magnus had not planned on terminating Bernie this early, although Alicia had argued for months that it was time. As Ponzi schemes went, this one had very little time to run, and closing it down now was prudent. Besides, she thought, before long Bernie would be whining about his cut of the Cayman account, and neither Alicia nor Magnus had ever intended to share that.

Bernie woke on the day of his death at 3:00 A.M. It wasn't that he was an early bird, it was just that he never slept anymore. He used to be a fat, pudgy kid too until the "ice" got him, the crystal meth. Now no sleep, no fat, and a constant buzz. Plus about $50 million in the Cayman account. Nothing could be sweeter, except for the ladies.

Bernie always thought of the ladies as soon as he awoke. The bedroom in the Palisades hills high above Sunset was dark and he could clearly hear coyotes and owls finishing pre-dawn kills. He lay back and planned. First, a buzz, then arrange for the evening's entertainment, then to work.

He showered quickly and went to the breakfast table to force down a bowl of cereal, a muffin, some orange juice. This part was boring, but important.

After the meal he put on strong Italian coffee. While it was brewing he poured some crystal into a teaspoon. He avoided the nasal membranes, nothing but trouble there. When the coffee was done he poured the meth inside, let it dissolve, then sipped it black. Whatever he was giving up in speed of effect he was gaining in long-term nasal health, a bizarre thought that made him smile.

After breakfast he logged on and read the overseas market reports, like any good trader. Twenty minutes later the buzz hit. He leaned back with relief. Fifteen hours of wired rushes ahead. Then barbiturate-induced suicidal blackness. Unless he drank more lines.

Maybe it would kill him and maybe it wouldn't. He'd take his chances.

Unlike the Drexel days he didn't have to get downtown until 5:30, an hour before the NYSE opened three hours ahead of him. He fueled the buzz with more cups of strong Italian coffee. By 4:00 A.M., the meth was biting deeply into his burned-out neurotransmitters, hunting for sustenance. That's when he made the call.

"Karen, how you doin', this is Walter."

"Walter, how are you? It's a little late."

"I know, this is for tonight." He was cruising now, the meth must have found someplace to feed. That was the problem, a scorched earth problem is the way he thought of it. Each day it took longer for the meth to find a home, each day it took more to get the job done, each day the buzz slipped off sooner. It was scary.

"Tonight? Oh, you mean tomorrow night. We're wide open, sweets. What would you like?"

The world was an oyster for a man on meth with $50 million in a Cayman account. A couple grand meant nothing.

"I was thinking maybe two girls." He got a sudden rush, the kind he loved.

"My, aren't we randy? You want anyone special or you want me to pick?"

"You go ahead, you know what I like."

"Okay, where? Over your house?"

"Yeah, is nine okay?"

"Perfect."

Alicia Kent drove from Bel-Air to Culver City, arriving about 8 A.M. The town was a beaten-up middle-class suburb of L.A., crisscrossed by major commuter surface streets. It was a town everyone ignored, and therefore a perfect spot to meet Howard Crabsucker.

Howard Crabsucker was the world's ugliest private detective, and one of the least successful. His head was pinched and frozen and seemed to sit as an unexpected growth atop his shoulders. His misshapen body was tiny and oddly twisted. His out-of-date suits hung on him with all the grace of a pair of pants thrown on a bedroom chair.

He smiled when Alicia entered and even his smile was odd. It forced his mouth into an unfamiliar position and it seemed to cramp as he did it. His smile also revealed his teeth, which didn't help.

Alicia held out a friendly hand. She actually enjoyed working with Howard. The odd detective was as loyal as a spaniel, and would do anything in the world she asked.

"You look happy this morning, Howard. Do you have some news for me?" The office was nestled above a 7-Eleven in a mini-mall. Outside the traffic noise was loud.

"He's been busy, our little bond friend." Crabsucker giggled.

"How so?"

He consulted his notes. "He's been buying a lot more meth than he used to. And when he buys, and gets a buzz, he calls Karen."

"And Karen calls you?"

"Yes, she does. Matter of fact, Bernie called this morning."

Perfect, Alicia thought. "What time?"

"Four A.M."

"Awfully early."

"Not if you don't sleep." He giggled again.

"What did Bernie want so early?"

"He wants Karen to set him up tonight at nine."

"Where?"

"His house."

Alicia thought for a second and that's all it took to plan it. "Who's the girl?"

Crabsucker waved his fingers. "Karen's choice. He wants two girls."

She smiled knowingly. "Such a slut, our Bernie."

"That's what Karen said."

Alicia was quiet again, the obvious solution running through her brain. Tonight's the night, like in the play. Yet how to coordinate it? Who would be the other girl? Not Roberta, she was busy in Long Beach.

"Okay. Tell Karen I'll take care of Bernie."

His breath grew fast and his warped smile appeared. "Tonight you'll do it, right? Am I right?"

"Howard, mind your own business," she snapped.

"I know you'll do it!" He almost hugged himself he was so happy.

"Howard, you're making me nervous. That's not good for you."

He laughed maniacally. "You'll be the girl, right? With one of your friends?"

"Howard!" she warned.

He gestured. "You'll need clothes."

"That's not a problem."

"Marilyn, let me ask you something."

She involuntarily blinked at the false name. She used so many it was hard to keep track. "What?"

"My bill's about twenty-five hundred dollars. I'll forget it, you don't owe me nothing. One condition."

"I'm listening, Howard."

"You let me watch."

This might be as sick as it gets. Yet she actually found herself smiling at the odd man's request.

"There's nothing to watch, Howard."

Even his laugh was odd. "Yes, there is! Yes, there is!"

"Anyway, if you're talking about Bernie, the answer's 'no.' Not that anything's going to happen anyway. Understand?"

"Okay, okay, I understand. You can't let me watch *that*."

"Right."

"I was thinking about something else."

Her eyes narrowed and she thought about how many people knew she met with Howard, and how many would care if he turned up dead. Not too many. Sorry, Howard.

"Something else? What?"

He gestured. "You have to change."

"We already covered that, Howard."

"So let me watch you change."

She stared in confusion for the full beat it took her to get it. Then she laughed so hard the tears flowed in cathartic bursts. When she saw Howard cackling along with her she laughed more. It was all a colossal joke. Say what you will about Howard, he made her feel better.

"Sure, Howard, you can watch. For free."

41

Stephanie Shane watched the pre-dawn glow spill into her apartment through faded windows and slanted blinds. She raised the blinds and saw garbage and newspaper trucks travel the empty streets like survivors after some cataclysmic devastation. The humans were all gone, hidden inside their concrete and metal caves.

In Stephanie's cave there were two humans, both naked and sweat soaked. She had made love to him in the warm, soapy water with a passion that went way past lust. When they left the tub, the floor was an inch deep in water. They slipped into the living room and in the next hour broke two lamps and a lovely vase. She bit her lip till it bled when Boyle took her the first time then screamed begging for him to do it again. She felt like a harlot and loved it.

Not that Boyle needed a lot of encouragement. For the first time in her life a man lusted after her because she was a woman, and not because of her rank, her father's rank or her pretty Annapolis grades. Boyle would have ravished her exactly the same way if she was a cashier at McDonald's. She wished she could stay in this room with him forever.

Her reverie was broken by his voice, waking slowly.

"Don't move. Please."

She closed her eyes and smiled. "Okay."

She felt his hands and shuddered anew. "All I can say is we'd make beautiful babies," he said. He rolled over behind her, the famous "spoons," and pressed against her. Her breath quickened as his amazingly strong hands roamed across her belly and breasts, like he owned everything he touched. There was an insolence in the way he touched her, a confidence. These parts of you are now mine, the touch said. And she agreed.

"Don't get too interested. We have to get some sleep before the flight."

He pressed against her more. "What makes you think I'm interested?"

"I don't think, I know."

"Well, you're wrong. I already used up all my energy."

"Really? So what's that I feel pressing against me?"

He pulled her closer and his lips moved softly to her ear, just like in back of John Bracca's couch. His teeth bit into her again. "Oh, that," he whispered. "Maybe you're right."

They slept like rocks until noon. Again, she woke first, this time timing her escape and leaping out of bed laughing, eluding the strong arms that snaked outward to suck her back into temptation. It had been a strange and powerful night, but now it was time to work. She ran into the bathroom and emerged twenty minutes later in a tan jumpsuit and soft black boots. She carried a dark satchel that included the essentials she might need for a week, including the two guns from John Bracca's apartment.

"Okay," she said, all business now. "You look real nice but it's time to go. Get dressed!"

A government car waited for them at the curb. The enlisted driver snapped to attention as Stephanie approached and his right hand flew to his cap. Stephanie returned the salute and climbed into the back seat. Boyle watched the whole thing with stunned amusement.

"This is unbelievable. You really *are* in the navy."

"I told you that. You have to start believing me."

"Why? Because you're such a truthful person? By the way, when do I have to start saluting?"

She flipped through her notes with her head down. Tommy Boyle would need some work yet. "Now would be nice."

The driver headed in the direction of Long Island but turned off long before JFK. After an hour signs appeared for Kelly Naval Air Station. The car stopped at a guard post and the driver handed over some orders. A marine examined them and the gate rose.

The car sliced through the barracks and administrative offices until it reached the tarmac itself. At the far end a T-63 idled quietly, a stairway ramp extending from the passenger door to the ground.

The military version of an executive jet had round porthole windows and room for fourteen passengers. It looked pretty skimpy to Boyle.

He coughed. "That's our plane to L.A.?"

"That's right."

"Uh, I don't know if I mentioned this . . . but I haven't been on planes that much."

She looked up, slightly confused. "What's that mean? You fought for seven years all over the country, Chicago, Atlanta, Las Vegas."

"I know, and every time I hated it. Before that I never flew *any-place*. I didn't like it then and I haven't done a lot of it since." He licked his lips. "I haven't done *any* of it since."

"So let's see if I get this. You're afraid of flying?"

"Not *afraid*, I didn't say *afraid*! But those planes are so small. What if the motor just quits. Are they safe?"

She patted his leg. "Trust me, they're very safe."

Her patronizing attitude infuriated him. "How the hell would you know? You've been on boats or behind a desk the whole time."

"They're called 'ships,' not 'boats,' and I haven't always done that." She actually hadn't done any boats, unless a nuclear-powered, 75,000-ton aircraft carrier qualified as a "boat."

"Well," he said, not giving it up, "how about the pilot? Is he experienced?"

"There's actually two pilots." She kissed him gently on the cheek. "Trust me, they're *very* experienced."

Before they boarded Stephanie walked around the jet, visually inspecting it. Boyle was right next to her.

"I'm with you. Let's check this sucker out. Do those wings look right to you?"

"They look wonderful. Let's go."

There was a marine steward at the top of the stairs and another crisp salute. This whole salute thing had gotten really old to Boyle. They didn't salute at the Paterson P.D. and he didn't see the need for it here.

"I hope we don't have to sit in the back," he said. "That's where all the bumps are."

"Don't worry, Tommy. I wouldn't stick you back there."

The ten minutes before takeoff were a complete blur to him.

Every seat in the plane was taken and he stood bewildered while
Stephanie turned left into the cockpit. The marine pointed and he
followed her in. She sat down next to a man flipping switches and
glancing at a clipboard.

"Hi," she said. "Lieutenant Commander Shane."

The man shook her hand. "Captain Al Compton. They tell me
you need a ride to the coast."

"Yes, sir. You sure your second chair doesn't mind?"

"Hell, no, he's happy for a few days off. We make this trip three
times a week. I'll pick him up the next round." He gestured at the
control panel. "You're checked out on these, right?"

"Yes, sir. We trained on these at Pensacola. I soloed in this."

The captain nodded. "But then moved on from what I hear."

Stephanie shrugged diffidently.

"You were on the Nimitz?"

"Yes, sir. About four hundred hours in Tomcats."

The man's face stayed fixed. "I never got to do that. Your father's
Admiral Shane, right?"

She kept it cool. She was used to the unspoken accusation. "That's
right."

He half-smirked, something else she was used to. "Well, ma'am,
I never flew off a carrier and my dad's not an admiral. So I'm just
gonna sit back and watch how the pros do it." He jerked a finger
at Boyle. "What about him?"

"He's with me. You mind if he sits up here?"

"Whatever you want, admiral's daughter."

Boyle was speechless and only vaguely following the conversation.
He was told to strap into the cockpit's third chair and put on the
headset the captain gave him. He watched as Stephanie fluidly
flipped switches and moved the throttle so that the twin engines
screamed ever louder as the RPM's rose. Captain Compton was talking to the control tower.

"Okay, you're clear," he said. "Take her up."

The blood drained from Boyle's face. "Take her up! Are you
nuts?"

The captain looked back quizzically. "What?"

"Tommy, it's okay. Look." She pointed to her left breast.

"So what! They're very nice! That doesn't mean you should screw
around with this plane!"

"Boyle, I was pointing at my wings, not my . . . never mind. I'll explain it up top."

"Up top! What do you mean up . . ."

He never finished the sentence. His angelic-looking paramour waved at the runway crew and pushed the throttle to full. The jet jolted as the brakes released and roared down the runway. At rotation speed she eased back and the front wheels lifted off the ground, then rushed vertically into the gray sky. She retracted the gear, smoothed out the tabs and the plane sliced through the early evening air. At thirty thousand feet she leveled off, set the computer to their flight plan and engaged the automatic pilot.

The captain's jaw was tight. "I got to admit, that was nice."

Stephanie turned to find Boyle still staring open mouthed at her.

"Now," she said. "What in the world were you screaming about?"

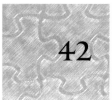

42

Alicia Kent expected that Magnus would remain alone and undisturbed on the floor of the room at the Hilton until at least four in the afternoon. It didn't happen. By noon Rosario Hernandez, the maid, had efficiently cleaned up every room on the floor except the one with the DO NOT DISTURB sign. She wanted to go home early because her new baby was sick. She decided to use her key.

She entered cautiously, more than once she had surprised guests in the middle of some pretty strange activities. She called out loudly and when there was no answer dragged her equipment in. She started in the bathroom and had that pretty much cleaned up when she walked into the bedroom. That's when she saw the man sleeping on the floor.

"Oh, I'm sorry, sir," she said quickly. He was an immensely fat naked man with the whitest skin Rosario had ever seen. When the man didn't answer, she peered closer, and that's when she saw the blood. Her screams were loud and long.

Hotel security was up there fast and a half hour later the uniforms from LAPD showed up. It took another hour before the homicide detectives from West L.A. showed up. The lead detective's name was Houlihan and he was a prematurely graying forty-five year old with jowly skin. He was cranky and eccentric, yet was also the most able murder investigator in the West District. He had no life, no family other than the LAPD, and it drove everybody else nuts. Houlihan was the sort of cop who was either sleeping, working or drinking. There was a legend around that he hadn't taken a vacation day in ten years.

"What do you got here?" he barked at a bored uniform.

The man checked a small pad. "The room was rented out at ten."

"To who?"

"Some company called Charter Properties, Limited. It was signed for by a woman named Mary Collins. Two desk clerks were on duty with about a billion Japanese checking in at the same time. One says Mary Collins was black, the other says no, she was white."

"Great. Did Mary Collins use a credit card?"

"All cash."

"Yeah, my name's Mary Collins too." Houlihan glanced at the body. "Who's Baby Huey?"

The cop shrugged. "He's not a guest. The doorman remembers him, though. I guess he's hard to forget."

"And?"

"He came in a cab just before midnight. Paid the cab, got out. The guy says 'Are you checking in?' He says 'no, just having a drink'."

"So did he have his drink?"

"Yeah. The bartender remembers him too. Two Beefeater martinis, dry, hold the olive."

Houlihan involuntarily licked his lips. He could go for a couple of Beefs right now. "Anything else from the bartender?"

"The fat guy downed them both fast. He looked like he had somethin' on his mind and was taking notes."

"He talk to anybody? Make any calls?"

"The bartender says he made a credit card call from the bar."

"Who'd he call?"

"We don't know yet. Bigelow's checking it out."

That information made Houlihan sigh with exasperation. Bigelow was his incredibly stupid partner. Giving information to Bigelow was the same as throwing it out the window. He pointed to the corpse.

"Look, you got a fat, naked corpse bleeding all over the hotel's rug. You got a broad that was in here that may be either black or white, you don't know which. The only thing we know about the dead guy is he likes Beefeater martinis. You think maybe it'd be a good idea to find out what number he called from the bar?"

The uniform wrote it down. Houlihan could be a jerk when he was hungover. "Yeah, I'll tell Bigelow to hustle."

"They're dusting and all around here?"

"They picked up a few things, the maid didn't clean up."

Houlihan looked around the room and mentally admitted defeat.

There wasn't anything to see. Whoever popped this guy was looking him in the eye, a friend. And yet the room was rented to a woman. How the hell did that fit in? A hooker? A robbery? Who knew.

"Let me know when you find out about that phone call."

43

Meza knew he had the hitter, the big strong one in the truck, and it was easy to follow her. The Range Rover was raised artificially high, so he could stay a quarter mile behind and still keep it in sight. At the first light, down at Sunset, he tucked his red hair back and snapped it with a rubber band. He felt under his coat and under the seat for the guns that were there, then got distracted while he wondered whether Christine would get home okay. The distraction surprised him. The girl was slowly, insidiously, getting to where he lived.

His quarry took a strange, tortuous path, traveling west on Sunset to the beach, then south along the PCH into Santa Monica. She stayed off freeways and picked up surface streets, sometimes cruising along Wilshire, sometimes doubling back on even more obscure side streets. As the streets became less traveled, it got harder to keep cars between them. He smiled, he was sure now he had the professional.

"Baby, you know what you're doing. But so do I."

She drove south through Venice, past the airport, all the way down to a working-class section of El Segundo ringed with stucco apartments and biker bars. Meza watched the Range Rover yank into the parking lot of a dark, one-story bar entitled, appropriately, "The Cavern." The woman got out, slammed the door, and went inside.

Now what the hell was this all about? Meza maneuvered his Buick Electra through the detritus of humanity that littered the parking lot. Some were leaning against rusting cars or bikes. Some were sitting on the black asphalt, contemplating the pain of existence. He parked in a corner of the lot next to a man who sat with a bottle between his legs, a baseball hat on and a long, black beard. His clothes were ruffled and swollen.

Meza got out and looked around, bewildered. What the hell did these bums have to do with a rich bond trader? The man with the beard scratched, took a pull off the bottle and cackled.

"You ain't even gonna make it to the steps."

Meza looked around slowly, then almost laughed. The Cavern was like a million bars he had been in, better than most in Paterson. And these bums could barely stand up, much less cause a problem.

"What're you drinking?"

"What do you care?"

"Don't be so nasty. I'm trying to be sociable. What is it?"

"I forget." The man looked at the label. "Seagram's something."

"That's a fine choice."

The man drank deeply. "When they whack you, don't bleed over here," he said amiably.

"Fair enough. That looks good though. How much for a drink?"

The man stared. "You want to buy a drink from me?"

"Sure."

The man coughed through broken teeth. "Look, just run. They're going to kick your silly ass till you bleed to death. They're already lookin' at you."

Meza turned. The drunk was right. The bikers were huddled, getting ready. Meza was surprised they weren't falling over their bikes.

"Man, that's some weird ducks. What's their problem?"

"I don't think they got a problem. You the one got a problem."

Meza pulled a twenty out of his pocket and stuck it in the man's shirt. "That's for the drink." He snatched the bottle away from the drunk and took a deep pull. He made a face. "God, that's terrible! That's not Seagram's!"

The drunk couldn't believe he had a twenty. "This probably ain't real either."

Meza gave the man his bottle back and walked toward the entrance. This whole thing made no sense. What in the world was this hitter doing inside a crummy bar when she should be downtown killing a bond trader? Maybe that's why Angelo wanted her checked out, she was scamming him. Then his thoughts were interrupted by dark shapes moving, like roaches when a light is turned on in a dirty kitchen. One of them, maybe the leader, slipped off his motorcycle and stood in Meza's path.

"Where you goin'?" the man said easily.

Meza looked him over. The man was drunk and fat, with reflexes that would look like slow motion to a fighter.

"I thought I'd have a cocktail." Meza pointed to the bar.

All of them laughed uproariously. "A cocktail?"

"Yeah, exactly."

"How you figure you'll do that?" The drunks laughed again as their leader moved in front of Meza. Damn, Meza thought, what a disgusting group. This is probably how the Berrigans wound up.

"Put one foot in front of the other, I thought."

"Maybe. But if they're broken feet that might be hard." The man widened his legs, bracing. Meza could smell the foul breath. It was a nasty experience. Nevertheless, he decided to try mercy for once. After all, he wasn't getting paid for this.

"I'm going to ask you nice to move. I think it'd be a good idea. I'll count to three."

The man shifted his weight. "Don't bother counting." He had a wrench and swung it. Meza ducked easily and the wrench flashed above him. The man staggered forward. Meza didn't want to hit him, he'd probably kill the poor rummy if he did that. So he just kicked the man's legs out from under him. The man fell hard, his forehead slamming twice off the concrete. He lay still. The parking lot got quiet, no more laughing.

Meza actually felt bad about the whole thing. He took out another twenty and tucked it into the drunk's pocket, then stepped over him and strolled into the bar.

Roberta had been jumpy when she entered the dark bar. The place smelled of stale beer and cigarettes, which just made her more nervous. She looked around for him and he was nowhere to be seen. She grabbed the bartender.

"Where's Marcus?"

"Relax, he just called, says he's tied up. You want a drink?"

"Yeah, Jack Daniels, rocks, with a twist."

Roberta sipped on the drink and looked around. The bar was empty except for the odd drunk or biker, plus some dirtbag with stringy red hair who came in and sat quietly by himself. Most of the men knew who she was and left her alone. One didn't. She felt a hand on her shoulder.

"Okay, baby, what's it cost?"

She had the ability to kill the man easily. She didn't have time.

"Go away," she said simply.

The man shifted, about to become more aggressive. The bartender put his hand out. "Hey, you, come here." The drunk stumbled over and the bartender spoke quickly into the man's ear.

The man, now very nervous, and very respectful, moved away.

It took another half hour for Marcus to enter, like a prince arriving for a coronation. He was black as coal, with a shaved head, cream double-breasted suit, red shirt, gold necklace, pink shoes and a white belt. He was a short man and his chest and arms were wide, muscle pumped in prison yards. His neck was nonexistent, buried inside a mass of shoulder.

Marcus owned the place and everyone in it, not officially, just in reality. He ruled by fear, because he was a psychotic multiple murderer, and everyone knew it.

He sat in a booth and Roberta came over. He was annoyed to see her. "What do you want?"

"I want to talk to you."

He nodded, in a drug-induced, sleepy sort of way. "I'm tired, baby. You want to talk to me? Then you better have somethin' for me."

"Don't worry. It's in my bag."

"Let's take care of that, then we talk."

He got out of the booth and kicked in the door to the ladies' room, where women rarely ventured. Roberta followed.

Meza watched the whole thing from his dark corner across the room. The bar was now empty and the bartender was in the back hauling boxes out. Meza wandered casually over to the booth Marcus had vacated and dropped a microcassette recorder into the booth. It was voice activated and very sensitive.

He went back to the bar and sipped on a Dewar's with a beer chaser. Marcus and Roberta came out ten minutes later, obviously buzzed, and slid into the booth near the black man's beer.

Marcus caressed her neck, first gently, then harder. "How much more of that crank you got?"

She pulled a packet from her jacket pocket and dropped it on the table. "Only the beginning, Marcus."

"Good, that's good."

"And now we have to talk."

"Yeah? So go ahead, talk."

She looked around. No one was paying attention. "This is the deal. There's a guy in Long Beach I'm supposed to give a lot of money to." Her voice dropped. "I want to rip it off. I need you to protect me from the bitch that hired me."

Marcus looked up. "Bitch?"

"Yeah, bitch. I been working for her for years. She thinks she's like a queen. She snaps her fingers and I'm supposed to jump."

The man laughed. "You? You don't jump for nobody."

"You got that right. But the money's been great so I do what I'm told. I been waitin' for my time, for some deal I could just move in on. I think I found it." She hesitated. "There's bucks in it, Marcus. But at the end I want her . . ."

"Gone?"

"Exactly."

He sat back, examining her, hunting for the lie. "We split the cash?"

"That's the deal. She has people that could come after me. So you provide protection, we split the cash."

Yeah, he'd split it. Maybe. "Okay, tell me about it."

She did, every detail, from Alicia Kent, to the murder of Magnus, to the horny engineer at the strip joint in Long Beach. By the time she was done, even Marcus got most of it.

"She's downtown on some other deal," Roberta concluded. "I won't see her till Thursday."

"How much you supposed to pay this guy in Long Beach?"

"Lots. Maybe eighty large."

"You meeting him tonight?"

"Yes."

The light from the bar glistened off his two gold teeth. "You better hope you pull this off. If you don't, I sell you to Oscar." He pointed to a man leaning up against the bar. The man had pasty white skin. His face was cratered with scars.

"Don't worry about it," she said.

"All right. One buzz before you leave."

They headed back to the ladies' room. When they were gone, Meza finished his beer and went back to the booth to grab the recorder. Again nobody paid attention.

He went out to the car, popped the micro-tape into a hand-held recorder, lit a cigarette and listened. He squinted at first as he tried to figure out what the Kent woman was doing. Then he got it. He leaned his head forward and banged it three times against the hard plastic steering wheel. The third time he hit his head so hard he opened a small welt on his forehead. He couldn't believe it! He had picked the wrong one!

He listened to the entire tape twice. Something was coming down tonight and the big hitter inside—Marcus called her Roberta—was going to try to rip off eighty grand. That got his attention. No reason he should let that slide by. Then he got to the part about Kent, and Roberta's plans for her. Even more interesting. What would Kent pay for *that* information? A lot!

He had to find Kent and fast if everything was coming down tonight. But where? Then he remembered Christine. Maybe she saw where the Mercedes was heading before she went home. He called Christine's house. There was no answer.

Christine didn't answer the phone because she wasn't home, and never had been. When Meza left her alone on the cold ground she just sat there and fumed. Who the hell did he think he was to tell her to go home! Christine never liked to be ordered around by anyone, not her mother, and definitely not by her newest boyfriend. So when Alicia came out and hopped in the Mercedes, Christine thought, he can stuff his stupid orders, I can follow people as good as him.

Alicia was as professional as Roberta and took a serpentine route out of the Bel-Air hills. She meandered down to Sunset, then over to Sepulveda, then south out of God's country and into God knows what. When the signs for Culver City appeared, Christine was as confused as Meza, wondering where the hell they were going.

She wondered a lot more when Alicia pulled into a mini-mall near Motor and Washington. Alicia got out of her car, looked in both directions and hopped up a set of stairs to Howard Crabsucker's office. Christine parked and wandered inside. It was hard to spend a half hour inside a 7–Eleven no matter what the excuse. She picked up merchandise, asked about the merchandise, occasionally bought some of the merchandise, and generally kept her eye on Alicia's car. After thirty minutes, Alicia came back down, got in her car and drove away. Very mysterious, Christine thought, but what the hell. She went running for the LeBaron.

44

Alicia Kent left Howard Crabsucker and drove directly to her downtown law offices. The traffic flow was thick and even Christine could follow without getting made. At Bunker Hill Plaza she entered a large brown building where the Los Angeles branch office of Hamilton, Purcell & Buck occupied the top eleven floors. The giant building looked embarrassed sitting there, as though it once thought it was coming to a great party, where there would be lots of buildings standing proud, shoulder to shoulder. Instead, like downtown Houston and Dallas, Los Angeles skyscrapers are now largely empty skeletons, peopled only by firms with long-term leases taken out in the heady days of the 1980s. Alicia Kent felt like she was entering a mausoleum.

Once on the forty-eighth floor she went directly to Magnus' office, behind which she knew was an exact re-creation of the dead man's secret New York conference room. Alicia punched in the combination only she and Magnus knew. She entered Magnus' cave and turned her attention to his *very* private computer.

The password changed daily and was known only to her and Magnus. She found the *L.A. Times* sports section and checked the handle at Del Mar; if she was in New York she would be checking the Aqueduct handle. She took the last five numbers of the day's betting pool and subtracted each of them from a number representing the five letters in V-I-P-E-R, disregarding whether the number was negative or positive. The last five numbers of the handle were 63870. The V-I-P-E-R numbers were 22, 19, 16, 5, 18. A little subtraction and she had 16, 16, 8, 2, 18. She punched the numbers in, then her own personal password, which was itself based on a randomly chosen word from an obscure Sanskrit document. After a moment the computer flashed: "Good morning, Alicia. Welcome to Los Angeles."

She pulled up the Cayman Islands account owned jointly with Bernie and asked for an account balance. She was pleasantly surprised; their crooked bond broker had been busy. The account showed a balance of $53,364,417.68, with a deposit at midnight of almost $700,000. A nice skim from two years of bond scams.

Alicia had had her own Cayman account for years that even Magnus did not know about. She told the computer she wanted to transfer the funds from Bernie's account to her own. After a moment's hesitation, she was asked for passwords. She ignored the request and asked for withdrawal authorization. Same result. Frustrated and concerned, she entered Magnus Purcell's password.

The computer refused again. She cursed so loud the world outside might have heard her were it not for Purcell's thick walls. She couldn't believe it, the son-of-a-bitch broker had demanded a dual password system for withdrawals.

When she calmed down she realized there was only one solution. In order to get Bernie's money she had to get Bernie's password. Tonight couldn't come soon enough.

It was after 4 P.M. when Bigelow got back to surprising Detective Houlihan with the phone information. It was close to the shift change and only a dedicated cop like Houlihan would still be interested. To a guy like Houlihan, however, the day had just begun.

"What the hell took you so long?"

"It's hard, sir, you got to make a lot of calls."

"To get one number?"

"Yeah, you got to call the phone company and they don't want to do nothin'. Then they say 'what credit card did he use,' which we don't know 'cause the guy's got no clothes on, forget a credit card. So they say wait and you get disconnected and you start again. The supervisors are dumber than the operators."

Houlihan's head was pounding beyond belief. "Just tell me what you got."

Bigelow flipped a pad. "The phone on the bar don't usually get used, so that's good. Between eleven-thirty P.M. and twelve-thirty A.M. there were six calls."

"And?"

"Two of the calls are to this number in Arizona. I call it, get the wife. She hasn't heard from hubby all day. I figure, bingo. She took the news hard."

"You told her? That her husband was dead?"

Even Bigelow was chastened. "Sorry, sir, I just wasn't thinking. You'll hear about it anyway, she's gonna write letters to everybody."

"Let me guess. It wasn't her husband."

"Yeah, after she got done screaming and the kids bawling I say, 'you gotta come in and I.D. the body, even though I admit it don't make no sense. I mean how many three-hundred-fifty pounders you think we got on ice?' "

"That's when she stopped screaming."

"Yeah, right away. She says 'what are you talking about, you moron? My husband weighs one-hundred-fifty pounds!' "

"She had the moron part right."

"Probably so. Anyway, that left four calls. The next two calls are off the same credit card as the husband of the screaming lady in Arizona, except to a number out in the Valley. So I call there."

"Why?"

"To check it out, you know?"

Houlihan sighed. "It's the same credit card as the one-hundred-and-fifty-pound guy from Arizona. What'd you think, he gained two hundred pounds between calls?"

Bigelow squinted. "I guess you're right. Sorry."

"Never mind, maybe the Arizona guy saw tubby at the bar. What's the guy's name?"

"Lewis. Delbert Lewis."

"So did you find Delbert in the Valley?"

"No, I got this lady. I say, 'This is Detective Bigelow with the LAPD. Is Delbert in?' "

"Yeah?"

"She goes, 'No, my *husband* won't be back for an hour. What is this about?' "

After a beat, Houlihan laughed so hard the pain in his head actually eased.

"And you were confused?"

"Way confused. The guy's got a wife in Arizona. So I figure maybe it's a different Delbert."

"Common name, could happen."

"Yeah, so I say, 'Your *husband*? Is this the same Delbert lives in Phoenix? Three kids, *wife* named Carlotta?' "

"Good move."

"I don't know about that, sir. She screamed louder than the lady in Arizona."

"And Delbert's whereabouts now?"

"Long gone. I don't think he's the fat stiff sir, I really don't."

"We got two calls left."

"Right."

"To where?"

He handed Houlihan a slip of paper. "One to London. All you get's a beep, like an answering machine. The other to a law firm downtown."

Houlihan got excited. "Get me a picture of Dale the whale that's not too disgusting, you know, not a coroner's photo or anything. Then find the address of that law firm." He thought some more. "Then we need to get their nighttime records, see who left a message at midnight. Then . . ."

"Sir?"

"What?"

"This'll shock you, but I already done the picture and address thing."

Amazing. Put a monkey at a typewriter long enough . . .

"Bigelow?"

"Yeah?"

"If you don't speak to me I'm either gonna die of this headache or shoot you, one or the other."

"The firm's name is Hamilton, Purcell and Buck. Here's the address. My car's outside."

Alicia was still sitting at Magnus' private computer when the screaming started. She had spent hours trying every conceivable way to get the Bernie access code. Magnus' office, nothing. Every password she could think of on the computer, nothing. In desperation she even called Bernie direct at work, said she was Magnus' assistant, asked for the number for the files. Bernie laughed and hung up on her.

By five she gave up and started thinking maybe she should forget Bernie and just concentrate on the beryllium deal. That one was worth a fortune and the Council would be generous. But the bond deal was even bigger, and just sitting there, one signatory dead, one soon to be, and the Council knew nothing about it. No, she would never walk away from that kind of money.

She left the hidden computer room and went down the hall to the office she used whenever she was in L.A. That's when she first heard the screaming.

"Alicia, Alicia!"

Someone was bellowing her name through the fog.

"What?"

The door to her office burst open. A young man stood staring at her, one of the new lawyers. He was a cute, little thing and she had given some thought to inviting him over, before she got tied up with burning Bernie.

"What?"

"It's . . . it's . . ." The fool was stuttering. Then the scream from the hall pierced into her brain.

"What is going on?" she thundered. This was nonsense. She had to think clearly. How *exactly* to do Bernie. How to make sure Roberta was on track.

The receptionist ran in, her face empty of blood, still screaming. Behind her were two men, one in a blue suit, the other teary-eyed, dressed badly in brown. Alicia stood up properly.

"May I help you?"

"It's Mr. Purcell . . . it's Mr. Purcell!" The woman's screams wouldn't stop. She tried to ignore them and concentrate on the men. They looked too official for comfort.

"What can I do for you?"

"Afternoon, ma'am. Detective Michael Houlihan, homicide supervisor, LAPD." He handed her a card and flashed the badge. "This is Detective Amos Bigelow."

Alicia glanced at the official documents and then back at Houlihan. "How can we help you, Detective?"

"I'd like to show you a picture, if I could, see if you can identify someone."

"Certainly."

Houlihan handed her a black-and-white photo of Magnus.

Alicia saw he was faceup, meaning the cops had rolled him over, and the picture was a full-body shot of Magnus in all his flaccid glory.

"This is disgusting. What is this?"

"I'm sorry, ma'am. Just look at the face."

"It's Mr. P! I know it's Mr. Purcell!"

"Marcia, be quiet. Let me look at this. Oh my God, she's right!" Alicia put her hands to her face. "Please take this away!"

"Sorry, ma'am," Houlihan said. "This lady says you work with this Mr. Purcell the most. That right?"

"Yes, of course. Dear God, can that really be Magnus?"

"Well, that's what you have to tell us, ma'am."

"I can't, I couldn't possibly. Oh, please take it away."

Marcia screamed some more. "I can tell, it's Mr. Purcell!" Jesus, Alicia thought, as the woman's howls bounced off the walls. Magnus had never said two words to the woman, couldn't have picked her out of a lineup if his life depended on it.

"Now, who exactly is Mr. Purcell?" Houlihan asked, his pen out. More and more people crowded her office. There was only one thing to do.

She rose. "He's . . . he's one of the name partners of our firm. May I . . . may I see that again?" Houlihan handed her the picture. "This can't be. Tell me it can't be." Then she dropped to her knees and toppled over, closing her eyes. It was easier to fake fainting than crying, she wasn't an actress after all.

Marcia, the distraught receptionist, brought her around after a good ten minutes, pressing a wet cloth against the back of her neck.

"Where am I?" Alicia said.

"Right in your office, ma'am. Sorry about that."

"That's all right, Detective. It's just . . . just such a shock."

"I understand. When was the last time you saw him, ma'am?"

"Magnus? I suppose Back East, in our New York office."

"You have any idea what he was doing out here?"

"I assume firm business. Magnus travels to our seven branch offices constantly."

"What kind of business was he in?"

"He is one of the name partners of this firm. A founder in fact. We work very closely."

"So he's a lawyer too?"

"Of course he is. I don't mean to be insulting, but he's not the type of lawyer you'd be likely to run into."

Houlihan smiled. He didn't like this babe already. "You'd be surprised the people I run into."

"Magnus is . . . was . . . an international tax expert."

"Hey, I know lots of those."

"I see."

"So what's so important he had to come out here?"

"As I say, it could be anything. Magnus had many Pacific Rim clients. Plus he was the manager of all the law firm's branch offices."

"But all these people say *you* worked with him closest."

"That's true, I suppose. On some matters."

"So you ought to know what was he's doing here, right?" Houlihan pressed, and looked dead into her eyes. They were bright and clear. He had seen lots of women faint after looking at homicide photos, more did than didn't on average. The thing was, their eyes weren't perky and smart after they got dragged to their feet.

"Detective, I've already said he had many clients that need service on the West Coast. I'm sure it was an important matter but beyond that I can't speculate."

"What makes you think it was so important? You just said he was out here all the time. Maybe he just wanted some warm weather."

It took her no more than a beat to think. "Just a guess. The circumstances."

His voice softened. "What circumstances, ma'am?"

She had stupidly opened a door for the man, she realized, and now tried to shut it quick. "The whole thing. When there was an emergency he'd do things like that, fly in, have a quick meeting at the airport, fly out."

Bigelow had been wandering around checking the view. Now even he stopped and squinted. Houlihan's headache disappeared entirely.

"What makes you think he died near an airport, ma'am?"

Alicia's shrug was so seamless the underlying panic was invisible. "He said it when he came in," she said, nodding toward Bigelow. "The Hilton, he said. I assumed he meant the airport."

Houlihan's eyes never left hers. "Bigelow, you say anything about a Hilton when you came in?"

The cop actually took off his hat to scratch his empty dome. "Gee, I must have, sir. How else would she know?"

45

When Roberta left Marcus she drove directly to Long Beach to finish her deal with John Doe. She met Jamaica at a coffeehouse about a mile from the strip bar. They sat in the front seat of the Range Rover while Roberta went over her checklist. The all-important brown briefcase stuffed with cash was hidden safely in the back.

"What's that?" Jamaica asked, pointing at the briefcase.

"Don't ask questions," Roberta snapped. She read her list carefully. If she did this perfectly, she could keep what Alicia paid her for the job *and* keep the money in the brown bag. After that, well, who knew how much money there was to make?

Jamaica licked her lips nervously. "Listen, can I ask you something? Just one thing?"

Roberta never looked up. "What?"

"It's about tonight. Any chance we can make . . . a small change?"

Roberta's head came up slowly. A pro like Roberta hated changes. "Just do what I told you. *Exactly* like I told you. No changes."

"I promise this won't screw anything up. It's just something I've always . . . well, always wanted to do."

This woman was starting to seriously worry Roberta. Now she *had* to know what the woman wanted. "Go ahead. What do you want?"

Jamaica told her and Roberta just stared. "Are you kidding?"

Jamaica retreated a little. "Well, if it's a problem, forget it."

Roberta actually smiled. "Why not? Sure."

Roberta and Jamaica arrived at John Doe's secret apartment just before ten. The night was moonless and the darkness hid many crimes. The apartment building was a cheap, boxy place, one in a

series in east Long Beach, largely nondescript. The freeway noise
from the nearby 710 was rumbling and constant.

"What next?" Jamaica asked. She was Roberta's loyal assistant
now, no more questions asked, just follow orders.

"You shut up and follow my lead."

They walked through the open lobby door and into the elevator.
Once upon a time the outside door had been locked and required
a buzzer to get in. Once upon a long time ago.

His apartment was 3-F. They rode to the third floor and knocked.

The door opened quickly. He was wide-eyed. His shirt was open,
the white T-shirt underneath it wet with perspiration.

"You're late. Why?"

Roberta pushed past him without answering. "Are you alone?"

"Of course."

She threw the battered briefcase on the couch. "Watch this," she
ordered Jamaica. She professionally inspected each room, returning
when she was sure they were alone. John Doe sat nervously in a pale,
beaten-up chair.

"Are you ready to do business?"

"Yes, certainly." The man tried to hide his fear. "You guys want
a beer or a drink or something?"

"Sure, John. Let's have a drink and relax."

John Doe's hands shook as he made the drinks. The ice rattled
as he handed over water glasses of Wild Turkey to the women. Then
he glanced at the satchel. Roberta knew he lusted after it.

"Don't be shy, John. Open it!"

He put the briefcase on his lap, gingerly, then flipped the latches.
"Damn!"

"Go ahead, count. Don't take my word for it."

He rifled through the bills. "I'm . . . I think it's all here."

"Don't think, John, be sure. I don't want you worried about anything. Take your time."

He did, his hands still shaking. "It's . . . it's beautiful."

That it was. The crisp green bills were precisely arranged, five
rows across, three rows deep. Fifteen rows in all. One hundred bills
per row, each banded in tight stacks of twenty-five. Every bill had
the face of Benjamin Franklin on it. One thousand, five hundred
hundred-dollar bills. A hundred and fifty thousand dollars in cash.

He took out a stack and reached for the wrapper.

"Don't touch the bands," Roberta barked.

"What?"

"You heard me. You can look, you can count. Don't rip the bands. Once you make your calls, you can rip whatever you want." She smiled and nodded toward Jamaica.

"Hey, John?" Jamaica said, moving closer. "Let's hurry up and get this done. I'm so horny I'm dying."

John Doe didn't need any more inspiration. All that cash and a grateful Jamaica besides. He sat at his desk and quickly dialed. Two thousand miles away, a man in Lima, Peru answered. John spoke in halting Spanish, to make sure the women wouldn't understand.

"Ricardo, this is Juan . . . I'm fine, thank you. I have received authorization . . . That's affirmative. The message is Crescent, Dolphin, Rice . . . Correct, C-D-R, Crescent, Dolphin, Rice . . . The delivery is authorized. Call this number when the plane arrives in Barbados. The same message will be given to authorize departure from there if everything's okay at this end."

After John hung up, the man in Lima made his own call and an aged 707 was towed inside a remote hangar. Rusting doors opened and a truck filled with twelve tons of nuclear-grade beryllium wheeled up to the cargo bay of the plane. It would take forty-five minutes to load the plane and another fifteen to get departure clearance. Then another couple of hours for the arrival in Barbados and the authorization to fly the second leg across the Atlantic.

Back in the secret, grimy apartment, John Doe spent his hour drinking Wild Turkey straight up and staring at the cash in the briefcase. At Roberta's direction, Jamaica stripped naked and danced for him. It was no big deal, she did it at the club all the time. John Doe had never been happier in his life.

"God, you're beautiful."

The dusky black girl knelt at his feet, then unzipped him. Roberta had ordered her to keep him occupied and she did a good job. She took him in her mouth and kept him there till the phone rang.

Roberta jumped up. "I'll get it." She listened quietly. "I understand," she said finally. "Thanks. I'll talk to you again in a few hours." She hung up and turned to the romantic pair.

"The seven-oh-seven just departed Lima. ETA oh-eight-hundred Barbados."

"Am I done?" Jamaica asked.

"Yeah, you're done." Roberta had her pad out and checked off items on the list.

Jamaica stood up and wiped her mouth. "You remember what I wanted, right."

Roberta looked up, confused at first. "Uh, yeah. No problem.

"I can do it?"

"I said no problem, didn't I?" She gestured to her bag. "In there."

John Doe smiled. "You can both do it."

Jamaica fumbled through Roberta's satchel. The .22 was small, feminine and efficient. It looked odd in her hand. She handled it awkwardly, because she had never held one before.

She pointed. "Like this?"

"Right," Roberta said. "Just put two behind the ear and we can get out of here. Do you think you can do that?"

"I think so."

John Doe suddenly got it and when he did he started to cry. His pants were at his ankles and his money stared at him from the open briefcase. The beryllium was in the air, now on the step at 33,000 feet, heading for Barbados.

"Please don't, I beg you. Besides, you *need* me. The man from Lima will call again! I have to authorize departure from Barbados to Lagos."

Jamaica moved behind him. She held the .22 a foot back from his head, near the ear.

"Is this right?"

"No, you have to grab his hair and hold it right against the ear. That way you can put two caps in without his brains flying all over the place." She turned to John Doe. "John, I was born, raised and trained in Argentina. I spoke Spanish before I could piss. I can give the departure instructions as well as you now. A lot better, actually."

"Oh, God, this is not funny."

Jamaica grabbed his hair. "Okay?"

"Yeah, that's good enough. Go ahead."

She fired once, closing her eyes, then again, this time with her eyes open.

"Cool."

Roberta examined the dead man. "Not bad." She grabbed the suitcase, closed it and slapped the naked girl hard on the ass.

"Get dressed and gimme that gun. Marcus is waiting for us."

Detective Michael Houlihan went directly from his confrontation with Alicia Kent to a bar. It was a simple bar in an Indian restaurant a few blocks from downtown. The bartender's name was Salameh and he wore a turban. All the cops called him "Salami."

Houlihan sat at the bar and Bigelow sheepishly crept next to him.

"Salami, I got a screaming headache. Make it a double."

His headache had disappeared an hour before when he caught Alicia Kent in a dead, cold lie. It came roaring back when Bigelow screwed the whole thing up.

"Bigelow, let me ask you something."

"Sir, I know what you're gonna say. I'm sorry, I really am."

Houlihan got his double Stoli rocks from Salami and drank it halfway down. He shuddered. God, he needed that. He checked his watch. It was after seven, hours after his shift ended. Good, he still had some control.

"Bigelow, you just *think* you know. Answer me this. How did you ever make this grade? Are you the dumbest homicide detective in the LAPD?"

"Sometimes I think so, sir."

"Salami, give the dumbest detective in the LAPD a beer. Don't let me get too close to the bottle. I may break his head with it."

Salami had learned how to be a bartender from watching Westerns. "You got it, pardner."

Houlihan downed his Stoli and pushed the glass across for another. "Bigelow, just tell me one thing. Why?"

"Sir, I never figured she was lying. You saw the way she was dressed, and that office?"

"Bigelow, there was no way you said anything about the Hilton when you walked in that room. Matter of fact you never said a word. I was with you every second."

"I think you're right, sir. I'm really sorry. But maybe we're still okay. If she knows the fat guy got it at the Hilton, and I didn't tell her, that must mean somebody else did."

"Somebody else did what?"

"Told her. And maybe that person saw something we can use."

The second Stoli was there. Houlihan did his duty, terrified that this mope was his partner, maybe someday standing between Houlihan and violent death.

"Bigelow."

"Yes, sir."

"I'm gonna try something here which I'm sure is a waste of time, which is to try to teach you something. Now think. If she knew about the Hilton, and you didn't tell her about the Hilton, how the hell did she know about the Hilton?"

Bigelow squinted, then brightened. "She was at the hotel by accident, meeting somebody on business, saw him come in the door."

"Try again, Bigelow."

He rubbed the cold beer against his face. "The fat guy called the office from the bar, we know that. Maybe they talked. He told her he was meeting some babe at the Hilton. Hey, maybe some guy! She's covering for him, wants to keep it under wraps because he's gay. The Hilton part blurted out."

"That's awful complicated, Bigelow. Think of something simple."

More rubbing. "Okay, simple. He gets there, goes to the bar, has his Beefs, calls the office to get her, she's not there."

"Simpler, Bigelow."

Bigelow was actually sweating at the effort. "Okay. He calls the office to check messages. Nothing more."

"Good. Then what's he do?"

"He goes up to that room . . . to meet . . ." He clapped his hands. "To meet her!"

"Bigelow, there's hope. What happens next?"

"They have *sex*! And if she's in the room when he gets it, she saw the guy who . . ."

"Bigelow!"

He rubbed the beer bottle against the side of his head, then his eyes widened.

"That's right, Bigelow."

"*She* killed him? But why?"

"Who knows. Did you check her voicemail?"

"Yeah, nothing from him."

"Ain't that weird? Guy comes in from the East Coast, calls the office, doesn't leave *any* messages for her, the one who works with him the most?"

"He didn't have to call her! She was waiting for him upstairs!"

Houlihan patted him on the shoulder. "Bigelow, all those people said you were dumb? I always sort of disagreed. Now make sure that room gets checked out for fibers, hairs, everything. She had to leave something."

"Yeah!"

"Who you got following her?"

"Jordan, just the way you said."

"Good." Jordan was Houlihan's best friend, to the extent he ever had a friend. Jordan was like a Commanche in an unmarked Mercury. Wherever Alicia Kent went, Jordan would be behind, and never get made.

Salami brought over another double Stoli and a beer without being asked. "On the house, pardner."

Houlihan was now five hours past his shift. It never occurred to him to go back to his empty, very cluttered apartment.

"Drink up, Bigelow. We got work to do."

46

Angelo Bracca was deeply in mourning. He sat quietly in an upholstered chair inside a darkened living room. On the coffee table across from him a tabloid headline said it all: "MOB KID AND SUPERMODEL GUNNED DOWN." The pictures had been taken while John was being wheeled into the emergency room on a white gurney. Natala De Marco walked next to him, covered with blood.

Angelo's men tried to take the paper away, but the old man refused. From the kitchen behind him he heard his wife's incessant wails. There were four women in the kitchen and two priests. Angelo didn't move, he just sat in the dark listening to the screams. His man came in, Anthony Constanto. Tony the waiter. Always there.

Angelo looked up, his eyes weak and bloodshot. He was expecting the worst.

"It's not that, Angelo," Tony told him quickly. "John's still in surgery."

"How about Nat? How's she doing?"

"Not too good, Angelo. Between her father and John . . ."

"Will she come out to see me?"

"I don't think now's the right time, Angelo. Besides, she wants to stay with John."

Angelo nodded slowly. "Anything else?"

"Yeah, Angelo, there's somebody here to see you."

"I told you, nobody." Angelo's voice was soft, which was dangerous.

"I know Angelo. I wouldn't ask except . . ."

"Except what?"

"Angelo, it's Nick." Tony the waiter hesitated. Ordinarily there was nothing unusual about Nick showing up. But something in Tony's voice said this was very unusual.

"So?"

"Angelo, he's drunk! He's even got a bottle in his hand."

Angelo's head raised slowly, and for the first time that day smiled. "You're kidding."

"No, it's exactly what I said. I told him to get out of here like that. He said, 'Just tell Angelo I'm here!' "

Angelo's smile broadened. "Get him in here."

Nick stood in the darkened room with Tony the waiter at his side and Angelo sitting in the stuffed chair.

"I don't believe it," Angelo said. Nick had a small bottle in his hand. He lifted it insolently.

Tony was furious. "Nick, what are you doin'! Angelo's son gets shot and you just walk in with a bottle like it's a party? You got no respect at all! There's damn priests out there!"

Angelo stood and kissed Nick on both cheeks. "Look at him, Tony. You're too young to remember what he was like. Nick the slicer! Ain't that right, Nick?"

Nick shrugged his beefy shoulders. "I don't know, Angelo, I don't remember much from those days."

"You know why he don't remember, Tony?"

"No."

"Nick was a drunk. A serious fall-down blackout drunk. Sober, the nicest guy in the world, like now. But not drunk, right Nick?"

"That's true, Angelo."

"When he's drunk he's a hitter like Meza. Maybe *better* than Meza! Nick the goddamn slicer."

Angelo held out his arms. Nick embraced him, burying his face in Angelo's neck.

Tony's eyes were darting back and forth nervously. "And now he's drinking again?"

Angelo took a long drag off the cigar he had burning in his ashtray. His eyes were bright and excited. "It sure as hell looks like it to me. Hey, Nick, you remember the Geronimo twins?"

"I remember some of it, Angelo. Not a lot."

Angelo laughed. "Tony, there was these two twins out of Garfield.

Name of Geronimo, like the Indian. They come and see me and Nick and tell us they want to expand into Passaic County. They got a dozen soldiers and we got two days to give up Paterson and Clifton."

"Yeah?"

"Yeah. So I just look at Nick and shrug. Nick leaves and that's why we got Garfield today."

"Why? What happened?"

"One by one he took 'em. Always the knife, right, Nick? A day later the Geronimos are goin' nuts. Five of their guys are sliced and three more ain't been seen. So Nick walks straight into their place in Garfield, just that damn bottle in his hand. They got four guys left plus the twins. Nick says he'll leave 'em alone but he wants it all, construction, union, the loans, the cops, everything they got in Garfield."

"And the twins just say okay?"

"Nope. One of their guys pulls a gun on Nick. The guy's in back of him, no way Nick can see. But he just spins and throws. The guy's now lookin' at a knife stickin' out of his chest. How the hell you do that, Nick? You got eyes in back of your head?"

Nick shrugged. "I don't know, Angelo. I always just know."

"Whatever, it works. So the Geronimos start screaming and tell their two last guys to open up. They do, about thirty rounds, right into the Geronimos!" Angelo laughed so hard he choked on the smoke.

"They killed their own boss?"

"Sure did. That's how we got Garfield. They work for us now!" Angelo stood and hugged Nick tightly. "So when his wife dies, Nick gets religion. He stops the booze and tells me he wants out of the life. I say 'no' but you don't have to hit no more, you done enough. We got somebody new maybe just as good as Nick. Just watch this Meza kid for me, I tell him."

"But . . . but he's drinking again!"

Angelo's smile was broad. "That's right! I think Nick's about to cut me some Russians."

The heavyset man drank deeply from the bottle, and his eyes were strange, ethereal. "I got to, Angelo. They shot John."

———

Alicia Kent was pensive as she drove away from her downtown office. Houlihan's visit had unnerved her and she wasn't used to that. She prided herself on instinctually recognizing danger, particularly danger caused by a competent opponent. Every instinct told her that beneath his sloppy clothes and bloodshot eyes Detective Michael Houlihan was a very dangerous man.

But first things first. She angled the Mercedes back to Culver City and mentally ran through her checklist. One, get Bernie's password and transfer the money. Two, make sure Roberta got the beryllium delivered on time. Three, get out of Dodge before that cop got any smarter.

She parked in front of the 7-Eleven to collect her thoughts. Out of the corner of her eye she saw a blue LeBaron pull in after her. She watched the driver steal glances at her. Alicia dropped her pad.

A girl got out of the LeBaron and scurried into the store. Alicia followed her in. Christine stood at the magazine rack pretending to read. Alicia walked directly behind her, crossed her arms and stared.

Christine tried to squelch the panic. "Something I can do for you?" she said, trying to sound hard.

"Yes. What are you doing here?"

Keep it cool, she thought. When in doubt attack. "What the hell you care?"

Alicia smiled. "Just a question. You're a working girl, right?"

Christine's outfits always led people to that conclusion. The only thing missing was a neon sign that said "hooker." She relaxed.

"Everybody's got to work," she said easily.

Alicia's voice dropped. "You want a job?"

Migo would kill her for this. "Maybe. As long as it's not too strange."

Alicia Kent glanced around the 7-Eleven. Empty. Back to Christine. "It's not strange at all, a very straight deal. We'll make at least two grand apiece for a few hours. The guy wants two girls. Interested?"

She acted on instinct. "I'm interested."

"Good. Stay here. I'll be back in an hour."

Christine looked her up and down. "I think you ought to wear something a little more exciting."

An hour later Alicia was back. She had changed out of her beige business suit and into a black leather skirt, heavy makeup and a pink vest with metal studs. She made sure Crabsucker got his wish. Like with Rudy Diaz on that long-ago bluff, she liked to pay her debts.

"That looks a lot better," Christine told her.

They piled into the Mercedes and Alicia drove slowly out of Culver City toward West Los Angeles. Once in the hills above the Palisades they would see an ocean filtered in the lights from the city and headlights snaking slowly along the PCH. Now it was just traffic, ugly traffic.

Alicia glanced at Christine, who was moodily staring out the window. The girl was beautiful and under other circumstances could be recruited by the Council and put to good use. But the Council could never know about this deal. No loose ends.

"There's some rules," Alicia said.

Christine woke from her daydream, an unpleasant one about a very angry boyfriend. "What rules?"

"Number one, we get paid up front."

"I like that."

"I thought you would. The guy is always on speed, and will be doing more when we get there. While he's getting buzzed you show the guy some stuff." Alicia wanted Bernie and the girl both naked. It would save work.

"Okay, I get it. What will you be doing?"

Once I get the password I'll shoot him like a dog, she thought, just before I do the same to you.

"I'll just wait, see if he gets off on you. He may not need me."

"Lucky you."

"Hey, I brought you the job."

"Fair enough."

A quarter mile behind them a cop named Jordan slipped through the L.A. night in an unmarked car. Alicia had no idea he was there. When he got to West L.A. his radio crackled.

"Jordan!"

"Yeah."

"This is Houlihan. You still got them?"

"No problem, Detective."

"Where you at?"

"Sunset, just near the strip. You wouldn't believe what hap pened."

"I ry me."

"After she left that downtown law firm she goes to Culver City and parks in this mini-mall. She goes to the second floor lookin' like a lawyer and a half hour later she comes down dressed all in leather. Then this other babe comes out of the store dressed just like her and they take off together. I don't get it."

Neither did Houlihan. Except now he was absolutely convinced he was following the killer of the fat man.

"Jordan, just stay with her."

"You got it, Detective."

High above the city, inside his glass and chrome aerie, Bernie the broker was ready. All his hard work had been finished hours before. The markets had closed on the East Coast at 4:30 P.M., 1:30 Bernie's time, and that's when he began what he called his "recon-ciliations." He was fast, had unlimited access to client accounts and was still skating along on his morning ice. It took him forty-five minutes to juggle the books so that the profits went one way and the losses the other way. At the end he pressed a button and another three hundred forty thousand disappeared into the account in the Caymans.

By 6:30 he felt great. The day had ended on an uptick and it took him a lot less time than usual to scramble the accounts. He paid some attention to the Pacific exchange, which closed later than the NYSE, but the plain fact was he didn't care that much. At seven he bolted.

"I am out of here," he announced breezily as he swept through the reception area. "The day's done."

He had to force himself to eat, otherwise he knew he'd really crash and burn. He vividly recalled the time a year ago when he didn't eat for three days over a long holiday weekend. The whole thing was just girls and ice. By the third day he was hallucinating, descending into a suicidal-homicidal blackness. He had a gun and huddled with it, naked, weeping in a corner. The girls took one look at that, grabbed his cash and bolted. Three times over the endless night he tried to pull the trigger, anything to ease the dark horror. Three times the gun he mistakenly thought was loaded just clicked. At dawn he finally passed out, scratching furiously at the imaginary bugs he was certain were eating him alive.

His source was the one who told him he had to eat, and since he followed that advice the full horror had not returned. By 7:30 on this night he was in a Chinatown restaurant in front of a bowl of food, praying he could stuff it down. He focused on the noodles, figuring that would provide the most sustenance. At the end, he washed the noodles down with a couple of beers and felt better, like he had done something healthy.

Once the food was in his stomach he drifted slowly back to the Palisades, stopping for a few pops along the way. Now the lights were down, the house was clean, the music was raucous and he was flying. He took a long, hot shower, put on a pale, silk robe which reached his knees and checked his watch. Any time now. He looked out the window and saw a silver Mercedes pull into the driveway. Two very exotically dressed women got out.

In the chase car Jordan parked a quiet quarter mile behind. He kept Houlihan advised.

"They stopped," he announced.

"Where?"

"Some mansion in the Palisades."

"Okay, stay back, don't get made."

Jordan was insulted. He didn't say anything.

"Sorry," Houlihan said. "What's happening?"

"Nothing, they just went inside."

Houlihan breathed deeply. He didn't care if his friend was insulted. "Be careful, Jordan."

47

Portov was beyond furious when he and his one remaining Russian gunman fled John Bracca's apartment. He was bewildered. Never in his life had an assassination failed when he was personally in control. And this hit did not just fail, it had turned into a complete fiasco. Now he had a dead doorman stuffed into a closet on the first floor and two dead Russians on the eighth. John Bracca was probably dead but Boyle and the two women weren't. That meant at least three live witnesses who could identify him to Angelo Bracca.

The Russian gunman driving the car was his best man, Viktor, born and raised in Yekaterinburg, about nine hundred miles east of Moscow, a town that is to Russia what the Chicago of the 1930s was to the United States. He had been personally recommended to Portov by Josef Alexeyev, and until now had been completely reliable. Portov's sullen silence was a shroud for the fury and confusion boiling inside the man.

"I think it's best you get out of New York right away," Viktor said in Russian.

Portov looked over slowly. "Great idea, Viktor. Where were those great ideas in John Bracca's apartment?"

Viktor kept his eyes straight ahead. "I was surprised by that police officer's tactic. I did not anticipate that."

No kidding, Portov thought, but not nearly as surprised as the two dead Russians on Bracca's floor.

"Just drive to the airport."

There was no traffic on the way to Kennedy at this hour. When the signs appeared, Viktor looked over quizzically.

"Drop me at the United terminal," Portov ordered. "I'll find something out of there."

"Where are you going?"

Good question. One possibility was back to London, to explain to the Council what had happened in New York. The other possibility was Alicia's warm arms. The second option was a lot more attractive than London.

"I'm going to Los Angeles. Sanitize my house, all the warehouses we ever used, everything."

"I understand," Viktor said. It was time to be useful. Who knew what Portov's rage might bring. "What else?"

"I want a lot of support in Los Angeles to make sure there's no more problems. Who do you have?"

"The best man possible. His name is Serge Belov. He is forty-six years old, mild mannered and frail appearing. He wears conservative, dark suits and thick glasses. His organization is small but first rate."

"Experienced?"

"Very. He was formerly head of Special Projects for Soviet military counterintelligence."

"What's 'Special Projects'?"

"They were responsible for interrogating suspected double agents."

"You mean killing?"

"Only after lengthy interrogations. Belov was an expert at avoiding early . . . early departures. Extremely active during the Aldrich Ames period."

Portov shuddered. There were so many double agents killed during the 1980's that the bloody trail ultimately led to Ames himself.

"That's fine. Have him meet me at the airport."

"All right. He's a cab driver."

Portov squinted. "A what?"

"A cab driver. It's a perfect cover. Most cab drivers in L.A. are Russian emigres."

"How long do you need to clean up here?"

"Give me three days."

"No more. When you're through, meet me in Los Angeles."

Portov jumped out of the car and ran to the United ticket counter. He had no bags. The monitor overhead showed the last L.A. flight had left forty minutes before. He scanned the upcoming departures then approached the woman behind the first class window.

"One way to Chicago. Name's Robert Daniels. Cash."
"Yes, sir."

Viktor was efficient as well as frightened and worked hard for a day and a half. Eventually he got to Portov's house in Little Odessa. Portov lived modestly in the same Russian neighborhood where he had been born. The white frame house was two stories high and had a gabled roof, with a pleasant yard in back.

It was deep night but Viktor parked a half block away and watched the street. Nothing. The neighborhood was still empty, barely stirring in the faint pre-dawn. He walked in the shadows past Portov's house, checked it out, then doubled back and quickly went around to the rear of the house. He fumbled with Portov's keys.

He was still fumbling when he felt rather than saw the shape near him, as dark and formless as the departing night. He spun to confront it, his face wet with sweat. He tried unsuccessfully to keep a tremor out of his voice.

"Who's there?" he barked in Russian. In this neighborhood, where even the menus are in Russian, there was never a need to speak broken English. This strange area of New York was as pure a part of Russia as Leningrad.

The shape moved closer and showed itself to be a man. He had something large in his left hand that looked like a club. Then the man drank from the club. It was a bottle, for Christ's sake! This was a goddamn vagrant in Portov's backyard!

"You're trespassing," Viktor shouted. "If you don't get out of here immediately, I'll have you arrested."

The man moved closer. "Talk English. Are you Portov?"

Viktor stiffened. Not a vagrant after all.

"What business is that of yours?"

The man's voice dropped. It was barely above a whisper. "Good. Keep it in English. Now, once more. Are you Portov?"

"I'm a . . . a friend of his."

"Where is he?"

Viktor still had the same semiautomatic he had used at John Bracca's apartment, now newly loaded. He licked the salt off his upper lip and touched it. It had a reassuring, calming effect on him.

The dark shape cocked an eyebrow curiously but otherwise never moved.

"I have a gun. My hand is on it now."

"I know, take it out and give it to me slowly."

"The only thing I'll give you is one last chance to get out of here. Once I pull this gun out, I'm going to use it."

"No," the dark shape said. "Once you pull the gun you're going to hand it to me. Politely."

Viktor had been in lots of violent confrontations, and had never seen someone so strangely serene. The two men stood quietly, unmoving, watching each other, the only sound soft breathing. Then the intruder raised the bottle to his lips, tilting it. Viktor yanked at the gun.

Later, when he thought about it, before he died, he could never remember seeing the stranger's hand move. But move it did, with snakelike speed. The knife sliced through the faint dawn, deeply into Viktor's arm. He screamed and the gun flew in a high arc, clattering to rest at the stranger's feet.

The Russian's arm bled freely. He ripped at his shirt, struggling to make a crude tourniquet.

The stranger picked up the gun and threw it into the yard behind him. He waited till Viktor's bleeding slowed.

"When you're through yelling I need to go in."

"You can't."

"Where's Portov?"

Viktor shook his head. The stranger sighed and showed the knife. It was a commando's knife, with a serrated edge. Viktor looked toward the yard. The gun was now very far away.

"I'm gonna ask one more time," the stranger said, his voice again soft as death. "Tell me where Portov is, then open the door with your key and show me through the house. If you don't, you'll bleed to death on this porch from a thousand cuts and I'll still search the house. Do you believe me?"

As one killer to another Viktor believed every word the stranger said. "Okay, no more with the knife." He grabbed his keys with his good hand and quickly opened the door. "I dropped him at the airport last night. I don't know where he went."

The knife caressed his throat and Viktor backed against the wall. A thin line of red appeared.

"Los Angeles," Viktor said quickly. "He took the first flight out to anywhere, I swear I don't know where. He's going there now."

The man smiled. "See how easy that was?" Viktor slumped, relieved, assuming wrongly that the truth would save him.

The stranger poked him gently with the blade. "Show me around."

"Sure, sure." Viktor gulped. "Just tell me one thing."

"What?"

"Who are you? Who do you work for?"

"Me?" The stranger drank some more. As the whiskey hit him he changed, becoming more focused, his eyes sharper, his mouth developing a cruel and pitiless cast.

"My name is Nick," the beefy man said. "I'm a drunk."

48

C hristine was brave until she got inside Bernie's house. Then she got very scared.

"I need to talk to you," she hissed at Alicia Kent.

Alicia was lounging on the couch, once again making her calculations. Christine's voice came to her out of a fog. "What?"

"I said I need to talk to you."

"What do you need to talk about? Count your money and make sure it's all there."

"That's not the problem. It's all there."

"So go make Bernie happy and let's get out of here."

That was the problem. She had to play for time. "What are you going to do?"

Alicia had that part precisely planned. She had a quiet .22 in her soft, leather bag. Once the girl and Bernie got started, she would walk into the bedroom and fire two small slugs into the back of the girl's head. Bernie would be terrified and realize that unless he gave up his precious password the next two bullets would be for him. If he still refused? Well she had other ideas. Maybe tie him up, pour some lighter fluid on his crotch, then hold a lit match in her hand. He'd talk once he saw that match. The only question was whether she'd drop it after she got the password.

"I'll go second if he's still frisky. You first."

Christine had run out of excuses. "I have to make a call first."

"Go ahead. Use his den."

"Okay."

She raced into Bernie's den and grabbed the phone. As she passed his bedroom, she saw him naked, carving lines from a pillow of white powder, spooning the lines into a cup of hot tea. Maybe she wasn't cut out for this life after all.

She called Meza's house first. No answer, and no answering machine! Then she dialed her own house and changed the message on the answering machine. "Migo, this message is for you. Don't get mad but I didn't go home like you said. I followed that accountant in the Mercedes except she ain't no accountant. Now we're together in the Palisades. Here's the address." She rattled it off. "She wants me to give it up to some bald guy in the other room for a thousand or two thousand or something. The guy's disgusting and I just saw him naked pouring some cocaine in a teacup. I'm scared and I may have to give him some just to stay alive. That doesn't mean anything between us. I love you and would never cheat. Bye."

Then she sat back on Bernie's desk chair, confused, exhausted, and starting to get seriously frightened.

In the sunken living room, under a twenty-foot impressionistic mural of a naked woman in congress with a pit bull, Alicia Kent hung up the extension. Her face was even paler than usual. How stupid could she be. Migo! Miguel Meza! The girl in the other room was his girlfriend. Miguel Meza!

She sunk against the soft pillows of the couch. "Now what?" she asked the empty room.

It took Alicia a good half hour to really calm down. In the meantime Bernie sat naked on his giant four-poster hollering disgusting suggestions. Christine kept making excuses and now Alicia knew exactly why. She beckoned to her.

"Have I ever asked you your name?"

"It's Jasmine."

"Jasmine, that guy in there is going nuts. You've got to do your job *now*."

Jasmine's eyes darted back and forth as she tried to think of another excuse. None came to mind.

"Don't worry, I get it," Jasmine said.

"You may get it, but the guy in there's *not* getting it and he's already *paid* for it. Look, maybe you can get him off easy."

"How?"

"Try to get him to do more dope. He's been going all day. He's got to crash and burn soon."

"Okay."

Christine/Jasmine marched bravely into Bernie's bedroom. His mouth was open and his tongue lolled. His naked, flaccid body was pasty. If he was ready for action, he didn't show it. His reason for living was limp, rendered useless by twenty hours of artificial stimulants poured into his tea.

Jasmine smiled. "All set?"

Bernie dribbled at the corners. "Yeah."

She doubted it. "How about if I undress? Real slow."

"Sure."

She did it like the movies, except *real* slow. By the end, a good ten minutes later, she stood naked before him and turned, giving him the full view.

"God, you've got an unbelievable body. How'd you get those bruises?"

"A client played rough. Is that what you like?"

Bernie looked down. "I don't understand this."

"Maybe you had too much of that." She gestured to the white cliffs of powder, waiting patiently for another trip into the hot tea.

"You might be right." He thought about it. "Maybe a little oral would help?"

No doubt. Christine's talents in that area could raise a corpse. "Maybe you should just rest first."

Bernie's eyes drooped. As he approached a full day without sleep, even the highest quality meth couldn't do the job.

"I can't believe you're going to frustrate him," a voice said.

Christine turned. Alicia was standing in the doorway, fully dressed, holding her gun. Christine had neither of those things. No clothes, no gun.

"What's with you?"

"Jasmine is such a silly name. What's your real one?"

Christine shrugged. "What's the difference? Everybody's got a made-up name."

"The difference is I'm holding this gun, and I want to know what Miguel Meza calls you."

Christine just stared, and called herself a stupid bitch in her mind over and over. The phone! The woman heard!

"Well?"

"He calls me Christine." She didn't want to think about what he'd really call her when he found out about this. Or what he'd do. She remembered his last threat: "You know those bruises on your ass? I ... ..." Well, good, she deserved it. From behind she heard harsh snores, the ultimate triumph of biology over chemistry.

"How did you find me?"

"Migo knew where you were. Some fat guy told Angelo."

Magnus. She wished she could kill him all over again! "Where is Meza now?"

"Can I put some clothes on?"

"No. Answer the question."

"He's back at his house."

Alicia shook her head. "Don't lie. There was no answer when you called." Christine heard an audible click. She was convinced if she didn't talk quick, she might never talk again.

"He's following the other one."

Alicia squinted, uncomprehending. "What other one?"

"The big babe in the boots and leather jacket."

"Roberta? Why is he following her?"

Christine shrugged. "He thought she was you."

The fog lifted. "He was assigned to follow a killer. Roberta looks more like a killer than me?"

"I think that's about it."

Alicia had to sit down. This was more than bizarre. "What to do," she asked herself again.

Christine put her hands on her hips. "This is really embarrassing. Can I get dressed?"

Alicia picked up Christine's clothes. "Are you strong enough to carry him?"

"Probably."

"Then do it. He'll be unconscious for hours. Take him to the car."

Christine hated being ordered around, by anybody. "What about my clothes!?"

The shot came instantly. The bullet whistled past her ear and shattered a mirror six inches behind her head.

"The next one's for you," Alicia said easily.

Christine grabbed Bernie. "I can carry him, no problem."

———

Six miles away Detective Michael Houlihan was as stuck in traffic as a man in quicksand. Nothing he could do would make a difference. His siren would just infuriate the other drivers and increase his headache. He called Jordan again. His friend was still sitting quietly outside Bernie's house.

"Anything happening?"

"Not really. It's getting boring." Then Jordan's voice changed. "Houlihan, you won't believe this!"

"What?"

"This is the most amazing thing I've ever seen!"

"Jordan, you're making me crazy!"

"Listen to this! There's three people coming out of this house. Two of them are bare-ass naked."

There was interference on the line, and what Houlihan heard made no sense. "Say again, Jordan."

"You heard right. There's a naked girl and you would not believe the body on her. She's dragging a guy out of the house and he's naked too. He looks like he's sleeping, or unconscious or something. The one that's dressed, she's holding some clothes, maybe for one of the naked people."

Houlihan's headache roared back with a vengeance. "Jordan, tell me exactly what the naked girl looks like."

"Looks like? You ever have a wet dream?" He went right to Christine's gory details and Houlihan could tell it wasn't Alicia.

"Okay, describe the one that's dressed."

Jordan did. No doubt. Alicia Kent.

"Jordan, listen to me. You got to be careful. That one that's dressed, she's dangerous, and I'm sure she's armed. She killed one guy I know about."

"Don't sweat, it's just some babe. Not bad, either, I wouldn't mind seeing her naked too. I'm not worried."

"Jordan!"

But Houlihan was yelling into a dead phone. The crack of interference was high and it took a good six minutes for the line to clear. Only when he finally heard the man's voice again did he relax.

"Jordan, you're about to give me a heart attack. What's happening now?"

"It's the strangest thing. They threw the guy in the trunk. The one that's dressed . . . well, sorry about this, you ain't gonna like this."

"What?"

"I think I got made, she's walking over here."

"Jordan, get out of there! Now!"

"Just one second, I want to find out what she has to say."

"Jordan!"

Later on, when he made his report, he wrote about voices, unintelligible, garbled, a series of pops, then silence.

"Jordan! Jordan!" Houlihan shouted until he was hoarse.

There was no answer.

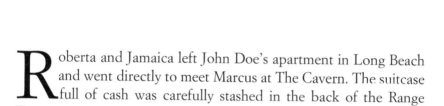

49

Roberta and Jamaica left John Doe's apartment in Long Beach and went directly to meet Marcus at The Cavern. The suitcase full of cash was carefully stashed in the back of the Range Rover.

Jamaica's head rested against the seat back. Her window was open and she gulped the rushing air.

"God, that was unbelievable. You think he knew it was real?"

"He knew."

"Oh man, that was great. You think I can do that again?"

Roberta kept her eyes forward. Jamaica wouldn't be doing much of anything once Marcus got hold of her.

"It's not always that easy. The trick is you don't get excited. You just do your job."

"Yeah."

Roberta pulled into the parking lot and nodded at the man standing quietly near the entrance. As always The Cavern was dank and smelly, although now more crowded. Marcus was sitting in his usual booth, his cigar blowing powerfully. A dusky girl with bare shoulders clung to his arm.

Roberta stood quietly with the briefcase. Marcus looked up quizzically and Roberta nodded.

"Get out of here," he barked at the dusky girl. She knew better than to argue. She was gone.

"What do you want to drink?"

"Jack Daniels, rocks."

Roberta sipped on the drink and tried to smile flirtatiously, which was hard when you looked like Roberta.

"You did him?"

"She did." A nod in Jamaica's direction, sitting at the bar as ordered.

Marcus' laugh was loud, "You're lyin'!"

"Nope," Roberta said. "She wanted to. She asked and I said okay."

Marcus rubbed his chin. "That's cute, but now you got a problem."

"I know. I was hoping you could help."

"I'll take care of it."

She let a beat go by. "All right."

"Let's see the suitcase."

She pushed it over. Marcus snapped the latch.

"Goddamn!"

"I know. There's seventy-five grand in there."

"Oh, man, that looks pretty."

"Yes it does. Now, Marcus, remember, we get to split it, fifty-fifty, like we said."

He sat back and rubbed his chin some more. "I ain't sure about that."

"Marcus!"

"Chill out, I said *probably* fifty-fifty. Plus, you said eighty, not seventy-five."

"Marcus, I did all the work!"

He leaned across the table and grabbed her lapel. "Tell me how much you took already."

She didn't say anything. His face darkened. "I'm waitin'!" He blew on the end of the cigar till it was red and glowing.

"I'm sorry, Marcus." She pulled out a crumpled wad of bills from her jacket and dumped them on the table.

He counted it. "Five grand. There *was* eighty."

Her voice wavered. "I'm sorry, Marcus."

He reached across the table. She flinched, then allowed her face to be stroked.

"It's not the end of the world, baby. You just got to pay for mistakes, right?"

Her voice was barely audible. "Yes."

"Right. So first, this is mine." He put the five thousand in his pocket. "Next we divide the eighty. Sixty-forty split. I get forty, you get thirty."

"Marcus!" She didn't comment on his wonderful addition.

"Shut up. You're lucky I don't take the skin off you for this scam. You hear me?"

Again softly. "Yes."

"Good, anything else?"

She gestured to Jamaica at the bar.

"Oh, yeah." Marcus could afford to be generous, take care of Roberta's problem for free. He wagged a finger and a biker came over. There was a whispered conversation and then Jamaica was gone. Never to be seen by Roberta again. Or anyone.

Marcus was again yapping at her but it was all about how smart he was and the women he controlled, the men he killed, things like that. Marcus liked to hear himself talk and she had heard it all before. She tuned Marcus out and did the count in her head. Forty large to Marcus left her with over a hundred grand. Not bad. And with Jamaica gone to dance again for John Doe, no one to ever question the count. If Marcus had been smart, he would have checked the count with Jamaica *before* doing her. But Marcus wasn't smart; he was dumb as a rock, which was why she chose him.

"There's only one more thing," she said dreamily, interrupting him.

"What?"

"Alicia Kent." She thought about the plane in the air and the millions somewhere being paid. "If you're willing to help me, there's a lot more where this came from."

Stephanie Shane landed the T-63 like a leaf drifting down from a tall tree on the runway of El Toro Marine Air Station in Laguna Niguel, California, about an hour south of Los Angeles. Captain Compton just watched, and kept his mouth tightly shut, like they all did when she showed what she could do.

There was a nondescript government car waiting for them in the parking lot. Boyle held out his hand, demanding the keys. Stephanie gave them over gracefully.

"Hey, you're the man."

He didn't do nearly as well driving off the base as she did flying into it. After two or three times circling the runway, he finally found the exit.

"You sure you want to leave? I was having fun."

He sighed. There was no need to respond. He was at the beginning of what promised to be a very bumpy road.

She had a map spread across her legs and she studied it. "Meza lives in West Hollywood. That means you get on the four-oh-five north to the ten. Go east on that for about twelve miles to La Cienega." She turned the map upside down. "Stay on La Cienega for four point six miles till you get into some hills. I'll give you directions there."

He stared straight ahead, gripping the wheel. She turned to him. "Questions?"

"What's a four-oh-five?"

She patted him lightly on the shoulder. "Turn left here."

Meza lived an hour from El Toro for anyone who knew what he was doing. Despite Stephanie's gentle instructions, it took Boyle two hours to make the trip without traffic. It was close to 9 P.M. when they got there, midnight New York time. He was both exhausted and starving.

The house was a 1940s-era bungalow on a street of modest houses. A steady stream of cars cruised slowly up and down. When Boyle got out to look at the house, one of the cars slowed.

"How you doin'?" a male voice said.

"Not bad, how about yourself?"

"How sweet of you to ask. Would you like a date?"

Boyle squinted. Hell, this was L.A., maybe they were all this friendly. "A what?"

"Hop in the car, we'll take a ride."

Just then Stephanie got out of the passenger side of the car.

"Oh, dear," the voice from the cruiser said. "What a shame."

"It doesn't look like anyone's home," Stephanie said.

"Plus this pond's got some weird ducks swimming around."

They rang Meza's doorbell to no effect. Boyle was moderately amazed that Meza even had a doorbell. They peered through the windows and saw nothing but emptiness. Once a phone rang six times and then stopped.

Stephanie sat on the ground. "I give up."

Boyle liked hearing that; after the airplane ride he needed an ego boost. One picks up a lot of tricks as a Paterson cop, and within ten minutes he had the back door open.

"And to think I thought you had no talent."

"That's not what you said this morning." And he was pleased to see pink rise in her cheeks.

Meza's house was as spare as a monk's cell. There was a formica table in the kitchen with metal chairs. The living room had a fabric couch, a television on a console, a ghetto blaster with a CD player and a table with liquor bottles. The bedroom had a bed, a nightstand and one lamp. Two small rooms were filled with duffel bags, sweats and fighter's tape. Boyle knew the look well. A lone telephone hung on the kitchen wall.

"I'd say he keeps a low profile," Stephanie said.

"Let's split up and search the place. We may figure out where he is."

"You'll search nothing!" a voice shouted.

They spun quickly and saw a man standing in the doorway. Boyle moved in front of Stephanie and reached under his jacket for the gun, then realized it wasn't there. "Who the hell are you?"

"My name is Mark," the man said, placing his hands on his hips. "The more important question is, who are you?"

It took a half hour for all the explanations and by the end everybody was still edgy. Mark still didn't understand what these two people were doing here, and Boyle *definitely* didn't understand what Mark was doing here.

If he wasn't starving Boyle would have spent more time figuring it out. As it was he decided to go for the refrigerator. Mark was still protective. "What, may I ask, are you doing now?"

"Trying to find something to eat. I'm dying. How about you, fake lawyer? You hungry?"

"Why?" Stephanie said. "Am I supposed to believe you can cook?"

He snorted. "Even Natala can cook. Not like me though."

He examined the refrigerator. "This won't be easy. There's sausage in here, that's a start. An onion, great. The zucchini's still in the wrapper. I see he still hates vegetables."

Mark sighed. "I try, believe me, I try."

Boyle squeezed a head of lettuce. "This is no good." He held up a tin. "Anchovies. Rusty metal, great fish, no problem."

He sniffed the open bottle of wine. "Vinegar city. Hey, Mark, you got any wine?"

Mark put his hands on his hips, "Yes, I have wine. I'm a *collector*. A red, perhaps, from the Trentino region."

Boyle slapped him on the shoulder. "Go for it, Mark."

Mark and Stephanie stood around the stove drinking red wine while Boyle worked. It was impossible that he could fight like an animal in Madison Square Garden, collect dead bodies off Paterson's dead streets and also be able to cook a meal from Meza's meager store. Plus there was that other thing in the morning. Stephanie decided she might be on to something here.

Boyle was actually proud of his abilities around a stove; in Patsy's house it was the only way he could eat. He started with the zucchini, trimming it into quarter-inch rounds. Then he salted the vegetable, wiped it off and filled a bowl with the vinegar, wine, pepper, bay leaves, lemon juice, juniper berries from a can, anything he could find. He boiled the whole mess and popped in the salted zucchini, mixing until the room filled with the smell of it. Then came the anchovies, layered over the vegetable in a flat dish. He let it stand.

"That looks magnificent," Mark gasped.

He wished he had more to work with but this would have to do. "Hey, sailor-girl, this is called sausage and peppers. Welcome to Paterson!"

She didn't say anything, just kept thinking.

Boyle sautéed and pierced the sausage, seeded the peppers and cut them into strips. He poured off the fat, popped in the onions and browned the whole thing, adding a pinch of worcestershire and whatever spices he could find. At the end he poured the whole mess over coarse brown bread and ladled out the zucchini. Mark and Stephanie sat down, took a sip of wine and just stared.

"Unbelievable," Mark said. "There's never anything in this house. It's like magic."

As hungry as Stephanie was she just sat, sipping on her wine and thinking. Boyle's hair was mottled and his clothes rumpled. He was already sporting stubble on that gorgeous face. He ate hungrily; as a kid he always had to gorge himself just to maintain weight. When he realized he was being stared at he looked up with the fork still in his mouth. "What?"

She leaned over, grabbed his hair in her fist and kissed him hard on the mouth, even though it hurt her to do it. He stiffened in surprise, then relaxed. The kiss lasted a lot longer than she first intended.

"This is so sweet," Mark said. "But I'm going to eat."

"That's just a thank you for the food," she said when she broke the kiss. "Means nothing."

He wiped his mouth with the back of his hand, his eyes locked on hers, which weren't moving either. Who knew where the whole thing was going to go.

"Eat your sausage, sailor girl."

50

Nick walked out of Portov's house in Little Odessa leaving a dead body on the kitchen floor. The sun was rising, cresting the buildings over Manhattan and landing bracketed and sullen in Brooklyn. Before he left, Nick called Angelo Bracca to tell him that one of the men who shot his son had died painfully. The old man cried with joy.

Nick left the house and followed a route very similar to Portov's. He drove to the United terminal and, ironically, but without importance, met exactly the same woman Portov had, and paid cash, exactly as Portov had. He caught the first flight out and after an hour layover in Chicago, landed at LAX.

The city was wrapped in mid-morning gunk and all but invisible as the plane descended. The smell when he walked out was an odd mixture of ozone and fuel oil. He jumped into a cab. The cabby's name was Ivan Petrovich, a former math teacher from the St. Petersburg suburbs. "Where to?"

"Where's the nearest Marriot?"

"About a mile away."

"Fine."

Nick checked in and again paid cash. He showered and took a two-hour nap. When he woke he went to the phone book, checked the yellow pages, found what he wanted, ripped out the page and went out to the street again.

"You know how to get to Norwalk?" he asked the first cab.

"Sure, as long as it's daylight."

"There's an army/navy surplus store at this address." He handed the cabby the page from the phone book. "Can you find this?"

"Sure."

The store had everything he wanted, hunting knives kept in

sheaths that could be strapped to a leg, folding knives that fit inside a jacket pocket, knapsacks, even the sharp edge of a bayonet if he wanted it. He passed on the bayonet and settled on the folding knife and field knife, plus a dark satchel to put them in. He already had his favorite with him, the serrated combat knife.

Back at the hotel he spread out his purchases on the bed and changed carefully: a dark suit, dark turtleneck and dark wingtip shoes with thick rubber soles. During the day he would wear sunglasses.

Once dressed he sat back, doodling aimlessly on a hotel pad. The Russian at Portov's house had taken a long time to die, and spoke freely in a futile attempt to save himself. Nick now knew everything about the mysterious Serge Belov and his Los Angeles–based Russian gang. He gathered his notes, pulled out four small bottles of Scotch from the mini-bar and filled a water glass. When he drank his expression changed, his eyes developing a cold, frightening focus. He put the dark glasses on, maybe to hide those eerie eyes, and went out the door of the hotel.

Meza spent the entire day and the beginning of the night trying to find Alicia Kent. He drove downtown to where Bernie worked and found nothing. He went back and forth from downtown to Bel-Air trying to get lucky and pick her up. Nothing. At 10 P.M. he gave up. He decided to go home.

When he got there, he was surprised, but not shocked to see Tommy Boyle quietly sitting at his kitchen table eating sausage and drinking red wine. There was a beautiful woman with tangled blond hair and green eyes sitting next to him. He had never seen her before and noticed her face was slightly discolored.

He walked in without ceremony and tapped Boyle on the back. Boyle just nodded. They had been through a lot together and didn't spend a lot of time being sentimental about it.

Boyle waved his fork over his shoulder. "Stephanie, meet the famous Miguel Meza, Migo to his friends. He kills people for Angelo Bracca or anybody else who pays him a lot. Migo, say hello to Stephanie Shane. She's a fake lawyer."

Stephanie found herself staring at the man she had heard so much about. It's seldom that people look exactly like their legend but Meza certainly did. He wore a rumpled, dark suit with a black shirt underneath it. His bright red hair was tangled and fitted in a ponytail. There was a day-old growth of stubble on his face, and a silver wolf earring hung from his left ear. He carried himself with a panther's grace, a killer's grace. Stephanie instinctually knew that every rumor she ever heard about Miguel Meza was completely true.

His voice, however, was gallant, soft and unthreatening, with a slight, almost undetectable accent.

"I'm happy to meet you," he said, holding out his right hand. The fingers of his left gently stroked her face, and she actually shivered at the touch. These brothers were good! "Did he do that to you?"

"Actually, yes."

Boyle waved Meza's look away with the end of his fork. "I'll tell you later. Did you hear about John?"

"No, what about him?"

Boyle told him everything. At the end, Meza was impassive, professional, knowing that soon enough he'd get the call telling him to respond.

"What's Angelo doing about it?"

"I don't know. We do know there's a woman out here who's working with the guy that shot John. She's the one who killed Patsy."

That news visibly stunned Meza. "A woman killed Patsy? What woman?"

Boyle again recounted everything he knew. When he finished Meza's look had blackened. He put a microcassette tape player on the table.

"Listen to this."

The tape was scratchy and there was a lot of bar noise but they could hear Roberta's voice clearly. Marcus did no more than grunt.

"Is that her? Alicia Kent?"

Meza shook his head. "No. I thought it was Kent but it's not. She works for Kent. She's doing some other deal out here."

Stephanie pressed. "What other deal?"

"I don't know." Meza wiped his hands over his face. He was beyond exhaustion. "I just want to grab some stuff and go over to Christine's. You guys can stay here."

Meza lit a cigarette and grabbed Boyle's wine glass, drinking it deeply as he walked to the phone. He pushed a button, the speaker phone wailed and he dialed Christine's number. Her answering machine picked up and they all heard her frantic cry for help.

Meza cursed and went running for the rooms where the small bags were stored. He grabbed a satchel, checked its contents, then sprinted for the door.

Boyle stood in his way. "Whoa, man, where you going?"

Meza's face was grim. "You heard that! Christine gave the address of that Kent woman!"

"Yes, I heard it all. Just don't go running out the door without thinking."

"I am thinking. I'm going to the address on that tape. And there's gonna be one real dead Kent lady when I'm done."

"What about the other hitter, the one you were following?"

"I don't care about her." He pulled away again. "It was stupid to follow her at all."

"Migo," Stephanie said softly. She touched his arm and he stopped, his eyes flat and dangerous.

"You're absolutely right to go after Kent. But remember, we're trying to get everybody she's working with. Just tell us what you know about the other one and we'll take it from there." She paused. "They all had a hand in Patsy's death."

It was smart to bring up Patsy's murder. Meza stopped long enough to point to the micro-recorder he had used to tape Roberta at The Cavern. "On that tape she says the name of a strip bar in Long Beach. That's where she met this guy John Doe the last time." He described Roberta's appearance. "That's the scam she's working. Go check it out. That's where I'd start."

"Good idea. Incidentally, does Christine have any clothes here I could maybe borrow?" Her hand swept over the tan flight suit.

"She keeps clothes in there. Help yourself."

"Thanks."

Meza turned to Boyle. "You got a gun?"

"No."

"You're a cop and you don't have a gun?"

"I'm actually not a cop anymore, remember?"

"I have some," Stephanie said. She turned over the brown satchel and John Bracca's two Glock 9 mms clunked out.

Meza inspected the weapons professionally.

"They're not bad but I got better." They followed him back into the gun room and watched him open a duffel bag.

"Here, take your pick." He turned the bag over and a varied collection of shoulder harnesses and semiautomatic handguns fell to the floor.

He turned to Stephanie. "I'd stay and help, I really would. But . . ."

Stephanie put her hand on his face. "Go help Christine."

Boyle was examining the guns on the bed, checking the heft. "Hey, Migo, you got any words of advice?"

"Yeah, you see a guy named Marcus?"

"Yeah?"

"Shoot first."

51

Supervising Detective Michael Houlihan found Jordan exactly as he expected to, slumped over the steering wheel dripping blood. The window on the driver's side was spotted with three small holes. Houlihan stood next to the car with clenched fists. Bigelow spoke quietly.

"I'll call it in, sir."

He was still standing there a half hour later when a car drove up and parked on the quiet street. A man exited and walked slowly toward him. The man wore a rumpled, black double-breasted suit over a black T-shirt. His shocking red hair was tied in a ponytail and there was an earring in the shape of a wolf hanging from his left ear. He was unshaven.

Houlihan watched the man approach. He looked to be in his late twenties and he walked with a light athletic gait. As he got closer Houlihan saw eyes ringed black from lack of sleep.

The stranger looked Houlihan over, then looked intently at the car.

"You a cop?"

"Yeah." Houlihan started to say more but didn't, frozen momentarily by the guy's attitude.

"Small caliber, I think."

"What?"

"The holes." He pointed. "A twenty-two maybe. Was he a cop too?"

"Yes."

"Friend of yours?"

"A real good friend." Houlihan was beyond rage and tried to hold it in, waiting until he could find out what the guy was all about.

The man turned to Houlihan. "You didn't find any more bodies? You didn't find a girl, did you?"

"No. You expecting a dead girl?"

"I was worried, not expecting."

Houlihan felt the reassuring press of the police .38 against his hip. You know the guy who did this?"

The man shook his head. "It wasn't a guy."

"What do you mean it wasn't a guy?"

"It was a woman."

Houlihan watched the man's eyes. They were calm, professional, and he knew a lot about this case. He knew, for example, that the killer was a woman. Houlihan's hand drifted to his gun.

"What do you do, friend? You're not a cop."

"No, I'm not a cop."

Houlihan yanked the .38 out and pressed it against the stranger's throat. "So how about we just freeze now."

Meza laughed. "Do I look like I'm gonna run?"

"Open your jacket. Real slow."

"Officer . . ."

"Detective!"

"Detective, think about this like a sensible person. I walked up here on my own."

"Last time. Open your jacket."

Meza opened his coat and spread his arms wide. The dark brown leather of the shoulder harness was clearly visible.

Houlihan grabbed the gun. "You're under arrest."

"Detective, can I ask you a question?"

"Ask whatever you want."

"The woman who murdered your friend has a girl with her, a real good friend of mine just like this guy was a real good friend of yours. You want to help find them or you want to stand here and waste time?"

Houlihan's angry response caught in his throat. An eight-hour-a-day cop would have snapped the cuffs on right away. Houlihan was a twenty-four-hour-a-day cop and there was something about this creep's attitude that got his interest.

"You okay, sir?"

"Yeah, Bigelow, fine," he shouted, still holding the .38 level. "Stay there till the backup comes." There was a hint of a faraway siren in the night air.

Back to the stranger. "What's your name?"

"Meza."

"What do you do for a living, Meza?"

"Does it matter?"

"Yes, it matters a lot. What's your first name?"

"Miguel."

The sirens were louder now. The two men stood in the dark street as still as Jordan, watchful.

"Okay, Meza, what do you know about the woman?"

"She's a cleaner, Detective. Supposed to be the best."

"Why do you say that?"

"I know a lot. If you give me a chance, I'll tell you a lot."

Houlihan breathed deeply and looked up to the Bel-Air house. Bigelow was standing stupidly at the crest of the hill, paying no attention. The sirens were less than a mile away.

"Miguel, give me your keys."

Meza blinked once, then handed them over.

"Hey, Bigelow!"

"Yes, sir!"

"I'm taking a ride. Take care of things here."

Detective Michael Houlihan drove in silence. Meza sat slumped in the passenger seat. Houlihan was thinking some about Meza, some about Jordan and a lot about how he was going to explain driving off with a guy who some people might consider a prime suspect in a cop killing.

Bernie's Palisades house sat on the spine of the Santa Monica mountain chain separating Los Angeles from the San Fernando Valley. Houlihan dropped onto Sunset and headed east, toward downtown. He drove in silence for fifteen miles until he was long past the parts of the city where the money lived. At Alvarado, where the gangs lived, Houlihan spoke for the first time.

"Meza, let's talk. I'm less than a mile from Rampart station. If I like what you say we'll see where it goes. Otherwise, I drop you off. Understand?"

"Yeah, I understand."

"How long you been out here?"

"About eight years."

"Where's home?"

"New Jersey, Paterson. Across the river from New York. About twelve miles."

"What's that, like one of those suburbs?"

Meza laughed. "No."

"How long you been in this business?"

"What business?"

"Don't lie to me, Meza, I'm too tired."

"Same thing, about eight years."

"What'd you do before that?"

"I was a fighter."

"Yeah? What kind?"

"Welterweight."

"You any good?"

Meza shrugged.

"I think you're lying to me, Miguel." They stopped at a light. Houlihan held his hands up. "Okay, let's do it."

"Detective, please."

"Meza, I'm not asking, I'm telling. We both use open hands. Take your shot, see if you can hit me."

This was like kindergarten. Meza opened his hands like the cop ordered and made a slight gesture with his right, a sort of half fake, not even much of a fake. Houlihan went for it like a trout for a worm and Meza slapped him across the side of his head with the left.

"Ow! That hurt!"

"Hey, don't blame me!"

"Ow, man, what are you, some kind of animal?" Houlihan held his head with both hands.

Meza didn't say anything. The light changed, Houlihan drove off and eventually stopped rubbing his face. "Okay, I believe that part. Were you a pro or amateur?"

"Both."

"Yeah? You ever fight in the Golden Gloves? I went there with my father once. That's the greatest event in sports. New York fight fans, Madison Square Gar . . ."

"Hey, Detective?"

"Yeah, Miguel."

"Can we talk about something else?"

52

After she shot Officer Jordan while he was sitting in his car, Alicia Kent immediately went back to the Bel-Air house to sanitize it and check for messages. There were no messages from Roberta, which infuriated her. She also tried to get Portov, no luck.

Christine was a prisoner and so exhausted by now she was beyond fear. It was hard work lugging Bernie's deadweight out of the Palisades house and into the Bel-Air house. She dumped him unceremoniously on the floor of the first bedroom she could find.

"Lift him up on the bed," Alicia ordered.

Christine flipped an impolite finger in Alicia's direction. "Screw you." She walked to a closet and flung open the door. "I'm getting dressed and if you don't like it shoot me." She noticed with satisfaction that Alicia's wardrobe was very high-end. And their sizes weren't that much apart.

"Not bad. Where do you keep your undies?"

When Alicia didn't answer she ransacked through some drawers. "Here we go. My, aren't we the little slut."

She selected a pair of black hi-cut panties and matching bra, then hunted for something loose to pull over it. Alicia had some wonderful cashmere sweaters and Christine got real comfortable inside one.

"Now if you shoot me it'll cost you a thousand dollars for the sweater."

All of a sudden Alicia didn't care. She got Christine this far and didn't need her naked for the rest of the night.

"Select whatever you want. You're going into a room with Bernie. Locked!"

Christine shrugged. "You know Migo is coming after you, don't you? He's *so* bad."

Alicia knew that a lot better than Christine did. "And what're you, his little plaything?"

Christine hopped onto the bed, stretching languorously. The cashmere sweater ended at the panties and that was it. "You better believe it. And I *like* that man to play."

"Does he love you?"

"As often as he possibly can."

Alicia realized there was both danger and opportunity here. Yes, Meza would come after her, no doubt about it. Yet as long as Alicia had Christine, she had a hostage.

"I'm going to lock the door. Let me know when he wakes up."

A licia used the next half hour to try to come up with a coherent plan. Goal number one, get the password from the unconscious Bernie. Number two, get out of this house before Meza tracked her down. Number three, find Portov and Roberta.

Her thoughts were interrupted by a banging on the door. "What?" she screamed.

"He's awake."

Alicia unlocked the door, her gun leading. Bernie lay in a flaccid heap on the floor. Alicia pressed the gun to his head.

"I don't have a lot of time."

"Is this a robbery? What do you want? I'll do anything." He was crashing heavily from his twenty-four-hour meth high. His eyes darted back and forth as the paranoia of the moment took him. Except, as the saying goes, sometimes even paranoids have real enemies.

"Bernie, this is not a robbery. I work with Magnus."

The little man just sputtered. "Magnus! Let me talk to him."

"He can't talk right now." That part was very true. "I only need one thing from you, your password for the Cayman accounts."

"If you really work with Magnus then let me talk to him."

"I told you, Magnus is . . . unavailable."

Bernie shook his head, the fog and pain starting to ease. "I don't know what this is about and I don't know you. But *nobody*, and I mean *nobody*, gets my password until I get my money."

Alicia Kent had to suppress the urge to just shoot Bernie on the spot. She only hesitated because she knew she'd be shooting her fortune into oblivion as well.

"Bernie," she said, in what she hoped was her most reasonable voice. "I'm going to ask you one more time. What is the computer password? What is the access code? If you don't answer me, I'm going to fire."

In retrospect, she realized her lack of attention was born of simple frustration at Bernie's intransigence. She never heard anything until the male voice spoke, startling her.

"You won't have to fire."

She flinched and started to spin. Then she smiled. The voice was deep and had a slight European tinge. She finally turned around and there he was. She wrapped her arms around his neck.

"Gregor, I'm *so* happy to see you."

Portov laughed easily. "And I you. Let me introduce you to my colleagues."

She looked at Portov's companions with the gun still in her hand. There were four of them standing there. Two had small automatic weapons that were pointed squarely at Bernie. She was safe now. She put her gun away.

"Alicia, this is Serge Belov. Mr. Belov, this is Alicia Kent, the most extraordinary woman I've ever known." Belov bowed. He was slight and pale, with thick glasses. He had a mild manner about him, like a friendly teacher. He carried a black satchel that seemed filled. He extended a hand.

"How do you do? I've heard so many excellent things about you."

"Fine, thank you."

Belov gestured toward the prone Bernie. "What do you need from him?"

"I need a certain account number. He won't reveal it."

Belov spoke directly to Bernie. "I really think you should tell her what she wants."

For some bizarre reason Bernie was emboldened by the man's quiet tone. He shook his head from right to left. "I'll never tell her. That's *my* money, not hers."

The Russian guards laughed. Belov smiled with genuine delight. "Really? Well, we'll see." He unzipped his satchel. "I think we have all we need here."

Alicia spoke quickly. "This house is no longer secure. Do you have someplace else?"

"Of course," Portov said, "the barracks. There's no one there now except two guards."

"Great. I assume he's a . . ."

"Professional, yes. Bernie will not be a problem."

"How long will it take?"

Portov turned to the pale man. "Serge?"

"Give me two hours." He pointed at Christine. "Is she mine too?"

"No," Alicia said quickly. "She's an extremely valuable hostage who must be kept unharmed. Just lock her in a room."

"Pity," the pale man said. He walked to Bernie, who was staring with wide eyes, his bravado gone. "Well, Bernie will do fine, just leave him with us. We'll have a wonderful time. Bernie, it was so nice of you to get undressed."

The "barracks" was really a corrugated tin warehouse in Inglewood, a broken city on the edge of South Central L.A. It sat next to a railway line where once upon a time trains came and went. Once upon a long time ago. Now the area was little more than an impoverished crime zone, ground zero for the L.A. riots in 1992. Once the Lakers played there but even they bailed a few years before. Now no one played there, except for criminals of all kinds. The Russians fit in perfectly.

There were thirty Russian gang members based in the barracks but most were now spread to the four winds. Three were with Portov and Belov. Most of the rest were out efficiently knocking off drug dealers in various parts of Inglewood and its environs. The Russians learned early that drug dealers carry a lot more cash than your average supermarket, are a lot easier to hit, and the cops care a lot less when one gets robbed.

The two guards remaining at the warehouse were in their late thirties and thick set. They had been in the country for three months, their English was crude and they were so low in the organization that they drew guard duty even on the dullest of nights. They sat on the concrete warehouse floor and spoke to each other in Russian, exchanging drunken memories of the glory days of the early nineties in Moscow, when good girls suddenly became streetwalkers and vodka was as cheap as bread. America was far different. Here the streetwalkers cost a fortune and even the vodka was expensive. Smoother, yes, but very expensive.

"So you think it was better then," one challenged, tilting up his bottle.

They both grinned. No. This was L.A., the land of no rules, of endless money, of opportunity, where anything was possible.

Once an hour a tour of the perimeter had to be made. Ivan, who was even thicker than his partner, checked his watch. He cursed amiably in English. In Russia, despite the propaganda, English was taught in schools and the military. It made it easy for Russian mobs to recruit.

Dmitri laughed and leaned against the stone wall. Half the bottle of Smirnoff was empty. "If you walk fast," he said in Russian, "it'll be over fast."

Ivan struggled to his feet groaning. He walked to the door, stretching, Dmitri's laughter loud in the background.

The warehouse was locked by a deadbolt on the inside. He slipped that and wandered into the night air, which rejuvenated him somewhat. A block away the nearest working streetlight sent glancing patterns onto the broken concrete driveway. There was no one out front, nobody had ever been out front.

He was about to leave the parking lot for the darkness of the perimeter when he realized the keys were still in his hand. He looked back to the open door. To walk back and lock the door would be good procedure but would be a hundred-yard walk for nothing. He continued his stroll.

Once away from the lights of the street, his world turned black. He had to feel his way around, sliding his left hand against the cold metal wall. There were trash cans back here, and rats, and his eyes strained to detect danger from the faint illumination fighting its way from the street behind him. He had a flashlight, of course, but that too was sitting exactly where he had left it, next to the vodka bottle. Russian curses as a rule are longer and more poetic than their English counterparts. He amused himself by uttering a string of them as he walked. By the time he got to the rear of the warehouse, all light was gone. The sounds now all seemed dangerous: his knee banging against a metal garbage can, the rustling of a rodent, the whispering wind brushing the clothes of a potential intruder. The noises were also insistent, and the shadows more ominous. He saw one and stopped, blinking at the darkness in front on him, watching as the dark shape shifted. It was a man. Ivan backed against the warehouse wall and sullened.

"Who are you?"

The shape didn't answer. A cold fear gripped him and he charged, firing the whole way. He closed his eyes just before impact. He smashed headlong into a metal trash can with a vinyl garbage bag sitting on top of it.

Ivan had trouble getting to his feet. The vinyl had burst after his aggressive charge and he was now covered with the remnants of a hundred fast-food lunches. His knee was swollen and throbbed with pain. He got on his hands and knees, then to his feet. There were no shapes back here, just his imagination. He limped around the rest of the perimeter toward the welcoming light on the street.

Ivan went in the warehouse door, closed it and snapped the dead-bolt. "I am an idiot," he screamed in Russian. He expected to hear his friend laugh; he wanted to tell him the whole story about charging the garbage can, like Don Quixote. Dmitri would like that story.

"Dmitri! Dmitri!" he shouted. He knew what he would find, his friend slumped against the wall, the vodka bottle in his hand, asleep. Dmitri was a good friend and would be a better one if only he could handle his drink.

Ivan staggered through the warehouse, partially from the effects of the vodka, partially from his swollen knee. The interior was littered with dozens of small crates used as lockers by the Russian gang members. The wall where he and Dmitri liked to sit was the farthest from the entrance. He turned the corner, saw his friend and laughed.

He spoke in Russian, as most of the gang did when they were together without outsiders. "Dmitri, you are an old man. You can't drink and you are no good on guard duty. Do you expect me to take the next shift?"

Dmitri lay slumped against the wall, the vodka bottle cradled in his arm. His head hung limply and his mouth was open. In the warped shadows of the warehouse, Ivan saw spittle dripping from the corner of Dmitri's mouth.

When he stood directly in front of his friend his heart froze. Dmitri's face was ash white and the spittle dripping from the corner of his mouth was bright red. He held the bottle near his chest, but his chest was open and the blood poured like a river to the smooth concrete floor between his legs.

Ivan had once been a dedicated communist yet now found himself making the sign of the cross. "Dear Jesus, sweet Jesus."

That's when he felt the presence near his left arm. He remained at attention, staring at Dmitri. Don't be afraid, this is the same as the garbage can, he told himself, a trick of the nerves. Then the presence spoke.

"Are you Portov?"

"What?"

The shape moved closer. "Are you Portov?"

Ivan knew enough English to get that one. "No."

"Do you know where he is?"

Ivan spun to face the intruder. He saw a beefy man in a dark suit, wearing sunglasses, sipping on a vodka bottle. *Ivan's* vodka bottle.

"I don't . . . don't know."

Nick sighed and reached for the combat knife again. Why did they always have to make it so hard?

53

Once Detective Michael Houlihan got done asking a half-hour of senseless questions, Meza finally got him turned around and headed in the right direction. Alicia Kent's Bel-Air house was dark when they got there except for a pale light near the back. There were high stone walls all around. Houlihan got out and just stared at it.

"How are we supposed to get in there? Ring the doorbell?"

"That ain't gonna work. We gotta sneak in. Can't we just hop the wall?"

"Meza, I can't do that, I'm a police officer. We got no warrant, we got no nothing." Houlihan looked around. "Besides, somebody'll see us."

"Not if we go around back."

"How we gonna do that?"

"Just follow me."

The Bel-Air Country Club was having a wedding party, now winding down. There was a band dressed in black-tie and a comedian. The bride and groom looked beautiful, and most of the remaining celebrants were ripped. Houlihan had never felt so out of place in his life.

"Are you nuts?" he whispered. "Where are you taking me?"

"Don't worry about it. Just try to look important."

Houlihan was plenty worried about it. He was out of shape, jowly and dressed like a slob, which was how he always dressed. His jacket didn't match his pants, his shoes were thick and worn, and his shirt protruded over his belly. His tie, vividly displaying multiple stains, reached only halfway to his belt. He was also ill-shaven, had rings around his eyes and needed a haircut.

"These people are going to throw us into the street."

"Don't worry, Detective, it's one in the morning and they've been partying all night. Just walk around like you own the place."

The men at the wedding were also dressed in black tuxes and their wives in shimmering gowns. Houlihan forced his to remain in long enough to check out a few of the bare shoulders. He couldn't remember the last time he hadn't just paid for it, or gotten a cop's freebie from somebody who charged for it. Yet here, the beautiful women held the arms of their men with light touches. It was a classy place, with classy people and Houlihan had no earthly idea how to act in a place like this.

Meza never had any such inhibitions. He put his fingers in his mouth and gave a sharp whistle. A waiter with a tray looked over quizzically.

"Over here, José, *por favor.*"

The waiter came over with a tray of champagne, asking no questions. Meza grabbed two and gave one to Houlihan. The detective might not know how to act but he knew what to do with the champagne.

"Damn, that was good."

"I told you. Follow me."

Meza led Houlihan through the celebrants and out the back door, into the darkness of the night. Meza pointed across a deep ditch to the black course on the other side. "See that bridge? We walk across the bridge, near that part with the flag—that's called the green—then we're right in back of her house."

"Yeah?"

"Yeah. So we check it out, maybe we break in and maybe we don't. Up to you."

Houlihan drank the rest of his champagne and threw the glass into the canyon. Meza did the same.

"Let's go."

Boyle drove away from Meza's house with Stephanie Shane in the passenger seat. Stephanie was now bedecked in Christine's finery, which was definitely a new look for her. The highlight was a short leather skirt that rested high on her bare legs. She also wore black boots and a blouse that was almost transparent. Boyle thought she looked just fine.

He followed Meza's instructions and found the Long Beach bar easily. It was like every strip bar in creation. A neon woman on the outside sign flashed red and green, green with clothes on, red not.

Boyle parked in a black asphalt lot between two pickups. The ocean smells from the nearby docks had an odd petroleum scent to go with the salt.

"Nice place," Stephanie observed.

"Yeah. You want to wait out here?"

"You've got to be kidding."

He was. "Okay, just stay close to me and be careful."

"I will. What do we do when we get in?"

"I get to be a cop again." He pulled out his wallet. "I may need to spread around a few twenties though." The wallet didn't look like it had a lot of twenties.

She smiled. "See that flight bag?"

"Yeah?"

"There's an envelope in there from the U.S. government. Take a peek."

"It's all hundreds!"

"That's right. I knew we'd need cash for something. Don't ask any questions. Just grab a bunch and put them in your wallet."

Not bad. Flies planes, looks great in a leather skirt and has a bag full of hundreds.

"Let's go."

Inside was about what he expected, naked girls dancing on a back-lit stage to loud music in front of a crowded bar. The current dancer was nineteen years old, half-black and half-Vietnamese. Her beauty would be enough to make any man crazy.

Stephanie watched him check out the dancer. "You like that?"

Boyle coughed. "Nah, it's just what they sell here."

She had to roll her eyes at that one. "Anyway, Detective, what happens when you stop looking at the stage?"

Good question. The bouncer at the door was lounging easily against the money cage. He was large and black, with languid movements. Boyle decided to go visit him.

"Time to spend some of this cash. You okay alone?"

"Sure."

Boyle strolled casually over to the bouncer. The man looked up quizzically.

"Got a minute?"

"No."

Nice guy. "This is important."

The man shrugged. Everything was important to somebody. Not much was important to him.

"I'm willing to pay."

The bouncer looked him over. "A cop. You should wear a sign."

"How can you tell?"

The man smirked. "If there was an elephant onstage, you know how I'd tell?"

"How?"

"I'd look up and say, 'Hey, look at the elephant dancing up there.' That's how I know you're a cop." Then he reached over near the cashier girl, grabbed a beer and took a long sip.

"So what? You hate cops?"

He put the beer down. "Matter of fact I do."

A hard case. Okay, Boyle had dealt with lots of those.

"What's your name?"

"Elden."

"Elden? What kind of name is Elden?"

"The name my mother gave me."

"Okay, Elden. Let me ask you something. You ever hear of a girl named Jamaica?"

The bouncer's expression never changed. He just sipped his beer.

"Elden, let me explain something. I'm not a real cop."

"No?"

"No, I'm sort of a detective."

"That's real interesting." Elden yawned. "Who's that you brought in? She want a job?"

"Don't worry about her, Elden, look at me." Boyle peeled off two crisp hundreds, put the bills on the bar, then grabbed Elden's beer and put it on top of them.

The bouncer shifted, interested. "Better be careful how you flash cash. Could get dangerous."

"What could happen, Elden, you'll reach down and grab it?"

"Could happen."

"Elden, get real." Boyle grabbed the bouncer's beer bottle and drank from it, then put the bottle back on top of the bills.

The bouncer involuntarily licked his lips. "You ain't a cop?"

"No, Elden, I'm not a cop, and she ain't lookin' for a job."

He gazed into space. "What do you want to know?"

"Jamaica. What do you know about her?"

"She works here."

"How long?"

A shrug. "Maybe a year."

"From where?"

"Who knows, Jamaica maybe."

"She have any friends?"

"Sure, everybody's got friends."

"Who?"

Another shrug.

Boyle reached for the bills. "Elden, you're disappointing me."

"Wait." The man's hand came down. The bills were underneath all the hands.

"What?"

"She had different friends. You mean people who worked here, customers, what?"

"Let's take customers."

"Lots of 'em like Jamaica."

"Names, Elden, names."

"Joe, David, Michael, Danny, Pete, Arnold, Eric, John . . ."

"John who?"

"Lots of Johns. Smith, Jones, Connolly, O'Neill . . ."

"How about Doe?"

He pulled out a cigarette and slowly lit it. "Who?"

"You heard. If you don't want to tell me that's fine. You must not care about those two C's, though."

"I care. Those C's are mine."

"So who's Doe?"

He blew the smoke toward the ceiling. "A guy. Like a million guys in here."

"I don't care about a million guys, just this guy."

"He's a bald guy. Kind of fat. White guy. Wore suits a lot."

Boyle gestured. "There's about a million of those in here now. Which one is he?"

"A guy went with Jamaica. You're starting to get boring. You sure she ain't workin'?" He grinned at Stephanie and waved.

"Then I'm sure. And two C's don't buy you telling me I'm boring."

The bouncer looked him over. There was a forty pound difference between the two men. He grabbed the bills and put them in his pocket.

"Elden, don't be stupid."

The bouncer put his hand on Boyle's chest and pushed. "Go watch the show. Those greens are gone."

Boyle was rapidly losing judgment. "Elden, you got two choices. Those C's go back is your best choice."

The crowd was watching the show on the stage. No one was paying attention to Elden and Boyle. It was empty near the door except for the girl taking the five dollars and she was reading a magazine. Stephanie stayed rock still, not getting in the way.

Elden pointed to the door. "Time for you to leave, my man. You're what we call disrupting things. Your lady can stay though."

He grabbed Boyle by the lapels and yanked. It was a bad move. A moment later Elden was on his knees, holding his gut, gasping to catch his breath. The two bills fell harmlessly to the floor. Stephanie leaned against the wood post.

Boyle waited until the big man recovered. "It wasn't my fault, man."

Elden choked. "Give me the money. I'll tell you what I know."

She was outraged, complaining all the way to the apartment house where Elden said Jamaica took her men.

"Can you believe how that guy talked about me? She workin'? She want a job? He thought I was a stripper!"

Boyle laughed merrily. "Hey, that's his business. Besides, you should be flattered. Elden wanted to put you onstage."

"Yeah, real flattered. And then you had to *hit* him. Is that the only way you know how to deal with people? Elden, you hit. The guy that got you suspended, you hit. You even hit me!"

"A false pattern," he said quickly. "Besides, you all lied to me."

"You hit people who lie to you?"

"Not always!"

She sighed and looked at the directions. "Turn here."

The apartment house was small, a two-story pink stucco shaped like an Italian townhouse. There was even a Veronese balcony on which Juliet might have stood if she lived in L.A.

"Nice place," she observed.

"Don't be so snooty."

"What now?"

"Elden says Jamaica was scared and wanted him to watch her back. She told him she was going to this apartment to meet a woman. By the description it's got to be Roberta, the one Migo taped. Let's go in, spread more of your cash and ask."

"Okay."

The apartment house was really more of a motel and sometimes rented by the hour. That meant it had a clerk who sat behind a desk. He was bored and wasted. Boyle felt like he was back in Paterson.

"Can I help you?"

"Yeah." Boyle casually dropped a hundred dollar bill on the desk. Again the interest increased immediately.

"Two women," Boyle said. He described both of them. The man concentrated.

"Jamaica, you mean."

"You know her?"

"Yeah, this was like her . . . you know . . ."

"Place?"

"Yeah, she came here to do guys upstairs. There's one there now."

"I want to surprise him." Boyle slid the hundred closer to the man, then added another, like a garnish.

"He's in three-F," the man said, snapping up the bills.

Room 3-F was on the third floor like it should be. They walked down the desolate hallway and stood outside the door, straining to hear any sound from within. No light escaped from beneath the door.

"Now what?" she whispered.

Boyle had the doorknob in his hand. He twisted it slowly, quietly, feeling it turn. When it stopped, he stopped, then pushed gently. The door opened.

"This is scary," she said.

"It always is."

He walked in after the opening door and she came in behind him.

The light from the hall created odd patterns in the dark room. There was a twisted sofa, a television that seemed to be sitting at a warped angle and a dead body. The dead body was naked and Stephanie, for all her training, screamed.

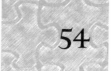

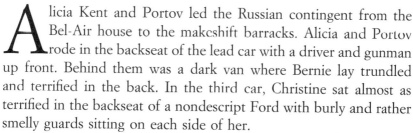

54

Alicia Kent and Portov led the Russian contingent from the Bel-Air house to the makeshift barracks. Alicia and Portov rode in the backseat of the lead car with a driver and gunman up front. Behind them was a dark van where Bernie lay trundled and terrified in the back. In the third car, Christine sat almost as terrified in the backseat of a nondescript Ford with burly and rather smelly guards sitting on each side of her.

The strange caravan arrived at the Russian barracks after midnight. All around them the criminals of the night were stirring, like jungle cats. Before the night was done, death would come easily and repeatedly throughout the city. On an average night there are five homicides in Los Angeles County, many of which occur in Inglewood. But the next two nights would not be average.

Alicia was appalled by the sight of the place, a corrugated broken-down tin shed in South Central next to a weed-covered rail line. The warehouse was shrouded in darkness, no help coming from streetlights long ago shot out. A shattered concrete driveway led up to a set of metal double doors. Portov slowed and the trailing vehicles parked in back of him.

"I pictured something a little more majestic," she said. Then she saw his face, which was stiff. "What's wrong?"

"There are at least two guards on duty twenty-four hours a day. They walk the perimeter every hour. At night they turn on arc lights." He looked around. "I don't see *any* lights."

Alicia Kent always assumed the worst. "Who besides me knows you're out here?"

Portov didn't answer, just pulled the Beretta 9 mm from his waistband and got out of the car. Alicia followed, staying slightly behind

him. Portov gestured and the guards from the trailing cars spread
out. Portov screamed, "Ivan!" There was no answer.

"Check the perimeter," he ordered. Three guards with drawn
weapons circled the building. Six minutes later they returned.

"Nothing."

The news seemed to agitate rather than calm Portov. He banged
the butt of his gun against the metal door three times. The noise
echoed loudly and then stopped. There was no further sound.

Portov took out a set of keys. There was a small door next to the
main double doors. "Stay here."

"Forget it." She moved closer to him.

He didn't argue. The small door was rusted and he had to slam
a shoulder against it. Once inside Alicia saw large metal grids filled
with makeshift pallets. The pallets stored sleeping bags and weapons:
handguns, automatic weapons, an occasional shotgun. This was a
soldiers' enclave, a crude one to be sure, but one that served Serge
Belov's interests well.

The interior of the warehouse was faintly lit by ceiling bulbs. Portov inched forward, leading with his weapon. He called out loudly
and his voice ricocheted off the metal walls. There was no response.

"Who's supposed to be here?"

"Two guards. New men. Ivan and Dmitri."

They didn't find them till they reached the far end of the warehouse. The two men were lying against a wall, sitting in a lake of
blood. Portov used his foot to prod Dmitri. The man's face was
ashen and he didn't move.

"He must have been shot many times," Portov said. He glanced
briefly at Alicia. "I hope this does not disturb you?"

It was a curious remark and she tried not to laugh, but a small
snort escaped anyway. "Don't worry, I'm fine." She grabbed Dmitri
by the hair and turned him.

"You're wrong about one thing."

He squinted. "Wrong?"

"They weren't shot many times."

"How can you say that? Look at all the blood."

"They weren't shot at all," she said easily. "They were stabbed."

The Russians gathered around and the anger erupted. Pallets were torn from the walls and shattered. Automatic weapons opened up on the ceiling of the shed. The curses were loud and constant, some in Russian, some English. These were soldiers and they wanted blood revenge. Belov grabbed Bernie and threw him roughly on top of the dead men. Bernie fell whimpering into pools of blood.

"Put him in that room," Belov ordered. Then he turned to Christine. "Put her in the room next to him, so she can listen."

Two Russian guards grabbed Christine by the hair and dragged her through a wooden door. She found herself thrown roughly into a concrete enclosure open at the top. On all sides were metal shelves stuffed with bedding.

A door clanged in the next cubicle and she realized with horror that she would now hear every whisper, every word. The metal scraped as the guards manacled Bernie to something. There was raucous laughter, the unzipping of Belov's strange satchel and some commands in Russian. Then came the screams.

There was a time Christine was known as the Babe Ruth of screamers, an actress whose howls always let the audience know the bad guy was around. Inevitably she was in a shower, or emerging from a lake, or getting ready for bed. As her agent always said in the pitch sessions, once Christine gets down to the skin, it's time for the earmuffs.

Yet nothing Christine ever experienced prepared her for this. Bernie's screams were not Hollywood screams, they were primal and guttural, laced with obscenities. They started slow and built, alternating between aggressive curses and abject begging. At their height they were sudden, piercing and violent, short-lived, signaling agony, unconsciousness, alertness, sobbing and begging, then great pain all over again.

Christine knew Bernie was in a no-win situation. The pain would continue as long as he refused to talk. But once he talked his life would end, maybe painlessly, probably not. And Bernie knew that too.

At one point she thought she was next. After an hour of horror, the door opened.

"Hello," Belov said. A guard stood next to him.

She lay huddled on the concrete floor with her jacket over her ears.

"Get up."

She took the jacket off and was relieved at the silence. She did as he asked.

"Very nice." Belov's hands swept languorously over her face, exploring her cheekbones, probing slightly.

"Don't touch me, you sick bastard."

His eyes brightened. "Such language. You will have to be punished."

"Yeah, right. Is it comfy under that rock, weirdo?"

Belov shivered. "She has such spirit. This will be exquisite. Tell me, why is the Kent woman protecting you? Are you really that important?"

Christine was a lot more frightened than she was letting on. The man's hands probed odd places, like her kneecap, the small of her back, the line of her jaw where it crept back to join the skull. None of it hurt, but all of it spoke of hurt to come, like a dentist's pick gently tapping an infected tooth.

"Have you ever heard of Miguel Meza?"

"Sorry, no."

"You'll be a lot sorrier when you meet him. He's my boyfriend. He works for the Braccas."

A shrug, a squint. "The name means nothing to me. If that's the only reason perhaps we'll risk her wrath." Another long glance and then he made a decision. "Would you be kind enough to undress? You can leave your clothes on that chair."

"In your dreams, you pervert."

"Then we'll do it for you." Belov gestured. The guard didn't move.

"Begin! Now!"

The guard remained still, his eyes fixed on Christine. "She mentioned the Braccas. That is a serious matter. Also I know that other name."

"What name?"

"Meza. He is a famous assassin."

Belov hesitated. "Is that true?"

"You bet it's true, sicko."

Belov glanced at the guard quizzically. "An American insult. Don't worry about it. Worry more about her friend."

"Can we investigate this famous friend? Find out if she's really protected by him?"

"Of course."

They left quickly, leaving her alone with her fears. Fifteen minutes later they returned. Belov's jaw was set, pinched in a tight line, turning blue from the pressure.

"Don't be so sad," Christine said sweetly. "You can always go in the bathroom and use your hand."

The guard dragged him away spitting with rage. Three minutes later she heard Bernie's voice.

"God, no!"

55

Boyle and Stephanie got out of John Doe's apartment fast. The last thing Boyle wanted was a long conversation with a couple of unsmiling faces from Robbery-Homicide. He'd get professional courtesy for about ten minutes. Then they'd want to know *exactly* what he was doing there.

Stephanie was more upset than she would have thought. Even with all she had gone through in the last forty-eight hours nothing prepared her for a dead body with bullets in the back of the head in the middle of a dark apartment. Her scream had been shrill and was still going on when he pulled her away.

"God," she said, rolling down the window and gulping the night air. "He was *naked*. Why was he *naked*?"

Boyle may not have ridden in a lot of jets but he had sure seen a lot of homicide victims. "It makes it harder to I.D. the body."

"And his head! You see that blood?"

"He was shot at close range."

The air calmed her somewhat. She breathed deeply and was again very happy to have Boyle next to her. "There's no chance it was a robber, right?"

"Right, there was no struggle. Plus a robber wouldn't take time to strip the victim."

"So it had to be somebody he knew, right?"

"Had to be."

"Alicia Kent," she said easily. "Or her friend."

"If I was working, that's where I'd start."

She got quiet, thinking it all through.

"I need to call this in. We need agents in here to help us."

"Great. Tell them to come to the bar where Migo made that tape."

"You got it."

Stephanie made her call to Braxton from a gas station near the edge of Long Beach, about a half mile from the apartment build ing where John Doe died. She again woke him up. Braxton listened with emotions that rapidly changed from concern to surprise to shock. The woman that was supposed to be so incompetent had managed not only to hook up with Boyle and Meza, but had now tracked down the dead John Doe. More to the point, neither Portov nor Alicia Kent knew how close she was!

"Where are you heading next?" he asked, hoping to keep the urgency out of his voice. "I'll have some agents from Los Angeles meet you there." That he would, just not the sort of agents Stephanie expected.

"There's a bar a couple of miles from here called The Cavern." She gave Braxton the address. "Boyle and I are going there now. The woman who's working with Alicia Kent hangs out there."

Braxton wrote it all down. "Just be careful."

"You got it."

Stephanie got back in the car and they pulled away. "What did he say?"

"He's going to have some agents meet us there." She yawned, trying to make her next sentence sound routine. "Incidentally, I want to go in alone."

He laughed easily as he drove through the black streets. "Right."

"I'm serious."

"You're not serious. You're crazy is what you are."

"Boyle, listen to me. If I go in there alone, I may get to talk to some people. If I go in there with you, I can't do that."

Boyle shook his head. "Forget it. You're not flying a plane. There's killers in there. You remember what you did when you saw that body?"

"Yes." She let a beat go by. "Boyle?"

It was the tone of her voice, quiet, reasonable, the calm before the storm. Boyle didn't yet know her well enough to know the danger signs. Duncan would have.

"What?"

"You know what I thought when I saw that body back there?"

"No."

"I thought these are the same people who killed Patsy and tried to kill John. If it wasn't for what you did, they would've killed me too."

"I know that."

"So may I tell you one thing?" she asked sweetly.

"Sure."

She took a big gulp of air. "Don't tell me what to do!" she bellowed. She was actually louder than Natala, Boyle realized, which he hadn't thought possible.

She lowered her voice. "Besides, remember Elden?"

"Yeah. So?"

"So Elden picked you out as a cop right away. That means we're either dead when we walk in or they all run. Am I right?"

He thought about that. She actually was right. "Stephanie?"

"What!"

"Ouch, softer please. Listen. Okay, you got a point. Here's a compromise. I'll drive there, park, you go in. Five minutes later . . ."

"Ten."

"Ten minutes later, *exactly* ten minutes later, I come in. We ignore each other unless I think you're in trouble."

She smiled and kissed him lightly on the cheek.

"Deal."

Stephanie was surprised at the darkness and smell of the place. It was close to 1 A.M. now and the bar was filled with grimy men in filthy clothes. In a booth in the corner a thickly muscled black man huddled with three girls. One wore a bomber's jacket, high black boots and a cowboy hat. She smoked a cigarette and drank her beer with three fingers on the neck of the bottle, tilting it upward and letting it drain into her open throat.

Stephanie felt oddly exposed and for an instant wished Boyle was with her. She sat at the bar. The man next to her was drunk.

"Hey, baby."

Hey, baby. What a line. "Hello."

The bartender came over to save her. "What'll it be, miss?"

Stephanie couldn't have flown for years with fighter jocks without learning about whiskey. And right now a jolt sounded great.

"You see that bottle there?"

The man looked over. "Chivas?"

"Pour one over ice." She looked around at the men already beginning to stare. "Make it a double."

It didn't take Marcus long to notice her. She sat sipping, wearing Christine's wild clothes, trying to ignore a guy telling her a long story about the navy. It was a different navy than Stephanie knew.

"Who the hell is that?" Marcus said at last.

Roberta's head swiveled and her eyes flattened. "Who cares. Don't you have enough right here?"

"Never enough, baby." He got up.

Stephanie was so intent on ignoring the navy guy she never heard him approach.

"This mope bothering you?"

The voice startled her and she turned quickly. He was enormously wide, his shaved head exuding menace. The only light near him was the reflection off the gold chain on his neck and the silver ring that hung from his ear. His iron-inflated muscles burst against the fabric of his suit. She knew exactly who he was and exactly what to do.

"Yeah, he is."

Marcus moved in back of the man.

"Hey chump?"

"What?"

"I think you had enough."

The drunk was insulted. "Why you say that?"

"You're falling off the stool."

"I ain't fallin' off nothin'."

"No?" Marcus grabbed the man's collar and yanked. The navy guy flew backward and landed hard. His head bounced twice, then lay still.

"Sweep him up," Marcus ordered. The bikers moved in. He sat down next to her.

"You never been here before, I would've noticed."

"Why's that, you come in here a lot?"

"This is my place."

She checked her watch. Five minutes to Boyle time.

"Really? Nice place."

He moved closer. "You workin'?"

She blinked, not getting it at first. Then she remembered the strip joint.

"Not anymore."

"Why's that? You could make serious bread. I tell you, baby, I'd have them in line." He opened his hands. "And I'm fair. I take half, no more."

She shrugged and sipped, tried to appear casual. She *definitely* did not want to know too much about her end of the deal.

"It's always the guy," Marcus said, being sensitive, figuring it out. "He use his hands too much? Have you out there too much?"

"Maybe." She looked over at the table where the women sat sullenly. "Those yours?"

"Yeah, all but one works for me. What's your name?"

She let a beat go by. "I'm Heather."

He held out a hand. "Marcus."

"Who're they?" She said it quickly, and she hoped believably.

"Them? They make up names, like Sunshine, Moonbeam, Crystal, all kind of names."

Almost to touchdown. She smiled, and it was a smile that made Marcus' handshake stay put, and start squeezing a little. "And their real names are Mary and Sue, right?"

"Yeah."

Three minutes to Boyle time. Now his other hand closed over hers, patting gently. She spoke hurriedly. "Really? Mary and Sue?"

"No, it's like . . . I don't know."

She bit her lip. This was like pulling teeth. "That one in the corner, the one that looks so mad, who's that?"

He took his hands away long enough to look over. "Her? She's mad at the world and everybody in it. Somethin' must have happened to her down where she come from. That's the only one don't work for me. That's Roberta."

Boyle cheated, waiting only nine minutes before stepping over the drunks and rushing inside. There was a guy at the door who gave him a look before he slowly backed away.

The inside of The Cavern was as depressing as Meza said it would be. He could barely make out Stephanie sitting at the bar. A thick-necked man hovered near her. Boyle remembered Meza's advice: if he saw a guy named Marcus, shoot first.

Stephanie saw Doyle out of the corner of her eye and involuntarily twitched. Marcus saw the move.

"Friend of yours?"

"No, I was just looking."

"Don't look there, look here. You want to work for me, baby?"

She shrugged. "I don't know, it didn't turn out so good last time."

Marcus put his arm around her and she could feel the scary strength in it. "Some men don't know how to treat a woman. I'm not like that."

"Do you treat *them* well?" She nodded toward the table.

"Oh, yeah, baby. They all love me. You want them to tell you?"

"Sure."

Marcus took her by the arm to the table where the women sat. On the way he gently kneaded her shoulder, and again she felt the frightening power of his hands.

The women shifted to make room for her. "This here's Heather," Marcus said. "She's gonna work for me. Tell her how good I am."

Two of the women laughed. Roberta kept her eyes straight ahead, her mouth pinched and angry.

"What's wrong with you?" he snapped at Roberta.

She turned to him. "Nothing. I just need your attention for awhile. You can hire hookers or strippers some other time."

Marcus' face hardened. The look scared the other two.

"He treats us fine," one said quickly.

"Yeah, real fine," the other chimed in.

Marcus didn't take his eyes off Roberta. "I don't hear you."

"I don't work for you, Marcus. I'm trying to get you to . . ." She never got the words out. Marcus grabbed her by the hair and yanked. Her head was pulled back and her neck exposed. He swept the table with his arm and glasses shattered. Marcus had six men in the bar working for him, biker types with stringy hair and fat bellies. They moved closer to get a better look.

"You don't have to do that," Stephanie said quickly.

"Shut up," Marcus barked. He suddenly seemed less sweet and caring. Now back to Roberta, his fist still in her hair. "You got some problem?"

Roberta cursed silently. She'd kill him later. Now she needed him. "No problem. We can talk later."

Marcus let her hair go and turned back to Stephanie. "See?"

"Yes."

He opened his hands, the businessman now. "You'd be special, baby, trust me. And we take care of our girls. My guys deliver you to the hotels and wait for you to come back. Total safety."

She swallowed hard. "Hotels?"

"Absolutely. I promise. No streets for you. All business guys. Nothin' less than five hundred dollars an hour minimum. Maybe more! You're special."

"What a nice compliment."

"Right! So even if you just do three a night, maybe five nights a week it adds up. Some of my girls make like five grand a week!"

"Who?" the two at the table wanted to know.

"Not you two! I'm lucky to find a trucker with a hundred bucks for you. But you . . ." again he stroked her, "oh yeah, baby, we can make some cash!" He gave her his best gold-toothed grin. "So we got a deal?"

"I'm not sure. I . . ."

She never got the whole sentence out. Marcus' hand grabbed Stephanie's pale curls and yanked. Now it was her neck exposed, her whimpering soft. Across the bar a chair scraped.

"Time to make up your mind, baby."

"We got a deal," Stephanie said. "Sure."

Marcus let go of her hair, then gave her a tap on the side of the face, just to let her know what a nice boss he'd be. The tap was a slap and audible. Again the chair scraped and this time it got Marcus' attention.

"What are you lookin' at?"

"Not much," Boyle said. His face was flushed. The look was way too direct for Marcus.

"Why don't you look someplace else."

Boyle turned around. "Where?"

"Don't worry about him," Stephanie said quickly. "Let's talk about us."

Marcus grabbed the back of her neck and squeezed. "Let me explain one thing. You work for me, you shut up till I tell you to talk. Understand?"

"Sure. It's just that . . ." He squeezed harder and she gasped from the pain. Now Boyle stood up. He felt the urge to rush and strike, like waiting for the bell.

Marcus recognized the challenge, in prison yards lots of fights started this way. "Didn't I tell you to look someplace else?"

"I think so," Boyle said.

"Tommy!" Stephanie shouted.

Roberta's head snapped. She got it right away, even if stupid Marcus didn't. These two were *working* together. It was a *scam*. "Do it, Marcus," she urged. "Do it!"

Marcus made a small gesture and the six bikers moved in back of Boyle. The road to the door was now completely blocked.

"You got a bad attitude," Marcus said. "That's a problem in here."

Boyle didn't answer. Roberta moved closer to Marcus. "You gonna let this chump mouth off like that?"

No, he wasn't. Marcus took off his leather jacket and threw it on the bar. Then he grabbed his dark pullover sweater from the back and yanked it over his head. He was now naked from the waist up, deeply cut with rippling muscles and scattered with prison tats.

"C'mere," he ordered Stephanie. "C'mere and get a feel of this."

"Sure," she said quickly. She rubbed her hands over Marcus' shoulders, biceps and chest. It was like touching a marble table top.

"You're so strong! You'll kill him!"

"I like the feel of those hands, baby. How 'bout you feel something else?"

Now Roberta *knew* she had an angle. "Yeah, Marcus, make her do it."

"No way," Boyle said easily. "You want it grabbed, do it yourself."

That did it. Marcus ducked his head and charged. The raucous shouts of the bikers were loud. Boyle skipped backward and threw a left at the top of Marcus' head, then howled at the pain. It was like punching a stone wall and he felt the bone in the knuckle of his ring finger crack. Marcus' face came up and Boyle got in two shots, both hitting square. Marcus staggered, bled freely, then roared. He showed a blade.

Stephanie tried to jump in between but Roberta threw her to the ground. She pinned her arm and pushed her face into the floor. "Is that your boyfriend?"

Stephanie winced at the pain. "No."

Roberta's lips moved closer to Stephanie's ear. "You're lying. Why were you following me?"

Boyle backed away from the knife, keeping it in sight. If it was just him and Marcus he'd have no worries. Then he felt the hands grab him from behind.

Boyle struggled but there were six of them. Soon he found himself pinned against the bar.

"I hope your momma kept pictures," Marcus said. " 'Cause she ain't gonna recognize you now."

licia Kent carried a highly-secure cell phone at all times and Braxton got her right away. He repeated the whole conversation with Stephanie, including where Boyle and Stephanie were now heading. Alicia said thank you, also in code, and hung up.

"Boyle and Shane are heading for The Cavern."

Portov gestured. "Just tell them where it is."

Alicia and Portov rode together in the first of three cars. The men in the other two cars loaded and rechecked their weapons. It was deep into the night when the caravan arrived in the parking lot.

"It's a dive," Portov said.

"Yes. Let's check it out and get out of here."

At the door they heard raucous cheers from inside.

"Somebody's having a party," Portov said. He gestured and two of his men went first. Marcus' doorman blocked the entrance with his arms crossed over his chest.

"Can't go in there, yet," the man said.

The Russian guard used the butt end of his AK-47 and the man went down hard. Then he tried the door. "It's locked."

"Get us in there."

The Russian fired a short burst of the assault weapon and the door exploded. Inside was a hell's broth of smoke, screams and smells. Portov and Kent pushed through to get a better look.

The fight was well underway. Marcus had made the mistake of approaching Boyle too casually and wound up getting kicked dead in the chest. In the resulting confusion, Boyle pulled away from the bikers and started to swing. The one on the left went down immediately but the one on the right got in a good shot with the pipe. Boyle dropped to his knees. He saw a leg come up and grabbed it, toppling the man. The pipe crashed again and he slumped.

He wouldn't have lasted very long with the bikers slamming him from behind. He was on his knees, bleeding, with Marcus approaching, when the Russians blew open the door.

His platoon twisted away from Roberta, "It must be the agents!"

It wasn't. Alicia moved regally through the throng of men. Roberta jumped to her feet and ran forward, casual, playing it cool. "Alicia! What are you doing here? I thought we were going to meet at the house."

Alicia Kent looked at her darkly. "What's going on?"

"There was a fight. This guy . . ." Roberta gestured to Boyle, "he got out of hand."

"Forget him. Where's the plane? Why haven't you called in?"

Roberta saw the murderous look in Alicia's eyes. She had seen it many times before. It held no mercy and always appeared just before a kill.

"I can't talk about that now."

Alicia's eyes darkened even more, becoming almost black. Serge Belov walked forward and stood next to her.

"Let me ask you again," Alicia said softly. "Where's the plane and what's happening?"

"Alicia, I told you. I can't talk right now."

"Why not?"

Roberta was confused and froze. Her voice had become a nervous stammer. "There's too many people here."

"Don't worry about the people. Just answer my question."

"Well, there's other things too."

"What other things?"

"Well, the whole money thing." Marcus decided to be a hero and moved next to her. He held the knife like a sword. Boyle leaned against the bar, dazed, gingerly touching the large bump on the back of his head.

Alicia Kent barely noticed him. All her attention was riveted on Roberta. "What possible money thing are you talking about?"

Roberta shrugged, and the small movement overplayed her hand. "I just think we ought to talk about it more."

The veiled blackmail was a big mistake. Alicia Kent gestured and Serge Belov moved, his hand slapping Roberta hard. Her head whipped to the side.

Marcus raised the knife, still too dumb to get it. Roberta

screamed, "No!" but it was too late. Marcus only got halfway to Belov before a Russian fusillade drove him back. He died with open eyes and slid down the far wall.

Portov came up to Alicia. "What do you want to do?"

Her eyes swept the room and her incomparable brain took it all in right away. She approached Stephanie first, held out a hand and gently helped her to her feet. "Good evening, Lieutenant Commander. You're much younger and more beautiful than I expected."

"Wrong girl. My name is Heather."

Alicia Kent smiled. "Heather? What a silly name." She gently touched Stephanie's face. "Yes, so very young, and so very lovely."

Stephanie shrugged, no longer interested in the game. "I'm older than I look, trust me."

Alicia Kent turned to Boyle. "Please tell me you're Meza. It would solve my biggest problem."

"No, my name is Heather too."

This time Alicia didn't smile. "We'll see how cute you are later, Boyle."

Portov got all the introductions he needed in John Bracca's apartment. He remembered Boyle well and kept a close eye on him. "Alicia, let's finish them and get out of here."

Suddenly in back of him there was a burst. Portov spun and saw one of the bikers holding his bleeding gut. The man had a gun in his hand, another fatal miscalculation. The other bikers now just cowered. No one would challenge the Russians anymore.

"Once again," Portov barked, "let's finish this now! I don't care what Braxton says, this guy's dangerous!"

Stephanie's shocked intake of air was audible.

"No," Alicia Kent said. "We can't."

"Why not?"

She gestured to Roberta. "I still don't know anything about the plane. Plus Meza is still out there. We *need* hostages."

Belov moved close to Stephanie and smiled. "Hello."

"Last time," Portov said. "What do you want to do?"

Alicia sighed. "The ones we need, bring them alive. The rest . . ." she glanced at the shuddering bikers, ". . . do what you want."

57

It was almost 3 A.M. when the entourage got back to the Russian barracks. They dragged Roberta off to one room to wait for Belov. They threw Boyle and Stephanie into another.

When the lock engaged she turned to him. The back of his head was still bleeding and his broken ring finger throbbed. He sat back on a packing crate and used his shirt to stanch the bleeding. She wrapped her arms around him, burying her face in his neck, feeling the warmth of blood that had drifted there. He held her as tightly as he could. They stayed that way for a full five minutes until she lifted her face.

He didn't say anything, just enjoyed the sight of that flawless face, now pink from her battle with Roberta. He kissed her with a gentleness that would not have burst a bubble.

When she shifted in his arms he took her face in his hands and kissed her eyes, her cheekbones, her neck, her ears.

She was murmuring. "Tommy, I love you, I really love you."

"I know, don't say any more."

It was a breakthrough moment, a tender one, something pure that should have stayed that way. But purity is also transitory and Boyle's hands took on a life of their own, moving perhaps involuntarily to the buttons of her blouse. They were both uninterested in the purity of the moment when the door burst open. Stephanie spun away and tried with only partial success to cover herself. The guard grunted with obvious delight and pushed a prisoner inside. The door slammed and the lock engaged with a grinding metallic sound.

"Hi," Christine said, sizing matters up pretty quick. "Am I disturbing something?"

A hundred feet away, in another part of the warehouse, Roberta was having a lot less fun. She had been pushed alone into a small cubicle ringed on three sides by concrete walls. The cubicle was the same as all the others except that Bernie the broker, naked and obviously tortured, lay dead on the floor.

Roberta had seen lots of dead men in Buenos Aires, once the capital of naked, tortured men, and knew precisely the techniques they would use to break her. She refused to allow her mind to anticipate horror, a trick drilled into her during Argentine military torture training. She knew her only chance was to refuse to give in to naked fear. She tried to put herself in that state of mind when Belov entered.

"I must say," Belov began, "you are a beautiful woman."

Roberta jammed her hands into the pockets of her black jeans. "Let me guess. You did that to him? Nice work."

The man's face registered no response. The guards shifted with anticipation.

"Yes, I did. He refused to give us information. Yet I have a question. Your tone is still rude. Why? All I have done so far is comment on your beauty."

She didn't need to look at Bernie again. She had been brought into this room to see him, to let her anticipate her own torture. She wasn't brought here so Belov could comment on her beauty. "Rude? Not at all. I was being complimentary. In Argentina this job would have been considered first rate."

Serge Belov put his finger to his lips in a thoughtful way. One of the guards smiled with interest.

"No, you were not being complimentary. You were being rude. And the last comment was sarcastic. I've been curious for years about how people perceive me at first, so maybe you can help. Do I appear weak to you? Is that it?"

"Weak, not at all. It takes a real man to do something like that." She gestured to Bernie, now barely recognizable as a human.

"Ah, more sarcasm. Did the Argentines teach you to always appear unafraid when in enemy hands?"

She didn't answer. Belov was already reading her mind, figuring out how to break her. It was getting harder to squelch the rising terror.

"But let's move on to something else," Belov said. "Will you give them the information they want?" Belov kept the request purposely vague.

"I don't know what you're talking about."

"Well, let me try again. They want to know the status of an airplane." He pulled out a small sheet of paper and read it word for word. "Will you tell them where the flight is now and what the departure authorization code is to cause it to go to . . ." He squinted. "Perhaps you can help me with this word." He showed her the paper.

"Lagos."

"Ah, yes, Lagos, Nigeria. The handwriting is so poor."

"Are you going to stand there all night and read pieces of paper to me?"

Belov smiled. "I hope not. But she did order me to ask you these questions." He made no threats. The shattered body on the floor spoke for itself.

"Tell her the answer is no. Torture won't work because I'll die first. She'll have to kill me."

Serge Belov smiled broadly. "Oh, my dear, I don't think it's she who will kill you."

58

Detective Michael Houlihan and Miguel Meza broke into Alicia Kent's Bel-Air house and spent an hour searching it. Everything they found made Meza more agitated, especially the blood on the white marble floor.

"Don't get too upset yet," Houlihan advised. "Let's stay cool for now."

They found Alicia's laptop Toshiba computer, turned it on, played with it, and found nothing. They ransacked her closet and trashed the expensive clothes, again finding nothing. In her office, they found a phone with multiple lines.

"Now what?" Houlihan said.

Meza picked up the phone, pressed the first line and hit the redial button. A digital display flashed and Roberta's phone rang. A mechanical voice told him to leave a message.

"Strike one," Meza said. He did the same with the second line and an operator answered. "The Hilton Hotel," Meza told Houlihan. "Ring any bells?"

"Lots. That's where she killed the fat man."

"Strike two." Meza tapped into the third line and again hit the redial button.

This time the phone rang seven times before a man answered. His voice was deep. "Da," the man said.

Meza let a beat go by, then talked rapidly in Spanish. The man on the other end was confused. "Talk in English."

"I am looking for Alicia Kent. Is she there?"

"Who are you?"

"I am her assistant. My name is Miguel Meza." He spelled it slowly.

"She is not here. She went to that bar, The Cavern. She'll be back later."

Meza pointed at the digital display of the phone number and glanced at Houlihan. Houlihan nodded.

"Take a message for the Kent woman. Miguel Meza says he'll meet you later. Whatever happens to Christine or Tommy Boyle happens to you. *Exactly* the same. Did you get that? Good."

Meza hung up. "Can you trace that number?"

"Hell, even Bigelow can do that."

"Good. Let's go find them."

By the time Houlihan and Meza reached The Cavern it was all over. They spent ten minutes examining the carnage and trying to interview the one biker left barely alive. Meza kicked Marcus for fun. Then they heard sirens.

"Let's get out of here."

They escaped from The Cavern barely a minute before a squadron of red flashing lights roared into the parking lot. Houlihan had long since stopped worrying about how come he wasn't with the other cops. He grabbed the radio. Bigelow's voice crackled through the speaker.

"Bigelow, Houlihan, what's happening?"

"Sir, where you been? Everybody's looking for you."

"Don't worry about it. Just tell me what you got."

"First, the guy's name is Bernie something. He has drugs all over the place."

"What kind?"

"Speed, mostly. Plus we found these papers."

"What papers?"

"A guy in the AG's office looked at them and he says Bernie was running some game. Me, I can't tell."

Big surprise. "Okay, Bigelow, forget about all that. I need you to get me an address." He rattled off the phone number of the Russian barracks. "Radio me back in five, then meet me there."

"You got it, sir."

———

Thirty minutes after they heard Roberta scream for the first time the lock disengaged. For most of that time the three of them sat in stunned silence, listening to the shrieks, refusing to add it all up. Then the door burst open again.

Alicia Kent walked in with a Russian guard next to her. She pointed at Boyle.

"I need to talk to him alone."

Stephanie stood up. "Why?"

"None of your business." She gestured to the guard. "Get them out of here."

The guard opened the door wider. Christine walked out last. "Keep it in your pants," she said breezily over her shoulder.

Boyle sat casually on a packing box, his back to the concrete wall. The bleeding in the back of his head had slowed. Alicia Kent sat near him.

"I want you to know," she began, "I have no quarrel with you."

"You could have fooled me."

"I had no choice but to take you as prisoners. Portov badly wanted to kill you at that bar for what you did to him in John Bracca's apartment. You humiliated him. Should I have let him get his revenge?"

"No," he admitted.

She moved closer. "I'll make this fast. I know you don't trust me but maybe this will make sense. Portov is not afraid of Meza but I have great respect for killers of his caliber." Not only respect, she had to admit, something more. Almost fear. Almost admiration. Could *he* be the one? Could she satisfy him the way Christine seemed to? She *knew* she could. "Anyway," she continued, "I want the three of you out of here safely. I have no interest in having Miguel Meza hound me to my grave."

"More likely, put you in it."

"Exactly. He's already called here to let me know he holds me personally responsible for your safety. I take that threat very seriously. But with a little cooperation from you, I can make my peace with Meza and none of you will be harmed."

He examined her, looking for the lie. She was eerily attractive and self-confident. She undoubtedly got what she wanted in life.

"Let me ask you something."

"Whatever you like."

"Why did you kill Patsy De Marco? He was a nice old man who never troubled anyone. Why did you have to do that?"

She squinted. She wanted to answer honestly but it was hard. It was such a long ago problem. "He just got in the way, I think. It really was nothing personal."

He laughed without humor. "Well, that explains it." He was about to get right in her face when they both heard an unholy shriek bounce off the metal roof. Even Alicia Kent, viper that she was, involuntarily glanced toward the sound. The scream was like the rumbling of an incipient volcano, heralding the horror to come.

"We have to move fast. Belov will start to flay her alive soon, tearing the skin off her in strips like he did to the broker. Roberta will tell us what we need to know but he will continue flaying till she's dead. Then it will be time to go."

"I can't wait."

"Yes, you can. After Roberta talks, Portov will kill you. I won't be able to protect you anymore."

"He'd be making a mistake," Boyle said without much conviction.

"Yes, but he's prepared to make it." The sounds of agony were weaker now. She opened her hands to ask the question. "To further his revenge on you Portov will turn Christine and Stephanie over to Belov. Are you prepared to allow that? To let Belov slowly flay them alive?"

That did it. Boyle tried to keep his face a set mask, but couldn't pull it off. The blood left his face and the flinch was obvious.

"We don't have to talk any more about that. You know what I'm saying."

"What do you want?" he said evenly.

Alicia Kent came closer. "I have a plan which will get you out of here and the women too."

"I'm listening."

"Good." Her voice was crisp. "Listen very closely."

Meza and Houlihan got to the Russian barracks shortly before Bigelow. They parked on an empty street three blocks from the Russian barracks, shut off the lights, then leaned against the car and smoked. Nothing moved.

Suddenly they were blinded by a high-powered light and a screeching siren. The car roared down the street at seventy miles an hour, hit the brakes and twisted to a stop. Houlihan jumped to his feet.

"Bigelow, you idiot, shut that thing off!"

The road got quiet again. Houlihan sat down and lit another cigarette.

"Hi, sir. Who's that with you?"

"Bigelow, don't worry about it. Just shut up and sit down." Bigelow did as he was told and the three of them sat on the concrete with their backs against the car. There was nothing going on. Meza was sick of smoking cigarettes.

"I have to do something."

"What?"

"Next time a guard comes out let's grab him."

Bigelow shook his head. "Sir, there was a memo about that. You see, unless we actually see a crime in progress . . ."

"Bigelow, shut up. What then?"

"We'll force the guard to tell us exactly where they're holding Christine and the others. I don't want to just go in blasting, we might hit the good guys."

"Okay, I agree. Then what?"

"We cut the lights, break in and take them all out."

Houlihan snorted. "Meza, there's only three of us even if you count Bigelow. There could be like fifty guys in there."

Meza wasn't thinking about numbers, he was thinking about Christine. And about what Boyle would do if their situation were reversed. "So it's ten apiece."

Bigelow took off his hat and scratched his head. "That's not right, sir. Three into fifty equals . . ."

"Bigelow, shut up."

Roberta gave up the information and her life at 4 A.M. Serge Belov was disappointed. "That was such a mistake. I could have kept it going for hours."

Once Alicia had the departure code she grabbed her cell phone and dialed. Four thousand miles away a pilot received the Spanish instructions and taxied a 707 charter onto a runway in Barbados.

He barked into his radio and received confirmation from a bribed tower controller. The fully pressurized jet took off over the Atlantic within fifteen minutes and climbed to thirty five thousand feet. The plane had enough fuel to reach the African coast. There, after one quick refueling stop, it would deliver the beryllium to Lagos, Nigeria.

As soon as the plane was in the air, Portov called Josef Alexeyev in Moscow. The pure Sarin had been delivered to Chile as fertilizer and made its way up the coast to Mexico in a small Cessna. The single-engine plane now sat on a runway in Tijuana waiting for instructions to make the forty-minute flight to a dirt runway on a farm in southern Arizona. Within six days the gas would be smuggled northeast, there to be released by the mysterious buyers into the air-conditioning duct of a midtown Manhattan office building crammed with thousands of unsuspecting workers. The German banker in Paris wired the funds as instructed and faxed confirmation to the Russian warehouse. The message was cautious.

> We will examine cargo on receipt in Lagos. If fabric is of quality discussed, we will confirm receipt to JA. JA will release beverages. Funds have already been released.
>
> Regards,
> Klaus

Alicia read the fax and relaxed. "JA" meant Josef Alexeyev. No problem.

Portov was standing nearby. "Is it all arranged?"

"Perfectly," she said.

It had always been hard for Bigelow to sit still and now was no exception. There had to be a better idea than this.

"Sir, I don't think we should just go beat up a guard. I think we should call for help."

Houlihan had rejected that idea all night, primarily because once he called for help he'd have to explain Meza. But now, with the dark warehouse filled with Russians, it suddenly seemed like a great idea.

"Who's back at Bernie's house now?"

"Detective Taylor took control."

"Damn." Houlihan hated Taylor and Taylor hated Houlihan and neither of them spent a lot of time trying to hide it from the other. But now he had no choice.

"Bigelow, get Taylor on the radio."

It took a good five minutes to get Taylor on and when he got there he was fuming. "Houlihan, where the hell are you? I got people all over this house and there ain't nothin' happening!"

Houlihan tried the tender approach. "Dave, listen to me. I need some backup in Inglewood but I really don't want to call it in yet. We're at a warehouse just past Florence."

Taylor snorted. "Houlihan, I been sittin' out here on *your* problem for hours. And it ain't the first time. How you ever made supervisor I don't know. I never saw you do anything worthwhile yet! Now listen to me! I want you back here and I want me gone. This is *your* problem and I want *out* of here."

Houlihan pressed. "Taylor, I know you wanted supervisor but this is different. Hang in there with me. This could be big for both of us."

"I know it's big," Taylor said. "We got a cop dead and you're gone."

"It's bigger than that. There's at least thirty guys in this warehouse."

"Yeah? What are the thirty guys doing?"

"I'm not sure, Taylor, but trust me, it's big."

The detective on the other end laughed. "Houlihan, you're nuts. Incidentally, who's the guy you drove off with?"

"Taylor, it doesn't matter."

"Houlihan, that's the only thing right you said. It don't matter and I'm going home."

"Taylor, listen to me. Taylor!"

He handed the radio back to Bigelow. "He cut me off."

Meza was staring at the house, smoking. "Forget it, I don't want a million guys assaulting anyway. Then everybody's dead." He gestured. "There's a guard, just starting his round. He'll come around the other side in three and a half minutes."

Houlihan sighed. In for a dime, in for a dollar. "Okay, Meza, let's do it."

59

There wasn't any champagne to drink so Alicia Kent and Portov sipped vodka in Belov's makeshift office. It was primitive, just a wood desk, crates, phones and fax, but for now it was fine. For the first time in a long time, the warehouse was quiet, no screams, no angry curses, no nothing. They clicked tumblers.

"Here's to us," Portov said and drank deeply.

"What next?" she asked gently.

Portov poured another for both of them. "I've chartered a G-Three to pick us up at LAX at eight in the morning. Do you have your passport?"

"Several. Where are we going?"

"First, Mexico City. We'll get even newer passports there. Where next? Do you enjoy the islands?"

She did enjoy the islands, for a week at a time, not a lifetime. "No, I think Paris or New York. Rome perhaps."

"You're not afraid of being detected?"

A smile. "The Council will protect me."

He laughed heartily. "Yes, we will. There's only one last detail."

"What?"

He gestured toward the locked rooms. "The cleanup will be messy."

"That's a mistake. If we harm them we'll have Meza chasing us forever, plus Angelo Bracca."

Portov drank the tumbler dry. "If I was afraid of Angelo Bracca or his crude people, I would not have ordered the death of his son."

Alicia knew he'd say that. "Well, we shouldn't do it here. I think you'll agree the body count is already pretty high. We need to take them someplace."

"I agree."

She smiled. "Plus, I'd like to . . . to participate."

He laughed heartily and his hand slid under her skirt to squeeze her bare thigh. She let him stroke. "You are a viper," he whispered

She leaned lower. "A viper with a bite!"

It took only ten minutes for Houlihan and Meza to get the Russian guard in the back of Bigelow's car. They let Bigelow have the first crack at getting information out of him. Bigelow played it by the book.

"Things will go a lot easier for you if you cooperate," he explained to the Russian. "We can put in a word with the D.A. Do you have any strikes?" In California a strike was a felony, and three strikes a life sentence.

The man just grunted. "No English," he muttered.

Meza yanked Bigelow out of the car and went right for the man's throat with a knife that Houlihan didn't even know he had.

"Sir," Bigelow shouted, "this is completely illegal!"

"Shut up, Bigelow."

The Russian stiffened, staring at Meza's eyes and the knife. He held up his hands. "You are the man who killed Ivan." Whatever that meant.

Meza just went with the flow. "That's right. Do you want to be next?"

The Russian shook his head. "What do you want?"

"How many men are in there?"

"Half of us. About fifteen."

Much better than thirty. "How many prisoners?"

"Four in all. No, three now."

Meza's eyes narrowed. "What's that mean?"

The Russian shrugged, a little too casually. "One died, a woman."

Houlihan never saw anyone move so fast in his life. Meza backhanded the Russian and screamed curses at him. After four openhanded shots the Russian was almost unconscious, slumped in his seat, his mouth slack.

"Meza, stop!"

Meza ignored him and whipped the .38 out of a shoulder harness. He pulled the Russian's hair back and stuck the Walther PPK in the man's mouth. There was a loud click.

"Meza, no!" Houlihan screamed again. He grabbed an arm that was rigid, stiff with clenched muscles and tendons. Everyone was breathing hard. Meza's face was flushed; the Russian's eyes were wide and he was shaking with terror. Bigelow was mumbling something.

Houlihan's voice was soft. "Let me, Miguel." He pulled the arm back and the gun left the Russian's mouth.

"How many women are in there now?" Houlihan asked gently.

"He's a madman!" the Russian screamed.

"Look, I'm trying to help you. How many?"

The Russian spoke fast. "At first, three women and one man. Now, two women, one man."

"What do the two women look like?"

"One is skinny and curses a lot. She slapped two guards and told Serge Belov that he should relieve himself in the hallway."

Meza relaxed. "Christine." He put the Walther back in its harness.

"What about the other one, the other *live* one."

"She is a beautiful woman," the Russian said. "She has twisted yellow hair and green eyes. She was seen kissing the man."

"That's Stephanie," Meza said, "the fake lawyer." He squinted. "She was kissing Boyle?"

"Now the dead woman," Houlihan said.

"She is the Argentine killer who worked with the Kent woman. She had information and Belov tortured her until she died."

They got quiet at that, each in his own way imagining the horror inside the warehouse.

"Sir," Bigelow said softly.

"What?"

"If they're doing things like that in there, shouldn't we do something?"

Meza pulled the Walther from his shoulder holster, checked it out and put it back.

"Houlihan, I think Bigelow has a point."

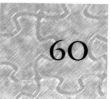

60

When they were ready to go they took the Russian's weapon and left him handcuffed to the door handle of Bigelow's car. The Russian breathed a sigh of relief. He had no doubt that his comrades would release him. He leaned against the car to wait.

He didn't stay relaxed long. The night shadows played tricks with his eyes and at first he thought it was a mirage, just the faraway light twisting through the branches of long dead trees. Then, to his horror, he saw that the moving shadow was neither a cloud over the moon nor the reflection of dead branches. It was a man.

The man was large and dark suited. The slice of moon that fought its way through the smog glistened off something in his hand. The Russian stiffened until he saw the phantom was simply drinking from a bottle. This was probably one of his own men, arriving late. But when the shape stood directly in front of him, he could see it was no Russian.

"Are you Portov?" the man said and drank again.

The Russian just shook his head. His mouth was heavily taped.

The strange man ripped the tape off so the Russian could speak.

"Are you Portov?" Now the guard knew that the metal glint was not a bottle. The man screamed, like Dmitri and Ivan had, just before the checkered night claimed him.

Portov entered the locked room with Alicia Kent at his side. Two guards entered in back of him with automatic weapons. Boyle, Stephanie and Christine sat on packing crates.

"I have some good news for you," Portov said.

Christine yawned. "What, she gave you something? Try penicillin."

Portov smiled, and enjoyed the thought of giving her to Belov, and watching. "No. We're going to release you."

Alicia Kent's dark eyes revealed nothing. Boyle adjusted the thin jacket he wore and tried to appear casual.

"So we can just walk out?"

"Not exactly." Portov paced, appearing to consider the question. "I doubt you'd be able to find this warehouse again. But just to make sure, we're going to drop you someplace far away."

"Like in a grave?"

Portov shrugged. "I could do that here. Besides, what's your choice?"

Boyle didn't have an answer to that, so he just shut up.

When the time was right, they pushed the three of them down the long corridor. The light from the ceiling bulbs was inconsistent. Two guards with automatic weapons led the parade. Two more followed behind.

Outside, under an ineffective moon, a stretch limo purred like a kitten, its doors open. Portov pointed and Alicia, Boyle, Christine and Stephanie got in the back. He followed them in and barked to the driver in Russian. The doors were shut and locked. There were no handles on the inside of the limo and the windows were blacked out. Portov pressed a button and a sheet of opaque glass rose, separating the passengers from the driver. The limo pulled away.

When the Russians and their prisoners unexpectedly emerged, it created a big problem for Meza, who was primed to cut the power and storm the place. Instead, when the creaky double doors began to open, he was reduced to diving behind the nearest garbage can he could find. When the limo pulled away, he whistled and the three men sprinted back to Bigelow's car. That's when they found the guard they left handcuffed to the door.

"Oh man," Houlihan said. "What is that?"

Meza spent about ten seconds trying unsuccessfully to make sense of it. "I got no explanation for this, none at all."

Houlihan spoke softly. "What now?"

"You want to drive with that? No. Let's take my car."

Houlihan jumped behind the wheel while Meza yanked a shotgun out of the trunk. Within a mile they caught the limo, which was meandering and not really trying to get away. All three of the men were quiet, checking and rechecking weapons. Meza was moderately calm because he had seen Christine alive. Only moderately.

"Houlihan?"

"Yeah?"

"If you had called in support, everybody'd be dead now, like Attica."

"I know. I thought of that."

"So I like it just the way it is. But whenever they stop, wherever they stop, we take them out. Agreed?"

Houlihan never blinked. "Agreed."

61

The limousine sailed through the harsh night out of South Central Los Angeles to downtown, then north on the Hollywood Freeway toward the fabled, fictional city. Halfway there it turned north again to Griffith Park, the largest urban park in the country, a massive, undeveloped blanket of land deeded to the city in the 1920s by one Colonel Griffith. It is now home to golf courses, equestrian centers, observatories, coyotes, hundreds of vagrants, bald eagles, red-tailed hawks, thousands of acres of woods and horse trails, periodic dead bodies and at least four Mexican gang shootings every weekend.

The city closed the massive park at night and guarded the entrance with a flimsy wooden barrier that resembled a railroad crossing. The limo accelerated and crashed through the barrier like it was made of papier-mâché. The big car took a left and wound its way up a steep mountain road. At the top it pulled into an asphalt parking lot. To the right was the Griffith Park Observatory, sitting atop the crest of the Santa Monica Mountains like a round, muscular colossus. The city spread out harsh and blinking in all directions. At the edge of the parking lot the road ended in a precipice, dropping long and lonely hundreds of feet to a roaring freeway far below. The hillside was twisted with brush and dried trees, exactly like it was when it served as a dumping ground for the Hillside Strangler during the glory days of the seventies. It still performed that grisly function from time to time for less celebrated killers.

Portov was pensive during the ride, staring wordlessly out the blackened window. As the car crested the hill it slowed. Alicia turned to him. "I think this is the best place."

"Yes," he said. "I imagine you would." His tone was stiff. Then he reached over, picked up her tan briefcase, and opened it.

"What are you doing?"

"Just sharing information, like we talked about. You don't have any secrets in here, do you?"

"Of course not."

Portov pulled out a one-page handwritten memo. He read it carefully.

"Problems?"

"Not so far. Mmm. Interesting."

"What's so interesting? It's just a checklist."

"I see all the accounts have been consolidated into a master account. When were you planning to tell me about that?"

"It's just a convenience. Royal Bank of Canada, Isle of Man. There's the account number, wire transfer number and authorization code."

"All the money's there now?"

"Bernie's funds have already been transferred from the Caymans. The beryllium and Sarin money were wired into that account by Klaus as soon as the plane left Barbados."

Portov pulled at his ear. "A small matter, but you should have told me." Then he stared at the roof of the car.

"Now what's wrong?"

"Probably nothing. The consolidation of the accounts? I'm sure you're right, perfectly routine. On the other hand . . ."

He looked down at the memo again. "What's that phone number on the bottom. The one in handwriting?"

"I don't know, it could be anything."

"Anything? Let's see." He grabbed the limo cell phone and dialed, then listened while the call went through. "American Airlines, how interesting. Just one second please." He pulled the phone away from his ear and looked at Alicia, his face darkening, then he spoke again. "Please do me a favor and confirm one first-class ticket from Los Angeles to New York in the name of Alicia Kent. Leaving today. Yes, I'll wait." He hummed and whistled with the phone at his ear. "No? Maybe it was misfiled. Do you show anything for Ms. Kent? . . . I don't know, let me see."

He hunted through her bag some more, then came out with her wallet. He flipped through it until he found what he wanted. "Here's her frequent flyer number. Could you please see whether any tickets at all have been purchased by this passenger in the last forty-eight hours. . . . Me? I'm her loyal assistant."

The limo rumbled quietly underneath them while Portov waited for his answer. Alicia sat wooden next to him. Boyle was relaxed, ready.

"Yes," Portov said finally. "I've got a pen. . . . Rio, you say! Via Mexico City. Two-day stopover. First-class, no less. That must be very expensive." Portov leaned back, stunned by the information. "I'd like you to check that carefully for me and confirm. . . . Thank you." He closed the flap of the cell phone and placed it carefully into its holder. Then he calmly put his hands in his lap.

Alicia had to break the eerie quiet. "Gregor . . ."

"Shut up."

The silence continued until Boyle stirred. The movement seemed to galvanize Portov.

"Let me state the obvious. I already told you there was a G-Three picking us up at LAX in the morning. Why would you book a commercial ticket?"

She waved her hands. "You're too suspicious. I booked it before you told me."

He turned and swung. She anticipated the attack and tried to deflect it. Still her head spun and the sound of the slap was loud.

"You are not only a viper," Portov said, "you are a lying viper." He breathed harshly. "The reservation was made one hour ago."

She said nothing. She just watched him, waiting.

"I anticipated this betrayal," Portov said at last. "You've betrayed others, why not me?" He reached into her bag again and this time pulled out a Colt Special Lady, a bright, stainless .38. "I suppose I should be interested in what your plan was but right now I'd rather just kill you."

She tried to grab for the gun but he pushed her aside easily. "This was so unnecessary," he said. He put the shining gun to her temple. There was a loud click. "What a mess this will make."

"Maybe not," a voice said. Portov froze. There was a .38 pressed against his own temple. He heard the same click.

"No," he said softly, disbelieving.

"It looks like a big 'yes' from here, Greg," Boyle said just as softly, and grabbed the man's jacket to press the barrel against the temple even harder.

Portnoy still had his own gun trained on Alicia. His mind raced with possibilities. Kent had obviously helped Boyle. Maybe the two of them were closer than he thought!

"I don't care if I die. I will kill this viper as my last act on this earth!"

"Oh, my God," Boyle said, the sarcasm dripping. "Wouldn't that be a shame."

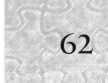

62

T he opaque interior glass shielded Portov from his gunmen and the two guards still didn't know what was going on. Once Portov's gun clattered in surrender to the floor of the limo Boyle pointed to the intercom.

"Tell them to shut off the engine. Speak only in English."

Portov did as he was told and the limo quieted, perched dark and motionless on top of the mountain.

Alicia Kent grabbed her bag. "Now it's my turn."

She pulled her cell phone out of the bag. The reception was pure from the top of this mountain. She dialed many numbers and quickly got the twenty-four-hour line at the Royal Bank of Canada on the Isle of Man.

"What exactly are you doing?" Portov said.

"You'll see."

She instructed that all of the funds be moved to a new account, one that was hers alone, that neither Portov nor the Council had anything to do with. Portov growled dangerously but remained still. Boyle's gun stayed trained at his head.

"We need a new password," she said into the phone once the transfer was complete. "Let's make it simple. Just call it Kent."

"Let's make it simpler," Boyle said. "We can call it Boyle."

"What?"

Boyle grabbed the phone. She cursed and lunged at him. The .38 swept from Portov's head to hers. She froze.

"Give me that!" she screamed. Portov laughed.

Boyle spoke into the phone. "To whom am I speaking? . . . Great. . . . Is the new account open? . . . Only when we agree on a password? . . . Okay. . . ." He turned to Stephanie. "Grab a pen."

"Okay, I'm back. How much is in there altogether? . . . That much? Wonderful. Now tell me exactly what I need to do to get the money out? . . . Really, that easy. Just call, give the account number and the password and that's it? . . . Sure, I'll hold." He put his hand over the mouthpiece. "They have voice ID. This is really high tech."

Alicia Kent howled again and grabbed for the gun. Christine and Stephanie jumped on her simultaneously and the three women wrestled furiously on the floor of the car. Boyle kept the gun trained on Portov, now quietly finishing his vodka. The man from the Royal Bank of Canada came back on the line.

"Sure, talk at the beep. . . . Okay. . . . This is Thomas Boyle. I am the owner of account number AJC-8764138-TWX. I hereby authorize the Royal Bank of Canada, Isle of Man branch, to allow deposits and withdrawals from this account. This voice authorization must be accompanied by the following password. . . ."

He looked down at the fight that was now becoming vicious. Alicia Kent had ripped Christine's blouse and was throwing some pretty fair rights. Stephanie was pounding Alicia in the back of the head. He cupped his hand around the phone and spoke quietly. "The password is 'Warm Breasts.' . . . Is it okay to say that? . . . You get a lot worse, great."

"So tell me, what do I do if I want to come over and take out a few hundred thousand, you know, some pocket change. . . . Sure, okay, and that's it? . . . It seems so easy, and you're so helpful. What's your name? . . . Bruce Lilliston? Fine British name. I'm going to write a letter to your superiors, tell them how helpful you were. . . . No problem, you're very welcome."

For posterity Boyle entered the number into the phone's memory and pressed the button terminating the call. Portov leaned back, sort of enjoying the irony of it all. "You're much more talented than we thought. We could make a lot of money together."

Boyle laughed easily. "Greg, I been there."

He looked down at the continuing fight. These women were really going at it. Alicia was holding her own but the tide was slowly turning. Christine had her hair pulled back and Stephanie was trying to get a good shot to the face. Alicia was reaching and scratching and all the blouses had ripped. Portov was as interested as Boyle.

"Try the left, baby." It was the first time Stephanie ever listened to him. Alicia slumped. The two survivors lay panting. Portov stared at the victors' heaving, now almost completely exposed breasts.

"Men are such primitive creatures. It's actually almost worth it."
He took another long sip.

"Greg, I think we finally agree on something."

A t Boyle's instruction, Portov ordered the Russian guards to
throw their automatic weapons out the window, get out of the
car and walk fifteen feet away. Once Boyle had them in his sights
he let everybody out. The lights far below blinked with a sheer,
dramatic beauty. Alicia Kent sat on the concrete, her back against
the limo. Boyle held the .38 Alicia had given him steadily on Portov
and the driver.

"Okay," Boyle said. "Take your men and walk to the end of the
parking lot. We're taking the car."

"You really think you can do that?"

"Trust me, Greg, it's a done deal."

"So very confident. Don't you think there's a problem?"

"What problem?"?

"Well, what about that car over there?"

Boyle spun and saw it. The roar of the freeway blocked all other
sound and he had never heard it coming up the long drive. Now it
sat there, watching him, like a large animal, its innards rumbling, its
lights shining.

"Now that's a problem," he said softly.

The doors of the car opened and three men got out. The high
beams blinded him. He heard the metallic click of hardware.

Boyle grabbed Portov and held him close. He put the gun to the
Russian's head.

"Don't come any closer! One more step and he's dead!"

Portov was a brave man. "Don't listen to him! There's only one
of him. Attack!"

Nothing happened for a moment and then a voice came from the
car. "How about I just waste you, right where you stand."

Christine ran forward. "I can't believe it!"

The smile left Portov's face. "Who is that?"

From the car a man walked forward. They could now see him
clearly in the smoky headlights. He had a long, red ponytail and held
a Benelli Super 90, a semiautomatic shotgun, casually at his side.
The driver mumbled to Portov in Russian.

"Da," Portov said.

Boyle tried to swerve but it was too late. The man had reached under the fender and now had a MAC 10 in his hand. Boyle couldn't get to him because Christine was in the way.

"Migo, down!"

"Fire!" Portov ordered.

The Russian guard braced against the car but was way too slow. Meza dropped the shotgun to his hip with almost casual grace and the Benelli roared repeatedly. The Russian guard was gone.

Christine ran and jumped in his arms, wrapping herself tightly around him. Meza kept walking, smiling now. When he got to Boyle he held out a fist. Boyle tapped it with his own fist.

"I get here in time?"

"Just in time, Migo."

63

Houlihan and Bigelow took charge of the Russian guards. Bigelow inspected the one who took the burst from Meza's Benelli. "This one's *real* dead, sir."

"Go ahead and cuff the live one, then let's get out of here."

"I doubt it," Portov said.

"Why?"

"Because this time I don't think those headlights are friends of yours."

Houlihan twisted and there they were. Once again the roar of the freeway below had masked the sound of engines coming up the dark, windy road. Once again the first they knew of the visitors was the glare of arriving headlights. The two cars had come up quietly, stealthily, barely causing the derelicts, coyotes and drunks along the way to blink. Bigelow dropped the cuffs. Nobody said anything, not even when the metal clanked harshly on the concrete.

The cars stopped but the headlights remained trained on them. Six men got out. Again there was the shattering sound of ordnance being readied.

"This can't be real," Boyle moaned. His head swerved rapidly as he hunted for cover and a way to get everybody down.

Portov chuckled at the delicious irony. "You should have accepted my partnership offer, Detective Boyle. I'm afraid I must withdraw it now."

The dead guards' automatic weapons were on the pavement, a MAC-10 and an Uzi. Meza grabbed one and flipped the other to Boyle. Boyle turned quizzically to Stephanie, who just held out her hand. Boyle gave her his .38.

"You know how to use this?"

She held the weapon high and inspected it, snapping the chamber. It was almost exactly like a naval officer's sidearm. "Just watch."

Portov moved to the car, where Alicia Kent sat. His voice was soft. "Please try to stay alive. I want to give you to Delov." She said nothing, just stared with flat, black eyes.

Meza had been spoiling for a fight for a long time, and now the odds were a lot better than back at the barracks. "You ready, Houlihan?"

"Yeah."

"Bigelow?"

"Yeah."

"Tommy, I know you're with me."

"Always, Migo." He glanced at Stephanie who nodded back. She was a soldier. She was ready.

One of the men screamed in Russian. "Gregor, where are you?"

Portov yelled back. "I am here. Kill them!"

The Russians opened fire. Boyle's crowd hit the ground and used the limo as a shield. Even Alicia crawled underneath the car. The Russian guard left alive was not so quick. He took one square in the chest from his own men. "One down," Meza said.

Boyle, Meza, the two cops and Stephanie returned fire immediately. One Russian ran for the trees and got cut down by Houlihan. The five that were left put their MAC-10s on full automatic and sprayed the limo. The car rocked with the shock of the high-caliber bullets.

Meza jumped on the hood of the car, lay flat and sprayed the Russian car. The headlights shattered and another Russian went down. Four left. Then Meza jumped off the hood and ran for a small copse of trees, firing the whole way. Halfway there he spun and dropped.

"No!" Christine screamed. She ran from the shelter of the car. Stephanie howled and grabbed at her. One Russian lay flat and drew a bead.

"Christine, stop!" Stephanie shouted. She tackled Christine and dragged her to the ground. A stream of .45 caliber bullets flew over their heads. The Russian crept closer, dropped to the ground again and this time wouldn't miss. Bigelow was closest. He dove, landing on top of the women and covered them with his body. The Russian's gun spurted and Bigelow's body jerked. It was impossible for Boyle to get to him. Stephanie saw the spark from the muzzle of the Russian gun and fired at the light continually until the magazine from Boyle's .38 was empty. The firing from the Russian stopped.

Three Russians left and one was Serge Belov. Belov was no hero; he ran from the cover of trees toward the car. Boyle recognized Belov from the warehouse and knew exactly what he had done. He stood and fired on full automatic for twelve seconds. Belov took eighteen rounds in the back.

Meza rose from the parking lot, limping, bleeding from the burst he had taken in the leg. He went right for Portov and held the Benelli to the man's head. "You got two men left. They leave now or you got no head."

"No."

"You know who I am?"

"Of course. You're Meza."

"Tell them to get out of here."

"No," said Portov.

Meza stepped back, fired and Portov wailed. He twisted, grabbing his shattered shoulder in agony.

"Tell them!"

Portov screamed in Russian. "Cease firing." The firing stopped.

"Tell them to drop their weapons and get out of here."

"They'll never do that."

"You want me to blow that arm all the way off?"

Portov quickly shouted in Russian. Two men rose from firing stations behind the trees. They kept their weapons and walked slowly toward the one car that still worked. A moment later, with squealing tires, they were gone.

Boyle stood up slowly. The air was dense with smoke. The groans and curses of dying men could be heard from the trees and under the remaining Russian car. The limousine was riddled with bullets and the passenger window was shot out. Miraculously, the driver's seat was intact and the tires still held the car up.

Bigelow had taken three high-caliber rounds in the back and was hemorrhaging badly. Houlihan called it in, then came back. Christine had Bigelow's head in her lap, speaking softly to him, running her fingers through his hair. Stephanie was working hard, ripping what was left of her shirt to find the pumping arteries and shut off the blood flow. It seemed she had been doing a lot of that lately.

"The more he moves the more he bleeds," she said. "Try to keep him still."

"No problem." Christine leaned over and kissed him deeply, Bigelow stiffened and then relaxed, remaining every bit as still as Stephanie could ever want. She wrapped the shirt around him and twisted hard, then tied the end around a hunk of wood.

Houlihan came over and Christine broke the kiss. Bigelow's eyes were glazed.

"I'm sorry, sir. I didn't mean to get shot."

"Shut up, Bigelow, you're a hero. Did I see right what he did?"

Christine was again stroking Bigelow's hair. "He jumped on top of me. He took the bullets meant for me."

"Sir?"

"Yeah?"

"Can I ask a favor?"

"Anything you want, Bigelow. I called it in, the ambulance will be here in a minute."

"I was wondering if it would be okay if she kind of . . ." He gestured to Christine.

"You don't need his permission." She kissed him again, this time harder.

Stephanie kept bandaging away. "If you want to switch, it's okay. He's cute."

64

Once Houlihan was sure Bigelow was well taken care of he went back to Portov.

"You're under arrest. You have the right to remain silent. Anything you say can and will be used against you in a court of law. You have the right to an attorney. If you cannot afford one, an attorney will be provided to you at public expense."

Portov's eyes were sleepy. "I have nothing to say. I'll talk only to my lawyer."

Houlihan was about to answer when he felt rather than saw the light at his back. Portov blinked. Houlihan turned and saw yet another car cresting the hill into the parking lot. "This is really getting stupid," he muttered.

Boyle came over. "Now what, more Russians?"

"Let's not take any chances." Houlihan got down on the ground with his gun pointed toward the car. Boyle stayed back with Portov. Alicia Kent had emerged from under the car and was again sitting quietly on the ground.

The door of the car opened and a man walked out with unsteady steps. There was a bottle in his hand.

Houlihan stood up and put his gun back in its harness. "It's just a drunk. They come up here all the time. This is exactly what I need, a DUI."

The man came closer. Portov leaned against the bullet-ridden limo, moaning from the pain in his shattered shoulder.

Houlihan shouted. "This is a restricted area, pal. I'll do you a favor and let you drive away. Just leave the bottle."

The man drank from the bottle. "Are you Portov?"

Everyone froze. No simple drunk after all.

"No," Houlihan said. "He is."

The man walked to Portov. "Are you Portov?"

Portov had a cigarette in his mouth and spit it out. It landed on the man's shoe. The man looked down quizzically. He sipped from the bottle.

Meza limped forward, stunned. Christine followed him, leaving Bigelow in Stephanie's care.

"Nick, is that you? Nick? What are you doing, man?"

"My name is Nick," the man said to Portov in a monotone. "I've been sent to see you by . . ."

He never got to finish the sentence before Portov sprang. He grabbed Christine and wrapped his good forearm around her throat. Meza brought the Benelli to his hip but there was nothing he could do. Portov backed toward the prone Bigelow, then dropped quickly and grabbed Bigelow's gun. He held the gun against Christine's temple.

"Everybody stay put." He backed away farther, toward the waiting precipice, taking Christine with him.

Everyone obeyed except Nick. He advanced slowly, unarmed. The freeway was roaring below and the lights of the city blinked far beyond. It was hard to hear.

When Portov was a safe distance from Meza he screamed at Alicia. "That limo still works. Bring it here!"

She stood and brushed herself off, glancing briefly at Boyle. "I don't understand you."

Boyle shrugged. There was nothing to say. She turned away, got in the driver's seat of the limo, brushed the broken glass off the seat and tried the engine. It roared to life.

Portov figured this was the best he could do. He'd jump in the car with Kent and Meza's woman, then get the hell off this mountain. He'd deal with the lost money later. He poked Christine with the gun. "Get moving."

Nick still approached like a zombie. When he was five feet away he stopped.

Portov held the gun steady, Christine's shoulder a brace. "Not another step. You want to die?"

Nick's eyes were red from liquor and lack of sleep. He stumbled slightly and his voice was slurred. "Let the girl go and I'll let you live."

Portov laughed. "You can barely stand up."

Nick smiled amiably. "Hey, I thought I'd ask."

Alicia Kent was sitting one hundred feet away, the motor purring in the big limo. There was something weird about the drunk, frightening. She thought about just driving away and leaving Portov on the mountain and then stopped. She watched the confrontation with mounting concentration as a new thought grabbed hold.

Portov jabbed Christine with the gun again. "Move!" He screamed at Alicia. "What are you waiting for? Get over here!"

What indeed. She leaned forward on the steering wheel, enjoying the engine's calming power. She spun the whole thing around in her mind and in a surreal way it all made sense. The strong, unafraid figure walking from the shadows, broken and drunk. Yet this was a man who feared no one, she could tell that, least of all Portov. He was a killer, that much was clear to her, even if Gregor didn't get it yet. But not a killer like her, a killer like Meza, ruthless efficiency inside a core of odd, perhaps even profane principle. A man who set his own rules, and lived in his own world. The man she wanted!

Then she looked up and saw that the strange man had turned, and was smiling at her, and he seemed to get it too.

Portov yanked at Christine and she made a small sound, which attracted Nick. He drank again, turned his back on Portov and tilted his head to the sky. He opened his arms and howled, his guttural scream long and loud, clearly heard over the roar from the traffic below.

Houlihan couldn't believe it. "Meza, what's he doing?"

"I got no idea, Houlihan, not a clue." But Meza, like all the others, didn't move, frozen while Nick made his play.

Only one of them understood: Alicia Kent. Alicia knew. She laughed and pounded the wheel. This was him! The one in the dream. He wasn't scary, he was just coming to take her home. Yes, someplace dark as death but that's where all the broken creatures went. Into darkness.

"You better shoot him, Gregory," she said to the empty car. "You better shoot him fast."

Nick again screamed to the night sky and everybody flinched. Portov just shouted, "Alicia, get that car over here!"

And then Nick moved.

Later on, when they were trying unsuccessfully to make sense of it, no one could clearly remember the sequence. Nick was screaming at the sky like a crazy man and Portov was shouting at Alicia. Then Christine made an unsuccessful move to break free. She stumbled and fell to her knees in front of Portov.

Nick could not possibly have seen that, could not possibly have known she was safe, his back was turned. Yet when he spun, the throwing knife flew end over end to the precise spot where Christine had stood an instant before. Now she was gone, and in her place Nick's knife was buried to the hilt in Portov's chest.

Alicia Kent shivered. "Oh, my God! What a magnificent man!"

Portov's mocking grin remained on his face until he looked down and saw the handle of the combat knife protruding from his shirt. He felt more shock than pain. The gun dropped from his useless fingers and he stumbled sideways, grabbing at the handle. He knelt at the edge of the abyss, bellowing uselessly against the roar of the freeway below.

"This is way past weird," Houlihan said softly. Still no one moved except Nick, who strolled casually to the limo. Alicia Kent sat waiting for him. He opened the door.

"Move over," Nick ordered.

Alicia Kent was completely at peace. "Yes, sir."

He got in and locked the door. The big motor was still smoothly running. He lit a cigarette.

She touched his arm. "I know who you are, and what you do." She had never heard of Nick, had no idea what he did for Angelo, but she knew.

Nick blew out the smoke. "You deserve to die. You killed Patsy De Marco." He turned on the radio. A soft jazz tune by John Coltrane came on.

"You killed before. Do you deserve to die?"

Nick's eyes were unfocused. "Oh, yes. Yes, I do. I deserved it long ago." She thought his face was beautiful.

"I wish I'd met you sooner, before Magnus."

He laughed. "Yeah, we could have killed together." He put the limo in neutral and revved the engine. "You ready?"

Alicia had never been more ready. Over the edge, just like Patsy, a perfect circle. She felt like a child, innocent, about to be purified.

"Ready like Freddy," she said and laughed, giddy and foolish.

Nick put the limo in drive and buried the pedal. The big black car lurched forward, accelerating rapidly. She saw the lights of the city beckoning, becoming more luminous, preparing to welcome her.

"Whoever you are," she said, "thank you."

Portov still knelt at the summit, pulling uselessly at Nick's throwing knife, now staring with disbelieving terror at the approaching headlights.

"Welcome to hell, Gregor," Alicia whispered.

Nick said nothing, just kept the accelerator pressed into the floor.

The edge of the cliff was less than fifty yards away. She felt an enormous sense of release, of demons long trapped within her being driven away. She thought one last time of a faraway and long-ago river. She had no problem dying with this man.

She shut her eyes and her world came to an end. The car smashed into Portov and propelled his useless body from the mountaintop parking lot to the freeway far below. She could imagine the blessed five hundred feet of hillside waiting to greet her. Instead, when she opened her eyes all she saw was his smile.

"I'll come visit. If they let me."

Meza ripped open the door. He grabbed the keys and pulled them out of the ignition.

"It's all over, Nick."

The bottle was half-full. Nick threw it on the pavement and it shattered. "I know."

65

The cleanup happened fast. Nick used the car phone to call Angelo in New York. Once again the old man cried.

"Do me a favor," Nick said at the end.

"Anything," Angelo said, "anything."

"My sister's worried. Tell her I'll be home tomorrow." Nick's sister was a good Italian girl who had cared for Nick since his wife died. Angelo had Tony the waiter sprinting in seconds.

Houlihan's call that a cop was down even got Taylor's attention. This time twisting red lights and screaming sirens fought for dominance with the developing dawn and the rumble of early commuters on the freeway below. The paramedics got Bigelow on a stretcher and even wrapped Meza's leg. Houlihan cuffed Alicia Kent and put her in the back of a squad car. He was about to order her taken away when Stephanie stopped him.

"Wait, I need twenty minutes."

The conversation took no more than that and then the squad car was gone. Stephanie immediately made her call. Her father, Admiral Duncan Shane, listened in shocked silence while his daughter told him all about Braxton, all about the Sarin, all about the beryllium, all about the dead bodies surrounding her, all about everything except Boyle. At the end her father's voice was clipped and official, struggling to keep his fury in check.

"I'll take it from here, Lieutenant Commander."

Ninety minutes later, and six thousand miles to the southeast of the Los Angeles mountaintop, two F-14s roared off the flight deck of the nuclear aircraft-carrier *Abraham Lincoln*, steaming with its battle group in the South Atlantic. The fighters flew in tandem, wing to wing, cruising over the Atlantic at a thousand feet for one hundred miles before rising vertically into the night sky. The pilots leveled off at thirty-five thousand feet and achieved double mach speed in under six minutes. They stayed at twice the speed of sound for the twenty minutes it took to reach the point of intercept.

The 707 aircraft was also flying at thirty-five thousand feet at five hundred miles per hour, or about a third the speed of the Tomcats. The intercept occurred two hundred miles off the west coast of Africa. The 707 pilots noticed nothing until the two F-14s blew by them over opposite wings before rising, twisting and bucking into the sky. The turbulence caused the jet to shudder violently and lose a thousand feet of altitude.

"What the hell . . . what the hell was that!" one of the pilots said.

Then the voice came on the radio. It was buttery smooth, Texan, slow.

"Barbados one-four-two, this is Lieutenant Commander Tolliver J. Jones the Third, firstborn son of Tolliver J. Jones, Jr., United States Naval Forces Atlantic Theater. You are being tracked by two F-fourteens from the aircraft carrier *Abraham Lincoln*. We have you locked on. I have two sidewinders right underneath me and my buddy Jerome has two more underneath him. Do you copy?"

The 707 pilots stared at each other. Then the captain grabbed the mike. "We copy! We copy! What do you want?"

"You are to immediately divert to the Canary Islands. We will give you coordinates. Respond by tipping your left wingtip. Repeat, your left wingtip. If you do not respond within thirty seconds, we *will* destroy you."

The captain yanked the stick to the left so hard the co-pilot almost lost his dinner. The wingtip dipped and the plane lurched again. "We copy. We copy. What are the coordinates?"

The voice sounded disappointed. "Sorry, Jerome. Anyway, the coordinates are as follows." Tolliver J. Jones III rattled them off.

"What is this about?" the captain said nervously; although both he and his bank account knew exactly what it was about.

"Just fly, Barbados one-four-two."

66

Homicide Detective Thomas Aquinas Boyle of the Paterson Police Department woke to the sight of a man staring at him from a ledge outside the window. The man smiled a gold-toothed grin and hit a lever. The rig on which he hung to clean the New York window lurched downward with a grinding metallic sound.

Lieutenant Commander Stephanie Shane slept innocently beside him. He reached for her and she was hot to the touch. He stayed still to avoid waking her, and watched her breathe, feeling rising excitement. She was naked, her only covering a thin white sheet tangled by her ankles, no doubt accounting for the gold-toothed grin on the window washer's face. Her arm was over her eyes and her breasts moved with every soft breath. A thin layer of sweat glistened in the pale hairs between her legs.

The tip of one breast was impossible to ignore. He brushed a hand against it, inviting it to respond. When it did he leaned over and gently nibbled. She moaned and her eyes opened.

"Tommy, no." Her voice was languorous, her smile a spoiled pout.

"No?" He nibbled more.

"Tommy, it's only"—she looked at the clock—"eight A.M.! We've only had *three hours sleep*!"

"That's not true. We were asleep before that."

"Boyle, we've been in this room for almost twenty-four hours straight! We got in at ten A.M. and . . . and . . ."

"Did it!"

"Don't be crude. We were . . . *together* till three. Then we got some sleep until five when we . . . we . . ."

"Were *together*."

"Exactly. Until eight."

"Right, and then sleep."

"Sure," she said, "till ten. And then . . ."

"Okay, I get it. So maybe we should . . . be *together* and then get some breakfast."

"Breakfast! I forgot, I'm starving! I don't know what I want more, to sleep or to eat."

"Or to be *together*," he suggested hopefully.

"Believe me, that's third." She looked down. "Boyle, are you *always* like this?"

"I've been waiting a lot of years. There was a buildup."

She groaned. "If I look horrible tonight you'll be complaining about that. Besides you're unemployed. Get some rest so you can get a job."

"Suspended, there's a difference. Besides, I have enough money to support us both for life."

"Yeah, but you stole it."

"From crooks, that's not stealing."

"Yeah, right." She yawned and stretched, a look he liked. "You ready for tonight?"

Angelo's party she meant. "Sure. I want everyone to see you on my arm."

"That's so sweet."

"It's the truth."

"And you think in return for that sweetness you're going to get some candy?"

"I was hoping."

She turned away from him again. "Forget it, I need sleep. Wait till after the party."

"After the party! That's eighteen hours away! What am I supposed to do for eighteen hours?"

She grabbed a box of Kleenex off the nightstand and tossed it over her shoulder to him.

"You are cold, really cold."

She laughed, mightily amused by her own joke. Her gorgeous bare bottom was staring at him and his right palm was near and he really couldn't be blamed. The loud crack seemed to shake the ropes on the window rig.

"OW! Boyle, you jerk!"

She turned and attacked him, punching and laughing simultaneously. They wrestled for thirty seconds and then she found herself locked in the embrace of arms that were all tendon and muscle and absolutely no give. She looked in his eyes and saw no mercy there. Oh, well, she thought, maybe I'll grab a nap later.

67

The ending was a lot simpler than everyone anticipated. Angelo closed Moska's for the evening and set the dinner for seven. Christine and Stephanie wanted to go shopping first in New York so the two brothers drove over to Jersey together.

"You ready for this?" Meza asked as he crested the George Washington Bridge and landed on Route 80 heading west.

"What, a dinner with Angelo? I can't wait. I love the Braccas now."

Meza laughed. He rolled down the window to flip his cigarette out. "No, I mean John and Nat."

"What about them?"

"I think Angelo's gonna wheel John out tonight and announce a marriage. Can you handle that?"

"Oh, man. He's still in a wheelchair?"

"Hell, yeah. He took about a million rounds."

That he had. "I never thought he'd make it to the hospital," Boyle said, remembering that night. "I guess he's hard to kill."

Meza got hung up in traffic and amused himself with amiable curses under his breath. "Ah, well," he said finally, "we're in no rush." He lit another cigarette. "How come you hate John so much anyway?"

"I just hate the Braccas. Not to dump on your employer or anything."

Meza shrugged. "I get along with Angelo, Nick too. If I like the job I take it. I think you don't like John 'cause you're jealous."

"Jealous? Of what?"

"Cause he's got Nat and you don't. Don't be such a pervert. It'd be like doing your sister."

Boyle snorted. "You're nuts. I think they're made for each other.

They probably fight like cats over who gets the mirror." Boyle grabbed one of Meza's cigarettes. They were jammed in traffic so he might as well breathe smoke as well as exhaust. "I don't get along with John for one simple reason. Because of them you lost everything we trained for. The Gloves, the Olympics, the pros, all of it."

Meza squinted. "Because of who?"

"John and Angelo. They spiked your test. I know you weren't using then, Migo. Those bastards just did it to make the bet easier."

"That's what's been bothering you all these years?"

"You're goddamn right it has. You were the best there was!" Then he had to grin. "Except for me."

Meza laughed. "Man, you been bent out of shape for nothin'. John didn't do any spike."

"No? Who did?"

"Me," Meza said simply.

T he traffic had come to a complete stop. Miles ahead they could barely make out the flashing red lights that had now closed all the lanes. Meza rested his head on the driver's side window, almost falling asleep. "What if all these cars just sat here and ran out of gas? Then what would they do?"

Boyle was slack-jawed, staring sightlessly. He had dropped the lit cigarette on the floor. Meza glanced over.

"What's wrong with you?"

"Me! You just said you spiked the test! What do you mean you spiked the test!?"

"I did. Angelo gave me twenty-five grand and a lifetime job. So I dropped a few sprinkles of coke into that jar they gave me. I didn't know if it'd work. I guess it did."

Meza's reasonable tone infuriated Boyle. "Are you nuts! It would have been me and you in the finals!"

"I think that was the whole point."

"But you fought that unbelievable fight against Lopez in the semis. He knocks you down in round one, he knocks you down in round two. Everybody thinks you're toast. Then you come off the deck and just crush him at the end of round three. Less than a minute left! That guy's still down. The paper said it was the best fight of the tournament."

"They're right. Lopez was as nasty as I ever saw. If I don't knock him out in that last minute, he wins that fight."

"So why did you spike the test? You get disqualified and I get Lopez all beaten up. He couldn't even see straight! I took him out at one-twenty of the first round."

Meza smiled at the memory. "Yeah. Lopez walked into that sissy left and it was lights out. He's a good guy. I went and looked him up a few years ago. He's a fireman over in the city. We got drunk together. He can't believe we both knocked him out. Nobody else ever did."

Boyle just slumped against the passenger door. "Migo! Me and you in the finals. Madison Square Garden, fifteen thousand fans, the whole thing on television! How could you throw a fight like that? Didn't you want to see how that would come out?"

Meza bristled. "I didn't throw nothin'. I never dropped in the ring and I'd never drop for Lopez."

Boyle retreated. "Okay."

"And as for you? One of us had to win, right?"

Boyle got it and nodded, slowly.

Meza shrugged. "And I already knew who would."

Boyle had to laugh at that. "You think so?"

Now it was Meza's turn to grin. "I don't think, I know."

The accident ahead and the fully blocked highway might keep things stalled for hours. "Really?" Boyle looked around. A lot of the drivers had already shut off their engines and were outside their cars, chatting with other drivers. The idea was just too delicious to Boyle, too immature, too infantile, too perfect!

"You know, it's never too late, Migo."

Meza turned slowly, blinked and then got it. His laugh was almost a cackle. "Right over there, on the shoulder?"

"Yeah." Boyle yanked his shirt and T-shirt off, then ripped the T-shirt in two. Meza knew what he was doing and did the same, the two of them howling like schoolboys. They were shirtless, and ready, the torn T-shirts wrapped thickly around their fists, makeshift gloves. Bare-knuckled they'd kill each other. This way there was at least a little protection.

Meza flipped the cigarette and yanked at the door. "Let's go!"

They walked into the party two hours later bloody and rumpled. It had been a hell of a fight and the men in the frozen cars were soon cheering like all fight fans do. A highway patrol car roared up the shoulder of the highway and ordered them to stop. Then the cop found out who the two fighters were and ran for the radio in his car. Soon there was a phalanx of squad cars and motorcycles providing a makeshift ring. The only problem was, there *still* wasn't a clear winner by the time the traffic got moving and the cops had to bring the whole thing to a close. They argued all the way back to the party as to who won on points.

"It's good you spiked that test," Boyle finally told him when they pulled into the parking lot. "I would've been feelin' guilty for years for droppin' you!"

Stephanie and Christine gave them holy hell when they saw them but eventually just rolled their eyes with everybody else at the story of the roadside battle. The party then got going good until Angelo stood on a table and banged a glass. The room got still.

"Everybody shut up for a minute. John's coming in."

Boyle hadn't seen John Bracca since the shootout and when Natala wheeled him into the party he was stunned. John was emaciated, the tendons in his neck clearly visible. The once olive skin was pale. When he lifted a cigarette to his mouth, his hand trembled. There was a good inch between his white shirt collar and his neck, and the elegant dark suit hung on him listlessly.

Boyle held out his hand and John shook it. "I'm sorry, man, I really am."

Bracca gestured dismissively. "Hey, I'm here, Tommy."

Boyle pointed to the chair. "Does this mean . . ."

"No, man, just for awhile. No big deal."

Boyle glanced at Natala. No one was talking anymore about the marks on Boyle and Meza. Now it was only about John. And it wasn't funny.

"He's had three operations, Tommy. He's scheduled for another in a week."

"Hey, John?"

"Yeah?"

"You walked in the way of bullets meant for her. It's all over between you and me, like it never existed. You know what I'm saying?"

John Bracca shrugged. There was an edge of pity in Boyle's voice and he didn't like that.

Meza was not the most sentimental of men. "How 'bout you guys hug by the bar?"

"That," John Bracca said, "is a very good idea."

By the time the party was over a lot of water had rolled over a lot of dams, but to Boyle's mind the night had a contrived quality to it. Angelo's toasts to Patsy, although heartfelt, were ironic. It was Angelo Bracca who found the old silk mill for Portov to begin with. And it was Angelo Bracca who would be, if Patsy had anything to say about it, last on the list of men to eulogize him.

So it was with a slightly empty feeling that Boyle rose at the end of the evening and shook everyone's hand. Angelo and Nick left first, then Meza, taking Christine with him to the airport. Stephanie kissed him and told him she had to go to Washington, she'd call him from there. Who knew what that meant. Natala hugged him through the sentimentality of a red wine haze and asked if he would give her away at the wedding. Sure, he said, as long as they play "Ave Natala" when you walk down the aisle. That got wine-drenched tears and hugs and then he wheeled John to his van. When the van left he found himself standing alone in the doorway. Then a hand dropped on his shoulder.

"Tommy?"

It was Angelo's brother Paul, John's uncle, the guy who owned Moska's. "Hey, Paul, great party."

"Glad you liked it. I got to like . . . shut out the lights, you know?"

"Sure, okay, sorry."

"No problem, Tommy. So if you could like . . ." Paul's hand fluttered toward the exit.

Boyle went out to the now empty parking lot. The Passaic River ran black and thick beneath him. The falls were six hundred yards away, lit to glowing by federal urban relief money. He leaned against the fender of his car and puffed on a cigar Angelo had given him, blowing the smoke lazily into the sky. Ten minutes later the lights of Moska's shut off and the parking lot darkened. It forced him to hop on the hood and lean back against the windshield, blowing tendrils of smoke into the cold glow of the bright moon. Twenty minutes later Paul came out, glanced quizzically at Boyle and jumped in his car. When Paul roared over the bridge, Boyle was completely alone. He sat Indian-style, smoking, staring at the roaring falls.

He saw the car long before it got to him, when its headlights crested the bridge over the river. She exited the car and her heels clicked on the harsh concrete of Moska's parking lot. Soon there were two of them sitting on the hood. She tucked her head against his shoulder.

"What happened?"

A sigh. "I thought about us the whole time. I didn't even get halfway to the airport. So I turned around."

He smiled and pulled her closer to him. "I'm glad."

She raised her head to look at him. "Can I ask you a question?"

"Sure."

"If I can't make it to the airport for a flight to Washington, how the hell am I going to do a six-month tour on a carrier? And what will *you* be doing for those six months? You can't even last six hours."

"Sure I can. Remember there was a time before you."

"That's what worries me." She nestled back into his warm embrace.

"I got an idea. I'll join the navy too."

She punched him gently. "It's not funny."

"Okay, you *quit* the navy."

"No, I want to fly. I *have* to fly. But I have to come back to you too."

"Yeah, right."

She gave him a theatrical sigh. "I'll be back. I promise. It's . . . it's just a little complicated."

Her tone was way too casual. "Oh, really?"

"Yes. The only way this can work is we both have to compromise. You know, give up something."

His eyes narrowed. All the red flags went up. "What do I give up?"

"Not much, just have a little patience."

"A little patience? I'm listening."

Now a fake shrug. "After my tour I'll make sure I get assigned to

New York. Duncan can take care of that. Then we can be together. You'll probably be long gone from Paterson by that time. Just stay someplace close."

He stroked her hair. "That's real interesting, doll, but in two weeks I'm off suspension. I intend to scrape Jack Ruffulo off a barroom floor and find the latest body. Believe it or not I *like* being a homicide detective. I like this stupid city. I even like Jack Ruffulo!"

"I understand that, I really do. It's like me and flying. We *have* to do these things. So all you have to do is wait for me."

He laughed. "Like a war bride?"

Exactly, she thought. "Not at all!" Her hand drifted to his leg, sort of by accident.

"I wouldn't be much of a detective if I didn't notice that."

She was incredibly insulted at the accusation. Her voice actually had outrage in it. "Notice what?" The hand drifted further north.

"You're so obvious it's pathetic."

"Pathetic? You think so? You think this is pathetic?" Her head raised and she whispered a suggestion in his ear.

"Very nice talk." He shifted, a bit more uncomfortable.

Her voice was soft, reasonable. "Let's say I stay on a carrier for one tour. That's six months tops, not a day more. Then I'm right back here in a heartbeat. Even Intelligence again if that'll get me into New York. You can wait that long, can't you?"

He coughed. The hand had not moved away. "Sorry, too complicated."

More drifting. Now very close. Don't give her the satisfaction, he ordered the troops. The troops were paying no attention, most actively planning a mutiny.

"Oh, my," she said, "how very surprising."

He glanced at the falls. No help there. Maybe Patsy was nodding, approving.

"Don't confuse things. One has nothing to do with the other."

Again the look of innocence. "Darling, I understand that completely. One has nothing to do with the other." Then, to his shock, he heard the raspy sound of a zipper.

"You're *so* evil."

An incandescent smile, as good as Natala's, *better* than Nat's. "Do we have a deal?"

"No way."

Pointing at the lie. "I'll seal it with a kiss."

The great falls were called that for a reason. The roar of the cascade seemed to suddenly resonate, the wide polluted river crashing
over the rocks and sending a hundred-yard strip of river pouring
into the gorge on its eternal journey to the sea.

He grabbed her insolent yellow hair and pulled it back, then
kissed her hard on her still-bruised lips. Her slight whimper, slight
moan, was hidden by the thunder of the river below.

"Ow," she said softly, when he broke the kiss, licking the tender
lip. Her breathing had quickened. "Is that a yes?"

Three thousand miles east of the Passaic River, in a sleepy London
suburb called Sunningdale, a general manager named Charles
opened a set of double doors leading to an ornate dining room. Nine
men sat pensively around a long marble table. A squad of servants
cleared away the dishes and replaced them with brandy snifters and
cigars. Then the great doors closed, and the Turk guards stood in
place.

Charles walked to the head of the table. "Welcome to our new
home. In the absence of a chairman I've been asked to administer
the election. In the last two weeks we have lost four members, Chairman Portov, Mr. Purcell, Ms. Kent and Mr. Yomoto. We also need
to elect a new chairman."

If the men in the room were stunned by recent events, they didn't
show it. This dining room, very much like the dining room at
Moska's, was not filled with sentimentalists.

Charles gestured and the Turk guards opened the double doors.
Three men and one woman entered.

"Let me introduce the new Council members. First, to replace
Gregor Portov, I have the honor of welcoming Mr. Josef Alexeyev
of Moscow."

The room applauded. Like Portov, Alexeyev was a beefy man in
his late thirties. He was conservatively dressed in a dark suit, blue
oxford shirt and patterned tie. A cell phone was clipped to his belt
and he looked every inch the western businessman.

After introducing an Italian and a Swiss, Charles turned to the
woman. "For the past five years Serena Grant has been the Council's
representative in Washington. In the recent unfortunate project, she

was responsible for informing the Council of the blunderings of the late Cameron Braxton."

Serena Grant walked forward and the men applauded. If Braxton were alive, he would have died again on the spot. Serena Grant was the lovely Georgetown waitress who had both slapped and captivated him, and who had once flirted with John Bracca at the El Cortijo. She was also the woman who executed Braxton, moments before the FBI arrived.

"Under our rules," Charles continued, "the chairmanship must rotate upon the death, incapacity or termination of the term of the existing chairman. The next nation in the rotation is the United States of America. There is currently only one American-born representative on the Council."

Now the men rose to clap. Serena Grant walked regally to the head of the table. She was thirty-two years old and looked even younger than Stephanie Shane, hiding the fact that she was as murderous as Alicia Kent. Her shoulders were bare and the scar of a deeply carved "X" was visible. She had wanted it on her face, demanded it on her face, to demonstrate to them all how ruthless she was, how self-mutilation wouldn't faze her. It was Charles who finally talked her out of it.

She held her hands out and the applause stopped. The men sat.

"Gentlemen, thank you for your support. Now let's turn to the problem of a very live Alicia Kent."